Cartier's
Hope

Center Point
Large Print

Also by M. J. Rose and available from
Center Point Large Print:

The Book of Lost Fragrances
Seduction
The Collector of Dying Breaths
The Witch of Painted Sorrows
The Secret Language of Stones
The Library of Light and Shadow
Tiffany Blues

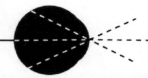

**This Large Print Book carries the
Seal of Approval of N.A.V.H.**

Cartier's Hope

A Novel

M. J. ROSE

CENTER POINT LARGE PRINT
THORNDIKE, MAINE

For Jillian S. and Sarah V.

Your enthusiasm, encouragement, help,
creativity, and friendship mean the world to me.

"My courage always rises at every attempt to intimidate me."

—JANE AUSTEN

Cartier's
Hope

HOPE DIAMOND COMING HERE

THE FAMOUS BLUE STONE BOUGHT BY A NEW YORKER—PRICE SAID TO BE $250,000

LONDON, Nov. 13—The report that the famous Hope blue diamond is going to New York is correct. It is in the possession of a member of a New York firm now on his way to America from London. The heirloom was sold by order of the Master in Chancery.

It was said that the price paid for the diamond was $250,000.

If the Hope diamond has been sold for $250,000, as reported, it has proved even more valuable than has hitherto been supposed, as the outside estimate placed on it was $25,000. The gem belonged to Lord Francis Pelham Clinton Hope, who was only allowed to sell it after a long legal fight.

It was not the size of the stone which gives it its value, but the fact that it is the only very large blue diamond known. It weighs 44¼ karats, while the next largest blue diamond, the Brunswick stone, weighs only 10¾ karats.

In 1688 Tavernier, the famous French traveler, returned to Paris, bearing twenty-five diamonds, which were all purchased by Louis XIV. A great blue diamond, weighing 112½ karats, was the chief of these gems. The process of cutting reduced its weight to 67⅛ karats. At the time of the French Revolution the diamond disappeared, but in 1830 the diamond now known as the Hope stone appeared in the possession of a certain Daniel Ellison. He sold it for £13,000 to Henry Thomas Hope, the London banker.

It is now regarded as certain that the Hope stone and the Brunswick gem were once a single diamond, and that this diamond was the long lost Tavernier stone.

PARIS JEWELER
TO OPEN HERE

Intends to Bring French Workmen
and Fill Orders Locally.

By Marconi Transatlantic Wireless Telegraph
to The New York Times

Paris, April 3—(By telegraph to Clifden, Ireland; thence by wireless.)—The Rue de la Paix is being moved to Fifth Avenue. Louis Cartier, the well-known jeweler in the Rue de la Paix, is to open a branch establishment in Fifth Avenue next Fall. I learned this week that he will not only have a shop there, but that he intends taking over several French workmen, so that all his work done for America will be done in America. It will not be necessary to send anything from Paris after the first outlay, which will involve several hundred thousand dollars. Pierre Cartier, one of his sons, is to have charge of the New York shop, together with Jules Glaenzer, an American, who has been with the firm for some time.

Many of the most famous pieces of jewelry in

the possession of the crowned heads of Europe, leaders of the American smart set, and celebrated actresses came from Cartier's. The enamel work of the firm is especially fine.

CHAPTER 1

New York City
February 3, 1911

Diamonds, scientists say, are the world's hardest material. And yet, like a heart, a diamond can break. When I was a reporter covering a story about the Hope Diamond, my research taught me that often a gem cutter will study a major stone for months, deciding where to strike, as cleaving is a precise and risky effort. If the jeweler misjudges, he can destroy the stone.

As a woman, I've learned the same thing. A single mistake can destroy a relationship.

Standing here in the cold, staring at the fountain in front of the Plaza Hotel, I try to pretend that I'm not really crying. That what look like tears are simply snowflakes melting on my cheeks.

But that's just another lie. And I promised myself that I was done with lies. Untruths, whether by omission or commission, are how I got here—a place I never wanted to be and from which I am trying to escape.

For weeks and weeks, my sadness has felt oddly comforting. A proof of love. A reminder that even if I have lost that love, I did have it once. And now the time has come to fight for it.

But am I willing to risk what is left of my pride? Willing to risk another failure even if there's little—if any—chance of winning that love back?

My father once said, *The fight is all*. But so far, this fight has laid me bare, stripped me of all pretense, and broken my heart.

The snow is falling harder now, dressing the marble woman in the fountain in a gown of white. As more snow catches in my eyelashes and hair and lands on my face, melting and mixing with the tears, I wonder if my father was right.

This spot on Fifth Avenue between Fifty-eighth and Fifty-ninth Streets has been the epicenter of my city and so many moments in my life. To my right is Central Park, all dusted with white on this early evening—the living, breathing forest that has always been my refuge. To my left, across the avenue and down a block, is my father's department store on Fifty-seventh Street, designed by my uncle and right in the heart of New York City's newest fashionable uptown shopping district.

If I look downtown a bit farther and west, if I crane my neck just a little, I can see the rooftop gables of the building that houses Pierre Cartier's jewelry shop.

But back to the fountain. In 1890, my father brought me to its installation ceremony. I was twelve years old. My sister was sick with a sore throat, so I was alone with him. My father spent a lot of time with me and always talked to me like an adult. He shared information about all the subjects he found interesting. The way fashions changed, how clothes and shoes and fabrics and jewelry were designed and made. How desire fueled commerce. What made someone want to buy something they didn't need.

He was a great reader, especially of history. Ancient Rome, Egypt, Greece, the Renaissance, and seventeenth-century France were some of his favorite periods. And as we stood with the crowd that night with the fireworks bursting overhead, he told me the story of the woman whose form graced the fountain. Elpis, a symbol of hope.

"The first woman created by Zeus, Pandora," he said, "had a jar—I believe it was a jar, not a box—that contained all the wonders of the world: life, renewal, love, generosity, wisdom, and empathy. Warned not to open the jar by Zeus, Pandora did her best to obey but ultimately gave in to temptation." Here he stopped to give me a stern look to warn me about little girls who did not obey their fathers. "When she opened the jar, all the elements flew out. Beauty is limited, our health breaks down, our love fades. And we die. But it turned out that one thing remained in the jar after all—the one thing left to all of us when we face the tragedies in our lives. A tiny creature named Elpis, also known as hope. She stayed in Pandora's jar so that she could revisit us after all our miseries. So that we can hope that the hard times will get better, hope that grief will soften, hope that terrors will quell."

As I remember this moment, my heart aches. How much love can you lose and still have hope that you will ever find love again? And if you do find it, how can you know that it will last for any time at all?

My father had tried to teach me that love, no matter how short-lived, was worth fighting for. Worth savoring. He always spoke of it with a wistfulness I never quite understood. For years, I wondered where his sadness came from. A successful businessman, father, and husband, he didn't seem to have had any tragedy in his life.

But that was a feeling. Not a fact. I am a reporter; I know how important the facts are. And when I discovered the facts of my father's past, they changed my life.

One of those facts was that my father had, indeed, endured a terrible tragedy a few weeks before he died. Another fact was that he had tried to hide it from me, as well as from my sister and my mother. Yet another fact was that in Paris in 1909, C. H. Rosenau sold a forty-five-carat blue diamond to Pierre Cartier, grandson of the French jeweler who had founded the world-renowned *maison*. It is another fact that in January 1911, Evalyn Walsh McLean and her husband purchased that same stone from Cartier.

Between those facts is a tale rich with revenge, robberies, myths, curses, psychics, lost fortunes, outright lies, murder, and heartache. And just a few months ago, it became my job as an investigative journalist to look at all the different facets of the story of the diamond originally known as the French Blue—but now known as the Hope—for a weekly magazine called the *Gotham Gazette.*

During the course of my probing, questioning, and reporting, I learned many things about history, power, jewelers, society, wealth, passion, greed, and love.

I started out the investigation, ironically, feeling quite hopeless myself, having lived a life that was dark and dreary. It's been a long and circuitous route to come to the end of the investigation. But therein lies my tale. A story that will come to its conclusion one way or another tonight and will very possibly change the direction the rest of my life will take.

My father told me to hold on to love even when the world around me tried to snatch it away. And I have. I've held tightly to its promise all these long months. I've imagined it wrapped up in some of the navy velvet my father's emporium sells on the second floor. Tied with a magenta ribbon from the notions department.

And tonight I will find out if I can unwrap it or if I will need to walk into the park across the street and find a soft patch of ground in which to bury it once and for all.

Like my father, I wouldn't give up what I've had for anything. But oh, how I hope that I'll find it again. When you fall in love, you aren't smart. You don't weigh the logic of your actions. You don't look at the man to whom you are giving your heart with the cold precision of a diamond cutter examining that rough stone. At least, I didn't. And so the man I'd given my heart to turned out to be a thief.

CHAPTER 2

New York City
October 1910

How many lovers does it take to turn a woman into a whore?

According to my mother, only one, if he turns out to be married and your affair becomes fodder for gossip in her social circle.

And how many sensational news stories exposing crime and punishment, fear and neglect and horror, does a reporter need to publish before she becomes a pariah in her own home?

According to my mother, also only one, if the story threatens to expose secrets of those close to your family.

My mother always judged me and was disdainful of my work. She only begrudgingly accepted it because my alter ego, undercover reporter Vee Swann, was a family secret. My father and my cousin Stephen had helped me come up with the pseudonym, and we were all careful to protect it.

While my sister, Violet, known by all as Letty, judged me, too, she also admired me for my career. Because of this, we got along fairly well despite being such opposites.

It was my sister—though unwittingly, of course—who in the end helped me plot how I would avenge our father's death, by asking me to lunch on a Wednesday in the beginning of October. While our lunching was not so rare an occurrence in the past, we had gotten out of the habit since she'd had her third child eighteen months before.

I was two years older than Letty. Everything about us, from our looks to our personalities and style, was different. She was elegant, with a grace that made heads turn. She had a charming sense of humor and that ability some people have to make you feel that every word you are saying matters intensely. She dressed impeccably in the brightest jewel tones. Her hair, twisted in a perfect blond knot, never escaped into unruly curls as my rust-colored locks did. Letty would enter a room on her husband Jack's arm, and all eyes would focus on her. I, on the other hand, drew a different kind of attention. It was curiosity, not admiration. If Letty was light and gossamer, I was dark and damask. If she was laughter and love, I was questions and fury. But we were both very stubborn, so sometimes we argued.

Like our mother, Letty was concerned about her place in society. She adhered to the customs of how one did things and was careful not to push the limits of propriety. It was as if our mother had bottled her values and Letty had drunk them down.

But I didn't give a fig about propriety or social mores.

So I admonished her that she was old-fashioned, a traitor to our sex for accepting our mother's generation's values. And she often had words about my lifestyle. Following my mother's lead, Letty didn't approve of my obsession with work and bohemian ways. Yet at the same time, she was excited by my escapades and always begged me to tell her everything I was doing.

Despite herself, Letty knew my heart, as I knew hers. Thus, we gave each other—and our opinions—a wide berth.

I did admire Letty for her charitable work. Indeed, I'd had a hand in her getting involved with it in the first place. When I'd first realized how much she was becoming like my mother and feared she'd turn into just another society matron, I'd taken action. In Silk, Satin and Scandals, the weekly gossip column I penned anonymously for the *New York World*, I'd written that according to rumors, Letty Garland Briggs had offered to take on the job of fund-raising chair for the Children's Aid Society and how proud her family was of her. In fact, I reported, Granville Garland, of Garland's Emporium on Fifth Avenue, was going to match all contributions for the year. I had gotten my father to agree first, of course.

He had thoroughly approved of my efforts with a twinkle in his eye. Only my father and my editor, Ronald Nevins, knew I was the voice behind the column. It was a necessary precaution, given that I regularly sourced my material by spying on my family, their friends, and their acquaintances. Mother and Letty wouldn't have been able to keep their lips sealed about it, nor would they have approved.

I'd started the column after graduating from Radcliffe. In 1900, it had been the only work I could find. I'd known I'd have to start with women's topics—all female journalists did. But I'd hoped to retire the column once my investigative work took off. By the time Vee Swann had made her mark by way of an exposé on abortion practices, Silk, Satin and Scandals had become so popular that Mr. Nevins begged me to keep writing it, reminding me of the good the column did: it could raise awareness of social ills and charitable efforts under the guise of gossip.

He was right about that. In addition to the Children's Aid Society, with my column, I'd been able to push my mother, my sister, and all their well-heeled friends and acquaintances into donating their time and money to the New York Foundling Hospital, the Jacob A. Riis Neighborhood Settlement, the Little Mothers' Aid Association, and more. Thanks to Silk, Satin and Scandals, noticing the world outside the List of 400 had become fashionable.

That Wednesday, Letty met me at noon for some shopping and lunch at the Birdcage, Garland's fanciful luncheon restaurant. Father's emporium was full of specialty venues for shoppers, each of them an homage to one of the women in his life. The Birdcage, so named after the dozen watercolor bird images painted by my mother that adorned its walls, served genteel dishes, including all my mother's favorites: bouillon with cheese straws, curried egg sandwiches, creamed chicken and mushrooms, and Orange Fool, a citrus custard flavored with mint that she adored.

The Library, where shoppers could stop and rest and have tea or cordials while browsing the stacks, had been created with me in mind and sold copies of all my favorite books. There they served a tea called Lady Vera, a special blend Father had imported from Fortnum's in England. It was a much fruitier version of Earl Grey, with notes of plum, orange, apricot, and peach. I drank it by the potful.

The Jewel Box was my father's nod to my sister. The furniture was upholstered in her favorite lilac color, and the walls were decorated with fashion illustrations of Letty modeling the *au courant* and affordable jewelry people flocked to Garland's to purchase.

My sister had wanted to stop there before we ate.

"I have a gift to buy," Letty said as we entered the cushioned enclave designed to look like a jewelry case. The lights had been specially designed by Tiffany & Co. to resemble faceted gemstones: rubies, emeralds, sapphires, topazes, and amethysts. The chairs were all gilded and upholstered with purple velvet-tufted cushions. The pulls on the drawers looked like bracelets, the knobs like brooches.

After inspecting the cases, Letty found something she liked and asked the salesman if she could see it.

"Do you like this?" Letty asked me, holding out her hand and showing off the seed-pearl bracelet with a small garnet clasp in a flower shape.

"It's lovely, yes."

And it was. Though the Jewel Box sold mostly trinkets and paste in order to keep prices low for customers, Father made certain never to skimp on quality. He only bought from the best jewelry makers and left the selling of fine gemstones to other New York merchants he knew, like Mr. Tiffany and Mr. Cartier, as well as Van Cleef & Arpels, Marcus & Co., Boucheron, and Buccellati.

The one thing we Garlands all had in common was a true love of beautiful things. From a fine silk robe to satin shoes. From an elegant lynx coat to a semiprecious trinket. From a necklace of perfectly matched Persian turquoise to a Burmese ruby ring to a brooch set with fire opals.

My family teased me that my obsessions didn't fit with my hardworking girl-reporter reputation. And they didn't. I was forced to eschew wearing most of my lovely things when I was at the city room or on assignment. A plain dress and wire-rimmed spectacles were as far as Vee Swann would go.

Except when I covered the social scene anonymously, in which case I could dress to the hilt in the kinds of clothes and jewelry people expected Vera Garland to wear. The truth was, I did love shopping with my mother or my sister, and I felt a bit embarrassed by it.

My father told me once, "Darling Vera, you are the daughter of a man who has built a department store that is a shrine to beauty. The daughter of a woman who dressed you in satin and cashmere from the day you were born. Admiring lovely things and wearing them are nothing to be ashamed of. It doesn't make you any less of a reporter."

But sometimes I found it hard to reconcile the incongruous halves of myself.

"Who is this bracelet for?" I asked my sister.

"It is Sybil van Allen's fortieth birthday at the end of the week. Were you invited?"

"I was."

27

"Are you going?"

"I am."

I certainly would be going. Sybil van Allen was in the midst of a very ugly court case with her stepfather over her deceased mother's art collection. The party was sure to offer up fodder for Silk, Satin and Scandals.

"What are you bringing as a gift?"

"To tell you the truth, I haven't thought about it at all."

"Well, you can give her this with me."

"Thank you, Letty."

"To repay me, I want you to come with me after lunch to Cartier's. Jack is having earrings made for me for our anniversary. I'm not sure about the design, and you're better at that than I am."

"Visiting a jewelry store is anything but a chore for me," I said, and we both laughed.

As we ate our perfectly cooked and browned Welsh rarebit, we talked about other upcoming parties that we'd both been invited to and gossiped about their hosts and hostesses.

Once the plates were removed and we were having coffee, she leaned across the table and took my hand.

"Jack said he'll be by on Saturday morning to help you clear Father's things out of the apartment," she said in an even softer version of her usually dulcet tone.

Our family home was in Riverdale in the

Bronx. Most days, my father commuted via train to the store on Fifth Avenue and back. But some nights, he stayed in the city proper in the penthouse apartment he'd had built at the top of Garland's Emporium. It saved him from traveling when he worked too late or there was inclement weather.

When he died, the Riverdale estate was transferred to my mother. The store and the land it sat on were left to my sister and me equally, with the stipulation that her husband run the emporium and that I be allowed to live in the penthouse indefinitely.

Almost nothing about it had changed in the months since. I'd moved into the second bedroom while Father was alive and remained there still. I'd left all his things in his room and hadn't touched his desk in the library.

Father had a housekeeper, Margery Tuttle, who came in each day to clean and keep the kitchen stocked. He'd never liked having the help around when he was there, so Margery would arrive in the morning after my father went down to his office and was always out by lunchtime. I'd kept her on, but I didn't need as much looking after and so had reduced her to twice a week while keeping her pay the same, as I knew my father would have wanted.

"You'll see," Letty was saying. "With Jack helping you empty the closets and drawers, it will be easier living there without it looking as if he's about to walk in the door any minute." At the thought, my sister's eyes filled, and the violet color for which she was named became more intense.

My father had been gone for almost ten months, but we both still missed him so much. I bit the inside of my mouth to keep my own eyes dry. "Jack is a godsend," I said. "It's so good of him to help."

"I am lucky," she said, and sighed. "Most men are difficult and quite full of themselves and must be endured. But Jack makes it easier than most."

I smiled at her. "You chose well."

She seemed about to say something, and I guessed it was about my unmarried state, but she must have thought twice, because she returned to the subject at hand.

"Do you think you'll come across anything special, hidden away? Any surprises?" she asked.

I examined her face. Did she know something? Sometimes she was more observant than I gave her credit for. Or was she just being her usual inquisitive self? Or was she a bit greedy? As much as I hated to admit it, she could be. Somehow, for all the money our family and her husband's family had and how well the store was doing, my sister never acted as if she had enough. My father had sometimes apologized for her, saying it was because she was the second child and all second children think they've missed out.

When I'd scoffed at this, he'd said, "It's true, Vera. Parents dote more on the first baby. With the first, everything is amazing and new. With the second, the love is every bit as strong, but the wonder is tempered. It was that way with you and Letty, and she senses it."

Now I asked Letty, "What kinds of surprises could Father have hidden away?"

"Oh, I don't know . . ." Her eyes lit up. "Presents he'd meant to give one of us at Christmas. Love letters from Mother from when they were courting. Or maybe there was someone before Mother whom he never told us about? Photographs of himself in college that we never saw. Maybe even a diary." She laughed. "Though I can't imagine anyone less likely to keep a diary than Father. Perhaps there is a painting he bought without telling Mother because it was too racy or avant-garde, and it's hidden in the closet?"

The waitress interrupted with our bill. There was no charge, of course, but we had to sign the receipt and leave a generous tip.

"I'll be sure to tell you if I find anything curious," I said as we got up to leave. "I never imagined our father as someone to keep secrets. Why do you think he did?"

She shrugged. "I'm not sure."

We strolled out of the Birdcage, across the

31

main floor, and out onto Fifth Avenue. We turned left out of Garland's and headed south.

"You're the one I'd expect to be on the lookout for secrets. What else is it you do as a reporter but search out the things people hide and expose them?" my sister asked.

"You're right," I said, a bit surprised at her insight.

Two blocks later, we reached 712 Fifth Avenue, where Mr. Cartier's shop was located on the fourth floor.

The original Cartier store had been founded in 1847 by Pierre's grandfather, Louis-François Cartier, in Paris and was now run by Pierre's brother, Louis. Jean-Jacques Cartier had opened the second store in London in 1902. Then, two years ago, the Fifth Avenue location had opened, the third in the Cartier crown. "A shop for each brother," the *New York Times* had reported upon its opening.

"Speaking of secrets, maybe Mr. Cartier will show us the mysterious Hope Diamond while we are here," Letty said as we walked into the building and approached the elevator. "Everyone is talking about it. It's cursed. Surely you've read about that."

"Who hasn't?" I asked. "But that's a silly rumor."

We entered the elevator. Letty requested Cartier's, and the operator pulled the doors closed with a metal *clang*. We rose jerkily upward.

"Father said it was quite controversial for Cartier to choose a fourth-floor shop instead of one on street level, but I think it was rather clever," my sister said. "There are never any crowds or people ogling through the window. The privacy is quite soothing. Not like our Jewel Box," she added.

"But Garland's doesn't sell the types of extravagant jewels Mr. Cartier does," I said.

"I wasn't criticizing Father's decision," she snapped.

I was about to respond, but the elevator had stopped, and the operator opened the gate for us.

I'd never visited the store and was surprised to see it was so much smaller than Tiffany & Co. on Thirty-seventh Street. Then again, Mr. Tiffany sold lamps, vases, dinnerware, silverware, and glassware, as well as jewelry, whereas Cartier's kept its inventory focused on jewelry and bibelots.

To my surprise, there was no sign that we'd entered a jewelry store at all. We walked into a carpeted sitting room with a scattering of delicate chairs and small tables, with soft green walls and curtains pulled back to reveal a view of Fifth Avenue below. Fine crystal chandeliers with multiple arms and rainbow teardrops of glass hung down, shedding a soft, warm glow.

"Where is the jewelry?" I asked.

My sister, who pointed to the elegant wainscoting, said, "There are drawers cleverly built into the paneling that pull out. You'll see."

A well-dressed man approached us.

Letty greeted him. "Good afternoon, Mr. Fontaine."

"Mrs. Briggs, how nice to see you. Can I be of assistance?" he asked.

"I have an appointment with Mr. Cartier," Letty told him.

"Of course. He's just finishing up a call. Can I offer you seats and some refreshments? Champagne, perhaps?"

Unlike American establishments, Cartier's followed its European counterparts and served champagne.

Letty said yes, we'd love some, and off he went. While he was gone, Letty told me that unlike the shop's jewelers and designers who had moved from Paris with Mr. Cartier to open the New York branch, Mr. Fontaine wasn't an import but a native.

"The only person you'll meet here who doesn't speak with an accent."

Mr. Fontaine returned with two coupes of pale golden liquid and a plate of thin cookies.

I took a sip of the dry, effervescent wine and thought of my father. He traveled to France twice a year, not just to see the latest fashions for the ready-to-wear department but also to bring back foodstuffs and liquors for both the store and his private stock. Cases of the best champagne were always included.

"Madame Briggs," Mr. Cartier said in a soft, heavily French-accented voice, as he walked into the viewing room a few minutes later. The jeweler was a medium-tall, dapper man with dark hair, a high forehead, and a strong nose. His dark brown eyes sparkled as he smiled at my sister.

"What a delight to see you again," Cartier said, bowing slightly and taking Letty's hand.

She greeted him and then introduced us. "Have you met my sister? Miss Vera Garland?"

I'd never been to his shop, but since he and my father were colleagues and friends, I'd come in contact with the jeweler several times socially.

"Yes, I have," he said as he took my hand. "It's lovely to see you again, Mademoiselle Garland."

"And you, Mr. Cartier."

The middle brother of the world-class jewelry concern, Pierre Cartier was well known in New York society not only as an entrepreneurial businessman and purveyor of magnificent gems but also as a benefactor of the arts. Together with his American wife, the heiress Elma Rumsey, he supported many causes, including the Brooklyn Museum and the Metropolitan Opera. The couple's names were in the columns at least once a month, as much because of the former Miss Rumsey's notoriety as her husband's.

By 1910, Cartier had already built quite a reputation for his New York shop, his largesse, and the parties he and his wife threw. I'd been to more than one of his galas with my parents at his Beaux Arts Parisian-style town house at 15 East Ninety-sixth Street, which was quite large, boasting more than thirty rooms, eleven bathrooms, and seven fireplaces. And Mr. Cartier had attended my father's funeral ten months before.

"So, you are here to try on your earrings, Madame?" Mr. Cartier asked Letty.

"Yes, your note said you wanted to check the way they sit on my ears?"

"Indeed. Let me go and fetch them and—"

"I was wondering," Letty interrupted, "if we could see the Hope Diamond as well. While we are here."

Did Mr. Cartier hesitate for a second? I wasn't sure, but there was the subtlest change in his expression. "I would be delighted. But let me warn you in advance, you mustn't touch it. I've devised a way you can try it on without coming into contact with it directly, but we have to follow strict precautions. While I act as its guardian, I must be careful that its curse doesn't rub off on my customers."

And on that ominous note, he left the room.

"What nonsense," I said to Letty once we were alone again. "Pierre Cartier, worried about a curse? Father always said he was the best salesman he ever met. I would bet that this is all part of his act."

"Quite so. Jack calls him 'the showman.' But even if this is all just to get attention for the stone, I wouldn't risk touching it, would you?"

Before I could answer, Mr. Cartier returned with a leather tray that he placed on the table before us. "Your earrings, Madame," he said with a flourish.

The earrings were displayed lying on dark gray velvet. They sparkled like delicate flowers moistened by spring rain. Amethyst petals surrounded a gold pink-sapphire-studded pistil. Delicate leaves with pavé emeralds peeked out.

Letty clipped on first one and then the other. After they were in place, Mr. Cartier studied them. Then he positioned the big oval table mirror so that it reflected Letty's image back to her. She turned her head this way and that and then looked at me.

"What do you think?"

"They are beautiful," I said, and they were. The emeralds and sapphires complemented her skin tones, and the amethysts matched her violet eyes.

"I think so, too," she said, beaming.

"I think they are sitting a bit too far back on the lobe. We can adjust that. Now, tell me about the fit?" Mr. Cartier asked.

As Letty focused, a tiny frown creased her

forehead. "They might be a bit too tight," she said to Mr. Cartier.

"Let me get our jeweler to adjust them."

He rang for Mr. Fontaine and made the request.

A few moments later, the door to the viewing room opened. I glanced over as a man ambled out, wearing a gray smock over black slacks. Everything about him was long and thin—his legs, his arms, even his hands. His black hair fell in waves over his collar. Despite his height, he moved elegantly, purposefully, without looking at either Letty or me but rather at Mr. Cartier.

"Ah, Mr. Asher," Mr. Cartier said, and he explained the issue with the earrings.

"I'd be happy to help adjust the clips," the jeweler said in a low, slow voice with an accent I couldn't quite recognize. A bit British but with something else mixed in.

"These are particularly lovely stones. Siberian amethysts are very rare," Mr. Asher said as he worked on the earrings with one of the tools he'd taken out of his smock pocket. "If you look deeply into the stones, you'll see that there are red flashes at six and twelve o'clock. These alternating zones of purple and blue account for the delightful and particularly velvety look that is the hallmark of a Siberian's quality. Christian bishops often wore amethyst rings, since its color symbolized royalty and an allegiance to Christ."

I tried to catch Letty's eyes. Was she as

surprised as I was that Mr. Asher was talking to us about the stones? Maybe I had been wrong to assume he was at a low rung in the hierarchy at the shop. Mr. Cartier appeared comfortable with his jeweler's recitation. In any case, Letty didn't notice me. She was too engrossed in listening and watching him work on her earring.

My eyes returned to Mr. Asher, and I found myself mesmerized by how his long fingers moved. Like a musician's, I thought, and for a moment, I remembered a man I'd loved long ago and how his fingers had moved on his cello . . . how his hand had held his bow . . .

Mr. Asher finished with one earring and offered it to my sister. She clipped it on.

"Next to your face, with the color of your eyes, the stones really are perfect," Mr. Asher said.

I had long since gotten over Maximilian Ritter but had never forgotten his sensuous beauty and how his touch had moved me as much as his music had. Since then, I'd never noticed the same grace in another man's hands, but Mr. Asher's made me shiver.

As if he felt me looking at him, Mr. Asher turned and met my eyes. His were dark green and unfathomable. Liquid mystery, I thought, and then wanted to laugh. I was beginning to sound like a stage review on one of the women's pages—and describing a heartthrob, no less.

"I think it's still a tad tight," my sister said, and

gave the earring back to him. "And thank you for all that information. I didn't know anything about amethysts before."

"Mr. Asher is our resident raconteur in addition to being one of our most trusted jewelers," Mr. Cartier explained. "Even I have learned innumerable facts from him. We call him 'the wizard' because of all the arcane and esoteric knowledge he possesses."

"Are there stories about amethysts?" Letty asked. She was flirting a little bit, the way she often did. I wasn't surprised. Mr. Asher had a certain charm, with that rakish smile and the way his green eyes sparkled.

"Oh, yes, they have a rich and storied history," he said. "In mythology, Amethyst was a Greek girl who had a run-in with Bacchus and was saved by Diana. The stone was said to have been one of ten in the breastplate of the high priest of Israel in ancient times. In 1652, Thomas Nicols, the preeminent lapidary, declared it to be of equal value to a diamond of the same weight. Mostly, it's believed to be a protective stone, one that helps rid the mind of negative thoughts."

"Stones have powers?" I asked.

Mr. Cartier answered, maybe to regain control. "*Bien sûr*. Powers and properties. Some that are considered occult."

"How very interesting," Letty said.

As Mr. Asher stepped forward, offering both of

the earrings to my sister for her to try on one last time, I caught a whiff of his scent. The metallic fragrance of warm rain mixed with smoke. And underneath those top notes, I detected a creamy amber. The combination stirred me. It was almost familiar, but I couldn't pull a memory of it. It was as if someone had planted the idea of this scent in me once, and now I had finally happened upon it.

While Letty looked at herself in the mirror and adjusted the earrings, Mr. Asher turned to me. "You should wear spessartite—rare garnets— often called mandarin garnets because of their deep orange hue," he said. "They are named for the Spessart district of Bavaria. They would pick up the russet tones in your hair and the fiery color in your eyes. Spessartite is known to be a healing stone and is said to stimulate the analytical properties of the mind."

"An excellent idea, Asher. I'll have to get some in and show Mademoiselle Garland. Mr. Tiffany favors them in some of his more colorful pieces, but I like seeing them in simpler settings."

Did I detect competition between Cartier and Tiffany? There was no question the two eponymous retail establishments were considered the best in the city, with Tiffany being a bit more of a household name due to its wider range of goods.

Mr. Asher caught my eye and smiled. He'd

noted Cartier's tone, too. An understanding passed between us.

My heart seemed to hold for a beat. I felt a flash of something as deep as the red sparkle in my sister's earrings. Were this man and I simpatico? No, that was ridiculous. We'd exchanged a quick glance that had lasted for mere seconds. This was the stuff of the sentimental novels that my sister read. Surely I was overreacting; it had been a long time since I'd had any kind of connection with a man. Except, if I were honest with myself, this was different. I felt him in my bones. And it scared me.

The men I met as Vera Garland treated me like a bonbon or an arm ornament, and they were not interested in talking about politics or social reform with a woman. And I couldn't trust the men I met as Vee Swann. Although I had more in common with other reporters and may have had some interest there, as a result, they instinctively always looked for the story, and I had secrets to protect. I never wanted to give any of them the opportunity to ferret out my true identity. That would be the end of my career, and I didn't want that.

"I'm sorry, but this one is still a tiny bit tight," my sister said to Mr. Asher as she took off the left earring.

Mr. Asher took it from her, made another adjustment, and handed it back.

She tried it again and announced it was perfect. "And now can we see the Hope?"

Mr. Cartier smiled. "Of course," he said, and turned to Mr. Asher. "Would you bring it out along with the bib?"

"The bib?" I asked.

"Because of the bad luck associated with the Hope Diamond," Mr. Cartier explained, "Mr. Asher created a metal bib for clients to wear. The necklace sits on that so the stone never comes in contact with your clothes or skin."

"But surely that's all the stuff of legend," I said. "Neither of you actually believes a jewel can bring bad luck." I looked from Mr. Cartier to Mr. Asher.

"The legends go back hundreds of years. It's my responsibility to take all precautions and protect my clients," Mr. Cartier said with the utmost seriousness.

"And you, Mr. Asher?"

That slight smile appeared on Mr. Asher's lips again. "Since I can't prove there isn't bad luck, I find myself left to believe it," he said, and then went off to retrieve the legendary stone.

"Let's go into the viewing room," Mr. Cartier said to Letty and me, escorting us out of the main showroom and into a smaller room decorated in the same colors and style but more intimate. He offered us seats at a French Louis XV desk and then turned to pull the drapes, casting us in shadow. Then he sniffed.

"It's a bit stuffy in here," he said. Opening a

drawer, he pulled out a leather-covered wooden box. From inside, he took out a stick of incense, which he lit and set to burn in a crystal ashtray. The scent of sandalwood and frankincense began to permeate the room—a mixture that at once brought to mind the mystery of a place of worship in a foreign and unknown land.

"The diamond has had quite a storied past," he said as the thin wisp of smoke filled the shadows, setting his stage. "And quite a legend has sprung up around it. Imagine, if you will, an ancient temple deep in the heart of India, where men and women had been going for years to pray and make sacrifices to their Hindu god. The year is 1668. A rather well-known merchant, by the name of Jean-Baptiste Tavernier, has traveled the Orient in search of rare and precious gems. Following rumors about a great diamond in the head of a Indian temple god, Tavernier finds the temple. This is an ancient and fantastical place. Entering, Tavernier sees only darkness, but he smells a heavenly incense not unlike the one filling this room now. Tavernier's senses open like a flower. The hairs on the back of his neck tingle. His eyes begin to adjust. And as they do, he can make out priests in attendance, tending to the shrine. They welcome him into the shadows and give him a tallow with which to gaze upon their treasure. He looks at the great carved figure of their god. He takes in the head and arms and torso, and then

. . . then his gaze rests on the stone in the god's forehead, between his eyes. The statue's third eye is a giant diamond. He can't look away."

Mr. Cartier paused for a moment. My brother-in-law had been right; he was not just a salesman but a showman, and this was a great performance.

"The diamond was most likely from the Kollur mine in Golconda, India. Tavernier stares at the crudely cut, somewhat triangular shape and is mesmerized by its beautiful violet color. He knows why the cut is so rough. The Indians put great faith in gemstones having protective powers against evil influences. And so when they cut a stone, they try to keep as much surface and depth as they can. They believe stones are like a Pandora's box. They absorb negative energy and keep it contained. So of course, the largest stones are the most revered and valuable.

"Tavernier can't take his eyes off the gem. He knows that no matter how long it takes, no matter what he has to do, he must have this diamond to bring back to Paris with him. This is something King Louis XIV, the extravagant Sun King of France, will reward him for."

I glanced at Letty, who was as enthralled as I was by the tale the jeweler was spinning in his delightful accent.

"The story of how Tavernier steals the diamond is quite violent. First, he pays off a guard, who lets him into the temple deep in the night when the monks take their rest. Oddly, he has no trouble plucking out the stone. The diamond just sits in a crevice in the statue. The monks were certain no one would ever tempt fate and try to steal a gem with such power, lest they be struck down and destroyed. The stories about the diamond's power had protected it for centuries. Until that very night.

"Tavernier runs out through the temple doors and into the black-as-pitch night, a pack of wild dogs chasing him back to his lodging, biting at his legs, rearing up and nipping at his hands. He barely survives the attack.

"The bad luck has begun.

"Tavernier returns to France with his treasure—a great violet-blue diamond weighing, we guess based on drawings, more than one hundred carats. The maharajas of India prefer their diamonds very large rather than brilliant, but King Louis is more interested in symmetry and brilliance than size. So Louis orders the diamond to be recut by his jeweler, Jean Pittan, who cuts the facets into several star shapes, sets the gem in gold, and mounts it on a stick made of precious metal.

"When he holds it against a gold sheet, a golden sun appears at the diamond's center, symbolizing the king's power and glory.

"Louis XV inherits the diamond from his father, and in 1749 has the diamond reset in an insignia piece for the Royal Order of the Golden Fleece, which he wears often and, it is said, with great pride. As an honor, for an appearance at court, the king allows a man close to him, Nicolas Fouquet, to wear it. Not long after, the king finds him stealing from the treasury and charges him with life imprisonment. Fouquet spends the next fourteen years of his life entombed in the fortress of Pignerol. The bad luck has followed the stone to France.

"Louis XV's grandson, King Louis XVI, is the next owner of the French Blue; his infamous wife Marie Antoinette's love of diamonds not only adds to her extravagant reputation but leads to her and her husband's unfortunate demise.

"In 1792, during the French Revolution, all the crown jewels, including the French Blue, are stolen from the royal treasury. We do not know precisely what happened to the diamond after that, but we believe it was smuggled out of France. There are stories that the English King George IV might have owned the stone for a time, since he was known to have an appetite for large gemstones. But we do know for sure that the diamond next surfaces in 1839, when it appears in the collection catalog of Henry Philip Hope, a prominent London banker and diamond collector. It is from him the diamond receives its current name. Although Monsieur Hope includes no record of this diamond's pedigree in his catalog, there is one stone of such distinct size and color it could only have been cut from the French Blue."

Mr. Cartier paused. My sister and I waited for him to continue. He had us in his thrall.

"I cannot, of course, vouch that Tavernier stole the gem from a Hindu idol or that he was cursed and chased by dogs or, as the story goes, torn apart by savage beasts on his next trip to India. But from all the research I have been able to conduct, the diamond has brought bad luck to those who have owned it and in many cases some who did no more than touch it.

"Let's look at what happened. First to Louis XIV, who died a horrible death from gangrene. And we all know about the knife blade that sliced through Louis XVI's and Marie Antoinette's throats. In the early 1800s, a Dutch jeweler named Wilhelm Fals recut the diamond, which was then stolen by his son. Fals committed suicide or died of grief over the theft in 1830. His son eventually killed himself. King George, also an owner, died penniless. Lord Hope's grandnephew and heir to the diamond had plenty of troubles. He was in a terrible accident, had his leg amputated. His wife eloped with Captain Strong. Hope also went bankrupt and had to sell the stone in 1902. One story claims an eastern European prince bought it for a Folies Bergère dancer and later shot her. A Greek tycoon bought it, and shortly afterward, he and his family were all killed in an automobile accident. The Turkish sultan Abdul-Hamid II had owned the diamond for only months when an army revolt cost him the Ottoman Empire."

With this, Cartier opened the leather-bound scrapbook I had noticed on the table. Each page contained a newspaper or magazine headline about the famous gem's history. Some were illustrated, others not. We perused the book while we waited for Mr. Asher to bring in the necklace.

From the *London Times*, Friday, June 25, 1909, dateline Paris. *Like most other famous stones, its story is largely blended with tragedy. Its possession is the story of a long series of tragedies—murder, suicide, madness and various other misfortunes.*

And from the *Washington Post*, January 19, 1908: *Remarkable Jewel a Hoodoo—Hope Diamond Has Brought Trouble to All Who Have Owned It. Deep behind the double locked doors hides the Hope Diamond. Snug and secure behind time locked bolt, it rests in its cotton wool nest under many wrappings, in the great vault of the House of Frankel. Yet not all the locks and bolts and doors ever made by man can ward off its baleful power or screen from its venom those against whom its malign force may be directed.*

Every gem has its own power for good or evil and this power never dies though it may wax or wane under the circumstances, may lie dormant for centuries only to reappear with redoubled energy when terrestrial and celestial conditions combine to bring into play the mysterious force beneath its glittering surface.

I guessed Mr. Cartier had every bit of this presentation staged, because just as we reached the end of that paragraph, he spoke: "I myself believe that superstitions of this ilk are baseless. Yet one must admit, they are amusing, and to use an old saying, it is better to be safe than sorry."

And with that, there was a soft knock on the door.

Mr. Cartier murmured, *"Entrez,"* and Mr. Asher stepped in, right on cue. Cartier's storytelling had been quite well done. I'd very much felt I was at the theater, and now the moment of the grand denouement had arrived.

Mr. Asher had donned a pair of white gloves and in his hands held a leather box that he placed on the table before us. I caught his eye, and he gave me the trace of a smile in return.

With a flourish befitting the theatrics, Mr. Cartier opened the box. "And here . . . is . . . the Hope Diamond."

Letty and I gazed down at the gem.

Indeed, the color was astonishing—not a sky blue but a dark, steely one. A true blue-violet stunner.

"Mr. Asher, please tell these charming ladies a bit about the gemography of the stone."

"A diamond starts out life as a piece of coal and transforms over millennia into a gem-quality stone. Its ultimate value depends on its size, quality, clarity, and color."

The Hope, partly because of its piercing color, did resemble an eye, and I imagined it in the Hindu idol. What mystery must have surrounded the stone when Tavernier first saw it in that holy place? I looked deep into its surface and in its facets imagined I could see the ages.

"What is so unusual about this diamond, if I may, is not only its size but its color," Mr. Asher said. "It has the depth and hue of a sapphire but also possesses the brilliance and perfection only seen in diamonds."

Letty reached out her hand toward the necklace.

"No, please, Madame Briggs." Cartier held out his hand to prevent my sister from touching the stone. "Please do not touch it. I wouldn't want to be responsible for anything untoward happening to you."

I looked at Letty and raised my eyebrows. The theatrics of Mr. Cartier's warning were a bit over the top. But I could tell my sister was already invested in the idea that ill will followed the gem's owners and those who came in close contact with it.

Like my father, I didn't believe in the idea of bad luck any more than I believed in the power of prayer or a God on high looking down on all

51

of us and making decisions about who would live or die, get sick or be well.

While the two of us shared our lack of faith, we mostly kept our conversations to ourselves, since Mother and Letty and my grandparents were all devout Presbyterians. Father agreed to attend church with my mother only when it was an occasion and even then refused to pray, much to my mother's consternation.

"Would you like to try it on?" Mr. Cartier asked Letty.

"I'm not sure. What about the bad luck?"

"That's what the bib is for." He turned to Mr. Asher, who pulled a flat metal necklace from his smock pocket. It was the same shape as the Hope but extended the stone's dimensions by at least a quarter of an inch on every side.

"This is a precaution," Mr. Cartier said as he gestured to the undernecklace. "It is made of platinum and acts as a shield between the Hope and your body without ruining the effect of being able to see yourself wearing the gem. I don't really believe it is at all necessary, but if there is such a thing as a curse attached to the Hope, it will protect you from having any physical contact with the diamond."

I wanted to laugh, but Mr. Cartier was taking this all quite seriously, as was my sister. Mr. Asher was fastening the bib around her neck, which prevented me from seeing his face or gauging his reaction. So I held my tongue as the jeweler closed the protective necklace's clasp and then turned back to the table.

Mr. Asher lifted the Hope Diamond out of its box and unhooked its catch. As he did, the necklace swung in the air. For one brief moment, I saw the blue diamond make contact with the strip of Mr. Asher's skin between the glove and his sleeve. He hadn't seemed to notice. But I had.

I looked over at Mr. Cartier. He'd noticed, too, and was frowning. Maybe he believed in the curse more than he'd let on. Or perhaps he was just pretending.

With care, Mr. Asher affixed the Hope Diamond necklace around my sister's neck and then positioned the mirror so she could see herself.

Letty was mesmerized by her image. She tilted her head this way and that as Mr. Cartier murmured words of admiration.

"The color," Mr. Cartier exclaimed with delight, "works so well with the color of your eyes. I wish the stone didn't have such a history of ill luck, or I would suggest to Monsieur Briggs that this would be a most perfect gift for you."

I stole a glance at Mr. Asher, who was studying the empty jewel box. Suddenly, he looked up. Like the diamond whose depths I could not read but found mysterious, his eyes were full of secrets, too. And as my sister knew, secrets were my downfall. I was pulled to them, fascinated by them. I often thought that yearning to know people's secrets was what drew me to being a reporter, not the other way around. What people kept protected and hidden inside them, what they were ashamed of, or what they felt was too sacred to share, gave you insight that nothing else did. I'd always felt it was only worth getting to know people if they had secrets, because only in the sharing could you discover someone's soul.

"There's been quite a lot of interest in the stone since we purchased it," Mr. Cartier was saying. "But it's not going to be easy to sell. How many women are there who would dare wear something so fraught with danger?"

"Vera?" Letty asked.

"Yes, dear?"

"What do you think? Would you be afraid of the bad luck? Would I be crazy to even think of buying this?"

"I don't believe in bad luck," I said, glancing over at Mr. Asher again, but he was looking past me. I focused on my sister again. "But that doesn't mean I don't recognize danger when I see it."

CHAPTER 3

Back at the penthouse, alone again, I opened a bottle of my father's best burgundy. I filled a crystal glass and took it into the greenhouse. I settled into my favorite rattan armchair, took a sip of wine, and looked up at the skylight. The colors were slowly shifting from sunset ambers to evening roses and violets. The color made me think about the Hope, but neither the diamond nor its bad luck held my attention anymore. The morning would bring my brother-in-law to help me begin the process of packing up my father's clothes and personal items.

That left the apartment intact for just one more night.

If I was good at pretending, I could have decided my father was simply away on a buying trip. But he wasn't. He was well and truly gone.

Over the last few months, my mother's most constant criticism of me was that by putting off the inevitable purging of his personal items, I was prolonging my mourning to a point that was unhealthy.

"Why," she had asked at our last family dinner, "aren't you more receptive when it comes to my suggestions? I have never wanted anything but the best for you. By waiting so many months to clean out that apartment, you are just delaying the inevitable acceptance of your father's passing. It's morbid, Vera. You are settling into becoming an old maid. Is this how you want to live your life?"

She was partly right, though I was never going to admit it. So in response I offered, "When will you stop despairing for my marital state and accept me for who I am?"

When I was younger, it used to take me a long time to give up hope. But I'd since accepted that my mother would never change her mind about me. To her and my sister, I was a traitor to my heritage and breeding. I was not fulfilling the role of a Garland Girl. Not following in the footsteps I'd been expected to follow in since birth.

But damn my heritage and breeding. I was an idealist—or at least, I had been until recently—and I wanted to change the world. I enjoyed my freedom, cared about my career, and vowed not to ever be subservient to any man.

My father had never argued with me about my life choices. Instead, he had given me all the support and extra love he could to make up for what my mother withheld.

Except then, in his own way, he abandoned me, too, and now, at age thirty-two, I was truly left all on my own, left with my idealism in shreds and my father's secrets to unravel even if I didn't yet know it.

They always say that bad things come in threes, don't they? But who are *they?* And where do these superstitions come from? I don't believe in superstitions, old wives' tales, or, as I had told Mr. Cartier as we looked at the Hope, I didn't believe in luck—good or bad—or anything really that I couldn't touch, taste, hear, or smell.

Like my father, I believed in logic. "Reason," he always said, "will never disappoint you."

Except that in succession, starting in September 1909, I had suffered three tragedies and with them a total loss of confidence and hope that reason would win out.

The first was work-related. I was investigating what I called "tenement babies" for the *World*, where, under my pseudonym of Vee Swann, I'd been one of the few female news reporters for the last eight years.

While there were laws in New York City forbidding children under fourteen to work in factories, there was none to stop parents from exploiting their young children's ability to work at home. If, that is, you could call the squalid and stinking tenements homes.

Children as young as three and four were put to work making artificial flowers, pulling bastings, and sewing buttons and tapes on gloves to bring in extra money, penny by penny.

My friend, social reformer Mary van Kleeck,

had written an article for *Charity Organization Quarterly* about the issue in 1908:

The evils of the system—intense competition among unskilled workers in a crowded district, low wages, unrestricted hours of work, irregularity of employment, and utilization of child labor—are the very conditions which make the system possible and profitable to the employer. Any effective attempt to improve conditions must therefore be an attack upon the sweating system. The manufacturer or contractor, whose employees work in their home, escapes responsibility entailed by the presence of workers in his factory. He saves costs of rent, heat, and light; avoids the necessity of keeping the force together and giving them regular employment when work is slack. And by turning the workers' homes into branches of the factory, he escapes in them the necessity of observing the factory laws. Instead of the manifold restrictions which apply to employees working in the factory, he is here responsible only for keeping a list of his home workers and he may not send any goods, which are named in the home work law, into a tenement which has not been licensed.

In my effort to research the injustice she'd outlined in her paper and write about it for the *World*, I'd gone undercover, as I often had before. In June 1909, I moved into a tenement on Ludlow Street, posing as a widowed factory worker.

As Vee Swann, I always wore a disguise. My cousin Stephen had gone to college with a woman whose father was one of the top costume designers on Broadway, and he'd helped create my alter ego's look. My wig was black, without any waves and with a bun that sat at the nape of my neck, nothing like my own auburn-red curls that I normally wore high on top of my head. As Vee, I also wore thick glasses. They were clear—since my eyesight was perfect—but no one looking at me would ever have suspected I wasn't half-blind.

As Vera Garland, I dressed well, indulged in jewelry, and always wore a light dusting of face powder, a brush of lipstick, and dabs of L'Étoile perfume that I purchased at the cosmetics and perfume departments of Father's store. But Vee Swann indulged in no such vanity. When I was reporting, I wore no makeup and donned only inexpensive dresses and shoes that I bought downtown. Even the least expensive clothes at Garland's were too fine for Vee.

I moved into the tenement with a small collection of belongings, bringing only two of my most worn dresses and oft-mended stockings. I pared down my necessities to fit into one ripped carpet bag I'd bought from a beggar in the streets.

After a few days of getting settled and watching the comings and goings in the tenements, I befriended my neighbors, the Danzingers, whom

I'd chosen to write about as an example of thousands of similar families. They included a mother and a father and four children all younger than ten. Two boys and two girls. All of them worked at home before and after school and over the weekends.

In the process of researching my piece, I fell hopelessly in love with seven-year-old Charlotte. This little girl made artificial roses out of rough red felt from dawn to eight a.m. and then went back to work as soon as she got home from school in the afternoon. Often she worked after dinner and late into the night. Charlotte was a winsome child with wide chocolate-brown eyes and a spattering of freckles across her nose. She spoke in a sweet, lilting voice and loved to laugh at her own jokes. We often sat on the front stoop of our building during her brief break after dinner, before she had to go back to her sewing. Charlotte would regale me with stories about the fairies who lived in the rocks by the East River and left children gifts during the night.

Early on, I started keeping wrapped candies in my pocket and would reward her with one at the end of each story. I began to notice that she would never eat the candy, just tuck it into her sleeve. Only after the fifth story and the fifth candy would she finally eat one.

Curious, I asked her why.

"I want to make sure there will be a candy

for all of us plus Ma, before I have mine," she answered while glancing up at the tenement window.

After that, I always gave her all five at one time, so she could enjoy hers with me on the steps.

I also bought secondhand books for her and her siblings to share, always picking out those I thought Charlotte would like the best.

To thank me, she made me little gifts of flowers with hearts embroidered on them. Her ability with needle and thread for one so young surprised me, until I discovered she'd been sewing since she was three.

"One day," she'd said as she handed me the third flower, "I'll have given you enough for you to have a bouquet."

"And I'll put it in a jelly jar and keep it forever," I said, kissing her on the forehead.

Charlotte moved my heart with her sweetness, sense of humor, and stubborn determination to do well in school no matter how tired she was, so she could write stories when she grew up. They'd all be about the fairies, she told me.

That summer, on Sundays when she had more free time, I helped her make a book to write her stories in. We sewed together the pages I'd bought for her and adorned it with a cover of blue felt.

She kept the handmade book in my apartment.

"So Pa won't see it and get mad," she'd told me. "He doesn't like me imagining all the time. He said it makes me work slower."

Her father was a drunk and a brute, and he didn't like my involvement with the family. He said the gifts of books and candy were me looking down on them. That they didn't need my charity. I never paid attention to his admonishments, which only increased his ire. He wasn't used to women not obeying him. But it was good for Charlotte, I thought, and her siblings to see that Leo Danzinger didn't scare everyone.

When Charlotte became ill that last Wednesday in August, I tried to intercede and persuade Danzinger to allow me to call her a doctor. He'd been drinking, as he usually did at night, and refused, slurring his words as he told me it was a waste of money. That Charlotte would sleep it off.

I went so far as to offer to pay for the doctor myself, but that only enraged Danzinger more. He shouted at me to mind my own business and forcibly pushed me out of their apartment. He shoved me so hard I lost my balance and tumbled down the stairs.

I was unconscious for hours. When I awoke in the vestibule at the bottom of the steps, I found it almost impossible to move because I was in so much pain. Something was wrong with my back. At dawn, our landlady finally opened her door to put out her milk bottles and noticed me.

I told her where to find some coins upstairs in my apartment. "Enough," I said, "to take a carriage to a doctor I know who will come and help."

When our family physician, Dr. Bernstein, arrived, he didn't recognize me at first. I whispered to him who I was and took off my glasses. Hurriedly, I explained about Charlotte, who I feared needed him more. I knew he was trustworthy, and besides, there was no time to waste. Even though he was shocked to see me in such a place and in such a state, he did as I asked and went up to see Charlotte before attending to me.

He returned after only ten minutes. Charlotte had not made it through the night, he told me, as he examined my bruised and battered body in the hallway. The little girl had died sometime before midnight. My physical pain was nothing compared to the emotional pain I felt hearing that. I was devastated to think that if not for her father's callous indifference, she could have been saved.

I'd broken two vertebrae in my back, so my editor assigned another reporter to write up the incident, and the article received a lot of attention. But I couldn't be reached for comment. I wrote to Mr. Nevins and said I was recuperating with my family and was taking a leave of absence from both my reporting and my column.

I moved back into my parents' house in Riverdale and stayed there for eight weeks. But even as my bones healed, my heart didn't. When I was finally well enough, I cloaked myself in the garments of Vee Swann and ventured downtown to the tenement house to see Charlotte's mother and siblings. I waited until I saw Mr. Danzinger leave for the night and then made my way upstairs, wincing with pain on each step. I had forgotten the stench of stale body odor, cabbage, and piss, and it made me gag.

Charlotte's mother opened the door at the sound of the knock, looked at me, and told me to leave.

"Please, let me come in, for just a few minutes. I want to help."

"You can't help. You didn't help before. You made everything worse."

Searching past her, I saw her other daughter, Alice, and her two sons, Bill and Henry, looking at me expectantly, hoping I had brought gifts. And I had, but Mrs. Danzinger wouldn't take them.

"I'm so sorry about what happened to Charlotte," I said. "I miss her so much. You must, too. All of you must."

Mrs. Danzinger's eyes filled with tears, but she didn't acknowledge my sympathy. "If my husband sees you here, I don't know what he'll do. Get out, and don't come back," she said, and shut the door in my face.

I left the bags of books and candy on the doorstep and made my way down the steps for the last time, thinking about the brown-eyed little girl who had dreamed of growing up and writing stories about fairies.

I wanted to help them but knew better than to openly interfere again. Instead, I had my father's charity reach out to Mrs. Danzinger, offering to help her if she wanted to have her husband brought up on charges or to take her three remaining children and leave him. She refused to do either.

When I heard that, I arranged to have the charity put her on its weekly delivery list, ensuring that the packages were given only to her and not her husband. We regularly helped hundreds of families with extra clothes, toys, books, and canned foodstuffs. I also made sure that once a month, Mrs. Danzinger received an envelope containing ten dollars, which she never refused.

Despite the fact that I had helped Charlotte's family, my spirit remained broken. Once I was able, I moved back to my rather unfashionable Chelsea apartment. I'd had the apartment for seven years. My mother had vehemently disapproved when I first moved in. She thought my disguise would be enough and didn't understand why I wanted to live among commoners—not that she called them that; she was too polite—but I knew that was what she thought. I'd wanted Vee Swann to have her own apartment, one she could afford. I'd decorated it with thrift-shop bargains. The kinds of cast-offs that fit Vee's salary. Despite the secondhand pieces, the apartment was cozy and welcoming, painted a warm peach, with lots of ferns and books and braided rugs. I'd found a couch upholstered in a leaf pattern and a green glass lamp in the exact same shade as the couch.

Once I recovered, I extended my leave at the *World*. Instead of writing serious stories for the newspaper, the column was all I was willing to tackle. Martha Sanderson and Fanny Ustead, two of my closest friends, both reporters, visited often. I made an effort to be cheery, but they knew I still wasn't myself. They took it upon themselves to urge me back to work, but I resisted. Faced with Charlotte's death and her mother's refusal of help to move her and her other children out of harm's way, I felt that all my efforts at shining light on injustice were a waste. I couldn't change anything. Not fundamentally.

Then the second tragedy occurred. Just two months later, in October, a fire gutted my apartment building. I wasn't hurt—I'd smelled the smoke and got out in time. But all the copies of all the articles I had ever written were lost forever. Charlotte's book of fairy stories and her bouquet of felt flowers, birthday cards from fellow journalists, photographs, souvenirs, trinkets . . . all the tiny, inconsequential things that go to make up a life's worth of memories—Vee Swann's memories—vanished in one night.

Without a place of my own to live, my father insisted I move into his apartment above Garland's, which boasted three bedrooms. Since he stayed there only when he worked too late to go home to the family manse in Riverdale, it was empty most of the time.

My father's penthouse had been designed by my uncle Percy, an architect who had also designed my father's store. Garland's was the first to move uptown to Fifth Avenue and Fifty-seventh Street—which in 1902 was shocking, since it wasn't yet fashionable to be up that far, and Uncle Percy had been bold and ultramodern in his designs both inside and out.

The apartment was even more splendid than the four-floor emporium beneath it. Perched high on the roof of the building, it had more windows than I'd ever seen in a New York City dwelling. It was like a mansion in the sky. Designed by Uncle Percy's friend, Louis Comfort Tiffany, each window was like a painting, framed by beribboned garlands of silver, blue, and lavender flowers with green trails of ivy. That winter, all the windows were laced with ice and glittered in the cold sun, splashing reflections of color onto the walls and carpets. Tiffany lampshades and tiles on the floor and in the bathrooms and kitchen echoed the silver, blue, and green color scheme, and the handsome furniture was all covered in dark sapphire and deep emerald velvets and silks. The drapes were heavy damask sapphire threaded with silver garlands—the store's logo.

A terrace wrapped its way around the whole apartment and on three sides was left open to the elements. Each spring, Father would call for a variety of bushes and flowers to be delivered. They would flourish and bloom in a riot of colors through the late summer.

On the east side of the terrace, my uncle had enclosed the outdoor space and erected a Victorian conservatory. Inside the greenhouse, a fountain sprayed water into another of Tiffany's fantasy creations, an iridescent mosaic-tiled pool surrounded by moss-covered rocks.

No matter the weather, we could sit on the rattan furniture among the palms and the orchids that my father tended like children, all thanks to the ingenious steam heating my uncle had installed.

Living there was healing, and I had finally started to feel like myself again when the third set of tragedies struck in early December. My uncle Percy died of food poisoning. He'd passed away during the night after a dinner, it was discovered later, that included oysters, which we all knew could sometimes be contaminated.

A week later, my father, who was only sixty-six and by all accounts extremely healthy, had a heart attack.

I had been out the morning it happened and returned home to find my father attended by Dr. Bernstein. He proclaimed it a mild attack and prescribed bed rest for two weeks, then a slow progression back to work.

My father chose to recuperate in the magical aerie at the top of Garland's. Every morning, department managers would visit to go over the store's issues and problems. Every afternoon, my mother and sister and Jack would arrive. At night, either Margery would make something or the Birdcage restaurant would send up dinner, and my father and I would eat on trays. He in his bed and me in the chair beside him.

After Father's heart attack, my work felt even less important. The only thing that mattered was tending to him and helping him recover. I couldn't bear to lose anyone else I loved.

But as it turned out, Dr. Bernstein's prognosis was wrong. Eleven days after the first attack, late one afternoon, after my mother and sister and Jack had left, I was sitting by my father's bedside reading out loud to him when he suffered another, much more severe attack.

I called Dr. Bernstein, who arrived within the half hour and saw my father alone. When he came out of the bedroom, he told me Father didn't want to go to the hospital. A nurse was coming to help me. I argued for taking him to the hospital regardless, but Dr. Bernstein shook his head and took my hand and told me that it was more important to let my father be where he was most comfortable. I, who always asked questions, who dug deep for information, who never settled on one answer if there was more to discover, didn't press. Nor did I ask if there would be any form of treatment. Or how much longer my father had. I didn't ask Dr. Bernstein a single question, because I knew everything I needed to know, and everything I didn't want to know, from the expression on his face.

I was with my father when he passed at nine that evening. Holding his hand, I watched his face and listened to his labored breath. How strange to be there when the soul takes flight. When a person goes from living to dead in a matter of seconds.

I never could have imagined what it would be like to see suffering calm. To see pain ease. My father didn't have any last words for me during those hours. But we held hands, and his fingers kept a slight pressure on mine, so I knew he was aware of my presence. Eventually, his hand stopped holding mine, and I knew he was gone.

I'm not sure how long I stayed there beside him. A half hour? An hour? Even after the nurse tried to get me to leave my father's bedside, I held his hand until I felt his flesh grow cold. And no matter what I did, I couldn't warm him. He'd left me in silence without any loving last words of advice or wishes or farewell.

But we had talked a lot in the days before. Had he spoken like a dying man? I hadn't thought so at the time. Rather, I thought he sounded like a man who had faced a crisis and it had made him contemplative. But looking back, I think he must have known how close he was to death all along.

The night before he passed, it was snowing. After our dinner, he said he wanted to have some port in the conservatory. He had seemed to be improving, and there was no reason not to indulge him. He walked a bit slowly but on his own, wearing one of the silk dressing gowns Garland's sold in the men's department. It was navy blue with a garland of green on the pocket and green piping along the edges. We sat under the gently falling snow, protected from the cold by thick glass and warm steam heat, and I thought he looked well, definitely less ashen than he'd been.

It's always lovely in the greenhouse, but with a full moon turning the icy frost silver and the little votive candles that were scattered about the room, that night was magical. We sat, silent at first, enjoying the port and each other's company, and then my father began telling me about my mother when they first met.

My father's family had owned a farm in Ellenville, New York. They weren't wealthy but were hardworking. When he began to shine in grade school, reading before most of his classmates and showing a great aptitude for math, my grandparents began to save up so they could give their only child the higher education he deserved.

Granville Garland did well enough in high school to get into Yale, where he majored in business with the hopes that he could turn his parents' farm into an even more successful concern. Those plans were abandoned after he spent a summer in New York working for Theodore B. Starr at his downtown store on Twenty-sixth Street and Broadway. The shop sold jewelry, silver, and clocks, as well as paintings, furniture, and sculpture. He told me that he felt as if he'd woken up after a long sleep. And it was that summer he discovered his aptitude for selling and enthusiasm for a city retail environment, as well as a real love for being surrounded by beautiful things.

During his second year at Yale, Granville roomed with my mother's older brother, Percy Winthrop, and they became fast friends. At the end of that term, Percy invited my father to his family's summer house in Newport. He told me that when he arrived at the Meadows and met Percy's sister, Henrietta March Winthrop, he was instantly struck by her beauty. She looked like a portrait by John Singer Sargent, he said, with her graceful figure, long neck, thick chestnut hair, and electric-green eyes.

"But it was her rebellious nature that made me believe I could be happy with her. She had such a fiery streak back then," my father said with a half-hearted chuckle. "Your mother was studying art and very determined to be a painter. A powerful determination, just like you have, Vera. That's why you two fight so much. She sees in you . . . the woman she might have been."

I couldn't imagine that. My mother was the epitome of a society matron. The proper fork was as important as her children's happiness.

"What changed her?" I asked.

My father shrugged. "Once we were married, she settled into the life that she'd been born to live. On our honeymoon trip abroad, she gave up oils for watercolors, and although I didn't realize at the time, that was a turning point. It wasn't submission. She just didn't *need* to become an artist anymore. She was Mrs. Granville Garland, and that, she once told me, was less arduous than struggling with her family to be taken seriously as an artist. I think as much as she yearned to make her own way, she just didn't have the mettle or the strength to keep fighting. But you do," he said.

"So she gave up her dream for the reality of

homes and children and dinners and teas and gowns. As if her rebellion was a costume, and she just took it off?" I asked.

"Don't judge her. Your mother was raised to conform. The effort to keep fighting in order to become someone else was too great for her in the end." He paused. "And anyway, I don't honestly think being that someone else would have made her any happier."

"What would have?"

"I hoped that I and the life I provided could have, but I failed." There was another pause, this one longer. "Hope, darling Vera, is the fire that keeps propelling us forward. We hope even in the face of impossibility, and that is as it should be. I think you've let its spark go out, haven't you?"

I shrugged.

"You need to admit it. You've given up since that little girl died, haven't you?" My father knew me better than anyone else.

"Maybe, maybe I have."

"Sweetheart, you have to forgive yourself. Even if you can't save everyone, you can make a difference. You have things to accomplish. I know you do. Reignite that spark, darling. And then don't ever let it die out again . . . Do you promise you'll try?"

"I'll do my best," I said.

He always had wine with dinner and port afterward. And the doctor had said it was good for him. So when he asked me for more, I was happy to oblige. He picked up his glass and looked at it in the candlelight, studying it as if there were words in the deep ruby-amber liquid. He took a sip. And another. And then resumed talking about my mother. But as it turned out, he was really speaking of his own failure.

"I really believed I could make her happy, trying so hard to be someone I wasn't . . . to be proper and conform . . . for your mother and your sister and you . . . trying not to . . . not to need all this so much." He gestured to the glorious greenhouse and the rooms beyond it.

I was confused by his comment. "Need this? What? The apartment?"

My father ignored my question. "I want you to really promise you will try and find your spirit again. Not just for the sake of your work . . . but for your soul. I don't want you to spend your life alone looking for perfection or wasting time avoiding hurt. To live a full life, you need a full heart. Even though a heart can break from loss, it's worth the risk. Even with my very broken heart, I don't regret a day."

If I were anything other than a reporter, I would have reacted to my father's death with sadness and grief, accepted his bequest of the apartment, and not paid much mind to the mysterious comments he'd made that night. He'd been, at that very moment, facing his mortality, after all. I would have considered his words a natural response to that.

But I am a reporter, and his cryptic confession continued to taunt me after his death. What had he really meant? It bothered me that I might never know. But with him gone, other than peppering my mother with questions—something that, based on past experience, I knew would only result in frustration—how could I find out?

And as for his plea that I not give up hope?

I tucked that away as a request that it was already too late to fill. My father was right: I had given up most of my hope the night Charlotte died. And then more of it when her mother refused help. And the paltry bit that was left? When I saw my father laid out in his coffin, his silver hair brushed back off a handsome face no longer animated, his always moving hands stilled and crossed on his chest, his aquamarine eyes closed against the light, what little hope I had left took flight.

CHAPTER 4

On Saturday morning, I woke filled with anxiety. My brother-in-law would be arriving at nine, and I dreaded our task of going through my father's effects. I didn't want to change how things were. Not in the apartment. Not in the curious existence I'd grown accustomed to. I spent very little time with other people, instead occupying my days reading the history books on my father's bookshelves and only venturing out at night to attend enough events to fill my column. Usually, that required going out at least twice a week. I'd attend a Broadway show or a ball or go to the opera or a concert. And as always, with my mother. Sometimes we were joined by my sister and Jack.

They say a child, even a grown child, always yearns for her mother's love. I wonder if another reason I continued writing Silk, Satin and Scandals was that it kept me connected to my mother in a way I was loath to give up, despite the disappointment, resentment, and pain that seethed between us. When we ventured out to events together, I knew I pleased her. During those outings, I was the daughter she'd expected me to be. Wholly and unconditionally. And while I so wished for her to be just as accepting about all the parts of my life, I decided to simply take what I could get—a glimmer of the way we once were, before I grew up and began to disappoint her.

My life was full of so many befores and afters, I realized, as I pulled an old shirtwaist over my dress to protect it from dust and cobwebs. There was my life before Radcliffe, when I was much less of a contrarian, and after, when I began to follow the path of my hero, Nellie Bly. Before my affair with the cellist, Maximilian Ritter, and after the devastating discovery that inspired me to truly go undercover. Before Charlotte died and after, when I lost faith in my ability to help those in need. And finally, before my father died and after, of which, at this moment, I had yet to know the outcome.

I hadn't moved any of my father's clothes or knickknacks or books. I hadn't gone through his armoire or his desk and separated his papers. I had rarely set foot in his bedroom, which was the first place Jack and I tackled when he arrived.

"You have been keeping this room like a shrine," my brother-in-law said as he looked around.

He walked to the closet, and as he opened the door, the scent of my father's cologne wafted out toward me. At first, it was comforting, but a second later, it was a mean reminder of what was gone.

Jack set to work, taking a shirt off its hanger and inspecting it for wear.

As the owner of one of Manhattan's most fashionable department stores, my father had the finest wardrobe. We decided Jack would offer the items in excellent condition to the employees, and whatever they didn't want he'd give to the Janus Shelter, which helped men find jobs and gave them clothes to wear. It was a charity my father had helped found—named for the Greek god of beginnings, choices, and doorways.

"Are you going to stay on here in the penthouse permanently?" Jack asked as he moved on to the next item of clothing.

"Yes, I think so. Why?"

"I'm not suggesting you leave, Vera," he said. "This is your apartment now."

"So why were you asking?"

"I just wonder if it's the best thing for you. You know, I only want to help."

"I do know," I said, because it was true.

Jack Baxter Briggs had been married to my sister for nearly ten years. He was two years older than she was, thirty-two, like me. He had become the chairman of Garland's Emporium even before my father passed on. After his first heart attack, my father had confided in me that he planned on slowing down, perhaps traveling more, and turning over day-to-day operations of the store to Jack. And why shouldn't he have?

Jack had been his protégé. The son of one of my father's closest friends, Jack had studied business at Yale University, like my father, and had gone to work at Garland's after graduating. His own father was a bit chagrined that Jack didn't want to follow in his footsteps at his bank, but Jack loved retail. And when he fell in love with my sister, my parents were overjoyed. My father never regretted not having a son, but at the same time, I knew he hated the idea that he wouldn't be able to turn Garland's over to someone in the family.

Letty and Jack married in 1900, had three children, and lived in Riverdale in a mansion abutting my parents'. My father had given the couple the land as a wedding present. Another parcel was bought for me at the same time, despite my protestations that I never planned to marry. I wanted my career, and working women were expected to give up their jobs upon marrying. Of course, some fought the convention and won, but it was a battle I didn't plan to undertake. My experiences with romance hadn't been very successful, as I seemed to have a knack for choosing the wrong men. I'd also argued about the gift of the land because I would die rather than live so far from the heart of Manhattan. I hated the quiet of the suburbs and craved the noise and activity that only a city like New York could provide.

"I think if you are going to continue living here," Jack was saying, "which was very much what your father hoped, then it's much healthier to clear out his things and make the apartment yours. I don't know why I didn't think of helping sooner. You shouldn't have to do it alone, Vera."

And that brought tears. Once Jack saw them, he dropped what he was doing and gathered me up in a brotherly embrace.

"Now, now . . . I'm here to help, OK?"

Through the tears wetting his jacket, I nodded.

"I'll come in every weekend if that's what it takes—"

I pulled away. "Oh, no, I could never ask you to take time away from Letty and the boys."

"I'm not giving up anything by helping you. Never think that. You're the sister I never had," Jack said. "And your father was closer to me than my own ever was. I want to do this. I know he'd want me to."

Unspoken was the actuality that my sister and mother had all but abandoned me in this task. My mother insisted that it wasn't my job and that I should just have her butler come and pack it all up. And my sister agreed with her. I wondered if the real reason was that she was actually too grief-stricken to help. Jack loved my sister so much he often ignored her faults. He was full of life and adventure, brave and creative and bursting with ideas about the future of retail and how things were changing. He was funny and irreverent and had a healthy skepticism about social mores and the ridiculous etiquette that my mother and sister lived by or the way they could distance themselves from situations they found uncomfortable or distasteful. A bit cowardly, one might say. And yet he looked at Letty with a supplicant's eyes. He adored her. Cherished her. As if she were the delicate flower she was named after.

I'd never met the favorite aunt Father had named me after. But he always compared her to a bolt of lightning. "Striking and bold," he said. "Vera commanded attention by making her own way."

I'd heard all the stories about how she'd opened up her own millinery store in the Bronx and designed the most outlandish hats and married a poet who was suspected of bigamy. Regardless of his questionable marital status, Vera and Stuart hosted popular literary salons and then died, together, in a boating accident off the Montauk coast, before I was born.

Letty and I had wound up with the names we deserved. And she had gotten the man she deserved, as well.

I thanked Jack for his kindness, and we continued on through the morning going through my father's things.

"Don't put those in the pile. I can wear them," I said, eyeing the soft gray and brown cashmere cardigans and vests that Jack was inspecting.

"But you shouldn't wear his clothes. We need to do this thoroughly, Vera. Not to chase out his ghost but to return the penthouse to a hospitable apartment instead of a place of worship."

We'd finished with the shoes, shirts, and casual wear and stopped to take a lunch break. After we ate the chicken sandwiches I'd had sent up from the Birdcage, we returned to the bedroom, and Jack started on my father's suits, dutifully going through each jacket and pants pockets before I folded and boxed them.

There wasn't much he found of note. Some coins. A business card. A cigar cutter. Nothing very interesting, until Jack fished out a key ring with a very small brass key on it. Examining it, he turned it over in his palm.

"Is that something to do with the store?" I asked.

"I don't think so. It's too small." He frowned.

"What's wrong?" I asked. "You look perplexed."

"It looks familiar, but I'm not sure why." Jack handed it to me. "Have you ever seen it before?"

I inspected it, then shook my head. "It must not be very important if he didn't tell either of us about it."

"Well, hold on to it . . . maybe we'll come across whatever it opens."

I slipped it into my pocket, and we went back to work.

SILK, SATIN & SCANDALS

In which your intrepid reporter fills you in on the most salacious and beautiful, glittering gossip in Gotham.

Continuing the saga of the last few months, namely the invasion of New York by Count Le Monte, I attended an event at the Waldorf-Astoria last weekend. It drew the most interesting fashions from Paris, along with the usual scoundrel or two. Dancing with more partners than this observer could count, Count Le Monte was dashing and daring with his entries and whispers. I was lucky enough to snag a dance of my own and quite taken with his fancy moves and oh so charming cologne. Vanilla, perhaps? But the real talk of the gala was Evalyn Walsh McLean, on the arm of her husband, sporting diamonds the size of eggs. Rumor has it that she has her eye on the Hope Diamond currently being seen by interested parties in Cartier's delectable shop, which resembles the perfect petits fours served at the Waldorf.

No stranger to the world of jewels or high fashion, I've seen my share of pretty baubles, but Mrs. McLean's outshone everyone's there. The newest, a diamond sautoir, was a wedding gift from her husband purchased from Pierre Cartier, whose fourth-floor store on Fifth Avenue is a veritable Tower of Jewels.

So to the real gossip: the ongoing divorce trial of Mrs. Penny Oakdale. The troops were out, and the courtroom gallery was full. Count Le Monte sat in the second row, throughout the afternoon. His pearl-gray morning coat from Savile Row pressed and fresh. The crease in his pants could have cut bread.

He waits to be called, as do we all, wondering just how far the attorney will go and how ugly this will get. But to date we are still being subjected to boring character witnesses for Mr. Oakdale.

We did spot some jewels and fashions worth noting. Mrs. Van Rensselaer is sporting a large diamond solitaire on her ring finger that she recently inherited from her mother-in-law. The firm of Tiffany & Co. the supplier. Mrs. Smythson was wearing an afternoon frock of green satin and black trim from Worth in Paris. And Mrs. Alstead was wearing shoes with the most unusual heel—at least two inches high.

CHAPTER 5

On Monday morning, a note arrived from Fanny and Martha insisting I meet them for dinner. I agreed, reluctantly.

When I'd moved into my father's apartment after the accident, I'd worried about how to conceal my Vera Garland identity from my friends, now that I had such an expensive address. I felt guilty about hiding the truth but at the same time was unwilling to jeopardize Vee Swann, as doing so would mean jeopardizing my career. My friends, of course, had no idea what I actually looked like or who I really was. They didn't travel in the same circles, and I was careful not to be photographed in public, often hiding behind a fan when I was at the theater or opera.

One of the interesting things about New York society was that people saw the world through their high but limited expectations. In my beautiful dresses, satin shoes, and fine jewels, with my auburn hair coiffed and my nose powdered, people only saw Vera Garland, the daughter of one of the wealthiest merchants in the city. But when I was dressed as Vee, no one ever noticed any resemblance to Miss Garland. Early on, I'd had photos taken of myself in both identities, then examined them to make certain they looked completely different. Even my body language changed depending on the role I was playing. Miss Garland exhibited careful posture and a slightly distant expression that suggested boredom, whereas Miss Swann's demeanor was assertive and challenging. She stood tall and held her head high while speaking.

To my coworkers, I was a fearless reporter determined to succeed.

To my mother's set, I was her spinster daughter who'd had a hushed-up love affair and never quite recovered. The same gossipmongers who whispered about me were all surprised by how quickly Maximilian married after our breakup. I knew the reason, even if they didn't. Having a bride by his January birthday had ensured that he received his grandfather's estate.

I gave Vee a background that was easy enough to keep straight, having her grow up in the town next to Newport—Middleton, Rhode Island— and coming from a family of doctors. I had her graduate from Brown University, since it, too, was close enough to an area I knew well.

I knew I wasn't the only reporter who worked incognito. For many women, it was often the only way we could get behind the scenes to carry out our research and investigations. But I've never known who or how many of them lived a truly double life like me. It all took an enormous amount of energy, which I only had a small store of after Father's death.

When I'd lived in my modest apartment in Chelsea, it had been easy to be Vee and transform into Vera for certain outings. A visiting spinster, even a well-dressed one, didn't interest my neighbors. But how to explain to my friends that Vee Swann was suddenly living in a penthouse above Garland's Emporium? I needed a story that would make sense. So I told them that my uncle was Mr. Garland's doctor and longtime friend and that Mr. Garland was looking for someone to organize his library. Since the businessman rarely stayed in the apartment but went home to Riverdale most nights, he'd offered me free lodging in exchange for cataloging his thousands of books.

It was only half a lie. My father did have an extensive library in the apartment, organized by a system only he understood. Whereas I could search for a title for hours and never find it, ask him where it was, and he'd go directly to the right shelf and pull it out.

After Granville Garland's obituary appeared in the papers, Fanny and Martha were naturally worried about my living arrangements and offered to let me move in with them. But the apartment they shared in the Second Ward on Maiden Lane down near the Fulton Fish Market was tiny and barely contained them. I told them that Mr. Garland's widow had asked me to stay on while she decided what to do about the apartment. I was to continue cataloging the books, and she liked having someone taking care of the plants. Mr. Garland, I explained, collected orchids and had a greenhouse on the roof.

Thus, I responded to Fanny and Martha's note from my elaborate lodgings high above Fifth Avenue, and two days later, I met them at Healy's Tavern on the corner of Eighteenth Street and Irving Place, where the adorably witty and kind O. Henry had treated us many times over the years. Before his death just a few months ago, he'd been writing a story a week for the *World*, which was where we all met and became friends. Mr. Henry had taken an instant liking to us, calling us the Three Musketeerettes, and gave us so much good advice, often peppered with personal anecdotes. One of his favorite tips had been to loiter in hotel lobbies. People, he said, tended to reveal their truest selves when not reclining in front of their own hearths.

Since those days, Fanny had left the *World* and now worked at the *New York Times*. Martha, too, had moved on and was at *Scientific American*, where she'd become an acclaimed investigative reporter writing on psychic phenomena. From articles on ghosts, mind reading, and Ouija boards to reincarnation and casting spells, she had done more to expose charlatans and scams than the police. Despite that, and being one of the senior staff, she still got paid far less than men who were her juniors.

The easygoing tavern that O. Henry had written about in his short story "The Lost Blend" was crowded that night, but the owner greeted us effusively and seated us before three other parties who were waiting.

After dinner, Martha said she had a stop to make and asked if we would mind walking with her. I wasn't paying much attention until we turned onto Twenty-third Street and walked east. When we stopped in front of number 126, the home of the Woman's Press Club of New York City, I asked my friends what was going on.

Martha took my arm. "We need you, Vee. It's time for you to come back."

"The club has more than one hundred and sixty members," I argued. "You all can't need me."

"No, but the action committee does. We need your ideas and your leadership. Please, just come in and listen to what's going on, and then decide."

I had created the action committee five years before to make noise and draw attention to the unfairness women reporters all too often faced. We wanted to change the culture and be treated the way we deserved. We were doing the same job as our male counterparts, and yet even though we did excellent work and were often asked to go on staff—which was indeed a high honor—we were supposed to simply accept that we would always be paid less than half what our male counterparts received. Raises, we were told, were out of the question. The attitude of our all-male editors and bosses was that we should be grateful to be employed at all.

The famous newspaperwoman and suffragette Rheta Childe Dorr, who was one of our club members, had once said that her managing editor believed women were accidents in the industry, only to be tolerated.

Yes some women were capable of rising to the top and becoming editors, but only of the pages that dealt with society and fashion, romance, and female health. Not one newsroom was led by a woman. Not one crime beat or political section. Not one financial section.

I thought everything about our situation was unfair and absurd. But even though we'd been trying so hard, we hadn't effected any change. Hell, Susan B. Anthony and Elizabeth Cady Stanton had begun fighting the battle for equal rights more than forty years before, and we still didn't even have the vote.

My father had always taught me to speak up and encouraged my efforts at the press club. So in honor of him, I followed my friends up the steps.

"I'm not making any promises to get involved in whatever this is," I said at the door.

"And we're not asking you to," Fanny said. "Just come in and listen."

She opened the door, and we walked inside the club that had been started in 1889 by journalist Jenny June. Also known as Jane Cunningham Croly, she had started the organization out of her home in order to help female members of the press who were not invited to join male press clubs. Her vision was that together we would encourage unity, fellowship, and cooperation within our ranks for those who were engaged in similar pursuits. The club organized social projects, raised money for journalism scholarships, offered lectures, and planned social activities.

We had also become active in the ongoing suffragette fight for equal pay and equal treatment. As reporters, we weren't just writing about the movement but were living the inequality ourselves. Newspapers and magazines were hiring women writers—more and more each year—but we were still considered second-class citizens. Not only paid less and treated unfairly when assignments and promotions were meted out, but we were also often sexually propositioned in exchange for getting better assignments and put in terribly compromising situations by our male counterparts. We were still, even after more than two decades of having female writers on staff who more than proved their mettle, expected to be thankful for the opportunity to write "women's stories" and not complain when men got all the "important" ones.

To take even a single step out of the girl ghetto took determination, moxie, and self-control.

By 1893, the club had swelled to more than one hundred members and moved from Jenny June's house into its present official quarters. Meetings were the second Saturday of the month for business and the last Saturday of the month for social activities. The club was open to us all week, day and night. It was a place where we could meet, commiserate, plan, complain, or come to work on articles if we didn't want to be at home or in the smoke-filled, male-dominated newspaper and magazine offices where we were often not welcome.

Fanny, Martha, and I walked inside and proceeded to the front room, with its terra-cotta-colored walls, cream-colored ceiling, and parquet floor. The atmosphere was homey and eclectic, since the four main rooms, plus the kitchen and bathroom, were decorated with member-donated furniture, china, rugs, and wall hangings.

Chairs were set up in the main meeting room, and more than forty women were already assembled, with seats for another dozen or so.

Martha, Fanny, and I sat near the front, where friends and colleagues I hadn't seen since the summer before I'd had my accident could see me. They waved or called out or got up to come say hello. Before she took the podium, Katharine Evan von Klenner, the club president, stopped to shake my hand and tell me I'd been sorely missed.

She began her formal welcome a few moments later.

"Good evening, ladies. And welcome back, Vee Swann. We're so glad you could make this special meeting of the action committee. As many of you know, a serious situation has arisen. For those of you who don't, and for the sake of clarity, let me outline what's occurred and where we are."

Mrs. von Klenner proceeded to describe the situation. In May, one of our esteemed members, Betsy Beecher, had been given a mediocre assignment to cover a charitable event at the Henry Street Settlement House. During the evening, she overheard a plan being discussed by a New York City councilman and the charity's lawyer to siphon off some of the funds raised and give them to the councilman's reelection campaign.

Betsy wrote up the story, exposing the plot, and turned it in to Hugh Packwood, her boss, the managing editor. There was no question that he was going to run it on the *Herald*'s front page, but he wasn't sure, he told her, whether he was going to run it with her name.

Not every paper had picked up the practice of having reporters' names on articles. The *New York Times*'s editor, Adolf Ochs, thought it interfered with the story and never ran a name, while the *Herald*, the *World*, the *Tribune*, and a few others did.

For a reporter, receiving that name recognition was a major accomplishment. Having it on a front-page story was a huge coup. And for a woman, it was even more of an achievement. It would be Betsy's first signed front-page story. A real triumph.

Packwood's decision, he told her, was dependent on whether or not she would pleasure him. "By hand or mouth is fine," he told her. "I don't insist you open your pretty legs for me."

Mr. Packwood had a long history of aggressive and improper behavior with Betsy as well as other female reporters. But nothing this blatant had been reported ever before. At first, Betsy thought he might be joking and tried to cajole him. When she realized he was dead serious, she refused.

The story ran without her name on it.

Betsy Beecher, like so many of us, was fed up. The suffragette movement that had begun in 1848 in Seneca Falls was only inching ahead. We weren't just dealing with ideological issues. We were affected every day in a hundred different ways, and Betsy had reached her own personal point of no return.

The press club had organized a network for club members, what we called the "survival chain." If one of our ranks encountered any editor or fellow reporter who made untoward sexual advances, made inappropriate comments, promised promotions or better assignments in exchange for sexual favors, or punished any one of us for refusing to engage in sexual activity, his name was circulated and entered in the dossier we kept in the library of the Twenty-third Street clubhouse.

We couldn't abolish brutish behavior. We couldn't have our editors and other reporters arrested for their actions. We couldn't get them fired or even reprimanded. But we could warn each other so we could be prepared.

So Betsy recorded her editor's name in our official file and wrote letters to friends and female reporters she knew, warning them about Packwood.

The following week, quotes from one of those letters wound up in an unsigned article in a rival newspaper. Had one of us betrayed Betsy? Or had one of the reporters she'd written to personally left her letter out where a male reporter had seen it and written it up? It didn't matter. Packwood saw it and fired Betsy.

"And now," Mrs. von Klenner continued, "Hugh Packwood has decided the best way to save his reputation is to destroy hers. Two days ago, Betsy found out that Packwood is suing her for defamation."

There were shouts of outrage.

Beside me, Fanny leaned over and said, "Isn't it disgusting? You see why you had to come back?"

Fanny was right. Mrs. von Klenner was right. We had to act. It was bad enough that we often were delegated to do stories men didn't want, or that we were treated differently, or that we were paid less, or that we were patronized or propositioned. But this was that much worse. This new development turned something immoral and wrong into something unconscionable.

Mrs. von Klenner continued by telling us that the brother of Caroline Middlestein, a member of the press club, had volunteered to be Betsy's lawyer, pro bono. Applause broke out.

"But is that enough?" Mrs. von Klenner asked. "Many of us think the time has come to take action. Too many of us suffer indignities because of our sex. Too often, we suffer and keep silent. We believe Packwood's aggressive act has to be met with a protest of our own, doesn't it? We can't sit by and watch one of our own have her efforts to do good and help the rest of us turned on its head."

I could feel eyes on me as Fanny and Martha and several other members turned in my direction. I knew what they were waiting for, but I was waiting for someone else to volunteer. We were still fighting the same battles we'd fought ten years ago. Five years ago. Nothing had changed.

I glanced down at my watch, wanting nothing more than to leave and go home. The timepiece was fancier than anything a reporter like Vee Swann had the means to own. When my friends had noticed it a while ago, I'd told them my aunt, the doctor's wife, had left it to me when she died. But it was my father who'd given me the gold square-faced piece from Cartier's in Paris. My father had been friends with patriarch Louis Cartier and had sold Cartier watches in Garland's until Pierre opened his New York shop. My father had given me this one in 1908 to celebrate a story I'd broken about unfair factory conditions. On the back was engraved, *There is nothing stable in the world; uproar's your only music.*

My father had first quoted the line in a letter he'd sent to me in college: *I've been reading Keats's letters. These words were written to his brothers. They made me think of you because you are so determined to make a difference, Vera, and shine a light on what is unfair and cruel.*

I'd be letting him down now if I left, if I didn't help. Mrs. von Klenner continued by suggesting that we begin a letter-writing campaign to the newspapers about how wrong Packwood's lawsuit was. Perhaps this was the motivation I needed to come alive again. But though my mind knew what to do, my heart lagged far behind. It wasn't ready for uproar, not poised or positioned for the fight ahead. Not yet.

But soon it would be.

CHAPTER 6

The following morning, I attended a fund-raising breakfast at the Waldorf-Astoria hotel for the Women and Children's Hope Society, one of the charities my father had founded. I was there as Vera Garland but, as always, kept an eye out on behalf of Vee Swann, who planned on writing up the event for her column.

When it was over, as I was leaving, I passed Mr. Cartier's jeweler, Mr. Asher, coming into the hotel.

"Good morning, Miss Garland," he said, stopping.

"Hello, Mr. Asher." I stopped as well.

He was holding a leather briefcase embossed with the name *Cartier* in the corner. I nodded in its direction. "A delivery?"

"Yes."

"Quite early."

"It's never too early for rubies," he said.

"Another stone I don't know very much about."

"They are associated with romance, of course, but they're quite mystical, in fact. A ruby is believed to darken when danger is near. Some say a person in possession of a ruby never need fear evil or misfortune."

"So if you held a ruby while touching the Hope Diamond, one would cancel the other out?"

He laughed, which pleased me. Maybe a little more than it should have.

"I don't suppose I might see your rubies?" I asked.

"Certainly not here on the street—"

I was embarrassed. "Of course not. I don't know why I even suggested it."

"I was going to say, not here on the street, but we could go inside if you'd like to see them before I take them up to our client?"

I said I would and followed the jeweler back into the hotel. As we walked, he shared another mystical tidbit.

"For obvious reasons, rubies have also long been associated with blood. Burmese soldiers believed wearing one made them invincible. Some actually inserted the stones under their skin, thinking it would keep them safe from wounds."

He'd led me to a corner partially obscured by palms, where we sat on a satin settee. In the shadow of the fronds, he unfastened the satchel and pulled out a maroon leather box, which he opened. He removed a bracelet composed of six diamond fleurettes with blood-red ruby centers, all set in platinum. The stones glittered in the soft light.

"Hindus referred to the ruby as the queen of stones and the stone of kings. They sorted them into castes the way they separated classes of people. Each ruby was rated by the purity of its color and its internal flawlessness. An inferior stone was never put in proximity to a superior one, for fear it would diminish the better stone's magic. These are as close to flawless as any I've worked with." He held out the ornament. "Would you like to see it on?"

I offered him my hand.

"Of everything, rubies are the stones that best symbolize love and passion." His fingers were surprisingly warm where they touched my skin, contrasted with how cool the platinum was. I looked down at the garden of sparkling stones encircling my wrist.

"What a lovely way to start someone's day," I said.

"Indeed."

He'd said something quite innocuous. A simple response to a simple comment. Yet the secret smile he'd added suggested he was talking about quite something else. Running into me?

I walked home wondering about Mr. Asher and his stories and how warm his fingers had been when they brushed against my skin.

Back at the apartment, I had sat down to read the morning paper and have some tea, when my brother-in-law rang up on the phone.

"I remembered why the key we found in Granville's suit pocket looked familiar," he said.

"You did? That's wonderful, Jack. I tried every

desk drawer in the apartment. But not a one was even locked."

"Because it's not a key for drawers but for the bookcases. I'd admired your father's cases in the library, and he had a set made for us. They came with a key like that, but I've never locked any of the cases so never paid much mind to the key. So that solves that."

I thanked him and got off the telephone, thinking it was anything but solved. Why did my father have the key to the bookcases in one of his jacket pockets instead of in his desk, where all his other keys were? And even more curious, I'd been taking books from the shelves for years and never noticed any of the cases locked. So why would he be carrying the key with him?

I retrieved it from my bureau and walked down the hall to my father's library, the only windowless room in the house. All four walls were lined with floor-to-ceiling glass-fronted bookcases with small brass pulls and, yes, little keyholes beneath them. How odd I'd never noticed them before.

My father and I shared a love of books and reading, and I'd spent hours in his library. He loved to search out books from his collection that he thought would be of interest to me, so that I could read them and we could discuss them. He often gave me lists of books for me to keep an eye out for at Conaway's or the public library—

both unusual secondhand tomes and new novels that I'd usually devour first and then give to him.

In the library were more than 160 individual bookcases, and I had no idea which ones, if any, were locked. If I'd worked without stopping, I might have done it in two hours or so. But too many times, as I stood on the floor or the ladder that slid around the room and tried each case, my eye would alight on a book that I'd remember my father commenting on or that just looked interesting, and I'd have to stop and pull it out.

After the first couple of hours, I had a pile of more than ten books stacked on the floor that I intended to read and wished for the hundredth time and for the hundredth reason that my father was still alive.

Looking at the pile, I tried to move to the next few cabinets without casting a glance over my father's eclectic collection. But I couldn't. He favored history, biography, art books, and fiction. And there were so many titles in every category worthy of a few minutes or so.

I'd see a word on a spine or a very elaborate binding and stop to pull it out, open its covers, and look through its color plates or read the first few lines, and before I knew it, I'd read a page or two. More than a dozen times, I read a whole chapter, getting lost in the words, or the story, or the idea, or the images.

I sighed over a portfolio of plates from the

Uffizi in Florence, a biography of Goya complete with reproductions of his etchings. I found what appeared to be a first-edition illustrated volume of Edgar Allan Poe's poetry. There was a book devoted to Leonardo's notebooks. I pulled out a history of ancient Egypt and another about the inquisition in medieval Spain.

And then there were row after row of wonderful novels. Since Father's death, I'd bought more than a dozen, most from our neighborhood bookstore, Conaway's between Fifty-fifth and Fifty-sixth streets. Every one of these books was popular, each had wonderful reviews, but I hadn't been able to read more than a few pages of any of them without being distracted by grief.

What was it about the books I opened that day that broke the spell? Was I merely ready? Or was it that these were *his* books, each chosen and placed there by him? Was it that connection that made every one of these volumes more precious? And so, as the afternoon slipped into evening and I disappeared to the far-off jungles of Africa in H. Rider Haggard's *She*, visited Venice in Henry James's *The Aspern Papers*, how could I not be transfixed at the opening of *The Leavenworth Case*, Anna Katharine Green's mystery about a man shot in his own library late at night? Not so very different from the one I was in now.

I still wasn't done searching for the locked case when the clock struck five. I knew for the sake of my back that I should stop, give myself a rest, and start again in the morning, but all I had left was the uppermost ten shelves on the west wall. So I moved the ladder over, climbed up, and began working my way across the top shelf first and then stepping down three rungs to the shelf below that.

Despondent that I'd failed so far in finding the right cabinet, I was six cabinets away from the end when I tried a brass knob and a cabinet didn't open on its own. This one *was* locked. And when I inserted the key, I heard the metal click.

After not succeeding for so long, I was stunned that the key had finally found its hole. My hand began to shake, and I reminded myself that I was on a ladder.

I wasn't the trembling type. Or, at least, I hadn't been. But the last year had changed me. I despised how lily-livered I'd become. Where was Vee Swann, the intrepid girl reporter, who'd put herself in the worst circumstance to get a story? I'd gone undercover as a factory worker to expose horrible conditions in the garment industry, as an indigent patient to find out how badly the poor were treated in city hospitals. I'd traveled with a wealthy woman as a lady's maid to understand what servants, especially women, endured. And while I'd known I was taking risks, the thrill of knowing I was accomplishing something was all that had mattered.

I felt a cold brace of fear enclose me as I finished turning the lock and opened the wood-framed glass front. It lifted up and slid back, disappearing into the cabinetry. As I held on to the ladder, I read the titles of the slim matching volumes that had been locked away. It only took seconds to realize I was looking at a set of Shakespeare's plays, bound in Moroccan leather with gilt letters. I assumed they must have been rare and very valuable.

Shakespeare had written thirty-seven plays, an odd fact I was surprised I remembered. There were fewer than that here. This shelf contained but twenty-five. Too many not to be part of a full set, I thought, and wondered if I would find the rest of the Bard's works on another nearby shelf. These were all histories and tragedies. I went down the line: *Hamlet, Antony and Cleopatra, Othello, Macbeth* . . . I pulled out *Titus Andronicus*, the last play I'd seen with my father. Bloody and violent, it was peppered with macabre elements of the absurd. Two of the many people who died were stabbed and actually made into pies that Titus fed to Tamora. My father and I had talked about it for hours afterward.

I opened its cover and examined the fron-tispiece. The publication date was 1860. Less than fifty years old. Not rare at all. Why, then, were they locked away? I flipped through the book, looking for something that would explain its protected location, but there were no hundred-dollar bills hidden between the pages. Perhaps one was hollow and contained some kind of treasure?

I was determined to solve the mystery that night.

I laid the *Titus* on the ladder step above me and pulled out the second volume on the shelf, *Romeo and Juliet*. I riffled through it but, again, discovered nothing at all.

Had my father simply locked the cabinet by mistake? But no, why would the key be in the last suit jacket he'd worn? Unless he'd been working on the shelves and strained himself in such a way that brought on the first heart attack?

As a reporter, I never had a problem coming up with questions. But my biggest flaw was how impatient I was to get answers. Mr. Nevins had told me time and time again that I had to temper my impatience, or else I'd overlook aspects of the story that were sometimes the most important.

I pulled out the third volume, *Hamlet*.

And before I even opened the book, I noticed something. With three volumes removed from the shelf, I could see that behind them was another row, double shelved and hidden from view. But not covered in the same leather as the Shakespeare matching volumes. These didn't appear to be part of any set.

My heartbeat accelerated. My father was not a

secretive man—or so I'd thought. Yet here was one locked case of books out of dozens and a concealed group of books. Why?

I removed all the Shakespeare plays, which, annoyingly, required me to go up and down the ladder about six more times. My back already ached from the hours of bending and stretching and climbing. But now wasn't the time to give in to my infirmity.

I climbed back up the ladder and peered into the cabinet, staring at a row of books of all sizes and bindings, few of the titles familiar. Carefully, keeping them in the order they had been in on the shelf, I took two or three at a time, depending on their heft, and carried them down the ladder.

Questions plagued me as I worked.

Were these insanely valuable books that he'd hidden in case of robbery? Possibly, but there were so many valuable paintings and sculptures and bibelots around the apartment, I doubted these books could be more precious.

Were they stolen? He had never stolen anything in his life. But perhaps someone else had. If so, who? And why was my father safeguarding them?

There wasn't a single answer that made any sense.

"What is the significance of these books? What did they mean to you?" I asked my father out loud. I admit I'd taken to talking to him occasionally. Living in his apartment, not having yet made it my own, it was easy to think he was just in the next room.

By the time I finished taking all the books down, my back was throbbing. But I was too driven to stop and take any of the aspirin tablets that would help. The drug would make me sleepy, and I wasn't ready to sleep. It was only five forty-five p.m. I had to know why my father had hidden these fifteen volumes away so that no one—even me—might stumble on them by accident.

CHAPTER 7

All the books were laid out on my father's desk, arranged in the exact order in which I had found them. I was warm and anxious from all the activity. I walked over to the corner of the library to the liquor cabinet and poured myself a few fingers of whisky. My taste for the fine Scottish aged blends my father so enjoyed was something else we shared but which my mother found unladylike and unacceptable. I had always ignored her pleas that I switch to sherry instead and remained faithful to the golden aqua vitae, as my father called it. Along with more affordable offerings, the finest whiskies and wines were stocked in Garland's wine cellar and spirits shop, along with gourmet foodstuffs.

Since my father's death, I'd replenished his liquor cabinet twice. Now I raised the Baccarat tumbler to my absent father.

"Here's to solving the mystery you've left me."

Now that I wasn't climbing up and down the ladder, I realized the room had grown chilly, but I didn't want to take the time to make a fire—the fiery malt would keep the edge off. It would help my back as well. I took a second sip and then reached behind me and put on the sweater I'd left on the chair when I'd come in.

It was my father's sweater. I'd appropriated it and started wearing it while he was still alive. Because of all the glass windows, the penthouse was a bit drafty, and I had borrowed quite a few of his cashmere cardigans and scarves. I was tall for a woman—five feet seven inches—but my father was taller by nearly half a foot, and his sweaters, even with the sleeves rolled up, fit me more like jackets. But I craved the way the soft wool cocooned me and how his scent of tobacco and cologne still clung to them. I'd dreaded that reminder of him disappearing along with everything else, and more than once, I'd dabbed a few drops of his cologne on his sweater to keep the scent intact.

My father's signature fragrance, Le Monsieur Gris, had been created for him by the House of L'Étoile, a fine French perfumer that had been making scents since before the French Revolution. With a base of citrus and neroli, Gris was a bold scent with a fougère accord.

I knew the language of fragrance from my father as well. Garland's boasted a very fine perfume and cologne bar in New York City, with scents imported from far and wide. While Saks Fifth Avenue and Gimbel Brothers also had extensive scent collections, our store was the only place you could buy L'Étoile scents without traveling to Paris. The same was true of the House of Guerlain perfumes we sold and the ancient oils and perfumes from the Florentine pharmacy of Santa Maria Novella, which had been making skin-care products and perfume since the sixteenth century.

I took one more sip of the Macallan and then began to inspect the books before me.

The first one was a water-stained volume of Plato's *Symposium*, bound in plain brown leather with letters that might have once been gilt but now were rubbed off. I looked through its pages, stopping to read a line here and there. The book yielded no clues to its importance.

I placed it to the right of where I sat.

The second book was a worn copy of Virgil's *Eclogues*, which I didn't know much about except that Virgil had lived in the first century BC. Not a fine book by any stretch, it showed signs of neglect. Not my father's fault, I was sure.

After riffling through the Virgil, I put it to the right of the Plato and picked up the third book— another ordinary volume, this one of Catullus's poetry.

So far, the books themselves didn't appear to be rare. And certainly, there was nothing untoward about owning the classics. There was nothing inside any of them. So why hide them away? I was more confused than ever.

The next book was *The Satyricon* by Petronius. I'd heard of it, remembering from some forgotten conversation that it was a salacious book about seduction and fornication and often considered the first novel written that historians were aware of. This volume was finer than the others, but its publication date was only twenty years ago. An expensive binding but not antique. I opened it to discover the frontispiece was illustrated with a violently pornographic image. I wasn't all that shocked. I'd seen similar images many times in the newsroom, despite my male counterparts trying to keep such things from me and my fellow female reporters. I took another sip of the liquor and looked at a few more of the equally disturbing engravings, then put that book aside and moved on.

The next book was unknown to me. *A Year in Arcadia: Kyllenion*, published in 1805, and written by Augustus, Duke of Saxe-Gotha-Altenburg. Old enough to be somewhat valuable, I thought, if, in fact, it was an important book. But was it?

The next few were more ordinary-looking, none of them a first edition or signed. All with obscure titles and authors. *Joseph and His Friend: A Story of Pennsylvania* by Bayard Taylor, written and published in 1870; *The Sins of the Cities of the Plain*, written in 1881; and *Teleny, or The Reverse of the Medal*, written in 1893.

The only thing I was certain of at this point was that my father had organized them somewhat chronologically, though the next three books were slightly out of order.

André Gide's semiautobiographical novel *The Immoralist* came next, published only eight years before, in 1902. I had heard of this book because it had created quite an uproar due to the main character's homosexual exploits. The story of a newly married man who found himself attracted to a series of four Arab boys had raised many eyebrows and caused endless gossip, as people wondered which parts of the semi-autobiographical tale were true.

Next to last was Oscar Wilde's *The Picture of Dorian Gray*, which had been written in 1890 and was the only one of these books I'd read.

Because of Wilde's libel trial, which had led to his indecency trial and subsequent imprisonment in 1895, the book had been very popular and the subject of much gossip. When my father had learned I was reading it, we had discussed it quite a bit.

Recalling those conversations, I searched my memory for any clue to the book's special meaning for my father but couldn't remember anything of note. I remembered we'd discussed the unfairness of the trial and the writer's sad fate. But we had frequently talked about injustice and the law's interference in personal freedom and liberty.

The next book I'd taken from the shelf was Edward Prime-Stevenson's *Imre: A Memorandum*. Even though it had been published just four years before, in 1906, I had never heard of it.

As with the other ten books, I leafed through the pages to see if anything had been tucked inside, sure that nothing would come of it. Until . . . there it was. The letter that changed everything. Explained everything. And turned my entire world upside down. The letter that would become the crucible of my life for the next few months. The missive that yet again separated time into *before* and *after*.

I was hardly a virgin. In fact, I was a thirty-two-year-old woman who'd had several lovers. I'd been a reporter for ten years and had exposed corruption and crime and gross injustice. I'd gone undercover, been beaten and threatened and nearly paralyzed. But nothing—not discovering my first lover's marriage, my fiancé's duplicity, or my own failing to save Charlotte's life—pushed my life into such a totally different direction as the letter I found in Prime-Stevenson's *Imre*.

December 4, 1909

Dearest Dear Friend,

By the time this reaches you I will be gone. No tears, please. No tears. I do this, as I have done everything, with great and deliberate thought. I have the bottle by my side—deadly nightshade—the perfect name for a poison that will deliver me into the arms of darkness. I want you to know I will have swallowed it down with a smile knowing it was a fair exchange for what we've been able to share, to have, to be to each other.

If our life together is ending sooner than we expected, so be it. We had so much more than we ever thought we would.

The bottle is dark brown without a label. Without a name. Fitting, don't you think? Like our love—without a label. Without a name.

I know you will try to blame yourself for what I am about to tell you, but that will serve neither of us. The world is not fair or kind to men like you and me. That we found each other at all . . . that we have had more than thirty-five years of happiness . . . what more could we demand of life? We have lived as others only dreamed.

But now that has to end. As it turns out, there was a spy in my house. My new manservant, Horatio, sold four of my letters to you to that scoundrel, publisher of the *Gotham Gazette*, Oxley. I know your pulse is starting to race now, but stay calm. Oxley does not know your name. The salutations on the letters were, of course, as always, Dearest Dear Friend. And each would have been personally delivered and tucked into your jacket pocket. If, that is, they had not been stolen.

At the beginning of October, Oxley came to me with an offer to advertise in his wretched magazine to the tune of 10,000 dollars.

When I said that I had no need to advertise, he showed me photographs of the letters and told me he was offering the ads in exchange for not exposing my illegal proclivities.

I haven't been honest with you about how bad my firm has been doing . . . I had every hope a few large commissions would be coming in soon. So I cleaned out my savings and paid him. And I thought it was done.

And, yes, I kept it from you. I didn't want to sully our times together. You'd just been to the doctor, who'd warned you about your heart. And besides, I thought the matter was finished.

Except it wasn't.

Oxley came back two weeks ago and

said he didn't think I'd taken out enough ads. He wanted another payment of the same amount. An amount I didn't have. I told him that.

He smiled and said that if I didn't have it, maybe my Dearest Dear Friend did and asked point-blank if the man I was involved with had money.

I realized then that he wouldn't ever stop—not stop demanding payments—not stop trying to find out who my partner in crime was so he could blackmail him as well.

Could I have come to you with all this? Yes. But where would it end? And could we ever be together again, for fear that Oxley's spies would discover you are my Dearest Dear Friend and I yours? And then what?

All this is why we haven't met in the last few weeks. I wasn't under the weather, I wasn't traveling. It was for fear Oxley was having me followed. For fear that he would learn everything we've so carefully kept hidden. And that fear is what brought me to my solution.

The truth is, you and I have been breaking the law. Unfair or not, it is the law. And we have seen what happens to men like us who are prosecuted and convicted. I will not go to jail and drag you there with me. The disgrace to me, our families, your store—so many people would be destroyed along with us.

No, we have been too caring and careful to ruin it all that way and pull everyone into the gutter.

And so it is time to bid you adieu. My Dearest Dear isn't strong enough anymore. Not now, not in this final letter. You have been the largest presence in my life, saturating every one of my days with color. You are my heart. My skin. My flesh. My blood. You are my passion and my love. You have been everything to me and more. And I am so thankful for all the precious moments we shared.

So with my undying affection—no, let me say it for what it truly is—with my deep and abiding love, I beg you to take care, dearest Granville—how odd it is to write your name out finally in this last letter—how careful we were to hide our lust and our love and how ignobly it all ends—with a scandal sheet and blackmail.

With love,
Your Dearest Dear

CHAPTER 8

I finished the letter and then read it again. I sat at my father's desk holding the sheet of paper, without moving—without breathing—for a long time. How long? Minutes? Hours, it seemed.

What was I holding in my hand?

The words were clear enough, as was their meaning, but I couldn't make sense of it. My father and another man . . . for thirty-five years? Since before I was born? Since before my father was married to my mother? How had he kept that kind of secret? Hidden so much of himself from us?

This apartment, I suddenly realized, must have helped. The separate entrance must have allowed him and his lover great freedom. And now all the nights he spent in New York City while his family was ensconced in Riverdale made yet more sense. But the machinations he must have gone through . . . the deceptions . . . the lies. How they must have taxed him.

I read the letter again. And then a fourth time. I laid it down on the desk and looked at the black letters on the fine, cream-colored stock. For the first time, I noticed the letter's date—December 4, 1909—the day of Father's first heart attack. Had the shock of receiving it, of learning his friend had killed himself, caused my father's heart failure? And about that, too—this friend had known my father had a weak heart. That was something else my father had hidden from all of us.

Had I known my father at all? Suddenly, I was furious. How dare he keep this secret? Have a separate life? How could he have put himself in jeopardy? What was this love? I'd never felt any emotion close to the one suggested in the letter. Why risk jail? Risk ruin? For another man?

I pushed the books onto the floor with one sweep of my arm. My father must have concealed them when I moved in. Hidden them from *me*. Shielded *me* from his other life.

I hated him then. For the deception. For the lies. I kicked at one of the books, and it flew up in the air and then landed, spine splayed, pages crushed. I kicked another, and it hit the leg of my father's armchair. I wanted to pick them all up and toss them off the edge of the terrace and into the street, to be trod on by horses and carriages and automobile wheels. I didn't care if I damaged the books. What were they but symbols of what I hadn't known? What I hadn't noticed? What my father's life had been and probably why it had been cut short, because surely if his friend hadn't killed himself, my father's heart wouldn't have broken?

I collapsed in a heap on the rug, near the pile of books, put my face in my hands, and wept.

It was as if he were dying all over again. My father had been gone for ten months, and now I was losing him again. Who he was, who I knew, what I believed about him—that was all ash now. The one person I was closest to in my family, in the world, was a stranger with a secret. A whole life that he'd kept hidden. I didn't even know the name of the man he'd been involved with. *Since before I was born.*

Still crying, I picked up one of the books, smoothing out the pages and putting it right. Then another. I got up and fetched the ones I'd thrown. I put all the books on my father's desk in two neat piles. As if they were nothing special. As if they were just books instead of the key to my father's life.

Once more, and for a final time, I read the letter, this time thinking of what it must have been like for my father to read it. Had it been delivered after the man had died? Did my father already know he was gone when he received it? Or was the letter how he learned of the tragedy?

He must have been so bereft. And how horrible that he'd had this great loss and hadn't been able to share it with anyone. And what a terrible time—to have it come the same week, wasn't it the same week, as Uncle Percy's passing? I had to think. Those few days had been such a blur because of my father's heart attack. But yes, it was the same week.

I remembered the conversation I'd had with my father the night before he died, when he had talked about trying to be someone he wasn't for my mother. Was this what he meant? Certainly, from the implications in the letter, I assumed so. But who was the man?

I had been a reporter since college, working on the Radcliffe newspaper. I knew how to look for clues and discover the truth. I just had to step back and get out of my own way.

I sat down at my father's desk and, drawer by drawer, started going through his papers.

After a half hour, I realized it was hopeless. My father had gone to so much trouble to hide the books and the letter from me, there wouldn't be anything left around carelessly.

But I needed to know more. I needed to know the rest of it. I thought about telephoning my brother-in-law, but what if my sister was there? If Jack knew the truth or any part of it, would he be able to speak in private from home? And if he didn't know? I didn't want to alert him that there was a secret. He wasn't good at keeping things from my sister. And what of my mother? Did she know?

I stood up and stretched my back. My eye fell on the corner table, where more than two dozen framed silver photos sat clustered together. I looked past the photo of Jack and my sister on their wedding day, to a portrait of my parents taken on their thirtieth wedding anniversary. I searched their faces, looking for a clue. What was their relationship really like? What did children ever truly know about their parents' marriage? My eye traveled over more portraits of family events.

If I could call and ask Jack about my father, surely there was someone who might know, who . . .

I was looking at a group photo taken at my father's sixtieth birthday celebration. My mother and sister and I were seated in the front row. My father was in the middle of a row of men standing behind us. On his right was Jack. On his left was Uncle Percy, on his right my uncle Malcolm. And to the left of Uncle Malcolm was my father's young cousin by marriage, Stephen Stillwell.

Like a son to my father, Stephen was my age and a member of the law firm that handled our family affairs. Yes, Stephen, of course! That's who I could talk to. He knew all the family secrets. If there was anyone who could help me and whom I could trust, it was Stephen.

I picked up the telephone and called the Plaza Hotel, where he lived. The switchboard operator told me that Mr. Stillwell wasn't answering, but they believed he was in.

Somehow, not being able to reach him made my need that much more urgent. I wrote out a note saying I wanted to see him, pocketed it, left the library, and walked toward my room, down the hallway, passing the parlor. The drapes were all open, yet night had fallen. The sky above was moonless and mysterious.

Stephen had lived at the Plaza Hotel, just a few blocks north, ever since I'd known him. A bachelor, he said it suited him to have all his needs so easily fulfilled. It was only just eight o'clock, so I decided I would walk over and deliver my note and wait. I hoped he might answer the door, read it, and come down.

I gathered my hat, coat, and gloves and left the apartment without stopping to check in the mirror to see if my hair was askew or my scarf was tied neatly.

At the Plaza, I sat in the lobby under the palm trees and nervously ran my fingers over the mohair velvet of the armchair. The porter came down and said Mr. Stillwell hadn't answered his knock but that he'd slipped the note underneath the door.

"Perhaps Mr. Stillwell slipped out for the evening without us noticing, Miss Garland."

I tipped him and stood up. I felt lost. The one person who knew me and my father well enough to talk to was unavailable. I walked outside. Even at that hour, Fifth Avenue was still busy with carriages. A well-dressed couple on their way somewhere special—dinner or the theater or the ballet—passed by me. They looked delighted with their evening. As they walked, he said something that made her laugh, and her diamond earrings caught the streetlights and glittered.

You never feel more alone than when you are surrounded by people who aren't the people you want to see. I was thinking about my father . . . about the letter . . . about the books, and I walked, not paying much attention to where I was going. Even as I wandered into the park, I wasn't focused on where I was headed, but my feet seemed to have a destination in mind.

All I could think was how much I wished my father was by my side so I could ask him to explain. I wondered if he'd purposefully left me clues or if happenstance had led me to the key, the shelf, and the letter. Had he wanted me to discover his secret, or had he simply been too ill at the end to destroy the evidence?

I shivered and pulled my coat tighter around me. Fall was upon us now. Before too long, winter would be here, the city cold and gray.

You have been the largest presence in my life, saturating every one of my days with color, the author of the letter had said. It was true. My father had been such a large presence in all our lives, and every day seemed diminished and less colorful without him.

So many images assaulted me as I walked. Pictures in my mind of my parents together at various family functions and events. Was his affection for this other man the reason that no matter how my mother might argue with him, he so rarely fought back? Was it the reason for the look of sadness in his eyes that I sometimes saw when he glanced at her? I'd come to believe my father despaired that the bright young girl he'd married had turned into a matron who cared far too much about what society said about her. Now I considered how very wrong I might have been. Was my father's friend the reason my mother clung so desperately to her societal rules and tried to impose them on all of us? Where we had to eat. What we had to wear. Whom we had to know. Where we had to summer. How many parties were to be had. Who had to be invited. What had to be served. Who had to make our hats and dresses, jewelry and luggage.

Was it all to create as much normality as she could in a world that made no sense to her?

Had my mother turned my father against her and then, in his loneliness, he had met this man? Or had he always been so inclined and had married to protect his reputation? Or to have a family? Had he been weak? Or stronger than even I could imagine?

I reached the Central Park Zoo and continued walking. I should have turned around and gone home. The park could be dangerous at night. But really, what could happen to me? I had walked every inch of it, exploring with my father since

I was a child. I couldn't get lost, even at night. And who would want to attack me, anyway? I was a middle-aged woman of no particular beauty. I carried no more than a dollar. If anyone approached me and wanted it that badly, they could have it. It hardly mattered to me.

There were quite a few people out strolling on the promenade, several with dogs. I suddenly, passionately, wanted one, too. A small dog that I could tuck under my arm. A companion for my long walks. Why hadn't I ever thought about it before? We'd always wanted a dog growing up, but Mother said they were dirty and made her sneeze, and that was the end of that.

When had I lost my desire for a pet? And not just that desire. Others as well. Had I been mourning my Charlotte, my career, and then my father for so long that I had lost the power to want anything?

I'd wandered into the Rambles, one of my favorite areas of the park. I'd never ventured there alone at night, and as brave as I thought I'd been five minutes before, I suddenly felt apprehensive. Too many shadows moved and whispered in the darkness, almost as if the trees and bushes had come alive. I could hear the rushing waterfall just a few feet away and saw the rustic bridge that passed over it. I knew where I was, but this sacred grove that Frederick Law Olmsted had created to resemble a picturesque forest glen had taken on sinister and foreign sights. By moonlight, the familiar had become something other and unknown. Off to the side, I saw two men walking out from behind a giant stone that my father and I had always wondered about— had Olmsted brought it from the Adirondacks or found it here?

The men averted their faces as they passed by me. I continued on, confused about why they'd hidden.

Another man, alone, was walking across the bridge toward me. A stranger, I thought at first. And then, surprised, as he came closer, I recognized him.

"Vera, thank goodness," Stephen said, relief in his voice. "I got your note. Why didn't you just stay? What on earth are you doing here at night?"

"How did you find me?" I asked.

"I returned just after you left. I asked the doorman if he'd seen which way you went, and he had. Then I asked another doorman further up Fifth and then another. I tracked you to the park. And then it was a guess based on your *World* article about your favorite Central Park haunts. Besides, I know how much your father loved this place and that the two of you came here often. But during the day, Vera! Don't you know it's no place for you at night?"

"Why? What do you mean?"

"Come on. Let's get out of here, and I'll

explain." Stephen took my arm. I was sure of the way, but so was he, walking us south without hesitation.

My father's family had always used the firm of Bowes and Stillwell, and in 1894, my father's aunt had married Mr. Stillwell, a widower with a seventeen-year-old son, Stephen. When the elder Mr. Stillwell passed in 1902, Stephen took over. He was not only a cousin by marriage and my father's lawyer but also a loyal and longtime friend. He often came to dinner parties and holiday celebrations in Riverdale and for weekends at the Meadows in Newport. For a brief time, and to my mother's delight, he even masqueraded as my suitor.

Despite Stephen's claims of confirmed bachelorhood, my mother had made many attempts to push the two of us together. Three summers after I had graduated from Radcliffe, she was more determined than ever to marry me off and cut my fantasies of a career short.

Seeing how unhappy I was with her meddling and complaining, Stephen had come up with a plan for us to engage in a pretend romance to take the pressure off. He confided that his family was pushing him as well, and so it would be a favor to him as much as it was to me. I'd come to value my own independence and freedom so much that I hadn't ever questioned his decision to remain single, but he'd told me his situation was more complicated. Stephen had a preference for men.

We played at being a couple for a full year, becoming even better friends in the process. We were ideally suited to each other. We were both avid readers, enjoyed the theater, opera, and ballet and talking politics and the law. Since Stephen was an excellent golfer and I loved the game, we'd often go off to the links and spend the day on the greens. All in all, it was a healing time for me, after having already been twice stung by affairs gone awry.

Even after we amicably called off our engagement, much to our families' dismay, we continued playing golf, having dinner together, or going to a performance of some kind, several times a month. That changed after Father's death. I had rarely seen Stephen since he'd presided over the reading of the will. Concerned, he sent notes and invitations every other week or so. Most often, I said no. It wasn't that I didn't want to see him. I wasn't trying to be antisocial. I just didn't quite know how to find my footing.

"You look quite peaked, Vera. I'm going to take you to a late supper, and you can explain what you were doing walking about town after dark like a madwoman."

We retraced our steps back over the bridge and through the winding pathways. Stephen didn't pressure me to talk about what had happened but instead told me anecdotes about Frederick Law Olmsted and odd bits and pieces about Central Park's creation.

Reaching the park exit on Fifty-ninth, we crossed the street, and Stephen ushered me into the Plaza Hotel and across the lobby into the restaurant. We were seated in a corner. Even before the waiter arrived with the menu, I told Stephen I wasn't very hungry.

"Do you want to order or have me do it for you? Because I insist you eat something, Vera."

I hated the convention of men choosing food for women—how on earth could they know what we wanted? So when the menu arrived, I perused it and ordered the lightest thing I could find, a fillet of fish. And when Stephen asked, I said yes, I would like wine.

He ordered the fish as well, along with a very good bottle of white wine from France.

"I have so many questions to ask, but let's wait until the wine comes," he said, as he took a carrot from the silver dish of vegetables presented on a bed of crushed ice that the waiter had brought. "I don't want to be interrupted. In the meantime, tell me the family news."

I filled him in with anecdotes about Jack and Letty and their children, until the steward returned with the wine, opened it, and waited while Stephen tasted it. After he nodded his approval, the steward poured and then retreated.

Stephen raised his glass to me but didn't make a verbal toast.

I took a sip. It was cold and crisp and delicious.

"This is so light," I said. "How did you learn so much about wines? I don't think you ever told me."

"No trying to distract me. I want to know what is going on. Your note said you needed to talk to me about something important, so why didn't you wait? And why were you wandering around Central Park at this time of night?"

"Yes, you said you were going to explain something to me about the Rambles," I said, ignoring his questions.

"You really don't have any idea?"

I shook my head. "No. I didn't think about where I was walking. I suppose I just wanted to be someplace familiar . . . someplace I used to go often with Father."

He cleared his throat as if he was buying time. "Well, I can understand your gravitating to a familiar area. And during the day, it would be fine. The Rambles is wonderful—unbridled nature right in the middle of our city. Birds, squirrels, rabbits, even foxes inhabit those nooks and crannies. And the waterfall is a wonderful spot to stop and ponder life's vicissitudes."

"Stephen," I urged, "I know all that. Just say whatever it is that you don't want to say."

"Yes, just say it, you're right. You're a

sophisticated woman. Vera, you, of everyone, are aware that every aspect of this city has its dark, ugly side."

I nodded.

"Well, the Rambles is a meeting place at night for men who don't have many other places to go to be with other men."

I took another sip of wine. "I passed by two men—out for a stroll—and they averted their faces. I wondered why."

"Probably, they were there for an assignation. And because it has that reputation, there can be quite a bit of rough trade in there at night, which is why it's so dangerous. That plus thieves, posing as interested men as a pretense to suss out potential victims, whom they beat up and rob."

"How awful."

He nodded. "Present-day legalities require the utmost discretion. Many men find themselves at a loss for how to meet others like them."

There was a sadness in his eyes that bored into mine. I could sympathize but not really understand. Yes, I was different from so many of the women I'd grown up with. But my dedication to my work and my negative views on marriage and the way it objectified women weren't against the law. I met men and spent time with them and had lovers, but I couldn't go to jail for that—only be gossiped about in my mother's circle.

But men like Stephen, who couldn't show any

emotion toward any man for fear. Men like . . . my father, who—my father? The enormity of the secret struck me anew.

I finished the wine in my glass.

"Vera, why did you want to see me so urgently tonight? What upset you so much to go wandering alone?"

"Going to the Rambles must have been unconscious, now that I think about it," I said. "Maybe I once heard about its nighttime purpose but forgot . . ." I shook my head. "Nothing is a coincidence, Father always said. Certainly, nothing that happened tonight has been. Have you read much of what this Austrian professor and doctor Sigmund Freud has written about the choices and decisions we make?" I asked.

"Actually, quite a bit," Stephen said.

"Well, on some unconscious level, I must have gone there to be among those men."

"Because?"

"Last week, Jack was helping me empty out my father's things in the apartment, and we found a key. We didn't know what it opened. And then today, Jack phoned. He'd figured out that it was a key to my father's bookcases. I immediately went to check. Only one case was locked, and inside I discovered a cache of hidden books and a letter." I shivered.

"Are you all right?"

"Yes, I am. Well, I think I am."

"Have some more wine."

He motioned to the waiter, who filled our glasses and took his leave. I took a sip.

"A letter?" Stephen asked.

I hesitated. To voice the words would make them real.

He took my hand, in a gesture of friendship and comfort. "You don't have to tell me anything you don't want to."

"No, I want to. My father always trusted you. Now more than ever, I know why. It's just not easy to say it."

"Take it slow. We're not in a hurry."

So I told him about the books and how I didn't understand their significance until I found the letter and put it all together. And then, in halting phrases, I paraphrased what the letter said.

"Oh, my God," Stephen said, as all color drained from his face. Anguish altered his features. "Why did Granville keep a blackmail plot to himself? How terribly guilty and confused he must have felt. I knew the wind had been knocked out of his sails when Percy died . . . we talked about the loss for hours, but—"

"Uncle Percy?" I interrupted. "He died the same week, I know, but how is my uncle's death connected to my father's friend's suicide?"

"Vera . . ." Stephen took a breath. "Vera, your uncle Percy was your father's friend."

"Yes, of course, they were friends," I said matter-of-factly.

"His *friend* from the letter."

For a moment, I didn't speak. My uncle? And my father?

"I don't understand . . . Are you saying . . . ?" I didn't finish my question.

"Yes, your uncle wrote that letter. Percy was your father's companion. For years."

"But Uncle Percy died of food poisoning," I said, focusing on the least complicated part of the whole mess.

"That's what was presumed, yes. But now, from that letter, we know his death must have been of his own making."

"I'm sorry, I'm having a hard time understanding. Uncle Percy is my mother's brother." This wasn't making sense to me. I loved my uncle. He was part of our family. A confirmed bachelor, he was always around, the first one after my father to show pride in whatever my sister and I did. When we were little, he attended every one of Letty's riding competitions. He read every one of my poems and papers and discussed them with me. He showed as much interest in Letty's obsession with dressage as in my obsession with social justice.

Stephen nodded. "I'm sure you've heard the story of how your parents met? Percy and your father were roommates at Yale, and Percy brought your father home with him one weekend to Newport. It became an easy solution to a more complicated problem. With your father courting your mother, no one questioned all the time he and Percy spent together."

"Yes . . . maybe at first . . . but my parents got married. Married!"

"Your father wanted to have a family."

"And you are saying his re—" I stumbled on the word. "His relationship with my uncle continued all those years?"

Stephen nodded.

"So my parents' marriage was a sham?"

"Hardly. Your father was very much capable of loving a woman. It's not unheard of. In fact, it's quite common. Look at Oscar Wilde, for example. He had a wife and children. For some of us, it's not either/or but simply a preference. Your father was like that. He cared about your mother deeply and treated her as well as any husband could. You know that, you've seen them together your whole life. And your mother cared about your father. She loved him. You know that as well."

"As much as she was capable of caring about anyone but herself," I said.

Stephen smiled knowingly. We'd had long conversations over the years about my impossible, selfish mother.

"Did my mother know about my father and Uncle Percy?"

139

"Years ago, your father told me that Aunt Henrietta knew about Percy's proclivities but not about his relationship with your father. Given that he was family, there was nothing suspicious about a bachelor like Percy spending all that time with his sister, his nieces, and his brother-in-law. I don't know if Aunt Henrietta ever learned more. She might have or not."

I was still processing all this information when our meal arrived. I looked at it as if I'd never seen food before, unsure for a moment about what it was or why it was being put in front of me.

I had no appetite. But Stephen insisted, and after I'd taken the first bite of the tender, buttery sole, I realized I was, in fact, famished. I'd been so busy with the books that I hadn't eaten all day.

As we ate, we continued talking about my father and my mother and her brother. Stephen continued to help me make sense of it all. I mused that making love with my mother was probably also easier on my father, since she and her brother looked so much alike. Only eighteen months apart, both had thick, dark brown hair and emerald eyes, high cheekbones, and full lips. They were both tall and graceful.

"But they were nothing alike personality-wise," Stephen said.

"No. Uncle Percy was lighthearted, and my mother is so serious. He was open-minded, while her mind is solidly shut closed to everything. She is a figure in society who measures herself against whoever comes to call and what invitations she receives and what people say about her, whereas Uncle Percy always said he didn't care a fig about what people thought of him, as long as he could build the buildings he wanted and explore his passion for art."

Ironically, it was my uncle whom people thought of so highly. Along with Stanford White, among his peers, Percy Winthrop was considered one of the most talented and forward-thinking architects of his time. But his vision for what buildings could and should look like was so avant-garde that he was never awarded the bounty of commissions he deserved. He refused to compromise for a job. And therein lay the financial position he must have found himself in when Oxley blackmailed him.

"What did you do with the letter, Vera?" Stephen asked, after the waiter had cleared our main-course dishes.

I had to think. "It's on my father's desk. Why?"

"You might want to give it to me to put in the office safe."

"My mother never comes to the apartment."

"No, I wasn't thinking of Aunt Henrietta. The letter is an indictment of Thelonious Oxley, and as such, it's a very dangerous and valuable piece of paper. An incitement of a crime."

I pursed my lips and held back my tears.

"I'm sorry, Vera. I don't want to make this harder than it already is. We don't need to discuss this anymore tonight. I'll have a messenger pick up the letter tomorrow morning."

"I do want to talk about it tonight. Explain the law to me like I'm a reporter, not my father's daughter or my uncle's niece."

Stephen smiled and squeezed my hand. "OK," he said. "Blackmail, or extortion, is a criminal offense wherein one person unlawfully obtains, or tries to obtain, money, property, or services from a person, entity, or institution, through coercion."

"So every time Oxley uses the gossip he collects to threaten someone into taking out advertising in his magazine, he is breaking the law?"

"Exactly."

"There have been rumors about Oxley's methods for as long as I've been a reporter. I never paid them much attention. Why do you think he hasn't been charged with breaking the law by now?"

"Because someone would need to challenge him in court. And no one will."

"Why not?" I asked.

"Because that person would have to admit to the deed that Oxley was holding over his head. Think about it—if the act is terrible enough to be used as a threat, then no one would want to publicly admit to it. What man is going to be willing to go into court and acknowledge that his mistress gave birth to his illegitimate child or confess that his business partner cuckolded him or that he had a hand in having his competition's factory burned down?"

"But if Oxley hadn't threatened Uncle Percy and Uncle Percy hadn't killed himself, then my father might not have had a heart attack and—" As much as I was trying to be a hard-boiled reporter, I couldn't hold back the tears anymore.

Stephen gave me his handkerchief.

"I'm sorry," I said.

"Don't you dare apologize. You've had a shock, and you need some time to let all this sink in. We both have. I had no idea that your uncle killed himself to protect your father . . ."

"Oxley is a monster to prey on people's secrets and get rich off their indiscretions. My uncle wasn't hurting anyone. I'm sure half the other people Oxley's threatened are just as innocent."

"Most are, some aren't. There's gossip that Oxley's taken money to keep quiet about information that would have sent some guilty men to prison."

"Well, that's just as bad, isn't it? Either way, he's evil."

"Yes, there's no doubt about that."

The waiter arrived to see if we wanted anything else.

Stephen ordered brandy and coffee, and I said I'd have the same.

"And one slice of your devil's food cake, with two forks," Stephen said as an afterthought.

The waiter left, and Stephen smiled at me. "Your father always called it—"

"Sin on a plate," I finished for him, with a little laugh. Indeed, my father had a passion for the dessert and often had a slice delivered to his apartment when he was working through dinner.

When the cake arrived, its chocolate frosting glistened.

Stephen held out a fork for me and then took one for himself. "In your father's honor."

We both took bites of the delicious confection, the bittersweet ganache complementing the light-as-air cake.

"I'd gladly go to hell for this!" Stephen declared, echoing the very words my father always said after his first bite.

I felt a wave of sadness wash over me. I had known that I would miss my father forever. That there would be moments every day when something I saw or heard or thought of would remind me of him. That I'd think of things I wanted to ask him or share with him and be at a loss that I couldn't anymore. I had known that there would be a hole in my heart that would never be filled, but I had started relaxing into the grief. Getting used to those terrible moments, as the urgent missing turned into a gentler ache. But this new information had rubbed my grief raw again. If my father had been able to confide in me, would he have been able to weather the grief of losing Uncle Percy?

"You totally believe that my uncle killed himself rather than be exposed as a homosexual and risk his reputation and my father's?"

"That and to protect your mother and both you and your sister from scandal. He was very brave."

"Brought down by a sniveling monster," I said.

My sadness slowly ebbed away as a wave of something else came sweeping in. Something I hadn't felt for more than a year . . . not since before Charlotte took sick and I had my accident. I was feeling the desire to fight back. A grievous injustice had been done that needed to be made right. I couldn't rewind time, couldn't bring my uncle or my father back . . . but I could prevent Oxley from doing this to anyone else. I was an investigative reporter. I had the knowledge and the means to get the facts about the story, to find the proof I needed and use it to bring Oxley down. As Martha and Fanny had reminded me, it was time to get back to work. Vee Swann was finally ready to reemerge.

CHAPTER 9

I remember well the circumstances under which my alter ego was born. It happened at an event unlike any Vee would ever be invited to. I was sitting on the porch watching the sun set over the sea, having tea and salmon sandwiches with my parents and Stephen at the Meadows. Letty, who was already engaged and eschewing college for society, was off somewhere with friends.

I had just graduated from Radcliffe, and while I'd wanted to look for a job right away, my parents had insisted that I spend two weeks in Newport, since I'd refused the European vacation they had tempted me with.

"So, Vera, which newspaper editors do you want me to speak with? I'll set up appointments for you with whomever you want," my father said. Since Garland's Emporium was such a big advertiser, he knew all the publishers in the city.

"I don't want to get a job because someone wants to keep your account," I said. "I want to do it on my own."

"But dear, they're going to know who you are as soon as you tell them your name," my mother said. "Why not let your father make the introductions? You don't want to be treated like just anyone applying for a job, do you? Though why you insist on going to work still troubles me. Do you know how competitive and cutthroat that world is? Women aren't really welcome. I've read that—"

"Henrietta, we've had this conversation. Let's not torture Vera about her choice any more than we already have. However, I do think your mother is right about one thing: they are going to know who you are anyway. Why not just let me make the introductions?"

Stephen was the one with the perfect idea. "Vera, you need a pseudonym."

"Of course! I'll take another name. Nellie Bly was a pen name, after all."

"Nellie Bly, Nellie Bly," my mother said. "Why couldn't you have a heroine like Mrs. Astor."

Stephen and I laughed at that.

"You'll be putting an extra burden on yourself by changing your name," my father insisted. "You know how few women journalists there are. You know what you're up against. At least, let me get you in the door."

"No," I said. "Things are changing. Maybe more slowly than we'd like, but there are more women getting reporting jobs all the time. No, no introductions, Father. I have to do this on my own or not at all. And under a different name. You know you would do the exact same thing," I said, certain it was true.

Mother, on the other hand, was quite relieved.

"What a good idea to have an entirely other name, dear," she said. "That way, the grit and grime of the city room won't sully your reputation or ours. If it doesn't work out, no one will be the wiser. And I won't have to keep explaining to people that no, of course, my daughter doesn't *have* to work. I was so worried that once people knew, they'd think I'd failed in introducing you to society."

My mother lifted her Limoges teacup to her lips and took the daintiest of sips. I wasn't surprised that she was so concerned about how our life looked to the outside world. With her impeccable blue-blood background and my father's success in building a small fortune despite his humble beginnings, her place in the hierarchy of New York's elite was secure—and she intended to keep it that way.

"If you must work, Vera, then by all means, do it without drawing any attention to me or especially your sister," she said. "I don't want her upcoming wedding sullied by gossip."

Stephen caught my eye and smiled at me, knowing exactly how I felt about my mother's concessions to society. As she sipped her tea on the stone patio of her Newport mansion, redecorated the summer before by the famous Paris firm of Allard and Sons, her Tiffany & Co. diamond ring glinted in the sun, and the Cartier pearl sautoir that hung atop her Worth day dress glowed. I was incredulous. How could my going to work possibly make anyone question this woman's position and place in society?

Yet I sighed to emphasize my point. "Don't worry, Mother, I won't be a threat to you or Letty."

"Why do you have so much disdain for the things that matter?" she asked in a woeful voice.

"That matter to you. They don't matter to me."

"We brought you up so that they should."

"*You* brought me up so that they should, but Father brought me up to think for myself and care about what's right and wrong, just and unjust."

She had a pained look on her face. "Why would you say that, Vera?"

"Because of how you have always treated me. Like I am my father's daughter, and Letty is your daughter."

My mother's eyes filled with tears—an unusual sight.

"Vera, you know your mother doesn't feel that way," my father said, stepping in and trying to keep peace between us, which he had to do far too often.

But I knew she felt that way. I was twenty-two years old at the time. Just home from Radcliffe with a degree in English literature and a failed affair with a professor behind me. I knew my mother didn't understand anything about me— from what she called my loose morals, to my decision not to enter into society, to my refusal to spend my time looking for a suitable husband.

"I just want you to be happy, Vera," she said, "and I'm afraid that being a renegade, while attractive to you now, will wind up making you an outcast and that when you finally decide to return to the fold, it will be too late."

"What is wrong with being a renegade?" I asked, meaning it. I actually hoped this conversation might lead to forging an alliance with my mother instead of continuing the push-pull of her efforts to get me to behave and become part of her world.

"You will wind up without the things that make a life worth living."

"And what are those?"

"A family, a place in society, friends. Admiration. The company of like-minded people. Amusements, not adventures. Men have adventures, Vera, but when a woman has them, they lead to heartache and scandal."

"It is 1900, Aunt Henrietta," Stephen chimed in. "We're in a new century. Women have been forging careers for a long time now."

"But another sort of woman," she said.

"You are such a snob," I said.

"Vera," my father admonished, "don't be rude to your mother."

"I'm not. I'm just telling the truth. And you both know it. Mother doesn't want anything to change." I turned to her. "You don't want the world to keep turning. You wish it was 1875, and you had just gotten married here in Newport, with everyone gathered to watch the ceremony and ooh and ahh over the flowers and the food and the gowns and the jewels. You wish time had stopped right then. When your crowd didn't really care about women getting the vote. Or wanting to work. Or making changes. When being a wife and mother was the pinnacle of success. You never had any fire in you to do anything but what your mother did and your grandmother—"

I had fully intended my father to interrupt and defend my mother again, even though I knew he approved of my forward thinking. But it was my mother who defended herself.

"That is enough, young lady. If I never wanted to pull up my skirts and pretend I was a man, it was because I was satisfied being a woman. If I didn't rebel, then it was because there was no cause. And I have no problem with your passions. I just wish they were better suited to those of a genteel woman. If you want to write, of course, you should write. But write poetry or novels. And I'm proud you care so much about those less fortunate than we are. But show your concern by volunteering with indigent women or orphaned children. There are very important charities that could use a firebrand like you."

"But I've never been a genteel anything. Not a genteel child or young woman."

She shook her head and gave a bitter laugh. "No, you haven't."

There was a gulf between us. Neither of us was able to meet even halfway. To me, she was the dissatisfied mother, always trying to turn me into someone I wasn't. To her, I was the daughter whom she smiled about when asked, waved her hand in the air like a delicate bird, laughed delightfully and quipped, *Well, you know girls these days . . . she's quite modern.* Acting for all the world to see as if she was proud of me, but I heard the hints of disappointment in her voice, even if no one else did. And so did my father. He'd do what he could to tell me not to mind. That, of course, she loved me and wanted the best for me and that she was just having a hard time adjusting to new thinking. Yet deep inside me, I knew she only wanted *her* best for me, and he knew it, too.

"Well, if we must disallow the Garland name from having its own byline, may I, at least, do the honors?" my father cut in.

"Of course."

"I christen you Vee Swann. Spelled with two n's. A swan, as we know, swims, flies, and walks. It is a beautiful, graceful creature of the earth, sea, and sky." My father raised his teacup. "To our duckling, who is about to swim into the pond of experience, where she is going to make a splash and become a swan, I am certain of it!"

Stephen raised his cup as well. My mother refrained at first but grudgingly did so after my father shot her a look.

Ten years later, here we were once again—this time, just Mother and me—having tea at the Waldorf-Astoria's Peacock Alley. Things hadn't gotten much better between us. We still didn't have an easy rapport. She was even more disapproving of my lifestyle now that I was a thirty-two-year-old spinster. And I was even more annoyed by her everlasting disapproval. She needed to accept that the world of 1910 wasn't the same world in which she'd come of age in the 1860s. That there were women determined not only to challenge the status quo but also to fight for change and damn the consequences. We wanted more. And believed we could get it.

It was in that spirit that I had carefully planned out my revenge on Thelonious Oxley. Our family would take the awful man to court for blackmail. I'd cover the trial as Vee Swann, making sure to expose even more than what witnesses would provide. But first, I needed Mother's approval.

"Mother, I need to ask your permission about something."

She gave me a surprised smile. She was wearing a navy-blue day dress from Paris. Even with all the frocks and finery at her fingertips in my father's department store, she still traveled across the Atlantic each year to order a new wardrobe. Today's ensemble was accessorized with sapphires that had once belonged to my grandmother and boots with mother-of-pearl buttons that matched the feather in her hat and the pearl buttons on her cream gloves.

To please her, I was wearing the kind of outfit befitting Vera Garland, a ready-to-wear copy of an olive Poiret dress trimmed in black fur. My boots were very stylish, olive leather with a jet buckle. My gloves were olive satin to go with the dress, and I carried a beaded jet purse.

I'd also worn the pearl necklace and matching pearl earrings my mother had given me for my twenty-first birthday, bought at Cartier's in Paris.

"How unusual, Vera. I don't think you've asked me for permission for anything since you were about five years old."

"Very funny, Mother."

She smiled. At least, we were off to a decent start.

"It's about Uncle Percy."

A soft look came over my mother's face. She'd loved her brother fiercely and had mourned him painfully along with her husband. Losing both of them so close together had been brutal for her— for all of us—to bear.

"Yes, dear?"

"I've stumbled on some information about his death."

"You've been investigating his death? Why?"

"Because I think there was more to it than what we were told."

"I don't understand."

"I don't think it was an accident."

She looked at me incredulously. "You can't be suggesting he was killed?"

"No."

"What, then?"

"Well, you and Father said he'd been taken ill, poisoned by something he ate . . ."

"Oysters, we believe," she said.

"I think there was more to it than that."

"What are you getting at, Vera?" she said impatiently. "Why are you dragging this out? Tell me."

I had hesitated only because I was trying to read her expression before I blurted out information she might or might not already have. I had no idea if she knew the truth. What had my uncle told her about his lifestyle? What had my father confided to her about himself? What had she guessed?

"To be precise, Uncle Percy didn't *become* ill."

She sighed with exasperation. "What do you mean?"

I just had to say it. "He took poison. It was self-induced—he did it on purpose."

She frowned. "No, Vera. Percy ate something that was bad, and while that might be considered self-induced, it was not done on purpose."

"It wasn't something he ate. He *drank* poison, Mother. And he did it completely with knowledge aforethought."

For a moment, her features contorted into an expression of anguish. I suddenly realized that I'd made a terrible mistake having this conversation with her in public. It was cruel.

"You are mistaken," she said, her face returning to a placid smile, as if she were talking about a new type of hybrid rose that avoids blight. "Percy was my brother. I know—I knew him. Your uncle would no sooner have taken his own life than I would."

"But he *did* take his own life, and he did it for probably the only reason you would as well—to protect his reputation and yours and all of ours. Mother, Uncle Percy was being blackmailed."

"This is ridiculous, Vera." Her voice was edged with annoyance. "*Blackmailed?* You've spent too much time around the newsroom. We are not that kind of family. We do not have those kinds of scandals."

I took a fortifying sip of the coffee I'd ordered even though we were having tea. My mother considered it bad form not to sip a delicate brew of lapsang souchong or Earl Grey along with the delicious little sandwiches, scones, and cakes that we'd barely made a dent in. And now I knew we wouldn't. I knew she wouldn't eat another bite. But would she allow me to do what I wanted? What I felt I needed to do?

"Mother, there is no question Uncle Percy was being blackmailed. I saw the proof."

I had decided only to reveal the necessary facts, which meant leaving my father out of the conversation if I could. First, because I had no idea what my mother knew or didn't about my father . . . about her husband. Second, because if she didn't know, I didn't plan on ever discussing my father's proclivities with her. I didn't need to bring him into this. In order for me to avenge my father's death, I only had to avenge my uncle's.

"All right, then, tell me, why on earth was my brother blackmailed?"

"Because of his . . . preferences," I said.

My mother didn't say a word. Was that because she knew exactly what I was talking about or because she had no idea?

"What 'preferences'?" she asked.

"He preferred men to women and was having a relationship with someone of the same sex."

My mother showed no sign of shock. Instead, she averted her gaze, looked across the room, peered into the cavernous space, and, ignoring every word I'd uttered, said, "I think that might be Lily Carnegie over there. Do you see her?"

"Mother? Did you know about Uncle Percy's interests?"

"I haven't seen Lily for at least six months. Not since she took her daughter on that grand tour. Do you remember yours the summer before you went to Radcliffe? We had such a wonderful time in Paris and Rome and London. Maybe we should go abroad again. You're not working, there's no reason not to travel. Maybe your sister will come with us. The children can go with Nanny in Newport and—"

"Mother, stop."

"What, darling? I'm just suggesting a summer excursion. Since your father passed away, I haven't gone anywhere, and it will be a year—"

"I asked you a question about Uncle Percy. Did you hear it?"

She lowered her voice, her eyes flashing anger at me. I knew she didn't want to discuss this at all and certainly not here. But that was why I had chosen this place, somewhere she couldn't run away from the conversation without causing a scene. And she hated scenes even more than unpleasant conversations.

"Yes, I am aware that my brother wasn't built like other men. He had different tastes. Some men are like that. Quite a shame, as my brother would have made such a wonderful father. Do you remember how he was with you and Letty?" Her eyes filled with tears, but those tears didn't fall. She had that much control over her emotions.

Then, using the silver tongs, she took a cucumber sandwich and put it down on her plate. She didn't pick it up to take a bite, however.

"Even if Percy was being blackmailed, he would have just paid them off. He would never feel the need to take his own life."

"He thought it was the only way to protect everyone involved. That if he didn't, the blackmailer would never leave him alone. Mother, I found out who was blackmailing Uncle Percy. I want to go to the police, accuse Thelonious Oxley, and have him stand trial."

My mother pushed her plate away with an expression of disgust, then looked at me. Her eyes narrowed, and with a voice that had dropped several octaves, she said, "You will do no such thing, Vera Garland. Do you hear me? You will leave this alone. Our family is not fodder for your career. Our shame is ours alone. I will not stand for you bringing any attention to our private battles. Your father and I supported Percy and cared for him deeply despite his . . . peculiarities. I will absolutely not stand by and allow you to destroy the reputation that we kept intact despite his own efforts to do the opposite. There is simply nothing left to discuss. Now, if you don't mind, I'm going to get up and go over and say hello to Lily, and when I come back, I want to talk about the upcoming season and what the magazines are showing. We haven't been shopping since your father died, and you are wearing a style that is at least a year old. And that simply won't do."

And with that, my mother stood, turned her back on me, and headed over to her friend's table.

CHAPTER 10

I left the Waldorf angrier than I'd ever been.
Over the years, I had made so many concessions to my mother for my father's sake. But
he was gone now. Was there still any reason for
me to respect her wishes? Did I really care if
she felt her reputation would be tarnished if the
family were to go public about her brother?

I crossed Park Avenue and headed west.

Maybe besmirching my mother's reputation
was something I secretly wanted. Hadn't I spent
the last eight years yearning to punish her in
some deep and painful way? Would this free me
from wanting to make her pay for what she'd
done?

Since the "incident," as I always thought of
it, my father had tried to help me resolve my
conflicted feelings about my mother. Yes, part of
me loved her, but another part of me would never
forgive her.

At home, I settled down with a glass of wine
and the newest novel by E. M. Forster, *Howards
End*. But I couldn't focus on Henry Wilcox and
Margaret Schlegel and their family dramas. I was
too consumed by my own.

During my junior year at Radcliffe, I had had
an affair with one of my professors, Thomas

Middletown, who claimed he was unmarried. As it turned out, he was not only well and truly wed but had a three-year-old son. After my experience with Thomas, more upset that I'd been deceived than heartbroken, I decided that I needed to focus on my career to the exclusion of all else. I wouldn't fall in love and certainly not consider marriage until I was well established as a reporter. While I did want to try my hand at romance again one day, I had come to understand that to establish a career in journalism, a woman required freedom. Social mores, a husband's needs, and a family's requirements would all get in the way and hamper my efforts. To compete, a woman had to be free to take chances and risks, move around without concern, keep her own hours and her own counsel.

I graduated at the end of May 1900, and by September of the same year, I had taken on my Vee Swann persona to protect and conceal the Garland family name and all the privilege attached to it. I had acquired my beloved apartment in Chelsea and gotten a job at the same paper that had once employed my hero, Nellie Bly. I'd been hired as a cub reporter at the *New York World*, albeit on the society page, but at least I had my foot in the door. While the *World* was often criticized for being too sensational, it was also known as an aggressive paper not afraid of publishing damning exposés, and my boss, the venerable Ronald Nevins, was known for being more open-minded when it came to women reporters.

That was when I met Maximilian Ritter. Max was the son of the railroad magnate Harris Jameson Ritter, but he'd walked away from his family business to become a cellist with the Philharmonic Society of New York.

My parents had a box at the Philharmonic, and I often attended with them. I enjoyed the music, and the gossip that flowed up and down its aisles provided plenty of fodder for Silk, Satin and Scandals.

My mother introduced me to Max and his mother at the season-opening gala. While Mrs. Ritter had come to see her son perform, her husband had remained at his club. It was known to all that he had disowned Max when he refused to give up his musical ambitions. I'd even written about it in my column.

Max and I had much in common. Only a year apart in age, we came from similar backgrounds but shared a desire to make it on our own without our families' help in fields not of their choosing.

We began seeing each other regularly that fall. By winter, when I wasn't in the newsroom, I was with him at his rehearsals, sitting in the empty theater and watching the amazing Gustav Mahler conduct. I was mesmerized by Mr. Mahler's dancing baton as he coaxed each note out of his musicians. It fed my soul and sent my imagination soaring.

I shared my Vee Swann secret with Max, and he found my desire to make it as a reporter admirable. He read all my art and architecture stories which I'd been lucky to get instead of just health and beauty stories and told me he thought I was the smartest girl he'd ever known.

Max wasn't my first lover. That honor had gone to the professor. And there had been a Harvard graduate student during my senior year. It wasn't that I was trying to break all the rules, they just didn't make sense to me. I didn't want to sit by the sidelines and do what was expected. I was surrounded by young women who did only that. Thoreau had said, "The mass of men lead lives of quiet desperation." And it was true for women in our set as well. I saw the proof every day. Even with money and privilege, so many women did as they were told, and their spirits withered as a result. Their spark vanished. I was not going to become like them.

After his rehearsals, Max and I would often go back to his rooms looking out on Gramercy Park and, after a light supper, invariably wind up in his bed. His apartment, which was nicer than mine in Chelsea but not of the caliber he had grown up with, was the same mix of bohemian and upper crust that he was. Fine paintings his mother had donated to the decor, and inexpensive Lower

East Side couches and curtains. But I liked the combination. It made sense, given his musical rebellion and still strong relationship with his mother.

Sometimes I would make him pretend that I was his cello, and he would sit me in front of him and play me until I reached my own kind of glissade.

Was it love? I thought so at the time, and that scared me, since I was determined no relationship would interfere with my career. But looking back, it was more of a good friendship laced with a lot of lust. It was also the first relationship I'd had with a man my mother approved of. Max might have been a renegade musician in a tuxedo, but he came with an unblemished family pedigree. Even if he was currently disowned, Mother believed that wouldn't last. She invited Max's parents to dinners and galas both in Newport and in Riverdale in an attempt to end the siege. She hoped I'd eventually settle down and marry him. That way, she said, I could feel happy I was with a man who was a nonconformist, and she'd have a daughter who was socially acceptable. We would both be satisfied.

Throughout the winter and spring, she continuously dropped hints about a possible engagement, while I insisted that I wasn't ready. Establishing myself as a serious reporter and not just another female fluff writer was incredibly hard. But I was determined to do it. It was what mattered. It had been my dream ever since I was a girl and read Miss Bly's groundbreaking exposé of Blackwell's Island Asylum.

Then, exactly a year after we'd first met, Max asked me to marry him. I immediately declined. I wanted to be with him, I said. Indeed, I was very happy with him. But I just wasn't ready to contemplate marriage. My career took precedence for the time being. He accused me of not being in love with him, and we argued. After that, we didn't see each other for more than a month. I was lonely and missed him but not as much as I thought I would. And that gave me serious pause. But then my mother invited him to our Thanksgiving dinner, and he arrived with a bouquet of flowers and an opal and peridot brooch from Tiffany's, along with an apology. He told me he was willing to accept my timeline. No marriage or talk of it for now. I forgave him, and we resumed our relationship.

Then, just after Christmas, I found myself pregnant. And miserable. I didn't know what to do. I'd never felt any pangs of desire to be a mother. I'd never wondered what it might be like to have a baby. My fantasies were all about having a byline at the *New York World*, doing the work my hero had done, exposing what was unjust and unfair. I'd spent years dreaming about that future and finally saw it in my sights. Having a child would derail all my plans. It was rare enough for a woman to retain a serious newspaper job after getting married. But a married woman with a child?

I stopped sleeping and lost my appetite. I didn't know what to do. I didn't tell anyone what was going on at first, as I hoped against hope for a miscarriage. After two weeks of misery, I broke down and told Martha. I knew she had done a story about nurses in one of the city's charity hospitals and hoped she'd be able to get me the name of a doctor who helped women in my situation.

I wasn't happy with my decision. But no matter how hard I tried to come up with one, there was no other solution I could think of that was acceptable. Carrying the baby to term and giving it up for adoption seemed an even worse scenario.

Martha tried to talk me out of such a drastic step, warning me with horror stories. Even with recommendations, some doctors turned out to be back-alley abortionists, she said. Many women died of botched operations and infections. Others survived only to find out the operation had left them sterile.

When I insisted, Martha went to her nursing contacts at the hospital. Two days later, we met at a tea shop downtown, and she handed me a piece of paper with the name and address of a reputable doctor who performed the operation after hours in his clean and sterile office. His price was steep, she said, and asked if I needed to borrow money. She couldn't imagine Vee Swann would have enough savings to cover the surgery.

I told her that the man who had gotten me pregnant was giving me the money. I hated lying to her, but I wasn't ready to tell her the truth about my identity.

While I didn't need Max's money for the operation, I thought it was only right to share my plan with him.

"It's wonderful that you're pregnant," he urged. "You can't terminate it. You can't do anything but marry me and have my baby."

"But we've talked about this, and you said you understood I wanted to focus on my career. That we both wanted to focus on our careers for now."

"Having a child doesn't have to change that," he said.

"You mean it doesn't have to change *your* career. But of course, it will change mine."

"You can keep writing, Vera . . . short stories or a novel. You don't have to be a reporter to be a writer."

I suddenly felt as if I didn't know him at all. "But you know that's not what I want to do. I'm a reporter. Max, this isn't what we planned."

"No, but plans can change. Think of how happy we would make our families!"

Max had a tell—it was, after all, my job to pay

attention to things like that. Since childhood, I'd been quite good at sensing people's moods and reading their facial expressions, and my abilities had only improved since becoming a reporter. Whenever Max wasn't quite telling the truth or had something to hide—no matter how insignificant—he would rub the calluses on his fingertips, which were thick and rough from years of pressing down on strings.

"Our families? Why bring them up now? What aren't you telling me?" I asked.

"Nothing, Vera. I very much want to marry you and start a family with you. We are so well suited to each other. This baby is coming at exactly the right time."

He began rubbing his fingers together. Something was wrong.

"Max?"

"This is what I wanted, Vera."

"What do you mean, 'wanted'? I don't understand."

He looked away for a split second.

"How could this have happened, Max? You've been using condoms. I pay attention."

His fingers were still moving against each other.

I suddenly had a terrible thought. Running to the bedroom, I pulled open the bedside table drawer. I grabbed the box with the four giant Xs on the top. Inside, the packets weren't neat, the way they would be coming from the manufacturer, but crushed with bent corners. I withdrew a sheath and examined it. At first, I didn't notice anything amiss. I turned it this way and that. Maybe I was mistaken and nothing was wrong. But as I folded it back up, I noticed something I hadn't seen before. The tip of the prophylactic had been snipped off, creating a hole. I pulled out each of the six remaining condoms, one after the other, growing more and more upset as I realized every one of them had been cut and rendered useless.

Sensing Max's presence, I looked up. He was standing by the door, staring at me.

"Why are these cut?" I asked.

Max looked sheepish.

I stared at this man whom I thought I knew so well.

"Max, why did you do this?"

"Your mother said you'd never listen to reason," he said with a shrug, as if he'd already lost the battle.

"Did you say my *mother?*" I couldn't imagine how my mother could figure into this.

Max just sighed. "What do you want me to say?"

"How about an actual explanation? I'm pregnant, Max. Carrying what will become a living, breathing baby. A sigh and a shrug of your shoulders isn't explaining anything. What does my mother have to do with any of this?"

"She and I . . . we talked . . ." he said haltingly.

I couldn't even imagine Max and my mother discussing the fact that we were having relations. Max was still talking, but I had a hard time concentrating.

"What?"

"Your mother thought that if you got pregnant, you'd change your mind and marry me. I didn't know what else to do. And your mother wants this for you so very much."

My whole body went cold, and I began shivering. There was still something unsaid, some explanation. I remained determined to end the pregnancy, but I had to understand.

"We've been so happy, Max. My career . . . yours . . . everything is fine. Why is getting married so important?"

"If I marry by the time I turn twenty-four, I'll inherit my grandfather's estate, and my father's disinheritance won't matter."

"An inheritance?" I'd never heard about this before.

"Yes. And then my father can do any damn thing he wants." The emotion coming out of Max's voice shut me out. He wasn't thinking of me. I didn't matter. *We* didn't matter. The baby wasn't something he wanted. It was a means to an end. It was all about the ugly situation between father and son, about money and social mores and acceptance. All the same ridiculous things that were so important to my mother.

I was still holding the box of damaged condoms. I threw it across the room, and all the packets rained down in an arc. I watched them fall. And then, as if I'd depleted all my energy with that one action, I sank to the floor, back against the wall, holding my belly.

He came over to me and sat down beside me and took my hand. I let him hold it. I didn't have the energy to pull away. The Max I'd known for more than a year was gone. I didn't know this stranger who was whispering to me that he was sorry. Who had tricked me and betrayed me. Made me question my ability to judge anyone.

"The thing is, Vera, it's not natural for you not to want to get married and be taken care of. Your insistence on being independent is a stage you are going through. You'll see. Once we get married and have the baby—"

"And you get your money?" Had he taken my silence for defeat and acceptance?

"Oh, Max. We're not getting married. And I'm not staying pregnant." I felt the tears welling up and refused them their release. "You should have told me about your situation. Not gone to my mother and taken her advice. She's wrong. You can't restring me like your cello. I'm not going to change. Not for her. Or you. Or this." I put my hand on my stomach.

He tried to take me in his arms, but I pushed him away. I got up, walked out of his bedroom and into the parlor. I took my coat and my bag, opened the door, and stepped over the threshold. I closed the door behind me and descended the staircase.

Outside, it had started to snow. I took in a deep breath of the cold night air and felt it burn. I could have tried to hail a carriage, but I wanted to feel the world around me. I wanted the snow to sting my cheeks. I kept going. One foot in front of the other. Slipping, then righting myself. My thoughts swirling like snowflakes.

My father had taught me a trick once after I'd had a terrible fight with my mother and I was overwhelmed with emotion. He'd said feelings sometimes can get tangled like threads. The first thing to do was to separate each thread and name the different feelings. Only by identifying each one could you make sense of them, find some kind of order, and figure out how to deal with the situation.

As I continued walking from Max's rooms to mine in Chelsea, as the snowflakes fell on my hat and in my eyelashes and the city's dirty sidewalks turned sparkling clean with the dusting of white, I tried to isolate what I was feeling.

First, I was afraid. I'd never had any kind of medical procedure and knew it was now unlikely that Max would be there to hold my hand and comfort me. I had to prepare myself that I'd be on my own.

Second, I was sad. I had trusted Max, and I'd been wrong. I was deeply disappointed in him. And in myself for not seeing him for who he was.

Third, I was angry. At Max for being so greedy. For going to my mother. For allowing her to use him. For this despicable thing he'd done—getting me pregnant to ensure a certain future. With no thought about me or the baby.

And I was furious with my mother for using Max. For seeing her opportunity and taking it, damn what anyone else wanted. Would she ever give up trying to bend me to her will? Trying to get me to conform to her standards? She had actually encouraged the man I was seeing to impregnate me rather than let me live the life I had chosen for myself.

"Well, you failed," I said out loud, as I kicked at the snow with my boot, slid, and lost my balance. I fell onto the sidewalk, right onto my coccyx bone. The pain was intense, and for a few moments, all I could do was sit there and try to catch my breath and wait for the pangs to subside. I looked up into the swirling night sky. So many flakes. As if all the stars were falling.

I opened my mouth the way I had when I was little and let the snow fall, feeling it land and melt in my mouth. But I wasn't little anymore. Not for the first time, I thought about going to my father and telling him about the pregnancy. Except I couldn't involve him in this. Pit him against my mother. I was grown up now. I'd chosen Max. I'd made my own mistake, and I would rectify it. I was capable. I was a working woman.

And then I had the idea that would change everything.

What if I wrote about it? Stunt girl reporters were always going undercover to get their stories. No one had yet infiltrated the abortion racket. I could go to several different doctors and play the part of a desperate woman trying to obtain medical care. I would expose the charlatans and bring forth the issue of unsafe, unethical practices.

The next morning, I went to Mr. Nevins and pitched the story, omitting my personal interest. I laid out my plan: first, obtain a list of doctors who provided abortions, then make appointments, then follow through right up to the procedure itself.

"How will you explain not having the procedure?" he asked, with a mixture of concern and admiration.

"I'll say I changed my mind," I said. It was partially the truth. I would tell all but one of the doctors exactly that. And with that one other doctor, whose name Martha had procured, I would go ahead.

"Are you sure you are ready to take on an investigative piece like this, Miss Swann? You haven't gone undercover yet, and for you to pick something so potentially dangerous worries me. Abortion is illegal. If any of these doctors become suspicious, your safety could be at risk."

"I'm ready."

"All right, Miss Swann. Be brave and be bold, but be careful."

It was a litany I was to hear over and over during the years I worked for him. And I came to use "Be brave and be bold" as my mantra when facing tension or danger while on assignment. I spent the next two weeks researching and made appointments with five doctors. By the end, I had the procedure done by the physician Martha's friend had recommended, Dr. Alfred Leighton.

The article, "The Abortion Factory," along with Vee Swann's first byline, appeared on the front page of the *New York World* a week after I submitted it to Mr. Nevins.

The story chronicled the various demoralizing, degrading, and dangerous ordeals women endured in obtaining illegal abortions. I described everything, from the one caring doctor who offered his help after hours in his clean and sanitary clinic to the butcher who operated out of a filthy tenement apartment with rusted utensils.

I wrote about the fear. The worry. The panic.

What I didn't write about were my feelings of anguish and abandonment after my womb had been hollowed out and the deed was done. Though I had acted on my own free will and was certain that I didn't want a child to derail my career before it had really begun—as much as I didn't want to marry at twenty-three and become a younger version of my mother—I still wept over my loss.

My mother had deceived me in a more profound way than I ever could have imagined. She and Max had plotted in a way that had put my very life in danger. And for what? So Max could claim an inheritance and my mother wouldn't have to be embarrassed by her daughter anymore?

When the procedure was over, after the nurse handed me a handkerchief to wipe away my tears and served me a cup of tea laced with whisky, I sat in the doctor's examining room recovering and thought about how I would confront my mother. I imagined what I would say. How to make her feel what I felt. How to communicate the depth of my despair and anger.

But in the end, I never did confront her. For the sake of my family, I remained a dutiful daughter. At least, on the outside. But my mother never had my fealty again. I continued to accompany her to the parties and soirees I needed to attend to keep writing my column. I attended family functions. But trust my mother? Admire her? Meet her with an open heart? How could I?

My anger at my mother grew as the child might have. No, I hadn't wanted a child, certainly not at that point. I'd never been drawn to motherhood.

I had another career in mind for myself. But despite that, something remained after the abortion—an image of a fat-cheeked baby with my eyes and hair . . . with Max's musical talent . . . with my curiosity. And I blamed my mother for my having to grieve over that baby, an infant I'd never know.

"The Abortion Factory" was a great success, and Mr. Nevins gave me more exposé assignments afterward. My career had taken a giant leap forward, and I embraced it, all the while keeping my scars hidden. No one but Martha knew how much I'd personally endured in order to write that piece.

I'd been lucky to have a decent doctor, but I'd become aware of how many women in my predicament hadn't. Some hemorrhaged to death after they left the surgery, alone in their rooms, ashamed and abandoned by the men who had impregnated them. Others thought they were fine until that night or the next day, when fever and infection would set in. And there were others who survived but had been mutilated and would never have children again. The tragedies were too many to count.

There is no easy solution to this nightmare, I wrote. *Having an unwanted baby that a woman is either emotionally or economically unable to care for is not the answer. Going through a pregnancy and giving up a child for adoption or, worse, to an orphanage can break a woman's heart in a way that she can never recover from.*

Surely as a society we must not just accept but understand that even if a woman is responsible for becoming pregnant, she should neither be punished nor risk losing her own life in an effort to alter the situation.

It is incumbent upon us in these modern times to figure out a safe and acceptable means for a woman to end an unwanted pregnancy without putting herself under a knife that might cut her very own life short.

There are kind and caring doctors performing the procedure safely and effectively, but when something is done under the veil of secrecy, things go wrong. Only the bright light of day and openness of our hearts and minds can protect the women who seek out an abortion as their only solution.

No one undergoes this surgery lightly. No one wakes from the procedure smiling. It is a last solution to a fate otherwise untenable. Only our willingness to challenge old-fashioned ideas can change its real and serious threat. Do we need to make the experience even worse? Women who undergo abortions will never forget what they have done. They will mourn and carry scars for the rest of their lives, if, that is, they even survive the procedure.

After the incident and my breakup with Max,

my personal hardship motivated me to become a journalist in the best sense—a truth seeker. Not just in exposés but also in Silk, Satin and Scandals. I didn't just chatter on about gossip but used the column to shine a light on causes and charities I cared about and hoped I was making a difference. Now it was happening again. The search for truth is not just a service for the destitute. Anyone can experience injustice, as I experienced it myself with Max. And so it was not all that surprising that I turned to journalism once more to find a way to avenge the deaths of my father and my uncle. If Mother refused to help pave the way, I would simply create my own path.

CHAPTER 11

The idea came to me as I read yet another newspaper article, this one in the *New York Tribune*, about Pierre Cartier's Hope Diamond and the terrible curse that might affect its sale price. Since arriving in Manhattan, the gem had rarely been out of the news.

Blue Stone Credited with Bringing Ill Luck to Its Owners, the headline read.

I thought about the diamond I'd seen, about Mr. Cartier's showmanship and his rarefied shop above Fifth Avenue. I remembered the mysterious jeweler who'd placed the necklace around my sister's neck. He'd seemed not at all concerned about any potential bad luck that might have tainted him when the stone touched his skin.

What if . . . what if . . .

I had no trouble getting an appointment with Thelonious Oxley, the editor and owner of the *Gotham Gazette*. Among the fourth estate, my pseudonym was well known. After eight years, Vee Swann had established a solid reputation as an intrepid reporter. But it was the mystery surrounding her leave after Charlotte Danzinger's death that, as Martha and Fanny had relayed, made her a curiosity and something of a legend.

For decades, the publishing industry had its

offices near City Hall so the reporters could be near the politicians. The *New York World* had remained on Park Row with the *New York Sun* and the *New York Tribune*. But in 1900, the *New York Herald* had moved to Herald Square, and in 1903, the *New York Times* had moved to Times Square, while the *Gotham Gazette* moved into the Decker Building at 33 Union Square West, facing a Frederick Law Olmsted open glade park.

When I arrived, I couldn't help marveling at the highly decorated building with Venetian arcades, cast-iron filigree, and Victorian Gothic detailing. A colorful Islamic minaret rose from the roof. Multicolored terra-cotta tiles covered the facade and continued inside to an equally ornate lobby.

Upon entering, I was confused. Decker was a popular piano manufacturer, and it appeared I'd wandered into its showroom. A salesclerk explained that the *Gotham Gazette* was on the sixth floor and showed me to the elevator.

The magazine's noisy offices were crowded with reporters—all male, from what I could see through the haze of smoke. A young man at the front desk asked for my name. Checking his calendar and seeing my appointment listed, he rose and ushered me into "the Bear's" office— that was what they all called him. I'd never met Thelonious Oxley before but had glimpsed him at various social gatherings. He was, indeed, a large, barrel-chested bear of a man, with thick black hair and a heavy black beard.

He watched me as I walked across his office, and as I approached, he stood and held out what I could only think of as a paw. His hand was easily three times as large as mine. I had a hard time looking at him and shaking his hand at that first meeting. Touching his flesh made me want to recoil. This was the monster who had blackmailed my uncle and caused him so much grief that he'd taken his own life. An act that had, in turn, broken my father's heart and I believed hastened his death. I was shaking the hand of the monster who had taken my father from me. I was staring into the eyes of the greedy bastard who bullied people into paying untold sums to keep their human frailties secret. I wanted to spit in his face for what he had done to my family, but instead, I allowed Oxley to hold my hand longer than was proper for a business handshake, smile at me somewhat seductively, and, with a soft Southern drawl that dripped like syrup, welcome me to his office.

I wasn't surprised by the flirtatiousness. I had come prepared. Mr. Oxley's reputation was well known among my circle of female reporters, who always uttered his name with loathing. He rarely took meetings with women writers, but when he did, he usually offered everything from dinners to dalliances, though rarely assignments. For those freelancers whom he did hire, he always paid late and rarely ran the stories. I now knew that was because he was collecting blackmail material.

At one of our press club meetings, Alice Little had told a story of traveling with a dozen other newspaper and magazine reporters accompanying President-elect William Howard Taft on a whistle-stop tour back in '08. Oxley had cornered Alice in one of the cars and tried to forcibly take advantage of her, but her trusty hatpin stood her in good stead. She stabbed him in the thigh as he lurched for her. He uttered a curse, backed away, and never went near her again. After that, hatpins became all the rage in the female reporting crowd. One could buy them for pennies in any New York emporium, but they were practically lethal if you knew how to use them.

"Well, well, well. It's certainly a pleasure to meet you, Miss Swann," Mr. Oxley said.

"And you, Mr. Oxley." My voice did not betray me. I had steeled myself for this moment, practicing at my vanity in front of the mirror to make sure I could say his name with a smile, not the expression of utter repulsion that I felt.

"Come, come. Have a seat. Can I get you some refreshment?"

"A glass of water, please."

I had planned on this, too, telling myself to take advantage of any pause, using it to take a moment to settle myself. Over the past days, whenever I had thought about my plan and become nervous, I'd removed my father's copy of *Imre* off the bookshelf, withdrawn the letter, and reread my uncle's suicide note. Though Stephen had suggested I store it in his law firm's safe, I had not been able to part with it. It had become my mission.

My anger and resolve had grown with all those readings, and I realized as I sat in Oxley's office that I was no longer nervous. This was the devil who had brought my family to its knees. He couldn't harm us anymore. It was my turn to harm him. And I was impatient to get started.

He went to the door and shouted out the order to his assistant—water for me, and he'd take another coffee. And then he returned to his desk and sat opposite me.

"So, to what do I owe this visit, Miss Swann?"

"I heard that you are open to pitches, and I think I have a lead on a story."

"Yes, quite true, but I had heard through the grapevine that you were no longer working."

"I haven't been, that's true. But I'm ready to start again. Just not full-time, and that's all that is open to me at the *World*."

"Quite a messy business with your tenement accident," he said.

"You know about that?" I asked.

"I doubt there was a newspaperman, editor, or publisher who didn't follow the story. When one of our own is struck down in the line of duty, all of us are struck down. And you aren't just one of our own. You were—*ahem*—you are a force, Miss Swann."

"You were right the first time. Past tense. It's taken longer for my back to heal than I or my doctor anticipated. But that's all behind me, and I'm whole again and with a doctor's letter to prove it."

I reached into my bag. I did, in fact, have such a letter. I had thought it wise in case the subject of my condition arose as it had.

"Not in the slightest bit necessary. I can see that a strong and wholly competent reporter is sitting opposite me. I'm excited to hear your pitch."

At that moment, Oxley's assistant entered with a tray. He placed my glass of water in front of me and handed his boss a cup of steaming coffee. I distinctly smelled brandy mixed in with the brew.

"Then I'll just jump right in," I said, and proceeded to tell Mr. Oxley about the Hope Diamond and how Mr. Cartier was merchandising it.

"I believe he's making up half of what he's saying about the curse and exaggerating the rest in order to trick someone into buying it just to defy the bad luck. I'd like to go undercover and see if I can expose the ruse before he sells it to some unsuspecting client."

"My, my, my . . ." Mr. Oxley was intrigued. He did everything but rub his hands together.

I had hoped the idea of a target as wealthy as Cartier would whet his appetite, and it looked as if it had. He leaned forward. His eyes sparkled.

"How do you plan on going undercover?"

"I will present myself as an heiress interested in buying the stone."

Oxley looked doubtful. And for good reason. I was wearing Vee Swann's modest and inexpensive clothes, thick eyeglasses, and dark wig. Scuffed shoes and an old handbag completed the disguise.

"You think you can convince Mr. Cartier of that?"

"I have a disguise or two I've used over the years. As well as a connected friend I can count on to present me to Mr. Cartier to ensure that he believes I am a woman of means."

"Disguises?" Mr. Oxley still looked doubtful.

"Yes, I had no trouble being a seamstress for two weeks in a shirtwaist factory, and I lived in a tenement as a widow and—"

"Yes, yes, I know. Your reputation precedes you. You have managed to be many things, Miss Swann, but all of them downtrodden and needy. Have you ever pretended to be one of the upper crust? That's a much tighter circle, where you are scrutinized and questioned in a way that no poor foreman just trying to keep his own job would question you."

"I have, yes. But sadly, the exposé I was working on didn't come to fruition. I wouldn't be here presenting this idea if I didn't feel confident. Besides, what do you have to lose? You don't pay up front, do you?"

"No, do you need the money?" He suddenly looked at me suspiciously. "It's been how long since your last article for the *World*?"

"Fourteen months. But no, I don't need the money the way you mean. I moved back home, and my parents took care of me through my convalescence."

"What do your folks do?" he asked. "Where are you from?"

"They live in Middleton, Rhode Island. My father is a doctor there. It's the town next to Newport and—"

"Yes, I know it."

"That's how I came to know some society people, including those I expect to help me with this story. My father is often called upon to treat them during the summer when they fall ill."

Mr. Oxley eyed me as if I were a filly he was considering buying. "How long do you think you need to do your research, write it up, and have this article ready?"

"Six to eight weeks."

"Well, I have to admit I'm intrigued. A story

like that would fit right in with what I like to publish and our readers expect to find in our pages. But I do have certain requirements for my freelancers."

"Yes?"

"You have to agree in writing that you won't tell anyone what you are working on until it is published."

"Of course." That was par for the course with any magazine or newspaper.

"We will settle on payment now, which I will guarantee, but you have to agree that after you turn the story in, if I decide not to publish it, you won't try to shop another version of it to other papers or magazines, as some writers do, and you won't discuss it at all."

"I'm not a neophyte. There will not be any question about the quality. You'll want to publish it."

"I trust that will be true, Miss Swann, but I have my reasons sometimes to hold a story back. So, I will need you to agree."

I had my own idea about why he was insisting on me not shopping the story if he didn't buy it. Once he read my Cartier story, he'd decide if it would be better as blackmail or as fodder for the magazine. Since I didn't want to give Mr. Oxley any reason to be suspicious, I reacted the way I assumed any reporter would, given the situation.

"I don't understand. Why wouldn't you publish

189

it if it meets the criteria we set up? I'm an established reporter. I'm not used to having my stories squashed."

"I don't explain myself, Miss Swann. Do you accept my terms or not?"

I had set a very difficult goal for myself. I needed to discover enough about Mr. Cartier's overblown sales techniques to write an article exposing his showmanship—even exaggerating if necessary—so that Mr. Oxley believed Cartier would pay to keep those methods secret. If, in fact, I succeeded and Oxley paid me but told me he wasn't going to run the story, I would need to go to Mr. Cartier and reveal all. I would hope he'd agree that suing Oxley would fit into his plans for generating yet more excitement around the Hope Diamond, and he'd happily go to court to expose Mr. Oxley's nefarious dealings. There were a lot of pieces that had to fall into place. And exactly how I was going to make sure they did promised to be difficult. But right now, I needed to take the first step and get the assignment. So I told Mr. Oxley that yes, I agreed to his stipulations.

"Well, well, I think we have a deal, then. Welcome back to the fourth estate, Miss Swann. I'm delighted you are reentering the arena with the *Gotham Gazette*."

SILK, SATIN & SCANDALS

In which your intrepid reporter fills you in on the most salacious and beautiful, glittering gossip in Gotham.

At the Metropolitan Opera's opening-night performance of *Madam Butterfly*, everyone's eyes were glued to the box of the recently widowed Mrs. Alfred Douglas, whose first name for the record is Marian. This reporter finds identifying women by their husbands' names archaic, especially when said men are deceased. That being said, Mrs. Douglas was entertaining a decidedly younger gentleman who was none other than the Broadway actor Stanford Clarke. The two had their heads together the whole evening, and one can only wonder at the romance they were so busy living out that they ignored the romance on the stage. Mrs. Douglas's ebony updo was adorned with a diamond and pearl tiara that matched her pearl and diamond sautoir and bracelet from the firm of Tiffany & Co. Her gems, some said, outshone the mediocre performance onstage.

The lovebirds probably were not whispering about the other piece of gossip very much on everyone's mind that night: the robbery of Mr. and Mrs. Harrison Todd's Vermeer painting, taken in broad daylight, so to speak, during the engagement party of their daughter Ruth.

The story, my dears, is that while everyone was raising a glass of champagne to the young couple, Ruth Todd and Peter Ridley, someone—probably one of the guests—was in the library cutting the canvas out of its frame. Since it's been quite a cold autumn, it would have been easy enough to hide the rolled-up painting away for the duration of the fete and then simply walk out of the house with it. Or at least, that's what this reporter and the police believe.

It's been quite the talk of the town that every guest has had a police detective visit them at their homes for questioning. (A very handsome detective, if you listen to the chatter.) But so far, there are no leads to the whereabouts of the diminutive painting of a woman sitting by a window reading a letter. A love letter, according to the symbolism of the work.

We can only hope the painting will soon be back in the library where it belongs, since the Todds are offering quite a reward for its return.

The engagement party itself was quite gay. The champagne was Dom Pérignon, and the bride-to-be wore an opulent silk dress in the same rose color as the hothouse flowers on the table. The gown was created for her by Lucille, and she sported a nosegay of sweetheart roses in the same delicious color at her waist. Miss Todd's engagement ring, which she showed off to all who cared to see, is a triplet with a Burmese ruby in the center flanked by two round diamonds, created by Marcus & Co.

So until next week, my dears. And remember, keep your secrets close to your vest, because this reporter has her eyes trained on you!

CHAPTER 12

The anger among the women in the press club's meeting room the next night was running high. The letter-writing campaign to protest Packwood's lawsuit against Betsy Beecher had failed. Not a single major paper had responded, and the editor's lawsuit was still moving forward.

We need to come up with a more powerful protest and need your ideas, Martha had written in her note asking me to come to the meeting.

Underlying her words was her admonishment that I had remained silent at the last meeting and that without my input, they had come up with only a milquetoast idea.

Since I was getting back into the investigative game for Oxley, I thought it would be smart to attend, and I was finally motivated. It was important for my colleagues to know I had fully come out of retirement. After all, I couldn't know what kinds of favors I was going to need in the upcoming weeks as I worked on my story.

There were more than fifty women at the meeting, forty seated, the rest standing in the aisles and in the back. Some of the best women reporters in the business, or "stunt girls" and "sob sisters," as our male editors and counterparts had taken to calling us, were there and desperate to effect change. I tried to curb my pessimism. Around me, these women still had the hope that I'd lost. They truly believed they could make a difference, not just by stopping Packwood's lawsuit but by improving how we were treated in our journalistic efforts and with the larger goal of bringing about equal rights for all women in all capacities. Being there that night among so many engaged, enraged, and determined reporters made me realize just how cynical and fatalistic I'd become.

Mrs. von Klenner took to the podium and commanded our attention.

"While we've been writing letters that haven't worked, our sister Dorothea Woods was taken off a story about the trial of a politician. When she came across information that guaranteed a front-page placement, a male reporter was reassigned."

Murmurs of outrage came from the assembly.

"How long are we going to accept being treated like second-class citizens in the newsroom? We get paid less, and we get assigned the least interesting stories unless we come up with them ourselves. Haven't we proved ourselves by now?" asked Caroline Middlestein, whose brother was Betsy's lawyer.

There was a chorus of *yay* and *hear hear* from the audience.

"It's all well and good to be outraged, but what are we going to do about how we are being treated?" shouted a woman whose voice I didn't recognize.

"What if we went on strike?" Dorothea called out.

There were many shouts of agreement.

Mrs. von Klenner reacted by holding up her hand. "While I understand the urge to strike, the problem is, would they even care? There are more than enough men to take our places. If anything, they'd probably be relieved."

"They would be!" Martha shouted.

"They'd celebrate!" Fanny agreed.

My friends were right. Female reporters going on strike wouldn't accomplish anything. But, I thought, there was something that would.

All my life, I'd seen my father's ads for Garland's in all the New York newspapers, but I hadn't ever really focused on the income ads generated until I read Uncle Percy's last letter to my father. Since then, I'd often thought about Oxley's scheme to get rich trading secrets for a high advertising spend.

Why not focus on that? We could trade something we believed in—integrity and equality—for advertising dollars. Despite my deciding to stay on the sidelines, despite my not believing anything would make a difference anymore, I stood up.

"Striking won't cause any change, but what if we get women *readers* to strike? Advertisers buy ads in the papers to lure women customers into their shops." There was quiet. I had their attention. "If women stopped reading the papers, the advertisers would see a decline in traffic in their stores. They'd be less inclined to buy ads. That would have a financial effect that no publisher could endure for long."

"You mean to threaten the papers with a loss of female subscriptions and therefore a loss in revenue from their advertisers?" Mrs. von Klenner asked.

"Exactly," I said, excited despite myself as I elaborated. "Once publishers see that if our editors continue to treat us like this, they will be risking their advertising dollars, they will have absolutely no choice but to force editorial to rethink their position. Even Prescott. No paper can exist without ad revenue."

Palpable excitement rippled through the room as we discussed the ways we might organize a protest and get the word out. I offered that I knew some people who wrote society columns and we might get them to mention the time and place.

"We would need to describe it in such a way that we could get it past our editors, who certainly wouldn't allow the mentions to run if they blatantly cried out against them," Fanny said.

"Let's call it a 'March for Equality' and make it seem like another suffragette effort and not let on what its true purpose is. We'll do that with the banners we carry and the leaflets we hand out."

"You're on fire. What's happened to you while you have been recuperating?" asked Elinor Edmundson, a society reporter who had always treated me with disdain. I wasn't sure why, but I suspected it was because she resented my lack of interest in my looks. Of all of us, I had always been one of the worst-dressed and most uncoiffed, eschewing the beauty tips, treatments, and products she wrote about so often. I found it especially ironic that Elinor was so obsequious to Vera Garland and her family when she wrote about them yet so dismissive of Vee Swann.

Ignoring her question, I continued on with another idea. "We should even take out ads for the march in the papers themselves."

"What if our editors notice?" Elinor asked.

"The ad departments and editorial are church and state," I said, trying to keep the supercilious tone out of my voice. "Editors never look at the ads, and the salesmen who sell them are so hungry they never really study them."

Half of them were advertising products that had no worth at all. I remembered Mr. Nevins quoting H. G. Wells, who said advertising was legalized lying.

"How much would advertising cost?" Fanny asked.

I knew because of conversations I'd overheard

between Jack and my father at the dinner table over the years, and so I told them.

"But how could we afford that?" Fanny asked.

"A patron?" Martha suggested.

"That's a ridiculous idea. Where would we get a patron?" Elinor said in her most annoying tone.

"I bet we could get a patron without too much trouble. This is a great cause, and there are many wives and daughters of wealthy men who suffer from the same kind of treatment in their families. I bet some of them would be willing to support us." I'd enjoy proving Elinor wrong. And I already had an idea for how to do so. I'd employ the same methods I'd used to help quite a few organizations that were in need. By embarrassing my mother and sister into helping in my column. I hadn't imposed it in a while, and it was time.

After the meeting, Fanny and Martha and I walked down to Greenwich Village and went to dinner at our favorite Italian restaurant, John's of 12th Street, and feasted on inexpensive plates of spaghetti and meatballs with homemade red wine. At first, our conversation focused on the march. Then we segued into discussing the suffragette movement's recent public events and how we could incorporate their efforts into ours. Having been stranded in a fog of medication and grief the last many months, I hadn't forgotten our camaraderie, but I had forgotten how inspiring spending time with them could be.

Our discussion moved on as Fanny told us the latest news in the Thompson trial, which she'd been covering for the last four weeks. Harold Thompson had kidnapped a little boy named Jimmy Campbell from his bedroom and held him hostage for one week. Although the Campbells had paid the ransom, Thompson had still murdered the six-year-old boy. He'd been the groundskeeper at the Campbell estate and had an affair with Sarah Campbell, the boy's mother. After Mrs. Campbell had ended the affair and fired Thompson, he'd taken his revenge.

Since the trial had started and the affair had come out in testimony, Donald Campbell, the boy's father, had left his wife.

"Sometimes it is hard to write the news," Fanny said. "Even though it's my job, I feel for Mrs. Campbell and can't separate myself from what she's gone through. Yes, she had an affair, but she didn't deserve to lose her son and now her husband. She's suddenly all alone and in mourning. All for having a six-week dalliance with the gardener."

"Which is exactly why they want us women covering these stories," I said. "It's our emotional connection and perspective that sell the papers."

"Women reporters are the ones writing the stories that boost circulation, and yet we're still relegated to sob stories and fashion," Martha said. "Our editors insist we can't take on assignments that could keep us out at night or take us away from our families. But our male counterparts have families and need sleep, too."

The waiter came and removed the plates.

"Have you heard that Helene Bishop is getting married?" Fanny asked us both once the waiter had left.

Neither of us had heard the news about the reporter who covered women's health for the *Tribune*. We fell into a discussion about marriage while the owner of the restaurant served us biscotti and small glasses of lemon-flavored liqueur that we dipped the cookies into.

"A victim of her romanticism," Martha said, and then took a bite of her sweet.

Martha was bitter about love. Before she'd gone to work at *Scientific American*, she'd been at *Cosmopolitan* magazine, where she'd had an affair with her editor. Once it began, he started treating her even worse than before, claiming that, like Caesar's wife, she now had to be above suspicion with the rest of the staff. So she cut off the affair. And he fired her for no reason, with no severance and no warning.

Fanny, a bisexual, was even more bitter about traditional romance than Martha. She had been raped almost five years before. Not brutally by a stranger but taken by force by a fellow reporter she was dating whom she thought she might be growing to care about. She'd gotten over it as well as could be expected, but she'd developed an edge and trusted women more than men now.

But weren't we all changed by the men we'd come in contact with? Certainly, there were good men out there, but those who took advantage of us were the ones who left scars on our souls and forced us to become suspicious and overly cautious.

That none of us three was married was atypical. We all found our jobs exciting and our careers daring. But if we married, our editors expected us to give up our work. And none of us was willing to do that. Trade in our typewriters for aprons? Our pencils for diapers? It was fine for the women who wanted it, but we had stories to cover and careers to pursue and changes to make.

"Helene's fiancé is a doctor, so he's well off. A widower with two small children," Martha continued.

"Two children? Then she's totally lost her mind," Fanny said, and we laughed.

"She's going to wind up a babysitter and a cook," I said.

"She claims he has a nanny and a cook and a maid. He's a society doctor. I think his name is Bernstein, or Bernstern."

I knew the name well. Dr. Bernstein was the Garland family doctor. And very much a society physician. He had overseen my back surgery and recovery after my fall and had assured me that because of doctor-patient confidentiality, he would never tell anyone about Vee Swann. But would that extend to his wife? Especially when that wife was also a journalist?

"It is possible," I said, remembering Dr. Bernstein the night my father passed away, "that Helene has found one of the good ones. If he has money, he won't expect her to be a slave to the children or the kitchen. There do seem to be some modern men who understand that not every woman wants the same thing. That some of us want to work and make a difference just like they do."

"Well, you won't find me testing those waters," said Fanny resolutely.

"No one would guess that you would. Not to mention how Susannah would react if you did."

We all laughed. Fanny's current female companion—the polite way of saying her lover—was a painter of some renown and as jealous as she was beautiful. Her temper with clients and friends and lovers of both sexes over the years was notorious. But in the last twelve months, she and Fanny, much to our surprise, had settled into a very domesticated arrangement. It seemed as if Fanny calmed Susannah while Susannah inflamed Fanny. It was what they both needed.

"Sometimes I think it would be easier to like women," Martha mused. "At least, the question of marriage and children and giving up your life for someone else wouldn't come into it."

Fanny sighed. "Like everything else, Martha, it only looks easier. We have our burdens. We have to hide our affection in public. No one thinks anything of a man leaning down and kissing his wife tenderly or taking her hand or a million other small niceties, but all of that is *verboten* to us."

"But the freedom," Martha continued.

"There is no freedom," I said. Both women turned to me. "There is no freedom for any of us. Whether we take women as lovers, or men. Whether we vow to remain unmarried, or marry a sophisticated, supportive man. Even if we dress as men like Malinda Blalock or Elisa Bernerström, who did it to fight in wars, or use male pen names like George Eliot or Charlotte Brontë, who did it to get published, we will still and forever be women, never liberated from our sex. Never freed from our way of loving and grieving and mourning. Never free from the power that men can exert over us. We are prisoners of our feelings. Of our attachments. Of our sentiments. We can pretend that we can do everything a man can do and more. We can insist we get the vote and the respect that is our due. But in the end, we will still be the ones to cook dinner and make the bed and weep over a novel and be called weak. We will still be forced to try to fight off a drunken coward who knows he is stronger than us and can get away with it even though he is a stupid lout and we are ten times smarter. We will stand up and fight for our sisters and our rights, but when the baby is sick, which one of us will not forgo all else to sit by its side? What man would do the same?"

Fanny took my hand. "Vee, you have to use that anger."

I shrugged. "I've always been angry at injustice," I said. "There's nothing different now."

"Yes, there is. I don't know what's changed in you, but the anger isn't impersonal anymore. It's not you looking through a window at a tableau you find disturbing. You're inside the house now. Don't be defeatist by thinking that what we do doesn't matter. That we'll never be free. We *will* be. We *have* to be. Even baby steps are still forward movement. Even if all we can do right now is fight for it, it's when we fight that we are really alive."

I went home that night and wrote and rewrote my Silk, Satin and Scandals column to include a rallying cry about the march. Finally, at midnight, when I read it over, I decided I had accomplished my goal. Surely, after reading about Letty Garland Briggs stepping up to spearhead the

March for Equality, my unsuspecting sister would, in fact, volunteer and become the patron of an army of women determined to fight the status quo and protect one of their own.

CHAPTER 13

After delivering the column to the *World*'s offices the next morning, I returned home and sat down at my father's desk. A strong cup of coffee by my side, I began taking notes and making a plan for how to get more information about Cartier and the diamond for my article.

What do I already know?

What do I need to learn?

How much material will be required?

The first thing I put on my list was to research the history of the Hope Diamond before Mr. Cartier had purchased it.

Who owns it?

When did it change hands?

Is there any truth to the story Mr. Cartier performed for my sister and me?

I also needed to visit Mr. Cartier and convince him I was interested in buying the stone to keep him from selling it to anyone else until I'd finished my article. That and my ultimate goal would require a balancing act. I had to play the part of Scheherazade but in the opposite way. To string Mr. Cartier along . . . pretend to be getting closer and closer to making the purchase but always wanting one more story from him . . . making him feel that his exaggerated tales were the way to reel me in as a client.

Meanwhile, I would need to check each of his narratives, proving through research whether they were myths.

As a reporter, I had always known that my job was to dig deep and ferret out the truth for the public. But this time, I had an ulterior motive. The article itself was just step one in a larger plan. Which may have been why this felt more like I was outlining a mystery novel. My mind was stuck in a muddle of plots.

Was there enough material to write an incendiary enough story?

Did that even matter? If Mr. Cartier was inventing stories, couldn't I, too?

I needed to remember that the end goal wasn't discovering the truth but convincing Mr. Oxley to try to blackmail Mr. Cartier. And then convincing Mr. Cartier that calling Mr. Oxley's bluff would bring even more attention to the Hope. Only then would I be able to expose the publisher and his diabolical schemes and in the process destroy his reputation and exact my revenge.

So what to do first?

Mr. Cartier had told my sister and me that the history of great gems was also the history of magic, alchemy, curses, shams, and superstitions. So I needed to acquaint myself with the annals of stones.

I spent the next two days in the New York Public Library, reading scientific treatises on different gems and their properties. I then perused current and older magazines and newspapers, looking for articles on the Hope Diamond specifically. There were quite a few mentions over the years but nothing of depth. And certainly nothing as dramatic as the stories Mr. Cartier had told.

In *The Scrapbook*, Volume 4, I read an article titled "The Melodrama of Diamonds" by Gilson Willets. It was subtitled "The Tragic Side of the History of Great Historic Gems—The Mystery of a Guillotined Court Beauty's Jewels."

The article romanced the history of the Hope, starting in the 1830s when Henry Philip Hope of Surrey, England, bought the blue diamond possibly from Daniel Eliason, an art dealer and diamond collector. In 1894, Lord Francis Hope removed the stone from his bank in order to give it to his wife, May Yohé, but there was no mention of a great curse on the stone. Bad luck visits most families over the years. It was foolish to assume a diamond could be blamed for the Hope family losing its money and May Yohé and her husband divorcing.

A Treatise on Diamonds and Precious Stones by John Mawe, published in London in 1813, gave me some insight into how people thought about gems a hundred years ago but yielded nothing spectacular. Nor did Harry Emanuel's similar book, written in 1867.

Natal Stones: Sentiments and Superstitions Associated with Precious Stones, by Tiffany's famous gemologist George Frederick Kunz, offered more help, as did several other articles written by him.

As I became more immersed in the material, I began to see how Mr. Cartier had taken bits and pieces from various sources to concoct his case for the existence of the curse. But nothing really surprised me until I came upon a pamphlet written by a well-known psychic that described the properties of different stones. Certain crystals told the future. One gem attracted unsettled ghosts. Another warded off evil energy. It reminded me a bit of the stories Mr. Asher had told my sister and me that day at Cartier's, and I made a note to search him out and see what else I could glean from his knowledge. But first, I wanted to get more information about how practitioners of the occult used stones.

The next morning, I sent a note to Martha, who had been writing about New York City's esoteric and arcane scene for more than two years, asking if I could take her out for lunch. She wrote back, saying yes, and at eleven thirty, I took the streetcar downtown to the *Scientific American* offices at 361 Broadway at Franklin Street. Upstairs, Martha grabbed her coat and bag, and we went to a restaurant a block away that she recommended.

Over our lunch of fresh salmon, mayonnaise, and salad, I asked her questions about the uses of different stones. Martha talked, and I took notes. Her latest investigation, she told me, was into a psychic who used crystals and certain gems to communicate with the dead. If I wanted to see the woman in action, Martha said I could join her at an event the next night. I readily accepted.

"What is this for, Vee?" she asked over a dessert of fried apple rings sprinkled with cinnamon sugar.

"I'm doing a story for the *Gotham Gazette* and need to learn all about gemstones, superstitions, and curses," I said.

Her eyebrows rose. "When did you get that assignment? We just had dinner two nights ago, and you didn't say anything. And you're working for Oxley? Couldn't you get your old job back?"

"I'm not sure I'm ready for the newsroom's constant pressures. Oxley was willing to hire me as a freelancer and—"

"You're fibbing. Not ready for the newsroom's pressures? Tell me what is going on, or I won't give you a whit of help."

There were parts of the story that I couldn't explain—after all, Vee Swann's father hadn't died. She was merely organizing a dead man's library. *She* wasn't out for revenge. So I told Martha the one truth in all of this that I could.

"I haven't completely recovered from the fall I took last summer. I still have bouts of pain and am afraid of going back to work full-time. If I did and had to take time off, I'd look weak and then get even less respect."

She nodded. "I know exactly how you feel. But I did some work for Oxley a while back. Don't you remember how miserable I was? He's not above putting female reporters in compromising positions. And then there are the ever-present rumors that he uses his army of reporters as spies to find stories he can use to strong-arm his victims into advertising in his magazine in exchange for keeping their stories quiet."

I knew that Oxley's methods were hardly a secret, but it was startling to hear Martha discuss them so casually.

"Yes." I nodded. "So I've heard."

"So why work for someone so disreputable?" She was frowning. But then, before I had a chance to answer, she started to nod and then smiled. "I know you, Vee. You aren't fooling me with your back pain. You want to expose Oxley's racket, don't you?"

Martha and I had been friends for a long time. I shouldn't have been surprised that she had guessed.

"Yes. I do."

"He is dangerous, Vee. Very dangerous."

"I've sparred with dangerous men before, you know that."

"And gotten your back broken in the process. I fear Oxley is a far worse adversary than Mr. Danzinger."

"I'll be careful."

"You can't be careful enough."

"I will."

"So how are you going to do it? What are you going to write about?"

I decided it couldn't hurt to tell my best friend my plan, as long as I left out the personal aspects.

"You're going to use Cartier to set Oxley up?"

"Yes."

Martha burst out laughing. "That's my Vee. Well, I'm happy to help you. A man like Oxley is bad for the industry. So what's your angle? What have you got on Cartier?"

"Not enough. That's why I need as much information as I can get about stones and superstitions. I've been reading up, but I'm still coming up short."

"What do you have so far?" she asked.

I told her as much as I had been able to pull together. Halfway through my explanation of what Cartier had claimed about the Hope's history, her eyes lit up.

"Some of that sounds very familiar . . ." She thought for a moment. "I know why! There's a very famous book with some of that story in it. Have you heard of Wilkie Collins?"

"I read *The Woman in White*, yes. But isn't that a fairly old book? I think critics called it the first mystery novel?"

"Exactly. Well, Collins also wrote *The Moonstone*, which was quite popular as well. And still is. I see it all the time in bookstores. It sounds as if your Mr. Cartier might be using some of Collins's story."

"How so?"

"It takes place at a country estate and is about the theft of a great blue diamond originally stolen from a Hindu god."

"I'll definitely get it," I said.

"Now, about tomorrow night," Martha said, and then gave me the address of the séance she would be going to and why she thought it might help me in my efforts. Indeed, it sounded perfect. The psychic used all kinds of precious stones to contact the dead. While Martha didn't think the woman was doing anything of the kind, she would be a wealth of information.

The next evening, I met Martha outside the psychic's brownstone on 143rd Street. The well-appointed sandstone building was decorated with sophisticated architectural embellishments. We walked up the six steps and entered an equally fancy vestibule and took a marble stairway up to a second-floor apartment.

As we walked through the foyer and into a high-ceilinged parlor, I smelled the exotic scents of vanilla and frankincense. The tall stained-glass windows on the back wall must have looked out onto a garden. Since it was dark out, instead of shedding the room in color and light, they created a closed-in feeling. A brown-and-red-domed glass chandelier cast a somber glow over a large round table and eight chairs. Tiny votive candles resting on the fireplace mantel sent shadows dancing on the walls. The joss stick I had smelled burned in its holder, sending a thin plume of scented smoke wafting upward.

Several people were already seated. A heavyset woman with hennaed hair, wearing a flowing cobalt-blue gown shot with silver thread, sat between two well-dressed men. One appeared to be around sixty and the other much younger, perhaps my age. There was also a couple who looked to be in their twenties and who appeared uncomfortable.

The heavyset woman turned out to be Madame Bunotti, who greeted us and then said we would wait a few more minutes for the last two people who were expected. She suggested we use the time to introduce ourselves.

"I'm Sally Frankel," Martha said, using the made-up name she'd created for her meetings with Madame. "And this is Annie Pearl," Martha said, coming up with a name for me on the spot.

A second pseudonym, I thought. As if I needed another.

We had just finished the introductions when a couple arrived. They looked to be in their forties, subdued and elegantly dressed. Both wore dour expressions and introduced themselves as Gertrude and William Albright.

Once they were seated, Madame Bunotti rose, went to an étagère sitting against the wall, opened its bottom drawer, and retrieved a round silver tray that she placed on the table. Next, she pulled out an ornately carved mahogany box and set it beside the tray.

She stood looking down at the casket as if in meditation but more to create a dramatic effect, I thought. Once she had all of our curiosity and focus, she lifted the box's lid. The overhead lamp shed light on its contents: a treasure of rainbow-colored stones, glowing and glittering.

She touched the tray. "We use silver as a base for each stone because it acts as a conduit, helping the spirits reach from their world to ours."

One by one, she pulled out different rocks and crystals, arranging them in a specific pattern on the tray while keeping up a running commentary about the power of each stone.

"This is to ward off the evil eye," she said, as she placed a large round piece of malachite in the center of the tray. "Its emerald-green color is soothing to behold, and it absorbs negative energy."

Her explanation reminded me of Mr. Asher's explanation of amethyst's properties.

"Now for a sprinkling of garnets," Madame said, as she created a circle around the malachite. Each deep-blood-red stone was approximately the size and shape of a raspberry.

"The garnet was one of the twelve stones in the breastplate of the high priest," she said. "From the Mayans to Native American Indians, mystics know it expands our awareness and helps us be more powerful. Garnets were used to protect soldiers during the Crusades."

Next, one by one, she withdrew eight clear, prism-shaped crystals. Each plinth, the size of her hand, appeared heavy from the way she lifted them. Walking back and forth around the table, she placed one in front of each of us.

"These are clear quartz," she said. "No stronger connection to the spiritual world exists."

Once she'd circled the table, she withdrew yet more stones and added them to her mosaic, explaining why she was adding emeralds, turquoise, tourmalines, and amethyst.

Finally, she positioned a large candle on either side of her arrangement.

"Now," she instructed, "place the forefinger of your right hand on the edge of the crystal to your right and the forefinger of your left hand on the crystal to your left, which will create an unbroken circle of connection both to one another and to the stones."

We did as we were told.

Madame then turned off the overhead chandelier. Next, she lit the two candles, both of which emitted heavy, fragrant smoke.

Then the show began. And what a show it was.

First, a soft breeze blew through the room, carrying the scent of roses with it, while far off in the distance, we heard the cry of a child.

Across from me, the Albrights looked at each other. She with an expression of hope, he with one of grief. The sound of the crying continued. Was it coming closer? I thought so.

"That's my baby," Mrs. Albright said, choking on a sob.

Her husband nodded. "It is, that's our boy."

Madame Bunotti, eyes closed, head bowed, began to speak in a high-pitched voice, her mouth hardly moving. It seemed as if the baby was inside of her and she was simply letting his voice out.

"Mama, Papa, don't be sad . . ."

The smoke from the two candles thickened and began to form into the shape of a child.

Mrs. Albright let out a cry as she pointed. "Oh, my, it's my Bobby! It's him, it's him!"

Suddenly, all hell broke loose. While the Albrights, Madame, Martha, and I remained at the table, the three other attendees quickly rose, two of them knocking back their chairs. The young woman ran to the wall and flipped the switch, turning on the lights. One man raced into a room beyond the parlor. The other man turned to Madame and, before she realized what he was doing, handcuffed her. Seconds later, the first man and the woman who'd since also left the room emerged, dragging a handcuffed man with them. The woman held a fireplace bellows in her free hand.

"Here's your son," the man said to Mr. and Mrs. Albright. "I'm sorry, but your baby is no more talking to you from the grave than I am."

He introduced himself and his partner as police detectives. The woman with them had been a decoy. The man in handcuffs was Madame Bunotti's husband and had been operating the special effects from the room abutting the parlor the entire time. The detective announced that they were taking Mr. and Mrs. Bunotti downtown to be formally arrested. Then he asked the Albrights to accompany them.

"We'd appreciate it if you would tell us how much you paid 'Madame' here for the opportunity to communicate with your child and make a formal complaint."

Once everyone was gone, Martha and I made our way downstairs.

"I can't believe you didn't tell me what was

going to happen," I said. "I was scared out of my wits!"

"I honestly didn't know that was going to happen tonight. I've attended two of these waiting for the sting. My sources simply advised me it might be one night this week, so I was prepared to keep coming back. I really brought you so you could listen to Madame Bunotti talking about the stones. I thought it might put you in the right frame of mind."

"I don't think Mr. Cartier is engaging in any séances."

"No, but from what you've described, is what he's doing any less disingenuous?"

CHAPTER 14

M r. Cartier greeted me warmly the next afternoon for our two p.m. appointment.

"It's a pleasure to see you again, Mademoiselle Garland. How can I help?"

We were seated at one of the delicate tables next to the windows overlooking Fifth Avenue. An associate had just arrived with a silver tray and carefully placed a glass of champagne and tiny madeleines dusted with powdered sugar in front of me.

"I have been thinking about the Hope Diamond," I said.

"It is hard to forget about it once you've seen it. It's quite a magical stone."

"It is. And my sister's thirtieth birthday is coming up," I whispered. "Knowing that he was ill, my father left me a special bequest to buy her something from him."

"Indeed, the Hope would be quite special. It is without a doubt one of the most precious diamonds I have ever seen. But have you considered the luck factor, Mademoiselle Garland?" he asked, shaking his head. "Not that your father was superstitious. Are you or your sister?"

"No, neither my sister nor I believe in luck. If

anything, I think Letty would like to have it just to prove how silly the idea of a stone bringing good or bad luck is."

"But so many people who have had extensive contact with the Hope have had such bad luck follow them."

"Why, Mr. Cartier, are you trying to talk me out of it? Do you already have a purchaser?"

"I have several people who have expressed interest, but the stone is still available. I'm not attempting to talk you out of it. But I do feel a certain allegiance to your father to be sure you are aware of the stories."

"Can you tell me how much you are asking for the piece?"

"We are pricing it at three hundred thousand dollars."

I raised my eyebrows. I had not been brought up in the retail environment for nothing, and I'd done my research. His quote was a third more than I'd expected. "Is there any room for negotiation?"

"Because of my relationship with your father, yes, there is. But I'm afraid not very much. I've already turned down two offers that were too low."

"I see," I said, and paused.

I had to make my interest seem real, and while my father was a very wealthy merchant, it wasn't necessarily feasible that he'd left enough for me to make that kind of purchase without deep consideration or help from another source.

"The only way I could manage that would be if my mother agreed to the purchase and joined me in buying it for Letty." My mother's inherited wealth was greater than anything my father had amassed. While her brother had sold off the stocks and bonds their father had lent him to finance his architectural firm, my mother had kept her investments intact.

Mr. Cartier nodded. "Of course. When is the occasion?"

"January fifteenth."

He nodded.

"Would it be possible for you to give me a week or two to discuss this with my mother? She might want to see the stone before she makes up her mind."

"Certainly. I don't want you to feel rushed at all, but as I mentioned, I do have other interest."

"Serious interest?"

"Yes, from existing clients who are very avid collectors, but I'm not at liberty to discuss who they are."

"No, of course not. Nor would I expect you to discuss my interest with anyone."

"Certainly not."

"May I see the diamond again?" I asked. "But out of its setting? I'd like to look at the stone itself and not as a piece of jewelry."

Mr. Cartier gave me a curious glance, as if my request had surprised him, but he didn't question me. He pressed a brass button in the corner of the desk, and a moment later Mr. Asher emerged from behind the showroom's door. He was dressed as he had been before, in dark pants and a gray smock over a white shirt and tie.

"Yes, sir?"

I watched as the jeweler's eyes moved from Mr. Cartier to take me in. I saw an ever so slight flicker of recognition. It made me feel much the same way it had the first time I was introduced to him. As if this meeting was happening on two different planes. The surface one and on a deeper, psychic level. Or perhaps Madame Bunotti's séance had affected me more than I realized. Either way, I felt silly. I wasn't a romantic. These notions didn't fit my worldview. I didn't see love as something ethereal. But here I was, unable to look away from this man's velvet-green eyes. I yearned to hear him speak with that curious accent. I craved a whiff of his fragrance to see if it was in fact as evocative as I remembered.

"Jacob, Mademoiselle Garland would like to see the Hope. Would you be so kind as to bring it out? Along with what you'll need to remove it from its setting."

Mr. Asher raised his eyebrows but didn't say anything. He just nodded, turned, and left.

"Hasn't anyone else asked to see the diamond on its own?" I asked Mr. Cartier, filling the quiet while we waited.

"No, actually. But I'm happy to oblige. It's a magnificent specimen. As scientifically important as it is beautiful."

Mr. Asher reappeared. He'd donned his white gloves and held a tray. I couldn't see the stone, but reflections from its facets sent rainbows dancing on the ceiling.

He set the tray down on the table in front of us. I saw he'd also brought out the metal bib.

"Would you like to try it on first?" Mr. Cartier asked.

"No, I don't think I need to try it on myself. I'd just like to study it. Without the setting. Is it difficult to remove?"

Mr. Cartier gestured to Mr. Asher.

"Not at all." I listened to his deep, slow voice and watched his graceful movements as he took the necklace from its satin-lined box. "This isn't necessarily the Hope's final setting," he said, "so we haven't secured it. The prongs are hinged."

I watched as he pulled back the first prong to show me. I leaned closer and inhaled Mr. Asher's scent. It was as unique and intriguing as I'd remembered. What was it about one set of ingredients that made them so powerful they could elicit an emotional reaction and another that left you unimpressed? Was it the cologne itself? Or was it the wearer's own aura that mixed with the oils to create the mystique?

"If you want to hold the stone, Mademoiselle Garland, I prefer you use these." Mr. Cartier held out a pair of white gloves.

"You don't trust me to know how to hold the stone?" I asked.

"No, please, don't misunderstand. It's the issue of bad luck. We don't want to be responsible for what might happen to you if you did touch the stone with your bare hand."

As I put the gloves on, he continued speaking.

"There's a newspaper article," he said, "that I want to show you." He opened the leather-bound book that obviously wasn't ever far from his reach and flicked through the pages. "This one, right here. May I read it to you?"

"Of course," I said.

He began in his charming accent:

Interviewed regarding the sale of the famous Hope Diamond, Miss May Yohé says she attributes all her troubles to that jewel, and prophesies trouble for the purchasers. "As Lady Francis Hope, I always felt a dislike for the stone, and I could never overcome the feeling and wear it in public.

"While I was wearing the stone I was in an absolute state of terror, and when I removed it to be returned to the vault of Lord Francis Hope's bankers I fell into spells of dizziness which I could not explain.

"Legends of Old India whence the stone emanated have come into my mind to account for this. The night before I ran away from Lord Francis I dreamed of the stone.

"Its shimmering facets reflected waves of light that seemed to beckon me, and I prepared to desert my home."

Miss May Yohé admits that she is poor and must sing in music halls for a very moderate salary, but says with surety, "I wouldn't accept the Hope Diamond to wear now even if they gave me as an inducement 100 pounds a year."

"Mr. Cartier," I said, "you have the most unusual salesmanship technique when it comes to selling this piece. Do you try to talk customers out of buying every one of your jewels? Is that the magic of the House of Cartier?"

Both he and Jacob Asher laughed.

"Mademoiselle Garland, there are so many beautiful magical stones in the world, so many in my own shop here, and not one of them has a curse attached to it other than this one diamond. I am not using the legend, as you put it, to induce a sale but rather to ensure that the person who does buy it does so knowingly."

"My father had many theories about merchandising. I guess this one does fit his *want* theory."

"What was his *want* theory? I'm not sure I ever heard him discuss it. I'm sure it was brilliant, though; he was perhaps the most astute merchant I've ever met."

I felt my emotions catch in my throat and for a moment didn't speak. "Thank you," I finally said in a low voice. I still had a hard time speaking of Father without tears. "He used to tell me that one of the secrets he had acquired over the years was that one could look at the world through the lens of desire and see how the two simple words *I want* have shaped civilizations. And that there is no greater way of making someone believe that they want something than to set up a situation whereby they think they cannot have the thing they so desire. Desire, my father used to say, is what puts food on our table."

Mr. Cartier nodded. "I agree with that."

"So by talking so much about the curse, you're doing that very thing. When you suggest to me, or anyone else, that this stone is *verboten* and not something I should want, you are setting up a situation where I find myself wanting it more and more."

"It's not often that I have a student of merchandising in my humble shop," Mr. Cartier said, with a small dip of his head as if he were bowing to royalty. "But please rest assured that I am not trying to trick you into buying this stone. I would never do that to your father's daughter."

With the gloves on, I picked up the Hope Diamond. For a few seconds, I forgot all the reasons for my being there. Forgot the sordid story of my uncle's death and my father's heart attacks. Forgot my plot to get revenge for those two men who wanted nothing but to love each other. I gazed into the depths of the violet stone and was lost in its sparkling, magical, colored facets. I felt as if I was holding desire in my palm. Hundreds, if not thousands, of years of desire. It was nothing but a rock, I thought. Yes, a very rare and beautiful one but a rock nevertheless. One people had stolen and died for, according to Mr. Cartier. I wished I could show it to my father, who so admired beauty. That wish quickly turned to anger, and the rage that had already been thrumming inside me hardened into even greater resolve.

I don't know how long I looked into the diamond's depths. Neither Mr. Cartier nor Mr. Asher made a sound to interrupt my reverie, but by the time I handed it back to Mr. Asher, something in me had changed.

The jeweler took the Hope without a word and reinserted it into its setting.

"Do you get tired of looking at it?" I asked him.

Jacob Asher finished closing the last hinged prong and turned to me. "No more than anyone tires of looking at a sunset or the stars or into a beautiful woman's eyes. The stone reveals more of herself to me every time I study her."

"So the stone is feminine? I thought that it was *le diamant*, not *la diamant*."

"Yes, in French, the word for diamond is very much a masculine noun . . . but I have a hard time seeing these mysterious, beautiful objects as anything other than feminine. A really fine diamond like this contains too many secrets to be masculine. It reflects a whole rainbow of infinite colors. That's not a man's way. And besides . . . I'm not French."

I wanted to ask him where he was from. To inquire about his accent. To listen to him talk more about diamonds and what he saw in them, but Mr. Cartier interrupted my absorption.

"Are you sure you wouldn't like to try the necklace on, Mademoiselle Garland?"

"I suppose I should."

"Jacob, the bib, please?"

As the jeweler stood behind me and attached the silver underpiece around my neck, I watched his reflection in the mirror.

"Mr. Cartier, if I were to say I wanted the Hope and offered two hundred thousand dollars, would you consider that?"

"No," he answered, then smiled.

Mr. Asher lifted the diamond and platinum necklace up and draped it on top of the bib and then worked the clasp at the back. As he did, his fingertips touched the skin at the nape of my neck.

"But I would consider two hundred fifty thousand," Mr. Cartier said softly.

I shivered at the feel of Jacob Asher's fingers as they lingered just a moment too long on my skin.

CHAPTER 15

That night, I went to *Swan Lake* with my mother, my sister, Jack, and Stephen, whom I hadn't seen since the night I told him about the letter. Though I was very happy to see him, Mother had, of course, extended the invitation without my knowing. She had never given up hope of sparking a romance between us.

Swan Lake was my favorite ballet and had been my father's favorite as well. In fact, I'm sure it had been the inspiration behind my pen name that long-ago afternoon at the Meadows.

We dined at home in Riverdale after the performance, Mother holding court as usual.

"I think you might want to get away for a bit, dear. Should we go abroad? You're so thin," my mother said, as the main course was presented.

"Yes, Mother, you've suggested that before. But the truth is . . . I don't have the time. I've gone back to work," I said.

Everyone at the table, including Stephen, was surprised.

"Good for you," he said.

"I thought you were going to stay away from newspaper work," my mother said. "Your back is healed, but you know Dr. Bernstein said it was a miracle, and you need to be careful."

"I'm not going undercover as a gymnast," I joked.

"There's no reason to be flip," my mother said, clearly not understanding the unintentional pun with "gymnast" and "flip" she had just made. "What are you going to be doing?"

"I'm actually going to be working on my old beat, doing investigative pieces. The twist this time is that I'll be undercover as Vera Garland."

Everyone looked confused.

"What do you mean?" Letty asked.

"I am planning on presenting myself as a society spinster in an effort to expose an extortionist."

"An extortionist? That sounds dangerous," my mother said, visibly upset.

"It could be," I said.

"But Vera . . ."

"Mother, I am a reporter. That's what I do. My job is to do whatever is required, be it dangerous or not, in an effort to bring the truth to the forefront. Stories like mine, like the ones other reporters are writing, can effect change. There are fewer children working in tenement factories because of Charlotte."

"I know, darling," she said, and patted my hand in a patronizing way. "And your father and I were so proud of you for that and all the other things you have done, but you aren't in your twenties anymore. It's time to settle down and really think about getting married. There is still a chance that you could find a widower who—"

"Mother, stop! Women don't have to be married to have a fulfilling life. I know you find that hard to believe, but this is 1910, not the eighteenth century."

My mother continued as if she hadn't heard a word I'd said.

"I had hoped that by now, your period of mourning for your father would be over, and you'd realize that you have one last window of opportunity. That won't happen if you go back to a terrible smoky city room or insert yourself into the lives of people who don't want you there and will take measures. Like Charlotte's father."

I felt deflated. Depressed by the weight of my mother's never-ending snobbery and old-fashioned beliefs. I wanted to shake her and wake her up. How could she remain stuck in a past that was growing ever more dim every day and not see the value in what I and my sister reporters did?

"Think of your mother like a silk dress from the 1880s, darling," my father had said to me once. "Beautiful but out-of-date about women's rights. She can no more reinvent herself than the dress can."

"But that's ridiculous," I'd argued. "The dress is not a sentient being. It is inert cloth. It needs a seamstress to remake it."

"I've tried to be that seamstress but realized long ago she can't be changed."

"Anyone can be changed."

"Not Henrietta March Winthrop Garland. She's determined, along with her set, to stop the march of time."

"Well, she can't stop me from jumping right in with both feet."

"No, darling, no one can stop you." He'd kissed my forehead then.

But someone *had* stopped me. A brutish drunk who needed his daughter's pennies to buy himself more drink. He'd refused to listen to me and bring in a doctor to see Charlotte and signed her death warrant by giving me a push down his stairs.

"Do you have a target for this extortion story?" my sister asked.

"I do."

"Tell us," she said.

"You know I can't, but it is someone in the press."

She pouted a little. As much as she was my mother's daughter, I knew she thrilled to my escapades.

Meanwhile, my mother was staring at me. Did she suspect what I was planning?

"What is it?" I asked her.

"Can't I be worried about my daughter?"

"Yes." I gave her a smile, touched.

"Please try to be careful, Vera," my mother said. "All right?"

I nodded.

"Will you go away to do your research?" Jack asked.

"Not this time, no."

After supper, Stephen took me home in his carriage.

"Will you tell me what you are planning?" he asked.

"Not yet, but I do need some information, and down the road, I might also need some advice."

"Of course. What information?"

"I'm going to need to educate myself completely about the ins and outs of blackmail laws. For instance, what would someone need to prove in order to charge someone else with blackmail to ensure conviction?"

The carriage had stopped, and because of the streetlamp shining through the window, I could see Stephen's eyes widen.

"This is about your uncle's suicide, isn't it?"

"It might be."

"It's too dangerous, Vera."

"Which of the stories I've gone after didn't sound dangerous?"

"But this is different, isn't it?" Stephen asked.

I thought a moment. "Yes, this time, it is personal."

CHAPTER 16

The following day, I called Cartier's and asked if Mr. Cartier was in.

"He is. Would you like to speak to him, Madame?" Mr. Fontaine asked.

"I would, but—oh, I have to call back. My maid has just come in with a message."

There was no one there with me. Margery wasn't due that day, but I needed a fast excuse to get off the phone. I didn't want to speak to Mr. Cartier, I just wanted to know if he was in the store. My first step required his absence.

The next day, I went through a similar charade, this time altering my voice. And the day after. On the third day, I was told that Mr. Cartier was out for the afternoon.

Finally, what I had been waiting for.

I opened my jewelry box and removed my pearls. They were a luminous, creamy white. The necklace had been a gift from my mother on my twenty-first birthday, and I never wore it unless I was in her company. While I appreciated its beauty, I found it too formal, too uniform. I much preferred the opal beads my father had bought me, with their dazzling whorls of color inside each perfect orb. The way they flashed orange and green, purple and blue, always amazed me. My father had told me the stones reminded him of me. Bold and different, he'd said.

In the kitchen, I took a knife and tried to scratch one of the pearls up near the clasp but couldn't get a good enough grip to do any damage. I found a jar and tried to smash the pearl but only managed a dent. Next, I tried with a frying pan and actually wound up smashing three of the pearls as well as the clasp.

The damage done, I placed the necklace back in its leather box, which I put in my purse. I dressed for the meeting and then walked the two blocks from my penthouse to 712 Fifth Avenue.

Upstairs, I was greeted by the always efficient and formal Mr. Fontaine, who asked if he could help me.

"I have a damaged pearl necklace. I'd like to have it repaired and restrung."

"Of course, Miss Garland. I'd be happy to take them and give you a receipt."

"If you don't mind, I'd like to speak to the jeweler myself. These pearls mean a lot to me, and I want to talk to him about how he is going to repair them."

"It would be my pleasure."

He acted as if there was nothing strange about my request at all. And perhaps there wasn't. I imagined they saw all kinds of eccentric women at Cartier's.

Within a few minutes, Jacob Asher emerged and approached me at the table by the window.

"Miss Garland," he said with a slight bow. "How can I help?"

"Well, as you can see, these pearls and their clasp are damaged."

He pulled out the seat beside me. "May I?"

"Of course," I said.

He sat down, pulled out a jeweler's loupe, and proceeded to inspect the pearls and the clasp.

I found myself sniffing the air to see if I could catch a whiff of his cologne—and I could. I let myself ride the scent for a moment, lost in its particular beauty. Like the man, I couldn't help thinking. *Handsome* was a more typical adjective to use to describe a male. *Rugged* was another popular word. *Virile* or *strong* were often used as well. *Beautiful?* Rarely. But those other words didn't match Mr. Asher's grace and aesthetic features. He was beautiful the way the Parthenon was. The way a Michelangelo sculpture was. The way a Beethoven symphony was. I shook my head. What was it about this particular man that so preoccupied me? His appearance? His exotic accent? The scent he wore?

I was still searching for answers when he finished inspecting my necklace.

"Yes," he said. "I do see."

"My mother gave me these pearls, and they mean a lot to me," I lied, and then wished I hadn't. "Well, to tell you the truth," I said, "actually, they mean a lot to her. These . . ." I pointed to the opals I was wearing. "These opals are what mean a lot to me. My father gave them to me. He bought them for me here."

"They are stunning. I met your father several times when he shopped here. And I helped him pick out those very beads. He had a fine eye. I'm sorry we lost him . . . that you lost him," he said with so much sympathy, and missed a beat.

I looked at him, and our eyes met. I knew in that instant that in his life, he had experienced the same sorrow I had.

For a moment, I forgot what I was there to do. Jacob Asher's words had reached out and held me, comforted me for a moment, and it had been most disconcerting. That he'd met my father and helped with the selection of the necklace I treasured so much seemed portentous.

"These three pearls should be replaced. Especially if your mother notices them." He smiled. "I've met her as well. One wouldn't want to disappoint Mrs. Garland."

I laughed. My mother would have said he didn't know his place and his comment had been presumptuous. It was. But that was just one more reason I knew I liked him.

"Yes, so the thing is, I do want them fixed, but I'd like to watch you repair and restring them."

His eyebrows arched. "That's unusual."

"Yes, I suppose it is. But my father got great pleasure from watching craftsmen work and often took me with him to see for myself. I've watched designers pin patterns in ateliers in Paris, shoemakers pick out leather skins and shape them into footwear in Florence, artists paint silk in a fan factory in Milan, others dipping marble paper in Venice . . . but I've never had the opportunity to see a jeweler at work. I suppose I'm carrying on my father's tradition. It makes me feel closer to him." I surprised myself with my outspokenness. Mr. Asher wasn't a confidant. I didn't need to give him a reason. And besides, the real reason I wanted to watch him was so I could try to get him to talk about Mr. Cartier's flights of fancy about the Hope.

My words clearly struck some kind of nerve with Mr. Asher. I didn't know how I knew it, but I saw it in his eyes and in the way he took a breath before telling me that, of course, I could watch him repair the piece.

"In the meantime, I'll work with our merchants to find matching pearls and stones for the clasp and will send a note when we have an assortment for you to look at."

"That would be most helpful, Mr. Asher," I said, and stood.

That was on Thursday. On Tuesday morning, I got a note from Mr. Cartier saying that my pearls were in and would I stop by at my convenience.

I sent a note back saying that I didn't feel well and would he mind sending Mr. Asher over with the pearls and giving him the address of the penthouse. I would be at home after two.

CHAPTER 17

When I opened the door, I found Mr. Cartier, briefcase in hand, standing there himself. I was disappointed and surprised and tried to hide my reaction, but my voice came out too high and loud as I welcomed him.

"Mr. Cartier! What a pleasure—I didn't expect you. Please come in." I gestured to the foyer.

He smiled charmingly. "I know it's unusual for me to do house calls," he said, as he took off his hat and held it in his hands. "But out of respect to your father, I wanted to take care of this myself."

"I'm flattered," I said, and led him inside. I offered him coffee or tea, and he said he'd prefer coffee.

I made it and brought it out on a silver tray, along with a plate of my father's favorite biscuits, which I kept stocked. We sat in the parlor, drank our coffee, and exchanged small talk for a few minutes.

"Now, for the pearls," Mr. Cartier said. "I fear the light isn't right in here to show them. Too many shadows."

I showed him both the dining room and the library, and he found them equally unsuitable. But the greenhouse with its skylights was perfect.

We settled into the wicker chairs in front of the

card table, and he pulled several items out of his briefcase. A maroon leather-bound notebook. A gold pencil. And two maroon velvet cases. He opened the notebook and then the larger of the two cases, which revealed my necklace with the offending pearls and clasp missing. He then proceeded to open the second case, which held about two dozen loose pearls sitting in a circular recession.

"I had your pearls cleaned. It was definitely time; besides, I couldn't match them without seeing their true color." One by one, he showed me the new pearls against my necklace and kept up a running commentary. "This one is a good match but perhaps a bit white. Your pearls have a slight creamy tint to them." He tried another. "This one is a better match in color, but it is ever so slightly larger."

And on and on it went.

"I had no idea it would be so difficult," I said, after we'd looked at them all.

"Yes, it is quite difficult to match pearls. Due to differing temperatures and conditions. Every pearl is unique, and it can take years to find a full set."

Now I felt guilty that I'd purposefully damaged three of them. I hadn't known what a complicated process this would be. And what a shame that, given how complicated it was, Mr. Asher hadn't arrived as I'd hoped. If I'd gotten him alone, I might have been able to make a connection with him that could have granted me access to behind-the-scenes secrets about Cartier and the Hope.

"None of these is one hundred percent perfect," he said. "They are a good match, but if you like, we certainly can keep looking."

"What do you think?" I asked.

He examined the pearls for a few moments.

"We could choose the ones that are closest in size rather than shade, since there are always shadows cast altering the coloring anyway. But that said, while they are a good match, I could do one more search."

If I said I wanted another search, I might get another chance to spend time with Mr. Asher.

"Maybe we should look a bit longer."

"I think that's the right decision. While I'm here, we should discuss the clasp," he said. "I wasn't sure whether you wanted us to repair what you had, or are you in the market for a different closure?"

I had meant Cartier to fix what I had, but now it occurred to me a new clasp gave me even more of a chance to draw out the process, which would buy me time with Jacob Asher.

"I think a new clasp. That one might be a bit old-fashioned now."

He looked delighted. "Shall we discuss designs?"

And we did for another half an hour, eventually settling on a few ideas, which he sketched out in his notebook and said he would have more formally drawn up so I could examine them in better detail.

Finished, he closed his leather notebook, swiveled the lead down in his mechanical pencil, and replaced both in his briefcase. He hadn't mentioned the Hope Diamond, and neither had I. Quite clever of him, I thought, because I assumed the Hope had been the reason for him coming here himself instead of sending Mr. Asher.

"This is a most enchanting room," he said, as he closed the larger of the velvet cases, the one holding my pearls. "What a delight to have such an elaborate garden in the middle of the city."

"My uncle designed it. Percy Winthrop. Had you ever met him?"

Mr. Cartier nodded. "Several times, yes. He was a true visionary. It must have been so difficult to lose both him and your father so close together."

"It was very difficult for us, yes."

"In times of grief, it's always such a blessing to have a sibling. My brothers and I—for all our competitive nature—are a family first. When tragedy has struck, we've relied on each other."

"Yes, my sister and I have as well."

"I imagine you must be close for you to be considering giving her such a generous gift."

Aha, I thought. He'd found a way to tie the conversation to the Hope.

"Well, my father wanted it to be a very special

gift, and my mother is intrigued by the idea. She just hasn't decided yet."

"I don't want to pressure you, but I should tell you that none of the interested parties has dropped out."

"The bad luck legend doesn't seem to be dampening enthusiasm, then?" I asked.

"No. If anything, it seems to be encouraging interest."

"Why, do you suppose?"

"I'm not sure. But honestly, if no one ever bought it, that wouldn't matter. For the House of Cartier to own one of the great diamonds in the world would be just fine."

"I think I'd like to take another look at that book of stories you have collected. I need to settle my mind about the legends and the myths. Try to separate the real from the exaggerated. Perhaps when you have the drawings for the clasp, you'll let me spend some time reading the articles you've collected?"

"Of course."

"And I would ask again that if any of the other interested parties becomes even more interested, you will let me know. I wouldn't want to lose it because I acted too late."

"As I promised before, I would be delighted."

After he left, I spent an hour in the greenhouse taking care of the plants. Pruning and dead-heading the flowers, shrubs, and trees were among my father's favorite hobbies. Since he'd passed, I hadn't taken enough care of his garden, and it was almost criminally overgrown and derelict. I resolved to spend time bringing it back to life.

As I worked on the wisteria, cutting back the tendrils, I thought about how poorly my plan to gather information about Mr. Cartier was going.

I'd always found in covering stories that you need to come at the truth from either underneath or inside. And Mr. Asher was inside. Maybe I needed to get a job as a charwoman, sweeping up the Cartier offices, I thought. Then I'd have access to everything.

I attacked the rosebushes next. My father favored antique roses, but how he made them flourish so high above Manhattan was a mystery to everyone who was lucky enough to see and smell them. Despite my neglect this past summer, they had bloomed nonetheless. Each glorious pink multipetaled flower giving up a wealth of perfume. I vowed that I'd do better for them. One summer of bad treatment hadn't killed them, but as with any of us, too much inattention could do irreparable damage.

Frustration overtook me as I put away the shears and gardening gloves. I'd thought an hour of gardening would help me sort out my thoughts. My father always said a brisk swim in the ocean or getting your hands dirty in a garden could clear up any messy, muddled head.

Except it hadn't worked for me. I still needed a plan to get to Mr. Asher. I couldn't just stand in front of 712 Fifth Avenue and wait for him to leave for the day and accost him.

But then again . . . why couldn't I? The simplest solution was often the best. The Cartier offices were only a couple of blocks from Garland's. Why couldn't I just be walking by and bump into him?

Was it too jejune a solution? I was ashamed that I couldn't come up with something better. Maybe I should wait until our press group met again and see if anyone had a more elegant idea.

As I closed the greenhouse door, I decided there was no time to wait. I needed to start getting material on Mr. Cartier now. I walked to the windows in the parlor and looked down at Fifth Avenue and across the street. I craned my neck as far as I could, down to Fifty-sixth Street and Cartier's.

And then I knew what to do. Conaway's bookshop was right there, directly across from 712 Fifth Avenue. And bookshops closed a bit later than other concerns to take advantage of those on their way home. I frequented it often. I tried to picture the inside of the shop. Was there a window looking out at the street? I couldn't remember. I shut my eyes and tried harder, but I just couldn't remember. I was always so content at Conaway's, browsing its shelves while the store's two tabby cats roamed. Mr. Conaway was a true bibliophile, who loved nothing more than to brew a cup of tea for a customer, sit with you in the armchairs in the back room, and discuss either latest offerings or old classics. He and my father had known each other for years, and my father frequented the shop even more than I did. I wondered now if he had helped my father amass his secret collection of homosexual literature.

Would the timing work? I tried to figure it out. Conaway's closed at six p.m., I believed. Cartier's closed at five. Mr. Asher would probably need to straighten up and attend to last-minute things for at least ten minutes before he left. So if I was in place by five, I'd probably be able to catch him on his way out.

At a quarter to, I shrugged on my coat to fight off the evening chill, went downstairs, and walked the two blocks downtown.

As I approached, I saw that Conaway's did, in fact, have a large picture window looking out at Fifth Avenue. I entered. Mr. Conaway was with a customer but waved hello. I picked up the first novel I found, *The Man in Lower Ten* by Mary Roberts Rinehart. The book was a best seller I'd heard of but hadn't read yet, and I was about to position myself in front of the window and peruse it when I had a better idea.

First, I checked my watch. Yes, I had at least five minutes to spare. I found a clerk and asked if the store had a copy of *The Moonstone* by Wilkie Collins.

"Indeed, we do, madam," he said, and went off to find it, returning in less than two minutes with a copy.

As I took it from him, I asked if he minded if I had a look first, and he assured me that browsing was more than welcome.

I took *The Moonstone* over to the window and positioned myself so that when I looked up, I could see the doorway to 712 Fifth Avenue.

To make sure that no one bothered me, I held the book at such an angle that made it appear I was reading but also gave me a clear view across the street. Mostly, I watched the doors to Cartier's building, but occasionally, I would look down at the book and read a sentence or two.

I address these lines—written in India—to my relatives in England.

My object is to explain the motive which had induced me to refuse the right hand of friendship to my cousin, John Herncastle . . .

I looked up and out the window. There was no activity at 712's doorway. I continued watching for another few moments and then looked back down at the book and read some more.

The Reserve which I have hitherto maintained in this matter had been misinterpreted by members of my family whose good opinion I cannot consent to forfeit. I request them to suspend their decision until they have read my narrative. And I declare on my word of honor, that what I am about to write is strictly and literally, the truth.

I looked up and out the window again. Still no activity. How long could I stand there and read the book before Mr. Conaway or the clerk approached? No sooner did I have the thought than the clerk came up to me.

"I'm so sorry, madam, but we will be closing in five minutes."

I'd thought the store would be open until six. Clearly, I'd guessed wrong. There was nothing to do but leave. Another plan derailed. Except first, I had to pay for the book. If Mr. Cartier was in fact borrowing its story, then I should at least read it.

I paid, took my parcel, and exited onto the street, walked to the north corner, and waited for the light to change.

"Miss Garland?"

I recognized the accent and turned to see Jacob Asher behind me. I sucked in my breath and then worried I'd let my astonishment show. And then I felt a wave of anger. I'd arranged for him to bring my pearls, and he had not done so. I should have at least wondered if that had been Mr. Cartier's choice, but instead, I assigned the blame to Mr. Asher.

"Good evening," I said a bit coolly.

The light changed, but neither of us crossed.

"I'm sorry the pearls didn't meet with your satisfaction," he said.

"They were fine," I said. "But Mr. Cartier suggested that if I wasn't in a hurry, he might find an even better match."

"And search we will."

"I had thought you were going to show them to me."

"I'm at Mr. Cartier's mercy." He gave a slight bow while that same rakish smile I'd seen before played at his lips. An expression belonging more to a lord than a servant. That he worked for someone instead of on his own suddenly struck me as incongruous.

The light had changed and now was back to green.

"Shall we?" Mr. Asher indicated the crossing.

With my first step off the curb, I tripped. My back had healed as much as it ever would, but a stiffness remained that sometimes caused me to be clumsy. Such things happened all too often and were very frightening.

As I lost my footing on the stone, I saw myself heading for the pavement. But before the expected happened, Mr. Asher's strong arms grabbed me and pulled me up and back onto the sidewalk.

He held me while my heart raced, my adrenaline pumped, and I fought to catch my breath.

"Thank you," I said, hearing my voice quiver.

"I'm just glad I was here to catch you. That could have been a nasty spill."

I became ever more aware of his touch, and it was making me uncomfortable. I stepped out of what now felt like an embrace. Instead of showing embarrassment, he raised a corner of his mouth in what looked like amusement. He reached down and collected the wrapped book I'd let drop and handed it to me.

"Your parcel?"

I took it. "Thank you again," I said, still a little breathless.

"Are you all right? Really?"

"I will be."

"Were you on your way somewhere?" he asked.

"Just home."

"Let me walk with you, then."

"No, no, please. I'm totally fine. It must have been my heel getting caught in a crack in the stone." I never spoke about my injury. Certainly not to strangers.

"Be that as it may, what kind of gentleman would I be to take a chance and leave you on your own?"

"I'm fine on my own." I knew I should allow him to accompany me, but I was uncomfortable around him now. I'd have to come up with another way to get my story without Mr. Asher.

"Think of what Mr. Cartier would say if I

abandoned a client on the street." There was a gleam in his eye. We both knew that the implication in his offer had nothing to do with what Mr. Cartier would say.

"Forget Mr. Cartier," he continued in a deeper and more intimate voice. "I wouldn't want anything to happen to you."

It was so outspoken and improper for him to speak that way to a client that I was startled.

He laughed out loud. "I've breached social etiquette, haven't I?"

"Well . . ." I found myself at a loss for words, which was quite unlike me.

"I don't much care for etiquette. And for some reason, I don't think you do, either."

"You don't?" Now, that was an odd thing for Vera Garland to say. Vee Swann was outspoken, but it wasn't done for a lady to speak in such a way. There was something in his manner and tone that made me react out of character.

"No, I don't. Now, give me your arm, Miss Garland, and let me walk you home."

There was no mistaking his teasing or his interest.

I offered my arm. Mr. Asher took it, and we began to walk down the street toward Garland's. The entire way, I was aware of the exact spot where our bodies were in contact, even through our winter coats and layers of clothes. November had arrived and with it the chill of late autumn.

I wanted to ask him why he'd been so sure I didn't adhere to a more strict code of social etiquette but was suddenly afraid I'd get a mundane answer, and I didn't want to hear him say anything ordinary.

I was thirty-two years old and had lived like an old maid for the last several years. It was too complicated for me to become close to any man . . . to take a lover or certainly to consider marriage.

If I met someone as Vera Garland, he would undoubtedly be from society, which would require me to conceal my occupation. If I met someone as Vee Swann, he would most likely be a fellow reporter or editor, perhaps a writer or poet, which would require me hiding my wealth and family background. The world Vera Garland lived in and the kind of fortune that she would inherit were bound to intimidate any man I might encounter as Vee Swann. Or else, it would tempt him to like me more than he might otherwise.

Rich or poor, banker or newsman, if either found out the truth, my deception would prove my undoing. It was one thing to be a reporter searching for the truth, but for that same reporter to be living a lie—how sympathetic would any decent man be?

Overall, I preferred mousy, bespectacled Vee. She was braver and bolder and far more interesting than Vera. She paid attention to the world around her in a serious, concerned, engaging way. She was angry and fought for what she believed in.

Vera was a fan of classical music, loved shopping for clothes and jewelry, enjoyed museums, and sped through book after book. She was sensitive to beauty and the arts. But without Vee's passions for truly making a difference, trying to effect change and help the cause of justice, Vera was a bit boring and even old-fashioned.

It's an odd thing to be able to examine two sides of your personality so dispassionately. My father and I had often talked about the two of me, laughing over who I might be at any given moment or in any situation. During one such conversation, about a week before he died, he told me that until I found a way to integrate these two women into one, I would never be truly happy. He made me promise that I would use his gifts to do that. I asked him what gifts, but he'd grown tired and never answered.

Now, as I unlocked the door to my father's apartment—my apartment—with Jacob Asher beside me, I wondered again what gifts he had meant. But then I stopped wondering, as I, Vera Garland, allowed a man into my home whom Vee Swann found interesting.

"You were so kind to escort me," I said. "Now that I'm safely delivered, would you like some coffee or tea? Or a glass of sherry?" And then I added, "Or a malt whisky? I keep my father's liquor cabinet stocked."

"I would appreciate the malt, yes. Your father's cabinet?"

As I led him inside, I explained about the apartment.

He followed me into the parlor, with its stained-glass-bordered windows, exotic decorations, and elegant furniture. He looked around, not saying anything for a few minutes.

"This is exquisite," he finally uttered. "Is that Tiffany glass?"

"Yes, my father was good friends with him. He created all of the lamps and glass in the apartment based on my uncle's designs. He was the architect Percy Winthrop."

"I've read about him," Mr. Asher said. "He was quite avant-garde, wasn't he?"

I nodded and finished pouring the whisky. I handed him one of the two tumblers. "Come this way. I'll show you the pièce de résistance." I led him to the conservatory with its pool and fountain and domed-glass ceiling.

"I feel as if I've walked into the English countryside," he said. "But one inhabited by a patron of the arts."

"Are you from England?" I'd been wondering about the unusual accent since the first time I met him.

"Not originally. I was born and lived in Odessa till I was fourteen, but my parents sent me to school in England and then . . ." He hesitated.

I sensed that he didn't talk about himself too often. And certainly not with clients, though I doubted he was still thinking of me as a client.

"Yes?" I encouraged.

He gave me a probing look, as if judging how serious I was about hearing his story.

"I stayed on in England after school and went to work for the jewelry firm of Catchpole and Williams. Then Asprey. After that, J. W. Benson. And I went to work at Cartier's when the shop opened in London, and when Mr. Cartier decided to open a New York branch, I accepted his offer to come with him."

"But didn't moving here mean being even farther from home?" I asked.

"Odessa?"

I nodded.

"There was no one left there by then. We had a small family. I was an only child. My mother died when I was twelve. My father died in 1904. I have a few cousins left in England but none so close that I felt compelled to stay there."

In 1903, I was already working for the *New York World* when the stories broke about the pogroms in Russia. I remembered reading about the horrific situation and the utter devastation and loss of life, especially in Odessa.

The anti-Jewish riots were part of a well-laid-out plan for massacre. The first attack was led by priests, with the mob crying out, "Kill the Jews!" According to the news reports I read at the time, the violence came as a total surprise, and the Jews were not prepared. Hundreds were beaten and injured. Many died. One of the worst things I read, which stayed with me for a long time, was that the police did nothing to stop the attacks, and at the end of the day, the streets were littered with corpses.

Over the next two years, more than six hundred other towns suffered the same fate. One of the women in our group of journalists had gone over to Russia. When she returned, she told us that the tsar was not only cognizant of but encouraged the riots and killings and gave clemency to anyone arrested for participating.

"In 1904? During the pogrom?" I asked softly. "I read the articles. Was your father a victim of the riots?"

Mr. Asher nodded. "Yes, while I was in London making pretty baubles for fancy ladies, my father's store was attacked. When he tried to stop the monsters from stealing his extensive stock of diamonds, they kicked him and beat him senseless. He was dead by the time he was found."

I put my hand out to cover his in a gesture totally heartfelt. For a moment, we sat there in silence, the terrible words hanging in the air of the fairy-tale greenhouse on the fifth floor of a department store, as far from Odessa as one could get.

"I will never forget what was done to him," Jacob Asher whispered in a furious rush of words.

"There is no end to the injustice and cruelty in the world, is there? It makes me wonder about faith and the human capacity for delusion. How can people hold on to their belief in a benevolent God when such things happen? And not just once but over and over from time immemorial?"

Mr. Asher gave me a curious look. "You are not quite what I expected."

I smiled. It was a familiar comment made by the few men who ever sat down and really talked to Vera Garland.

"How is that?" I asked, knowing but curious how he would respond.

"I don't want to be insulting, Miss Garland."

"Don't fear, Mr. Asher, you can't be more insulting to my kind than I am myself. And please, if we are going to converse like intelligent beings rather than mannequins at a ball, do call me Vera."

"Vera." He said it as if he was tasting the name. "I like your name. It has energy."

"As did the woman I was named after."

"Vera, then. And please call me Jacob."

"So tell me, Jacob, what is it about me that you didn't expect?"

"An unorthodox conversation about religion while sipping fine whisky in a magical aerie. It's far from what I would have anticipated when I caught you on the street."

"I don't think that orthodox conversations are worth having. Nor is sipping ordinary whisky. And I hate stuffy rooms."

We both laughed, and it felt good after the serious talk we'd been having.

"My mother and my sister, to a slightly less degree, can be quite aghast at how I behave, but I've been rebellious to one degree or another since I was a child. Going the same way as everyone else is hardly an adventure."

"And is having an adventure that important?"

"My father always used to say that we were given only one life and that our job was to experience its infinite passion."

"And have you done that?"

"I have tried . . . I'd stopped for a while . . . but I'm thinking about returning to the land of the living."

"Well, that pleases me," he said.

There was no doubt he was flirting. Seducing him had never been my plan. Even though I knew a reporter or two who'd exchanged sex for information, I'd never stooped to that level to get a story. It would go against everything my friends and I were fighting for. So while I certainly hadn't considered entrapping him, charming him couldn't hurt my effort to get to the truth about Cartier. That the jeweler was handsome and well spoken would make my job easier. Perhaps even pleasurable, I thought, as I took another sip of my father's liquor.

"Forgive my asking, but I'm intrigued by your earrings," he said then.

I felt my earlobes, not even remembering what I was wearing.

"They were my grandmother's," I said. "I know they are only paste, but I loved her so much, and she gave them to me. And honestly, I can't tell the difference." I realized what I'd just said. "I'm sorry. I shouldn't say such a blasphemous thing to a jeweler, should I?"

"Not at all. There is a great art to paste jewelry. My grandfather excelled at it. Do you know much about it?"

"Very little other than knowing the value of a paste piece is lower because it's just glass."

"Well, it is glass, yes. Lead glass made when—" He broke off. "Is this boring?"

"Not at all. To tell you the truth, it's society talk that bores me. I'd much rather talk about invention or innovation or science or art and design . . . please continue."

"The ancient Romans excelled in creating colored stones from a highly polished glass paste. There are wonderful examples of their lapis lazuli and emeralds in the British Museum.

But it was in the eighteenth century when paste was perfected. We don't know who is responsible. There are conflicting stories. Some say it was a goldsmith in Vienna named Joseph Strasser in 1758, and others say it was a French jeweler named Georges Frédéric Strass in 1724. The closeness in their names always struck me as very strange. But either way, the result was leaded glass polished with metal powder that produced stones that matched the diamonds and other gems in the crown jewels. To the naked eye, even jewelers couldn't always tell the paste from the mined stones. And they were very valuable, always set in real gold or silver. More recently, Daniel Swarovski, a man living in Austria, has invented a glass-cutting machine that creates even finer stones. But I like to think my own grandfather's secret formula creates the most realistic paste. He taught my father, who taught me. He called it 'evil knowledge.' "

"Why is it secret? And why evil?" I asked.

He shook his head and frowned.

"What's wrong?"

"It's not something I talk about. Ever. I've already said more than I should." He seemed genuinely confused by the turn the conversation had taken.

"Why did you decide to, then?"

"I honestly don't know, Miss Garland. Maybe this fine whisky has loosened my tongue."

"If you get tipsy that easily, you should take care. And it's Vera."

"I don't easily get tipsy," he said in mock indignation.

"I'm still intrigued, though. Why is the formula for the paste a family secret?"

He sighed. "If I told you, then it wouldn't be a secret."

"But it's the formula that is the secret, correct? Not the reason to keep it a secret." I laughed. We were being a little silly, but it felt good. "Certainly, you can tell me why it's evil?"

"That I can. The ability to create glass stones that mimic real stones worth thousands of times more could be used for very nefarious purposes of all kinds."

I realized instantly what he meant. "Oh, yes, I see. Like an art forger, you could be a jewelry forger."

"I couldn't be," he said quickly. "But yes, someone could."

"Of course. I didn't mean to imply . . ."

He laughed and waved his hand. "Would you like to hear one of my favorite stories about paste jewelry?"

I nodded.

"Its popularity reached its height during Victorian times, when a secret language of stones was created by a jeweler on Bond Street. He assigned a different romantic message to each colored gem. A customer of his was courting a young woman against her parents' wishes. So he taught her the code and bought her a new piece of paste every week, speaking to her through the colors. But as it turned out, the young woman's mother knew the code as well and confronted the young man and insisted he break off the courtship immediately."

"What happened?"

"The next day, the man delivered the final gift—a very real and very valuable diamond—and they eloped that very evening."

"True love conquers all," I said, with a bit too much sarcasm in my voice.

Jacob raised one of his fine dark eyebrows. "Such cynicism."

"I've earned it."

"Ah, that makes me sad."

"Why is that?"

"Because love *can* conquer all."

"Has it for you?"

The light was growing dim in the conservatory as dusk settled on the city. Jacob didn't answer me right away, and for a few silent moments, we sat as encroaching darkness enclosed us.

"You haven't answered my question," I said.

Jacob reached out and took my hand and brought it to his lips.

"I am taking a chance here that I'm not insulting you, Vera. But I would like to invite you to go for a walk with me on Sunday and then have dinner."

"And why would that be an insult? Usually, women are flattered when attractive men ask them out."

"Well, I'm aware of social conventions, and it's not done for a member of the Four Hundred to be seen with a member of my class."

I laughed. "Which is exactly why I'd be delighted. You'll find that nothing pleases me more than defying convention, much to my mother's chagrin."

"And your father's as well?"

"No, he encouraged my wild abandon."

"You miss him. I recognize the tone in your voice. It's what I hear in my own voice when I speak of my father."

"I do miss him. Every day. The worst part is that he shouldn't have gotten sick. He shouldn't have died. It was this whole rotten world and its antiquated beliefs and conventions that sent him to his grave."

"What do you mean?"

I shrugged. "The specifics don't matter anymore. But the injustice does."

Jacob looked at me with deep understanding in his dark, dark eyes.

"You and I, Vera, might have more in common than I ever would have guessed. We have both lost our fathers to the same terrible world. Both of us are angry survivors."

"Angry survivors . . ." I thought, and nodded. "Yes, that's what I am."

And then he leaned forward, and there under the shadows of the palm trees and hanging vines, with the scents of roses, dahlias, and lilies perfuming the air, Jacob Asher kissed me. And I didn't think I'd ever been kissed quite like that before. It would have been brutal if it wasn't shared. It would have been harsh if it wasn't so passionate. It would have been foreign if we both hadn't been through the same war.

Lovemaking can be gentle. It can be a game. It can be frivolous. Or desperate. Or an escape. Or boring. I'd had all kinds. But what Jacob showed me was the one kind I'd never experienced. A soulful, painful kind of lovemaking that comes from despair and shouts to the world that you still exist, that you are not giving up, that you are going to grab what you can and make the most of it, because waiting on the other side is nothing but oblivion, and damn, you are not ready for that.

CHAPTER 18

I had not been prepared to respond to Jacob Asher. I had certainly not intended to take him to my bed. Yes, when I'd poured him a glass of my father's best whisky, I had hoped to charm him, to forge a bond, but not to seduce him. I was caught off guard completely when he aroused my feelings and sensations. And it had been so very long since a man had done that—or I'd allowed one to. All the way back to Max. After his betrayal . . . well, it was easier to close myself off than to risk my body or my career. I had been lucky that the operation had gone off without a hitch and I had come out whole and ready to return to work after two days, but I might not be that lucky a second time.

Jacob and I lay in my bed afterward and looked up at the dark sky through the glass skylights that each bedroom in the apartment boasted.

"Doesn't it get cold during the winter?" he said, asking the most pedestrian of questions. This suited me; in fact, I liked it. I preferred to eschew romantic murmurings. I'd found that nothing said in the heat of passion or its afterglow was anything other than a reaction to blood boiling and pleasures exchanged.

"You'd think so, wouldn't you, but my uncle

ordered every skylight and window made with double glass panes so the rooms stay warm. When it snows, you feel as if you're inside a snow globe."

"Well, I've very much enjoyed being shaken up in this snow globe with you," Jacob said softly.

"Ah, you've gone and done it."

"What?"

"Said one of those things people say after."

"What do you mean?"

"Love chatter," I said, and explained my theory about the falsity of things said when the flush of pleasure is still upon you.

"Are you really as cynical as all that?" he asked.

"I'm afraid I am. Does that disappoint you?"

"I suppose it does a bit. I think that chatter is wonderful. That romance is wonderful. It's one of the things that makes this miserable world worth living in."

"In your own way, you sound as cynical. No wonder, though, considering what you've gone through."

"Do you have a kitchen here?" he asked.

"Yes." I started to get up. "What would you like?"

"No, just tell me where it is. I'm going to make us something to eat."

I laughed. "There's not much in there. I

usually ring down to the restaurant before it closes and have them bring up something I can heat up for dinner. But you were here, and I forgot. But if there was a stocked larder . . . do you cook?"

"I do. The winter I was ten, I broke my leg in a silly ice-skating accident and—you don't need to look so worried."

I knew about broken bones and surgery and must have made an anxious expression, because he pulled back the covers.

"It's fine, don't worry," he said, and showed me a perfectly formed naked leg. "It healed, but the recovery was long, as were our winters. So our cook taught me how. That, along with reading, saved me from complete boredom. I've since taken it up as a hobby."

"Well, if you are hungry, I can call down. They've only been closed for a few minutes, and someone will still be there."

"Why don't you get dressed instead, and I'll take you out to someplace festive, and we'll drink champagne and make cynical toasts not tinged by romance? Unless, that is, you've changed your mind about that."

"And why would I change my mind?"

"This won't make any sense to you. It doesn't to me, in fact. But I think that we may be awfully well suited to each other, and if you agree and are willing to spend more time with me, I'd like to show you that there's another way to think."

"One thing I think is that I may never have come across anyone like you before."

"No, I imagine in your set, there aren't many scrappy, Russian-born, British-schooled jewelers with a chip on their shoulder."

"A *diamond* on their shoulder," I said.

He laughed.

I think it was his laugh, not the passion we'd shared, that was what finally broke the ice in my veins and endeared him to me. He was a man who had been dealt terrible blows. Who had lost his parents and made his own way and had nothing handed to him. And yet his laugh was totally innocent and without guile. It was a child's joyful glee. The kind of laugh I'd heard my young nephews release when I tickled or teased them. That this man could utter that same crystalline laugh filled with delight caught me by surprise. I desperately wanted to laugh like that. I wanted to be at peace with the terrible injustices that I saw and lived and wrote about and that made me furious—just long enough to laugh the way Jacob Asher laughed.

Self-conscious about the scars on my back, I pulled my dressing gown on quickly. But he had a jeweler's keen eye and inquired.

"What's happened to your back?"

"It's not very gentlemanly to ask such a question," I chided.

272

"Probably not, but as we have already established, I'm not very gentlemanly."

"I fell down a flight of steps, broke two vertebrae, and had to have surgery."

"My goodness. Is it still painful?"

"A bit, but I cope. It's the stiffness that is more difficult to deal with. I don't quite bend the right way anymore. And I'm still prone to falling. It only happened just more than a year ago. That's why I got so anxious on the street when I tripped before."

"Can I see the scars?"

"Why?"

"I want you to be comfortable about it with me."

I stood where I was, looking at him, not quite knowing what to think.

Jacob got up. He was naked and made no effort to shield his body. And it was such an elegant body. Most of his height was in his legs, which were long and lean, with strong calves and thighs. He had a flat stomach and a well-defined chest. Seeing him standing there, I felt my breath catch in my throat. As he came toward me, my fingers itched to reach out and trace the long lines and inhale his scent, now mixed with mine.

I protested as he started to undo the sash on my dressing gown. I didn't want to be looked at in the light. I wasn't young. I wasn't comely. And my scars had healed badly, leaving red, thick lines on my skin.

"Every diamond," he said, as he ran his fingers over the scars, "has flaws. There is no one hundred percent perfect stone. Nature doesn't allow it. Not in stones, or flowers, or us. The flaws don't make us more beautiful. I hate that philosophy. It's ridiculous and not true. But the flaws are part of us. They *are* part of what gives us our character. And they need to be acknowledged, too."

His hands left my back and came around to my breasts.

"Your breasts, however, are perfect . . ." His hands moved to my shoulders. "And so are your shoulders . . ." His hands moved down to my arms. "As are your arms and each finger . . ." He pulled first my right hand and then my left up to his mouth and kissed each finger. And then he walked behind me and kissed the scars. Next, he put his hands on my hips. "Your hips are perfect . . ." And he kissed the small of my back and then turned me around to face him and buried his face between my legs, and he didn't say anything else for a time. And neither did I.

We did eventually go out to dinner, to a small French restaurant a few blocks downtown. And it was while we were eating that I finally asked him what it was like to work for Mr. Cartier. I felt almost guilty pumping him for information, but I wasn't about to abandon my plans just because Jacob and I had—had what? I wasn't really sure, and thinking about it made me nervous. I didn't want to like this man that way. I didn't want to like any man that way.

"He's quite a fair boss. I was happy to follow him to America."

"Didn't you have ties in England? You'd lived there since you were fourteen, isn't that what you said?"

"None that couldn't be broken. Or in my cousin's case, none that couldn't stretch. I'd never put down any really permanent roots."

"Why is that?"

"I suppose because of what I saw when I was growing up."

"What do you mean?"

He thought for a moment, then asked, "Have you ever heard of a plant called the Wandering Jew?"

I said I hadn't.

"It's very pretty. Green and purple, well-formed oval leaves. Very common, too. You've probably seen it and not known what it was called. Anyway, it is very hardy and resistant to neglect. There are several stories about its name. The one I prefer is that it's named after Moses and the Israelites wandering in the desert for forty years, because it's a plant that can grow anywhere—in the warm or the cold, in pots or in the ground. It adapts the way we Jews have had to adapt to new places throughout our history, because we were never welcome to stay in any one place long enough to put down roots before we were thrown out."

He was somber as he sipped his champagne. He looked around the room and nodded at the gaiety and frivolity on display.

"Look at them. Do you think any of them have any idea what it is like to have your home taken from you, your possessions stolen, your very life snuffed out for no reason other than the religion your ancestors were born to? Even if you don't care about that religion or believe much in any God, it doesn't matter. You're still a target. An outsider. A foreigner." He turned back and looked at me. "I'm sorry. I didn't mean to imply that your set are callous."

"Oh, but we are, Jacob. We are. But at least some of us have a conscience and are aware of how callous we are. Aware of how protected our money has kept us. My father didn't come from society and never forgot it. The more wealth he amassed, the more he gave away. For every dollar he put in the bank, he gave one to the charities he helped found. He abhorred that our society takes so little care of the impoverished."

"He founded charities; that's quite impressive."

"My brother-in-law who runs Garland's now is in charge of them."

"What are their missions?"

"The Janus Society helps men who are down

on their luck get back on their feet with clothes and short-term loans. The other, which demanded more of his time and energy, helps women with children who find themselves without support. My father and uncle started out by building one apartment house for them and helping them find work. Now there are a dozen apartment houses and a garment factory on Spring Street that trains the women and gives them work. There's a nursery and a school in the same building. So the mothers have their children close by and know they are taken care of. If the children continue in school through twelfth grade, we have scholarships so they can go to college. The charity also employs a woman who helps anyone not going off to college find apprentice positions. The first shelter, which was built twenty years ago, had room for ten women and their children. Today more than twenty women and their children are in residence at any one time. A woman will typically live in a shelter apartment for two to five years. By then, she's usually well established and earning enough to move to better accommodations of her own. Which makes room for a new family. No men are allowed to live in any of the apartments. Not even allowed to visit. Too many of the women have been abused or taken advantage of by the men in their lives. They can court, of course, and if they decide to marry, they move out."

"What an amazing accomplishment. Your father must have been a wonderful man."

"Oh, he was. He cared about the charity so very much. He created some very special traditions my brother-in-law intends to keep going. My favorite is the Christmas gala that Garland's throws each year for every family who is either currently living in the society's apartments or has previously. The restaurant downstairs, the Birdcage, becomes a holiday extravaganza decorated with trees, wreaths, and a Santa doling out presents to all the children and mothers. My sister and I were brought in to help the first year—dressed as elves—which my mother never approved of, and she wouldn't come."

"She didn't approve of the charity?"

"The charity was fine. She has a substantial inheritance, and she was fine with Father doing whatever he wanted with what he earned. It was us mingling with the poor that disturbed her. As if their poverty was contagious, and we might catch it."

"I know the type," Jacob said with disgust, and then realized his rudeness and apologized.

"Don't worry. I feel the same way. I love my mother because I am her child, but I don't have very much respect for her. She can be dangerously snobby and stuck in her ways. For instance, she helps with charities but from a distance, holding her nose. Nothing like my father, who was happy to sit with the men and women he helped. Having tea with them. Listening to them. Caring about their problems."

"What is the charity called?"

The irony hadn't struck me until that very moment. "The Women and Children's Hope Society. Quite a different kind of Hope from the one you showed my sister and me," I said.

"A much finer one," he said. And then looked down at the menu. "Should we order? I'm so hungry." He gave me a sly smile. "I wonder why."

SILK, SATIN & SCANDALS

In which your intrepid reporter fills you in on the most salacious and beautiful, glittering gossip in Gotham.

The daughter of the scion of a very well-known New York department store was seen leaving Mr. Cartier's fourth-floor establishment recently in a blue-green taffeta dress and black fur jacket. Her hat, from Garland's, but of course, sported a plume of peacock feathers, the iridescent greens and blues a perfect match for her frock. This reporter has heard Mademoiselle, as the ever charming and very French Mr. Cartier must call her, is one of the parties considering purchasing that oh so unlucky Hope Diamond.

One can only imagine why the stone, with its history of tragedy in its wake, would be of interest to anyone. Life throws enough bad luck at us all, doesn't it? Especially when these days, the theft of important and even not so important jewels has reached epidemic proportions.

Just last week, it was reported that Eva Stanton, returning home on the luxury liner *Amerika*, had over $80,000 in jewels stolen while the ship crossed the Atlantic. The police believe the thieves were part of an international band of thieves who have been helping themselves to expensive items onboard ships as well as ransacking hotel rooms both here and abroad. Among the gems Mrs. George Stanton lost was a pair of diamond and emerald earrings and a matching bracelet made by the French firm of Boucheron.

The Plaza Hotel, the site of several robberies in the last year, has hired a crew of detectives and plainclothes police in an effort to dissuade thieves. There's gossip there, too, my dears, since one of the recent guests supposedly had quite a liaison during her stay in the hotel with one of those burly boys hired to protect her and her ilk. I can't mention names, but she's a Boston Brahmin living on the West Coast now. And she's very much married to a very much older man who is very much self-made and often is seen himself with Broadway Babes on his arm.

And last, but certainly not least, yours truly is taking part in a very important protest— the March for Equality. Come join us next Wednesday starting at noon at Broadway and 34th Street. We need you all to cheer us on as we take on the establishment of the Fourth Estate who refuse to give us gals equal pay and equal credit for our stories and who expect us to turn the other cheek when their hands roam too far and their libidos get the better of them. To show your support, all you ladies out there should boycott the newspapers you read—just like this one—until they institute fair practices. Let the publishers know you're on our side. If we are the fairer sex, treat us fairly! See you at the march!

CHAPTER 19

"I read you are interested in Mr. Cartier's Hope Diamond," my luncheon partner said to me three days later. "Is your interest really serious?"

"Yes, Letty's birthday is coming up, and she was so enraptured with the stone. I've been thinking about it."

"It's a serious gift for one sister to give another."

"I know, but it wouldn't be from me, exactly. Father set aside a sum for me to buy something special for Letty when she turned thirty."

"But my dear, it's supposed to be nothing but bad luck. That's why I'm so upset that Evalyn wants it."

We were at a birthday fete my mother was throwing for one of her cousins, Nancy Thane. The woman I was talking to was a dear family friend, Mrs. Thomas Walsh. Aunt Carrie to my sister and me, though we weren't at all related. The Walsh house and ours had sat side by side in Newport for most of my life. Though Aunt Carrie's children were much younger, our two families began mingling when I was but a toddler. They were invited to the same parties and belonged to the same sailing and golf clubs. I'd always liked Mr. and Mrs. Walsh, adored them, in fact. Aunt Carrie had always been a much more fun and nurturing alternative to my own mother. There were never many rules at her house. Carrie taught Letty and me to sail and ride horseback and fed us when we were hungry instead of just at mealtimes. As a girl, I'd often confessed my hopes and dreams to her, and she always responded with an openness I found both comforting and refreshing, as opposed to the loneliness and isolation my mother's chiding instilled in me. Like my father, the Walshes hadn't come from money but had worked their way to their wealth, Mr. Walsh having been an Irish immigrant who literally struck gold. I often thought back to the many picnics we used to enjoy on their lawn, eating food that Carrie had prepared herself.

Our family had recently been to the wedding of their daughter, Evalyn, to Edward McLean, whose father owned the *Washington Post* and the *Cincinnati Enquirer*. Our lives were further connected, unbeknownst to either family, through Vee Swann. After my abortion exposé was published, the Cincinnati paper offered me a job to work undercover and write about "coal widows." These were women whose husbands worked in the mines and left them for long periods of time. The series of articles examined their poor living conditions and described how they coped while taking care of their families on their own.

I had been happy to leave New York for even a brief period, to put distance between Max, my mother, and me. I'd never confronted my mother about her role in what had happened to me, but she'd guessed based on Vee Swann's article for the *World*. Rather than apologize, she defended her position, saying that she believed I would be happier if I was married. I told her *she* was the only one who would be happier if I was married. The conversation did nothing to melt the iceberg that had wedged its way between us.

"How can I persuade Evalyn not to buy that cursed diamond?" Aunt Carrie seemed so disturbed. My heart ached for her. She'd lost her husband just eight months before, and she'd only recently begun venturing out. No wonder she was overly anxious.

"I wouldn't worry about all the bad-luck stories," I whispered. "If I tell you a secret, will you promise not to share it?"

Though I was reluctant to reveal to anyone the facts and clues about the Hope that I was gathering for my plan against Oxley, Aunt Carrie was different. I wanted so much to ease her anxiety. She nodded, and I trusted her.

"I heard half of those stories are made up. A friend of mine says they are too similar to the story in a book called *The Moonstone* by a British writer named Wilkie Collins."

"I read that book ages ago. Are you serious?"

"Yes."

"I want to believe you, Vera. I do. But ever since Vinson died, I am much more superstitious." Her voice caught in her throat. It had been five years since the terrible accident in Newport that killed her seventeen-year-old son and caused grave damage to then nineteen-year-old Evalyn. "I see a psychic regularly, and she's very afraid of the diamond."

"But Aunt Carrie, so many psychics are nothing more than charlatans."

"Of course, there are some who have no scruples. But I only consult with Madame Marcia Champney. She is the best in all of Washington, D.C. You should come to visit and meet her. You'd change your mind."

Aunt Carrie leaned closer to me and whispered, "She warned me about the accident weeks before it happened. I forbade Vinson to take out the car, but . . ." She stopped speaking for a moment to calm herself, but before I could think of a way to change the subject, she continued. "Madame Marcia has told me that I have to do everything in my power to prevent my daughter from touching that vile diamond. She claims it contains centuries of evil, and no good has ever come to anyone who has owned it. Thomas has spoken to me through Madame, and he agrees. The stone is evil."

"There's no such thing as an evil stone."

"Of course there is, Vera! Haven't you read the papers? Why, my own son-in-law's family paper has printed several stories about the ill fate that has befallen people who have possessed the stone."

"Just because the papers print it doesn't make it gospel." I smiled inwardly. I would know. But there was no reason she would believe me just because I said it was true.

"Do you have your heart set on buying Letty the stone?" she asked.

"No, just toying with the idea for now."

"I might have a proposition for you."

She had a gleam in her eye. "I was just thinking . . . you're such an enterprising young woman, and you live in New York where the stone is . . ."

"Yes?" I was intrigued.

"Do you know about paste jewelry?"

"I do. I learned about it only recently, in fact." Jacob had not only mentioned paste to me just days before, but he had given me a full lesson on it.

"Well, here's my idea. Since Evalyn seems to be serious about buying that damned stone, maybe I can somehow secretly replace the one she buys with one of paste without her knowing it. To protect her."

"Spoken like a devoted mother. But how would you do that?"

"I'm not quite sure yet. I've thought about

approaching Mr. Cartier and offering him some kind of deal, but I've asked around, and those who know him say that he's not the kind of man who would be amenable to pulling a trick like that on a client. And Evalyn and Ned are his clients, and I'm not." Aunt Carrie shook her head in despair. "Can you think of any way for me to do it?"

"You are really serious, aren't you?" I asked.

She grasped my hand. "You don't have children, and you haven't lost a sister or brother . . . Yes, I know you lost your beloved father, but that is in the natural order of things. A child knows that she will outlive her parents. Even though it was tragic and too soon, it's not the same as . . ."

Tears came to her eyes. She opened her pocketbook and withdrew a handkerchief. "I can't describe what it was like to lose my son, Vera. All the light went out of the world. I wouldn't want my most hated enemy to endure it. And now my daughter's stubborn obsession with beautiful things is pushing her toward tragedy. I just know it. I won't be able to bear it if anything were to happen to her. She's practically crippled from the accident as it is and in so much pain . . ."

Despite being at a party with people all around, Aunt Carrie broke down in sobs. I helped her up and escorted her to the ladies' room, an elaborate peach-and-green salon with a sitting room as well as a lavatory. The attendant there asked if she could get us anything, and I asked her to bring a glass of brandy and a cool cloth. The cloth first.

After receiving it, I pressed it to Carrie's temples while she lay back against the peach-striped silk cushions on the settee. When the attendant came back with the brandy, I helped Carrie sit up so she could take sips of the liquid fire.

In a few minutes, she had calmed.

"I am sorry, Vera."

"No need to apologize."

"I'm simply beside myself. With Thomas gone . . . and now Evalyn has her heart set on buying that stone and—"

I feared that continuing to discuss it was going to set Aunt Carrie off again, and before I knew what I was saying, I told her I would help. "I'll figure out a way to work with you on your plan. Together we'll make sure she doesn't touch the blasted thing. Bad luck or not."

I wasn't sure how I was going to accomplish it, but maybe Aunt Carrie's needs and mine might dovetail in a scheme that would enable me to write the salacious and compromising story that would finally bring about Mr. Thelonious Oxley's ruin.

CHAPTER 20

At noon two days later, I joined the other journalists at the press club to prepare for our March for Equality, in protest of Betsy Beecher's firing and the mistreatment of all women journalists.

We had an hour in the auditorium to organize before we headed out. A subcommittee had made up placards and had flyers printed that included sample letters for sympathizers to send to publishers, along with the addresses of the ten most highly circulated newspapers. We each took a sign and a handful of pamphlets. We had chosen the lunchtime period because more people would be out and about to see us. At twelve thirty, we left the building on Twenty-third Street.

It was a chilly November day, the week before Thanksgiving, but our energy kept our chills at bay. We walked east toward Fifth, planning on reaching as far uptown as Central Park.

Fanny and Martha and I were in a line toward the front.

My sign: *Women reporters get the same news.*

Fanny's: *Equal pay and equal opportunity.*

Martha's was the line I'd used in my column, which I couldn't take credit for, obviously, but pleased me nonetheless: *If we're the fairer sex, treat us fairly*.

As we made our way, we declared our mission, shouting, "Newsmen of quality don't fear equality!" "Equal pay every day!" and "Women reporters' rights are right!"

Hundreds of women stepped out of stores and homes to cheer us on, and a few dozen joined us. I recognized a handful of society ladies from galas and soirees and made a note to applaud them in my next Silk, Satin and Scandals column.

Of the many men who came out to see what we were doing, few supported our cause. Most shouted epithets as we passed.

We were a disparate group of female journalists of all ages and levels of experience, from wet-behind-the-ears twenty-year-olds to gray-haired matriarchs, cub reporters, and editors of women's pages, all keeping up with aplomb.

"The crowds aren't as big as I'd hoped," Martha said as we passed Thirty-fourth Street.

"Equality for female journalists isn't exactly top of mind for most," Fanny countered.

"It would be if people realized the changes we have helped bring about," Martha said.

"Would it?" I asked. "Sometimes I think we think more highly of those changes than the people they affect."

Fanny took my arm in hers. "Even if they do, we know what our kind has done since Nellie first went undercover in that madhouse for ten days. They call us stunt reporters, but laws have been changed because of us, Vee, and you know it. Many factories are safer, awareness of the plight of women sex workers is up, people have gone to prison for running slave trades. So many tenement landlords are being more reactive or forced into being reactive because of the articles you wrote about Charlotte and her family . . ."

I did know it. Everything she was saying was true, but it wasn't enough. Never enough. There was so much unfairness and so many problems and so little power. All we had was the printed word.

We'd reached Forty-first Street and were waiting at a traffic light when a man on the sidelines began shouting at us.

"Why aren't you all taking care of your babies? Go home where you belong!"

We'd discussed the importance of not engaging with hecklers, but it was difficult to ignore the nasty comments. But we did and just kept marching. He continued following us, shouting at us.

On the next block, three more men joined him. And then a few more.

By the time we reached Forty-fourth Street, there were more than two dozen men following us, walking beside us, heckling us. The jibes getting nastier and nastier.

"You're too ugly to find a man, so you're trying to be one!" one voice yelled.

"The only job you're good for is spreading your legs!" another shouted.

"You are no better than the heathens and whores you write about!" came a harsh voice from the crowd.

Some of the younger women in our group were becoming frightened. I noticed two crying, with a third consoling them. I wondered if they were going to drop out, but instead, they linked arms and kept going.

Fanny was seething. "A bunch of know-nothings. We have to get rid of them."

"No, we have to ignore them," I said.

We crossed Forty-fifth Street. A crowd of female office workers was standing on the next corner—young girls, all excited to see us, cheering us on.

Our band of male followers caught sight of them and stopped. So did I. Martha and Fanny did as well.

"What are you little ladies doing out here?" the male leader asked.

"You should go back to looking for husbands. You're not going to get more money any more than you're going to get the vote. You don't deserve it," another taunted.

"You are only good for two things," a third said again. He'd been chanting it for blocks now.

The women office workers started to argue with the men. Martha and Fanny and I broke out of the march and stepped up onto the curb. Our leaving the group alerted the rest of our tribe that there were rustlings that something was afoot, and the march slowed.

"Girls, go back to your office," I said to the troupe. "These are not gentlemen, and you don't need to engage with them."

"Who are you calling names?" One of the men turned on me.

"Girls!" I ignored the lout. "Please, we don't want any trouble. You need to know when to fight and when not to. These lowlifes are not worth your time."

"So now we aren't worth their time?" one of the men jeered.

I pleaded with the women for a few moments longer, while we all tried to ignore the comments the men continued hurling. They were a rough-looking group, with caps pulled low over their eyes, foul body odor, and breath that smelled of beer. They were probably agitators, I thought. Hired by politicians or businesses—depending on the situation—to break up peaceful marches like ours.

After the office workers finally heeded my warning and left, the men turned on us.

"Why'd you go and do that?" one of them said. "They were just getting cozy with us."

Ignoring him, I said to Martha and Fanny, "Let's get back to the march."

We hurried toward our group, the men at our heels like angry dogs. The marchers hadn't completely stopped but had slowed down for us, and we had no trouble rejoining them at the rear. But the men remained with us, intent, it seemed, on causing trouble, and began their own chant.

"Back to the kitchen. Back to the bedroom. Back to the nursery. Back to the kitchen. Back to the bedroom. Back to the nursery. Back to the kitchen. Back to the bedroom. Back to the nursery. Back to the kitchen. Back to the bedroom. Back to the nursery!"

Onward we walked, holding our signs higher the louder the chant grew. But as we continued, additional men on the street joined in, until there were more men than women marching. The men sounded so menacing that the female sidewalk spectators didn't want to have anything to do with us and shrank back.

"Why do these men hate us so much?" one of the younger reporters asked me.

"We threaten their way of life. Even the poorest of them can be the boss of a weak-minded woman," I said.

"Back to the kitchen. Back to the bedroom. Back to the nursery . . ." Their chanting continued, their cries even louder than before, drowning out ours completely.

I turned around to see how many there were. Then I poked Martha and Fanny. "Look!"

There had to be at least a hundred men following us and shouting at us.

"What should we do?" Martha asked.

"Keep going," Fanny said. She pointed to the crowds on the street. "They may be quiet now, but they're witnessing this. They're understanding it's what we deal with every day—an angry, insecure mob of men who want to stop us."

For all our bravado, I was growing more frightened by the second. An angry man or two was one thing, but a seething mob was something else. And while we believed we were equal in brains and abilities, few of us were physically equal to these men. Fewer of us still knew how to use our fists to defend ourselves. How was this going to end? We were certain to get hurt unless we could curtail the rising passions.

"I have an idea," I said to Fanny. "This is ugly and getting worse. I think we should change our route and march toward the next precinct house. Do you know where it is?"

Among the three of us, we didn't, but I went off through our crowd, asking other women, until one said she did know and that it was on Fifty-second Street. I hurried to the front of our crowd, to the club president, Katharine Evan von Klenner, who was holding a banner with the press club secretary, Louise Talesnick.

"You hear that roar behind us?" I asked Katharine.

"Of course! We can't see that far back, though. What is it, a dozen or so men?"

"That's how it started. We've estimated it's now close to a hundred. And all of them are angry. Some of them have clubs. Some, I'm sure, have guns."

"We didn't realize it was that dangerous," Louise said.

I told them our plan, and they agreed to it. So I returned to the back of the line, and we all kept marching.

We were only two blocks from the police station when the incident occurred. The men were not just behind us now. They were also walking alongside us. Two or three abreast, so we were surrounded by them.

Nervously, I watched the women around me. I took in their anxious glances to the right and left where the men were. I saw some of the women gripping each other by the hand. A few were openly weeping. Others had their heads down, trying to put one foot in front of the other and keep going without losing their tempers and shouting back.

But there was one woman among us who couldn't ignore the agitators anymore. I was standing just behind Betty Cantor when she began shouting back at one of the men marching alongside her.

"Go to hell! You're not better than me, you just think what you have between your legs makes you better!"

The man rushed up to her. He pulled her sign out of her hands, held it like a weapon, and smacked her over the head with it. She crumpled and went down. The man started to beat her, even though she was prostrate on the sidewalk. A dozen or so women quickly mobilized around her once they realized what had happened. Two jumped on the assaulter from behind, and two others jumped on each side of him. They worked at pulling him off Betty and pushing him away, hitting him with their fists and their placards, raining punches on him.

If there had only been one or two men versus the women, it might have ended there, but we were outnumbered. As angry as we were, the men who had seen one of their own get beat up by a group of women became incensed and descended on us.

A blur of men swarmed through our ranks, shoving us away, pushing us to the ground. They grabbed our signs and snapped them in half, ripped our banners out of our hands and stomped on them. They got their hands on our flyers and threw them underfoot. Some of the women tried to fight back but were met with fists. I didn't see any of the men strike the first blow, but damn if they weren't willing to strike back with double the force once attacked.

I can never forget the sound of the shrieks and cries as some of us refused to back down. We were not unscathed. But we were undaunted. Despite scratches, bloody noses, pulled hair, punched guts, few of us fled despite being overpowered and outnumbered.

Our plan worked. In less than five minutes, five policemen on horseback and a paddy wagon descended on us. I believe only their swift arrival prevented the melee from becoming tragic.

Except they weren't there to help us. They rounded us up and arrested us for disturbing the peace—not the men!

"You realize that if you arrest us and put us in jail, our editors are going to be delighted," I said to the officer who took my name. I spelled out "Vee Swann" and asked him to get in touch with Ronald Nevins at the *World* to post bail. Even though I wasn't currently writing for Mr. Nevins, several of us here were, and I knew he would come through. "You are giving them headlines to run."

"That may be, ma'am, but I'm still going to do my job."

"We're going to write about everything that happens to us," Fanny said.

He ignored her.

"You are making a mistake," I said.

But either the policemen didn't care, or they didn't believe us. "It's not fair," one of the younger reporters griped, and I laughed sardonically, hearing the leitmotif of our lives expressed with such innocence. Could she truly be surprised by the unfairness? Had she really expected something fair and right and true to happen?

Well, that certainly wasn't what occurred. With a brutality that was unnecessary, while the men dissipated and disappeared, the police pulled and shoved us, dragging us up the block and a half to the station house, arresting every one of us. None of us tried to get away. We all knew that what was happening to us was a story. Too good a story to run away from.

We were fifty strong, and the jail cells in that precinct house couldn't hold more than twenty, but they shoved us into the stinking, slimy, filthy cells anyway. We couldn't even all sit down.

We were members of the press; we knew our rights. The courts were open till four p.m. for our contacts to post bail. But the hour came and went. Our next hope was night court, created three years before to handle bail and releases after regular hours.

But the hours wore on, and we remained ignored. No one brought us water or food. The police acted as if we didn't exist at all. Six o'clock slid into seven. None of us had imagined when we started our march that this was where we'd be so many hours later. When eight p.m. rolled around, we were still behind bars.

I don't know what was worst—the heat, the hunger, the thirst, or the stench. Old urine and stale body odor plus cheap perfume and the smells of more than four dozen angry and frightened women crammed into two cells, each with space too small for ten.

We organized a schedule so that a third of us could nap at a time. That required the other two-thirds to stand at even closer quarters to make room for those getting their rest. We also kept the police busy, calling for them to take us to the bathroom. We'd concocted a plan to ask one at a time and always wait ten minutes between requests, to keep the officers in charge on their feet and hopefully annoyed.

It worked too well. After hours of them escorting us back and forth to the lavatory, the chief of the station house came to talk to us— or, rather, yell at us—that he wasn't going to put up with our shenanigans, as he called them. We could ask all we wanted, but there would be fifteen minutes set aside every two hours, and those who needed to use the facilities could use them then, or they would have to wait until the next two-hour stretch was over.

We demanded water. Received none. Demanded food. Got none. Several women fainted, and the police did nothing when we asked for medical assistance. It was that time of month for at least half a dozen of us, but no provisions were made.

I had done many things as a reporter in the ten years since I'd been working, but I'd never been incarcerated. I'd visited women in prisons and wasn't surprised by the horrific conditions. From reform schools to orphanages to factories and tenements, filth and squalor and rot were ubiquitous. But it was very different to be locked inside the jail cell knowing I was powerless to leave.

That we were treated with so little respect didn't surprise me. Or any of us, really. We'd all been victims of misogyny, sexual harassment, male dominance, racial or sexual slurs in our jobs and personal lives. But two things did surprise me.

One was how quickly we began to stink, shoved up against one another in the small, windowless cells. Second was how distracting it was to be hungry and thirsty. Even when I'd gone undercover and had lived in almost abject poverty, I'd always had water to drink, and I'd always made enough money to afford a can of beans, a loaf of bread, or an apple. Even if the bread was a little stale and the apple a little mealy, I could eat.

So while I'd been hungry before, I'd never focused on the feeling for long. Few of us had ever been in situations where there was no possibility of nourishment. And that awareness was what made it so unbearable there.

We'd met up at the club at noon, and most of us hadn't had anything to drink or eat for at least an hour before that, since we'd been in transit. We'd marched for almost two hours before our arrest. And by the time we were all locked up, another hour had passed. So by six p.m., we were all hungry and thirsty, and by eight, our stomachs were growling. Of course, I'd skipped dinner before without noticing or caring. But knowing I had no access to food put me in a state of crisis.

Our helplessness worked against us.

What woman hasn't felt helpless? Who of us hasn't felt defenseless against fate? Against illness? Against cruelty? Against someone bigger, stronger, more ruthless, or cruel? A sexual predator? A thief? An angry husband? A drunk father? A jealous brother? A thwarted lover? And now we could add power-hungry policemen to our list of men who take advantage of their place in society.

They reveled in what they were doing. Laughed at us. Berated us. Taunted us. They were nasty to us and took pleasure in our discomfort.

When morning came, we were all released, simply informed that the charges had been dropped. We found out later that the mayor had been pressured by the city's newspaper editors and had ordered the chief of police to handle the situation immediately and as quietly as possible.

But there was nothing quiet about what came next.

Those of us who had regular jobs went straight to their city rooms to write up the incident, each trying to scoop the other. As much as we were sisters in arms, we were still a group of competing reporters. Someone was going to be first, and everyone wanted to be that someone.

For us freelancers, there was no reason to fight the clock. We went home to bathe, dress, and eat. Most of us then went to see our editors at magazines and newspapers about longer stories on prison reform, women's rights, the anger of the mob, the lack of protection for women marching . . . there were endless angles to pitch.

I had my platform—Silk, Satin and Scandals— so I stayed home. First, I took a long bath, and then I made eggs, bacon, toast, and coffee. Still sitting in the dining room, which I also used as an office, I poured a second cup of coffee and went to work. I sat at my typewriter and composed a column for the next two hours. Not my usual fare—there was no description of pearls or silks. I wrote about the women from the upper echelons of society who had joined the march and described what they had seen.

Since I didn't need any more material for my column, I wrote a note to my mother saying that I wouldn't attend the opera with her that evening. I knew she'd be annoyed that she'd lost her companion for the night. I also knew she wouldn't worry. Her motherly concern was not as strong as her displeasure at having her plans changed.

That task completed, I penned a two-page article about the violence at the march and the way the police had treated us, which I thought would be of interest to Mr. Oxley. Then, dressed as Vee Swann, I left the apartment by way of the tunnel.

When my father had first showed me the secret passageway that led out to Fifty-eighth Street, I'd questioned its function. He'd told me it was a safety precaution. There were thugs and robbers on the streets of New York, and as someone who owned such a successful store, he was a target for all kinds of criminals.

But after I'd found the letter from my uncle, who had built both the department store and the rooftop apartment, I believed the tunnel had been designed for quite another purpose. It had allowed my father to come and go without being noticed and must have given my uncle the same kind of access.

I found it very convenient for Vee Swann's comings and goings as well. No one paid any attention to the plain, black-haired woman walking out of an alley behind the Fifth Avenue store. Surely, anyone who might have noticed the spinster carrying a sewing box would have assumed she was a seamstress. But had they opened the box, they would have found the envelopes I delivered to my editor at the *World* once a week. Added to that, they would have been able to identify the author of Satin, Silk and Scandals, which many readers were not only curious about but also anxious to learn. Over the years, its anonymous author had not only entertained but angered and embarrassed many.

That week's installment would prove to be no exception.

After delivering the column, I walked over to the *Gotham Gazette* offices. Mr. Oxley saw me immediately, read my article, and rubbed his hands with delight as he read through it a second time.

"Great job. This will ruffle a few feathers at City Hall. Are the same rate and caveats I offered you for the Cartier piece all right with you?"

I said yes and asked him when it would run.

"Is there anything in here that you have exclusively?" he asked.

"I'm not sure why you are asking." Though I had a very good idea why. Surely, if I had lied and said yes, he would have taken the article to someone in city politics and tried to make a deal. He'd agree not to run it, for this favor or that promise or political ads during the next election.

"Don't let it bother you why I'm asking. Just tell me," he said.

"No, we all were there and were treated the same way. I saw and heard the same things as everybody else. It's simply my interpretation of what happened."

"Then we'll run it in this Friday's edition of the magazine," he said. "And thank you for bringing it to me first. I know you have relationships around town with other editors."

"But none with your circulation," I countered, flattering him, as was my intention.

"How is your Cartier exposé coming?" Mr. Oxley asked.

"A little more slowly than I'd hoped, but I think you are going to be very pleased," I lied. There was no exposé yet. I was concerned that I hadn't come across anything other than exaggeration, and that wasn't salacious enough for Mr. Oxley to use to blackmail Cartier.

"Well, we need your piece before he sells the stone."

"That won't be a problem," I assured him.

Of course, it wouldn't, since Vera Garland could always engage in a bidding war with whoever else wanted the stone, submit the article, and, when the time came, pull out of the negotiations.

Finally returning to my apartment, I crawled into bed. Exhausted from the ordeal of the day

307

and night before, I slept from three that afternoon straight through till six the next morning. I woke up refreshed and walked to the newsstand to buy all the morning editions, to read the various reporting about our arrest and incarceration.

Each paper reported the story differently. Most editors had allowed their female reporters to express outrage and fury over how they had been treated by police, shining the unflattering light on them that they deserved. Some articles, written by male reporters who had not even been present, painted a very different picture of unruly women breaking the law. But in all cases, it was exactly what we had predicted and warned the police about. More than seventy-five percent of the papers led with a firsthand account highlighting how New York City's police had mishandled the situation and contributed to the brutality we'd endured. It wasn't that the majority of the editors were sympathetic to our plight—certainly not. Very few were. Hell, they were as responsible as anyone for our need to march in the first place. But they were newspaper men first and foremost, and they knew what sold papers. And sell they did.

At a little after noon, I met with Fanny and Martha for lunch at Dorlon's Oyster House on East Twenty-third street. We celebrated the attention the march had garnered with a bottle of champagne. As Fanny pointed out, the vile heckling men had done us a favor of sorts. Without them, our efforts might never have made the front pages.

When I returned to the apartment, there was a note from Mr. Cartier. Slitting it open, I thought back to my meeting with Mr. Oxley and how I'd exaggerated my progress on the story. For a moment, as I pulled out the note, I wondered if the bad luck surrounding the Hope Diamond might have been true and if it had begun for me.

I had been arrested, after all. And for the first time. But then again, everyone was released, and no one had been badly hurt. No, it wasn't bad luck. I knew better.

I needed to focus on finding the story—and soon. Mr. Oxley had reminded me that time was of the essence.

I looked down and read the note. Mr. Cartier had written that he had more pearls and would like to show them to me, along with a design for a clasp. Was I available at four thirty that afternoon?

CHAPTER 21

I sent a note back to Mr. Cartier saying that I could be there at five. It was a bit late for an appointment, but I wanted to be his last customer of the day so he wouldn't be in a hurry to finish up with me. Maybe I could get him to open up a bit about the Hope and reveal something I could use.

When I arrived, I was happy to see there were no other customers lingering. Mr. Fontaine offered me a seat and refreshments. I accepted a glass of champagne, and while we waited, I tried to engage him in conversation about the diamond, but he wasn't forthcoming. In fact, he seemed to grow slightly uncomfortable when I brought up the Hope. I wrote that off to the stone's storied past.

Mr. Cartier joined me at the stroke of five and brought two cases and a sheaf of drawings with him. He opened the case with much fanfare and showed me a new group of individual pearls that he felt were a much-improved match.

I agreed.

Next, he laid out the drawings.

"Here we have three choices for your clasp. Whichever one you choose, we can work it so you can remove it to wear as a brooch."

The first was in the shape of a flower, with diamond petals and a single pearl in the center.

The second was also diamonds and pearls but in the shape of a delicate bow. The third was not a drawing but a finished piece. A diamond pavé heart with a flashing opal at its center.

"This is a piece we just finished working on and were going to show for the holidays. I included it since you had mentioned opals were among your favorites," Mr. Cartier said.

But I hadn't told him, had I? I'd mentioned that to Jacob. But my father had bought opals for me from Mr. Cartier.

"How clever of you to remember. And it's perfect," I said. Thrilled, in fact, that this charade had yielded a new piece of jewelry I'd actually enjoy wearing.

"Mr. Asher can string the pearls and attach the clasp while you wait, if you like. It will take less than a half hour."

Thirty minutes would allow time for Mr. Cartier to give me another look at the book of press clippings on the Hope. I said I'd wait.

"And might I browse through the book of press clippings on the Hope once again?" I asked.

"Of course," he answered without hesitation, and handed me the leather-bound journal, then took the pearls back into the workshop.

He returned about ten minutes later. "Can I get you more champagne while you peruse?" he asked.

I demurred. "No, but I would like to discuss

some of these articles about the Hope with you while we wait."

"It would be my pleasure to answer any questions you have," he said, with a slight bow of his head.

"I've thought about it quite a bit."

"I would expect so. It's quite a purchase." He smiled.

"And I've continued to discuss it with my mother. She's now open to the idea of sharing in the purchase. But she asked me more about the actual incidents of bad luck than I could really remember."

"Does she believe in luck?"

"No, she's very pragmatic. Do you?"

"No." He laughed. "Or else I never would have bought it. But as we've discussed, gems are such miracles of nature that it is easy for people to assign all sorts of powers to them."

"I've been studying up about that. In fact, there is a novel I found, a British novel, about a woman who becomes obsessed with her gems to the point of being enslaved by them. Do you know the book?"

"I do."

"I wonder how common that is."

"More than you think. The desire to possess beauty is a very natural one. The entire art world is built on just such a structure. But I found that novel a bit of an exaggeration."

"Fiction often has to be exaggerated to make its point," I said.

"Very true. As many as there are who believe the stories about the Hope are fact, an equal number believe they are nothing but fiction. Either way, there is no question that it is a magical, stunning stone, and whoever owns it will become the custodian of that magic and beauty."

And then, ever so gently, he moved into a sales pitch.

"Of all the people I show it to, the number of my clients who are put off by the tales of ill fortune is equal to the number of those who are even more intrigued because of the stories. One, in particular, seems to be determined to own it just to stare bad luck in the face and laugh at it, as she put it."

"That sounds as if you have found a buyer." I guessed he was speaking of Evalyn Walsh McLean.

"I have two clients besides you who are seriously considering the stone. One has yet to convince her husband that it's a sound investment. The other is traveling, and I expect to hear from him in two weeks."

"You did promise to give me fair warning when you get an offer."

"I did. I'm not expecting a bidding war, but of course, Mademoiselle Garland, it's always possible. I am confident the sale will be concluded by the end of the year."

At that moment, Jacob came out from the back of the shop, holding the velvet tray, much sooner, to my dismay, than thirty minutes.

"Ah, Mr. Asher, thank you," Mr. Cartier said.

I was trying not to meet Jacob's eye. I didn't want to give Mr. Cartier any idea that there was anything between us, for fear I would put Jacob's job in jeopardy. With Cartier's Old World values, I was certain he would never approve of our liaison.

"Good afternoon, Miss Garland," Jacob said, making the exact opposite effort with a gleam in his eye, suggesting he found the game entertaining. "I think you'll be quite pleased with these pearls. Like satin on your skin."

The low, slow timbre of his voice rocked me, bringing back visceral memories of our hours together the previous week. Damn, I did not want to desire him. I did not want him to get inside my head. If anything, I wanted to get inside his and learn Mr. Cartier's secrets so I could use them. I didn't want to yearn for the feel of this man's fingers moving up my leg and down my neck. I didn't want to smell his scent and remember how he set my insides aflutter.

I crossed and uncrossed my legs, as I felt a flush rise up my chest and neck, and knew that my cheeks must be turning pink.

"Let me see, please," I said, trying to focus on the pearls.

Jacob looked at Mr. Cartier, as if for permission to approach, and Mr. Cartier nodded.

Jacob came up behind me. He lowered the strand of pearls around my neck and then carefully closed the clasp. As he did so, his fingers caressed the back of my neck for but a second. Quick enough to be certain Mr. Cartier didn't notice. Long enough to set my skin on fire.

Without meaning to, I let out a little sigh. Behind me, I felt Jacob's breath on my neck.

Mr. Cartier assumed the sigh was caused by my looking at the necklace and said, "Yes, they are stunning, aren't they? Your mother was quite definite when she originally chose them that they be of the very best quality."

In the mirror, I could see Jacob was looking at me with a sparkle in his eye. He was teasing me. He knew exactly why I'd exclaimed. And when Mr. Cartier turned to get a jewel box from the cabinet behind us, Jacob winked at me. By the time Mr. Cartier turned back, Jacob had already moved away and was awaiting further instructions from his employer.

There was nothing servile about Jacob's stance. No sense that he worked for Mr. Cartier as much as he worked with him and was simply giving Mr. Cartier the courtesy of pretending to be in charge. I wondered how Jacob managed to give off the impression of independence and deference at the same time.

"Thank you, Mr. Asher," Mr. Cartier said, dismissing him.

As Jacob turned to leave, I couldn't help but play with him a bit.

"Interesting accent you have, Mr. Asher. You sound British, but . . . there's something else in your voice I can't quite place."

"I was born in Russia and educated in England."

"How fascinating. Thank you."

As he started to walk off, I asked Mr. Cartier, "Has Mr. Asher been with you long?"

"A year in London and then since I opened up here in New York."

"He must be very good for you to have brought him overseas," I ventured.

Jacob had reached the door now, and I saw a hitch in his step and imagined that he was smiling.

"Yes, Mademoiselle, Cartier's only employs the very best. My father taught us that. Mr. Asher comes from a long line of jewelers."

Mr. Cartier wrapped up my parcel, and after we arranged how he would bill me, I took my leave.

Since I had errands, I didn't go back to the apartment right away. It was almost six thirty when I reached my front door and realized I'd left my satchel at Mr. Cartier's. I needed to retrieve

316

it as soon as possible. Inside was a notebook belonging to Vee Swann. How would it look if either Mr. Cartier or Mr. Asher opened the satchel to find a mix of papers with both Vera Garland's and Vee Swann's names on them? I might be able to explain my way out of it, but it would certainly raise suspicions.

I walked the two blocks back to 712 Fifth, hoping that someone would still be there. Jacob had told me he often worked into the night. As I opened the door to the office building, I considered that I might have actually left the bag there on purpose. It had, after all, given me this excuse to go back. I didn't like to think my subconscious mind was playing games like that. If I wanted to see Jacob, wasn't I confident enough just to send him a note? Except I didn't *want* to see him. I didn't *want* to like him. I just wanted to get information from him. He was too clever, too caustic, too rakish for me to want to associate with him for any other reason.

My frustration that I still didn't have anything about Mr. Cartier's tactics to base my story on was very much on my mind. I needed to discover something—and soon—if I was going to write an article scandalous enough to give Mr. Oxley reason to believe he could blackmail Cartier. And that was what I was thinking of as I got off the elevator and walked to the jewelry store's door and rang the bell.

Jacob opened the door a few moments later, obviously surprised to see me.

"Vera? What is it?" he said, his voice tight.

"Is something wrong?" I asked.

"You need to leave," he said in a rush. "You aren't supposed to be here."

I could tell he was agitated and uncomfortable. Maybe the reason was exactly what I needed for my story. "Why?"

"We're closed . . ." He hadn't opened the door any wider and stood blocking my entry.

"Seriously, you're not letting me in?" I was hurt. I'd thought he'd be pleased to see me. No, I thought. I couldn't allow myself to be hurt. I could not become confused between what I wanted professionally and privately. I'd committed the cardinal sin of involving myself in the life of a source before. How could I be doing it again? Losing my objectivity with Charlotte and not seeing danger when faced with it had been my undoing. I could not allow history to repeat itself now.

"I left something here. I'll only be a moment," I said, and pushed past Jacob, who didn't have the wherewithal to stop me.

I walked over to the table by the window where I'd been sitting to look at the pearls. Yes, there it was. I reached down and retrieved my satchel.

"While I'm here, I need to talk to you about something else. A favor for a friend." I wasn't quite sure how I intended to use Aunt Carrie's request to help me get what I needed, but I hoped that in discussing it with him, I could maneuver the conversation when and if I saw an opening.

"I very much want to help you in any way I can, but we need to make plans to see each other later this week. I have work to finish now, and it's imperative that you go and allow me—"

His words were interrupted by a loud banging and then the sound of glass shattering. I swung around in its direction to see the front door flying open and a blur of three men running into the room. The reporter in me sprang into action, and instead of cowering, I stepped back against the wall and took in the men, knowing I needed to see them in order to describe them. They had brown skin and wore black silk turbans with black handkerchiefs tied over the bottom halves of their faces to mask their features. They were shouting, but I couldn't understand all of their words because of their accents, which I identified as Indian.

Even I had no problem identifying their weapons. Each of them had a shining silver gun. One was pointed at Jacob. Another was pointed right at me. Before I could do anything, its owner approached, grabbed me around the waist, and pointed the gun up to my forehead.

"Do not move," he shouted at me, "and you will not get hurt!"

Of course, I wasn't going to move. I remained exactly where I was and watched as another of the black-turbaned men interrogated Jacob at gunpoint.

"Where is the Hope?" he shouted.

"I'll tell you if you let the lady go," Jacob said.

"Get us the stone, and everything will be fine!" the second man shouted.

"I'll get you the stone, just let her go."

"No, first you give us the stone!" the man shouted. "She is insurance."

Jacob looked from the man holding the gun on him to me. And then, in one swift, almost impossible move, he pushed his captor away with a giant shove, took a flying leap, and lunged at the man holding me.

The bandit let go of me and lashed out at Jacob, smashing him in the head with the weapon.

Jacob staggered and fell to the floor.

"We have to get out. This wasn't the plan," the man who had been holding me said. But I wasn't paying attention to him or the other men with him. I was down on my knees, focused on Jacob. A flurry of legs and feet rushed past me in a *whoosh*. So many, it seemed. And then they were gone. And Jacob lay on the floor of the shop, his beautiful face battered, the wound in his head staining the cream-colored carpet a dark, rich ruby.

I opened the door and screamed for help.

CHAPTER 22

The last time I'd been in a hospital was after I'd fallen down the steps of Charlotte's tenement. Being back in that same atmosphere, smelling the antiseptic, hearing the padding of the nurses' shoes on the marble floors, sensing the desperation, brought up terrible memories. But there had not been anyone else to accompany Jacob in the ambulance. It had taken ten minutes to get from the store to Beth David Hospital at 321 East Forty-second Street. But then there was no one else to follow the gurney as the medics took him inside. And then there was no one to wait with Jacob's unconscious form until a doctor arrived to examine him.

I was in shock, and a kind nurse who'd guessed as much made me a cup of hot sweet tea and sat with me as I drank it. It helped, but my shock was replaced by worry about Jacob. How bad was the wound? Why was he still unconscious? How long could he stay that way without being permanently affected?

The nurse did what she could to reassure me that long periods of unconsciousness after a blow to the head were not uncommon. She said that his color was good, as were his vital signs, and that was important. But, she did caution, only a doctor would be able to fully assess the situation.

After she left, I sat in the cold, sterile hospital room alone with Jacob. I stared at his bandaged, still face and went over and over the events to make sure they were cemented in my brain so I'd be able to write the story. I had a scoop, and as soon as I was sure Jacob was safe and in good hands, I would file it with my editor at the *World*. A break-in at Cartier's, an attempt to steal the Hope—that was front-page material. Even though I wasn't currently on assignment, I knew Mr. Nevins would welcome the exclusive.

So while I waited, I borrowed a few sheets of paper and a pencil from the nurses and wrote up the robbery, including as many details as I could remember. I had Vee Swann interview Vera Garland at the hospital after getting a tip from someone in the police department about the break-in.

I finished the piece by nine p.m., just as the nurse came back with an orderly. They were taking Jacob to have his head X-rayed. Beth David was known for being one of the first hospitals in New York to use the new technology, which had been invented just fifteen years before. For the first time in history, doctors could look inside a patient and see if there were fractured bones.

A half hour later, I was still sitting in Jacob's

room when some nurses wheeled the trolley in. This time, a doctor accompanied them.

I stood up.

"I'm Dr. Simon Lipskar," the man said as he offered me his hand.

I shook it.

"Are you Mr. Asher's wife?" he asked.

"No, a friend. I was with him when it happened. He doesn't have any family in America. How is he?" I had hoped that Mr. Cartier would have arrived by now, but he hadn't. There was no one but me to hear the prognosis.

The doctor looked grave. "We saw a small fracture in Mr. Asher's skull . . ."

I gripped the back of the chair.

"Are you all right?" he asked.

I nodded. "Please go on."

"A skull fracture is a break in the bone surrounding the brain. It is common in cases where there has been blunt force applied."

"So if it's common, he's going to be all right?"

"We can't know yet. Only time will tell us."

"But he's going to come out of this . . ." I searched for the word.

"He's in a coma, which happens often with skull fractures. And while these kinds of fractures can cause brain damage, there's every reason now to assume Mr. Asher will pull through fine."

"Brain damage? Do you think he'll have brain damage?"

"Miss Garland, I wish I could be one hundred percent certain that he won't, but it's only been a few hours since the injury, and we can't tell anything yet. We have to wait until he comes out of his coma in order to discover what kind of brain damage there is, if any, and if it is permanent."

I sucked in my breath and then wasn't sure I remembered how to exhale.

I heard the doctor from far away as I battled a wave of dizziness and felt the room tipping up to meet me.

Strong hands gripped me and pulled me back.

"Nurse," I heard the doctor call out through what seemed like a wall of cotton.

I wasn't aware of anything that happened after that, until I woke up with a start, smelling something strong that stung my eyes and nose.

"There now," the nurse I recognized from before was saying. "Just breathe, that's it . . . in and out . . . deep breaths . . . in and out." She turned away from me. "Doctor, she's come to."

The doctor approached, pulled up a chair, and, sitting beside me, took my pulse.

"What happened?" I asked.

"You fainted. But you're fine. You didn't fall. I caught you."

And then I remembered what he had been telling me.

"Jacob? You were saying that he—"

"Not yet. We can go over all of that later. Nurse, can you get us some sweet tea?"

She left, and while she was gone, the doctor continued to monitor me and ask me questions.

"Were you hurt in the robbery, Miss—"

"Garland. And no, they didn't touch me. Jacob—Mr. Asher stepped in. That's how he—" I started to cry.

The doctor spoke in a soothing voice. "You've had a blow as well, even if it wasn't physical. I know you want to stay here, but after you drink this tea . . ." The nurse handed him the white china mug, which he handed to me. My second of the night. "After you drink this, we can call you a carriage so you can go home and get some sleep. There's nothing you can do for Mr. Asher tonight, and I fear your nerves have taken a severe beating. Just sit here for a moment. I'm going to get you some Veronal tablets to take when you get home. They will calm you and help you sleep."

When he returned with the packet of pills, I told him that under the circumstances, I thought I should remain with Mr. Asher at least until Mr. Cartier arrived. Reluctantly, he backed down and said he had other patients to see to but he'd be back to check on Jacob, and me, in an hour.

"And," he added, "if you need anything or see any change in Mr. Asher's condition, please let the nurse know."

I sat, holding the tea mug, staring at Jacob. I couldn't take my eyes off the rise and fall of his chest and wished I believed in a greater power so I could pray to God to make his eyes open. I found myself crying.

Who was this man who I suddenly realized mattered so much to me? What about him, as opposed to any other man, made him special? I barely knew him. What is it that makes us react this way to someone, as if you've met the other half of your heart, when you never even knew any part of your heart was missing? And now that I had met him, what if I lost him? Before I could tell him? Before I could thank him for saving me?

When the nurse came in at ten thirty and saw how upset I was, she sat down beside me and spent some time assuring me that full recovery was possible. She had seen people get up and walk out of a room after a "deep sleep," as she called it. And then she repeated what the doctor had said, that nothing about Jacob being unconscious for a few hours or even a day or two precluded him having a full recovery without any brain damage.

"But there has to be something I can do. A specialist we could call in? My family has connections with doctors who—"

"This is the foremost hospital in the city for brain injury. Your friend is in the best of hands. I know how hard this is, but waiting is all you can do," she said. "Our job is to watch over him and keep him comfortable."

"Can he hear us?"

"The doctors say no." She made a face as if they were fools. "But every nurse you talk to on this ward will swear he can. So you just keep visiting and talking to him. I know it makes a difference. There are some nurses—mind you, I'm not one—who believe that in these cases, if the patient is hovering between staying here with us or letting go, our voices can be the factor that keeps them tethered to their corporeal bodies."

"You mean talking to him can keep him alive?"

She shrugged. "So some say. But they're more spiritual than I am. They also believe in ghosts, some of them. But never you mind that kind of talk. Right now, you talk to your friend, but don't forget to take care of yourself in the meantime. Make sure you eat and get some sleep. Listen to the doctor. I've seen lots of loved ones wind up exhausted and dehydrated and needing almost as much care as the patient."

"I will."

"I don't know if you are so disposed," she said, "but some people like to pray. There is a chapel downstairs if you'd care to visit. Even if you just need a break from this room, it's very peaceful and has a beautiful stained-glass window and lovely flowers that keep the air sweet."

"Thank you, but I think I'll stay here for now," I told her.

At eleven thirty, Mr. Cartier finally arrived. As it turned out, he'd been at a gala, and the police had not been able to locate him. So when he flew into Jacob's hospital room, he was in tie and tails. He didn't see me at first, just hurried to the bedside and took in the sight of his trusted jeweler, eyes closed, head wrapped in a bandage. Mr. Cartier's back was to me, but I heard his intake of breath and then a small moan.

"Jacob, I need you. We have a problem," he said.

"Mr. Cartier," I said in a soft voice, not wanting to startle him.

He turned. Clearly, he was astonished to see me in the room. And perhaps embarrassed that I had heard him.

"Mademoiselle Garland? How is it that you are here?"

"I was there, in the store with Jacob, during the robbery attempt."

"The police told me he's unconscious?"

I explained what the doctor had said.

"And the robbery, you were there? But not harmed?" He searched my face.

"No, not harmed. Only Jacob was hurt trying to stop them from hurting me. It all happened so fast. Even before they could take anything."

"How do you know they didn't take anything?" Sweat popped out on Mr. Cartier's forehead despite the chill in the room. I didn't know him well at all, but in the few times I'd met him, he had seemed nothing if not the epitome of calm deliberation.

"I didn't see any of them leave the showroom to go into the workshop," I said, but as I did, I wondered if I was certain. "Except . . . I'm not sure, now that you ask. I don't *think* I saw any of them leave the showroom. Have you been back to the store? Did you check? Did they take anything?"

"I have been there," Mr. Cartier said anxiously. "The police had me check our inventory."

Which didn't entirely answer my question.

"I don't understand, Miss Garland. Why were you there?"

His diamond studs and cufflinks twinkled obscenely. The contrast between this lively, dapper man and the pale, unmoving Jacob was stunning.

I explained that I had returned to the store to retrieve my satchel and described the rest of what had occurred. Just the retelling brought it all back, and I started to shake again.

If he was surprised that I had chosen to stay at the hospital by Jacob's side, he didn't mention it. It would have been improper for him to question me, a client, anyway. Perhaps he assumed that since I had been present during the altercation, I somehow felt responsible for Jacob's injury.

"And you are all right?" Mr. Cartier asked.

"I will be. It's Ja—Mr. Asher whom we need to worry about."

"Yes, of course, but you as well. Have you seen a doctor?"

"Yes, and I'm really fine. In shock but unhurt."

Mr. Cartier gestured to the chairs. "Let's sit. Or should we go outside? We don't want to disturb Jacob. I have some questions to ask you, if you don't mind."

"Actually, the nurse said it's good for us to talk in here and for us to talk to him. They don't have medical proof, but they believe it helps keep patients tethered to their bodies, was how she described it."

Mr. Cartier asked me more questions about the incident, and as he did, he became more distraught. "That you were present during the intrusion is something I don't know how to apologize for. Something I can never forgive myself for. This whole night has been a disaster."

He wrung his hands. I'd read the phrase but had never seen anyone do it. It was every bit as disconsolate-looking as it sounded.

I assured him that he needn't apologize. But he remained extremely distressed. I wasn't clear which was more upsetting to him, Jacob's infirmity or that I had been in the shop and at risk. Or was there something else he wasn't telling me?

Finally, after yet more apologies, he insisted on having his car and driver take me home.

"You don't need to remain here now that I'm here, Mademoiselle Garland. I will make sure that Mr. Asher receives the best of care."

"Do you need me to help contact relatives or friends about his condition?" I asked. Of course, I knew Jacob had no family here in New York, but for propriety's sake, I kept that knowledge from Mr. Cartier.

"Jacob has family in London but none here in New York. I will make inquiries tomorrow and see if I can contact them. As for friends, I don't know. I don't pry into my employees' personal lives."

Since Mr. Cartier insisted and I had no reason to object, I agreed to take his car and driver home. I didn't want to leave Jacob, but Mr. Cartier's presence meant I might have just enough time to meet the deadline for the morning paper.

At home, despite the hour, I called Mr. Oxley and explained that I had an exclusive regarding Cartier's that I was going to give to the *World* since it was a daily. I wanted to make sure he'd understand and promised him that I wouldn't reveal anything that would compromise the longer piece I was writing for him. If anything, this was going to make that article even more salacious, I promised.

After he gave me his blessing, I sat down and typed out the story of the attempted robbery of the Hope Diamond from the jewelry concern of Cartier's on Fifth Avenue and Fifty-second Street and then, despite the late hour, found a carriage to take me to the offices of the *New York World*, where I had the carriage wait while I arranged with a messenger to deliver the envelope to Mr. Nevins.

I returned home for the second time that night. I considered taking the tablets Dr. Lipskar had given me but remembered how awful the drugs for my back had made me feel the next day. So instead, I drank some of my father's best brandy and finally got into bed at two thirty in the morning.

Sleep was elusive, as I'd known it would be, and at five thirty, I gave up, got dressed, and went back to the hospital. Mr. Cartier was gone, and I found myself alone with Jacob once again. I felt less worried sitting by his bed. At least, there I could see that his color was still good and his breathing was regular. Dr. Lipskar came by at eight, and after he examined Jacob, I pressed him with a reporter's tenacity for some kind of prognosis.

He told me the same thing he'd told me the night before. There was no way to know when, or even if, Jacob would awaken. Just as there was no way yet to determine how serious the blow to his head was or if he would have any kind of damage. When I asked for statistics and probability, he simply refused to speculate. Brain injuries, he said, were very unpredictable. There simply was no way to gauge the severity of the blow.

He left me to my vigil. While I sat and waited, I replayed the scene of the intrusion and subsequent events over in my mind. Even when I'd written up the story, something about it had bothered me, but I couldn't figure out what it was.

Jacob and I had been talking. There was a commotion. The door burst open. Three men ran in. All of them were Indians wearing turbans and handkerchiefs over the lower halves of their faces to mask their features. Each had a gun. One demanded the Hope Diamond, and another threatened me. It was chaotic. Frightening. The gun in my face was all I could see. And then Jacob shouted and pushed the man who held him at gunpoint. He then leaped onto the man who was holding a gun on me. I remembered the sound of the gun as it hit Jacob's skull. A loud crack. And then him falling to the ground. The men ran. A door slammed. Except, now that I thought of it, it seemed as if the slamming had come from the wrong place, behind me. Not in front of me, where the front door was. Was it an acoustical anomaly?

There was no way to confirm the sequence of events with Jacob unconscious. He was the only one besides me who'd seen what happened. Then again, if he were awake, my questions would have only made him suspicious.

Mr. Cartier arrived at ten, holding that morning's edition of the *World*. I'd forgotten to go out and buy a paper to see where Mr. Nevins had placed it. There it was, front and center on the front page.

"Miss Garland," he said, surprised to see me. "I certainly didn't expect you to be here again."

"I feel as if this is somehow my fault. Mr. Asher stepped forward to protect me. The least I can do is sit vigil at his sickbed." I pointed to the newspaper. "Is that an article about the attempted robbery?"

"Attempted? No, didn't you know? The Hope Diamond was stolen last night."

"*Stolen?* While I was there?"

"Yes. I assumed you knew."

"No. I remember the thieves asking Jacob where the stone was, but I don't recall him telling them."

"I'm sure it was very chaotic and frightening, Mademoiselle Garland."

It was, but I was a reporter. I'd tried to stay focused, even though I was scared. Was I confused? Or had I missed something?

Mr. Cartier said he was going to look for the doctor to get an update on Jacob. He left the newspaper behind, and I picked it up.

The *World* had printed my story but with a different ending, and they'd attributed the reporting to another reporter, Robert Parrish, who must have contributed to the ending, and Vee Swann. I scanned the copy. The theft had been reported at ten p.m. after the police tracked down Mr. Cartier at a dinner party and accompanied him to his store so he could ascertain the damage.

The theft of the Hope Diamond was probably on the front page of every newspaper in New York, perhaps the whole country and, I guessed, a few in other parts of the world.

When Mr. Cartier returned to the room a few moments later, I was still reading the article.

"I'm sorry those reporters badgered you. Did they find you, here at the hospital?"

"Yes."

"How can I apologize? It's my fault you are getting all this unwanted attention in the press."

"Hardly. It was just bad luck that I was in the wrong place at the wrong time. And I don't care about being in the papers. It's Mr. Asher whom I care about now—" I nodded toward the bed. "He stepped in front of the burglar to protect me in a moment of pure bravery, and for that effort, he's lying here. With God knows what kind of skull fracture. If I hadn't been there, he would have cooperated and never been hurt."

Tears came to my eyes. What I didn't say to Mr. Cartier was that no one had ever acted so selflessly toward me. And the man who had done it was someone I had gone after in order to take advantage of him. A man I had allowed to seduce me, and yet I still planned on trying to get information out of him for my own purposes. And now, all because of me, that man was lying, unmoving, in a bed not ten feet away, possibly damaged for life. If I hadn't been so determined to get my story . . . if I had not gone back to the store and been there when it was burgled . . . if Jacob had been alone when the three bandits showed up, he would have just given over the diamond. Wouldn't he? No one would risk his own life for something he didn't even own. For something that at the end of the day was nothing more than a shiny lump of coal.

Mr. Cartier removed a snowy-white handkerchief from his jacket pocket, handed it to me, and checked his watch.

"I have to get to the store. Please allow me to drop you off at home on my way there. I spoke to the doctor, and Mr. Asher's condition is unchanged. He assured me there's nothing either of us is doing for him by staying here."

"Thank you," I told him, "but I want to stay. It seems so sad that he has no family or friends to be with him. Of course, you can't spare the time, you have a store to run, but I can."

I stayed with Jacob, trying to read but mostly staring out the window. At one thirty, realizing I was hungry, I went downstairs and ate a sandwich in the cafeteria. Afterward, on my way back, I stopped at the newsstand and bought all the papers.

The afternoon editions carried yet more stories about the theft of the Hope Diamond, all enumerating the terrible luck befalling the stone's owners, including Mr. Cartier's unfortunate current situation. As I finished one article and read the next, I found myself itching to put on my Vee Swann outfit and investigate along with all the other journalists, but I knew I had to remain Vera in order to accomplish my long-term goal.

I read the *Tribune*'s story, which quoted one society matron, Mrs. Patrick Lenox, as saying, "Why anyone wants the thing is beyond me. There's enough bad luck in the world without inviting in even more."

Another article quoted Mr. Cartier himself: "While there are people who will shy away from purchasing the Hope because of the superstition surrounding it, several new parties have come forward expressing interest in the stone when the police recover it. There seems to be a certain type of woman, a very modern woman, who wants to turn the idea of bad luck on its head. On her charm bracelet, she has golden amulets of the number 13, and she wears upside-down diamond horseshoes."

The headline in the *New York Times* read: *After Hope Robbery Armed Guards at Cartier's*. The article elaborated on the new security measures Mr. Cartier had put in place and would increase when the stone was returned. "Once the Hope is home, Pinkerton men will cover the shop twenty-four hours a day."

Most papers included sidebars about the history of the stone, repeating the stories that Mr. Cartier had been telling since purchasing it. Mr. Tavernier was back in the news almost three hundred years after he'd stolen the gem.

Mr. Nevins had sent word that unless he heard from me, he'd be putting Robert Parrish on the Cartier story. I wrote back and told him that as much as I wanted to do more, I didn't want him to count on me. Every word pained me to write. But I knew how imperative it was for me to keep my goal in sight. I also got a note from Martha, who was especially curious to know why Vee wasn't collecting more bylines. I wrote back telling her I was working on another angle that would take more time. I never liked lying to my friends, but what could I do? It was crucial to hide my identity, especially now.

The robbery also sparked a series of articles about other great jewel heists through the ages, as well as stories examining the myths, facts, figures, and science of gems. The theft reached above and beyond every exaggerated tale that Mr. Cartier had ever pulled out of his leather-bound book. It gave the Hope even more attention.

All afternoon and that evening, Jacob remained unconscious. I left the hospital at eight p.m., went home, slept fitfully, and returned the next morning by ten, to find his condition unchanged.

The day progressed as it had the day before.

At four p.m., one of the nurses came into the room holding an afternoon copy of the *New York Times*. The headline read: *Cartier Pays Ransom: Hope Home Safe*.

The article was sketchy, leaving out certain details at the request of the police, who were still hoping to apprehend the criminals behind the kidnapping. It bothered me that I wasn't out there covering the story. That my name wasn't in the paper. I would have been more persistent with the police, not giving up until I got more details. But my frustration was wasted energy, and I knew it. This wasn't the time to focus on small victories. I had a much larger one to devote myself to.

According to the information they were willing to share, at seven o'clock on Wednesday evening, the night after the theft, Mr. Cartier had received a note offering to exchange the stone for an undisclosed amount of cash. An address was given and the time of eleven at night stipulated for the exchange.

Even though the note warned Mr. Cartier not to bring in the authorities, he had gone to the police. At the appointed hour, Mr. Cartier's chauffeur—that night, an undercover cop—dropped him off two blocks away from the address. On foot, the jeweler walked, alone, to number 193 Grand Street in the heart of Little Italy in downtown Manhattan. The tenement was next door to Ferrara, the bakery famous for its cannoli and espresso. Cartier had been instructed to place the cash in a galvanized milk box sitting on the stoop.

Upon opening it, Cartier found a package with another note. This one explained the diamond was inside and further instructed Mr. Cartier to leave the money and exit the area immediately. It warned that the building was being watched from neighboring rooftops and apartments, and if anyone approached to retrieve the cash, they would be shot.

Mr. Cartier did as he was told and retreated.

The police, however, remained in place, waiting in shifts all through the night for someone to come fetch the money. All remained quiet until dawn, when they watched the milkman arrive, leave four bottles of milk, and depart.

Thinking the milkman was in on the heist, the police apprehended him. But the poor man didn't have the ransom money on him and claimed he hadn't seen anything in the milk box. Just four empty bottles beside it.

At that point, the police inspected the scene and discovered the milk box on the stoop had a false bottom. Removing it, they found a hole and looked down into the building's basement. Upon further examination, they found the basement opened up into a back alley, which must have been how the thief had absconded, undetected, with Mr. Cartier's cash.

I was standing outside Jacob's room, waiting in the hallway while Dr. Lipskar was examining him, when Mr. Cartier returned to the hospital early that evening. He said he was surprised to see me there again. I didn't bother offering the same excuse again and just told him how relieved I was for him that he'd gotten his stone back.

"Thank you, Mademoiselle, but Mr. Asher's recovery is more important than the Hope's. How is he?"

"There's no change. The doctor is in there now."

Mr. Cartier became quite distressed and went inside Jacob's room to talk to the doctor. After the doctor left, I went back in to find Mr. Cartier standing at Jacob's bedside.

"Did the doctor say anything?"

He shook his head.

"No change and no news. I'll stay with him this evening, Mademoiselle Garland. Please, go home. It really is quite unusual for you to remain here. I would hate for your vigil to be misinterpreted and for any rumors to start."

"Mr. Asher saved my life," I said.

Outside the window, sunset was turning to dusk. The bruised blues and grays of evening taking over from pale peaches and golds.

"I appreciate your concern," I said, "but truth be told, I don't have much of a reputation to worry about. An unmarried woman past a certain age is simply not fodder for the gossips. I've pretty much been written off."

"You say that almost as if you like it," he mused.

"Well, I do like it that no one is waiting for me to do the right thing anymore. I have my charitable efforts with my sister, and I'm satisfied with my life."

"That's quite admirable, Mademoiselle."

"Do you really think so? I believe I hear hesitation in your voice."

"It's hardly my place . . ."

"Oh, please . . . If you have something you want to say to me, say it. I looked into the barrel of a gun earlier this week. Your place? That hardly matters to me."

"You and I are close to the same age," Mr. Cartier said. "I recently married and had a

342

daughter, so I say this to you as a friend, if I may . . ."

"You were my father's friend. I'd be honored if you were mine also."

He bowed his head for a moment, then continued. "You shouldn't give up on the idea of marriage, on the idea of a family. The world can be very lonely without someone to share it with, whereas with the right person, all things become possible. Hope is restored." He smiled a little, chagrined, I think, that he'd used the word *hope*.

"I appreciate that. I do. My father often expressed similar sentiments. But I've been spoiled. My father treated me as an equal. He taught me to expect that from a man. I haven't met many men who would appreciate the work I do—" I stopped, realizing I'd slipped and referred to my career while speaking as Vera Garland. For a moment, I held my breath, wondering what Mr. Cartier would say.

"But surely most men would respect your charitable work?" he asked.

"Yes," I answered, relieved. The slip had frightened me. I was tired and had been careless. "Many men would, but . . . but only up to a point. They'd have expectations of how their wife should behave. I don't know if I can explain this, Mr. Cartier. I read constantly. I fight for causes that I think are unfair. I speak out. I argue. I've learned over the years that men who sit beside me at dinner parties find my spirit quite attractive, but they also see it as a challenge. They want to tame me. They wouldn't want the mistress of their house and the mother of their children to embarrass them. No, I'm simply not made for the life I was born to live."

"But surely you can step out of society. Cities like Paris and London and New York are filled with free spirits and bohemians breaking convention," he said kindly.

I nodded. "I suppose so."

"Forgive my impertinence, but I think you have closed off a certain door. I don't know why, and I am not asking you to tell me. But as someone who knew your father, who has met you and watched you here, I see a sadness in you. Don't allow it to define you. Choose happiness, Mademoiselle."

Choose happiness. The phrase stayed with me as I left the hospital that night. It remained as I arrived home, ate some dinner, changed my clothes, wrote, and then filed a Silk, Satin and Scandals column on women about town who were all showing off their Cartier jewels as if that somehow connected them to the robbery and contributed to their stature. Done, very late that night, I returned to Jacob's bedside.

CHAPTER 23

My vigil continued for two more days. On the third, the police came to the hospital to ask that I accompany them to the station to see if I could identify a man they'd taken into custody as one of the thieves.

As I was escorted through the precinct house, it occurred to me that I had never been in a police station as Vera Garland, member of society, and what very different treatment I was getting from that accorded to Vee Swann.

It was all so unfair, I thought, as the captain apologized for interrupting my day. But what *wasn't* unfair? Since I had been a very little girl, I must have uttered that phrase more than a hundred thousand times. But it was what I saw. At every turn. Every day. On every street corner. In every factory and municipal building. In every restaurant and music hall. Not all people were given a fair chance. Or given the same respect. Or treated equally, even though the Constitution of the United States deemed it should be so.

The suspect sitting at the wooden table had the same hair color and skin color as the men I'd seen in Cartier's shop on the night of the robbery. He spoke with the same Indian accent. But he wasn't one of the men who had burst into the store. He was too short. Too stout. And he had a scar that cut through his right eyebrow. I would have remembered that.

The police captain encouraged me to be sure. But I was a reporter, trained to remember details. I couldn't tell them that, but I didn't doubt my memory.

"I'd have recognized that scar," I told him. "It's like a horseshoe, which is a symbol of good luck."

The irony was astounding.

Reluctantly, they let the man go, and he gave me a grateful look as he exited. Fortune was smiling on someone, I thought. Though I could only imagine how difficult his life was here in New York as an Indian man. He would always stand out. At least, as a woman, I could fade into the sea of other women.

My sister's anniversary fete was on the fifth night after the robbery attempt. The plan was for all of us to attend a performance of *La Bohème* and then have dinner afterward. I'd spent the day at the hospital but had left at six to return home and change, which gave me barely enough time.

As I screwed the post in my pearl and diamond earrings, I stared at myself in the mirror and realized how tired I looked. How red my eyes were. How pale I was. Every step at my toilette was an effort and felt like a waste of what little energy I had left. I was putting on jewelry and perfume and a fancy dress and elegant shoes, when all I wanted was to be sitting at Jacob's bedside, holding his hand and whispering to him. Begging him to wake up. I wondered how I was going to get through the long evening without bolting.

I arrived at the Metropolitan Opera House on Broadway and Thirty-ninth Street with fifteen minutes to spare before the curtain. As I walked through the lobby and upstairs to our family box, I took notice of who was there for my column. I mentally made notes about everyone I said hello to. What designers they were wearing, what jewels they had on, who was with them. I was having a difficult time concentrating, though. My thoughts remained with Jacob, alone in the hospital room with no one by his side. What if he woke up confused? Who would answer his questions? Who would talk him through what had happened? I should be there. I was the reason he was hurt.

"Vera, you're late," my mother said when I arrived at the box. Letty, Jack, and Stephen were already there, talking to Aunt Carrie who had her own season seats.

"I was visiting someone at the hospital."

My mother frowned as she took in my clothes and hair and jewelry, assessing me. "Your dress is wrinkled, and your hair looks quite disheveled. It looks like your ordeal at Cartier's has left you the worse for wear."

"It has," I said as I sat, but I didn't offer any further explanation.

"What were you doing at Cartier's, anyway? You aren't serious about buying that stone, I know you aren't."

"It's all part of a plan, Mother. For an article I'm working on. That's why I was there."

"Putting yourself in danger for an article? Really, Vera. Again?"

"Father wouldn't be criticizing me if he were here. He'd been proud of me. Just once, could you try that?"

Before she could respond, Letty interrupted, leaning over to kiss me hello. She took both my hands in hers and squeezed them.

"I'm so glad you're here," she said. "We all are just so thankful to see that you are all right."

"Happy anniversary," I said to Letty, and then looked over at Jack and wished him the same. I turned to Stephen, who reached out for me and pulled me into a hug. I hadn't expected to react emotionally to his embrace. I hadn't realized how exhausted and raw I was. But as soon as I felt his arms around me, I started to cry. And as hard as I tried to stop, I couldn't.

"Do get a hold of yourself, Vera," my mother said. "You're drawing attention. People will gossip. If that awful columnist is here, she'll surely write about you. She always focuses on our family if she can."

My mother's jibe at Silk, Satin and Scandals would normally have delighted me, but I hardly registered what she was saying. I was emotionally scarred and scared, and Stephen's embrace had given me the sanctuary I needed to finally let go.

He took me by the arm and turned to the family. He told them not to worry if we weren't back in time for the first act, and then he escorted me out of the box and downstairs to the club.

The Metropolitan Opera Club was a private men's supper club founded in 1893. My father was one of its founding members, along with my uncle and Stanford White, who had designed the miniature stage where vaudeville was performed while members dined after the opera.

I'd been there many times with my family, but it had always been crowded. Now our footsteps echoed in the cavernous space. Stephen ushered me to an empty table set with gleaming crystal and silver.

He pulled out a seat for me. "Stay here," he said. "I'll be right back." He went off through the double doors to the kitchen. He was gone for only two or three minutes and returned with a chilled, opened bottle of champagne along with two glasses.

He poured the pale yellow wine and handed me a coupe.

"Take a sip," he said.

I obeyed.

"And another."

I obeyed again.

"Now, I want you to tell me what is going on. If you are writing an article, why were you at Cartier's dressed as yourself so late at night?"

"I had been at the shop for a repair during business hours and left my satchel there. So I went back for it. That's why I was there when the thieves arrived. I was simply in the wrong place at the wrong time."

Stephen knew me well enough to know that I was still holding back.

"All right, but why were you there earlier?"

"I'm writing an article about the superstition surrounding the Hope Diamond, but I'm working undercover—as Vera Garland, a lady of independent means interested in purchasing the legend."

"And why were you at the hospital today? Were you visiting the jeweler the article mentioned? Is he still in a coma?"

I nodded and felt my eyes fill with fresh tears. I didn't trust my voice to explain further.

"Do you have feelings for this man?"

"Yes, we've spent some time with each other."

"In a romantic way, you mean?"

I nodded.

"Oh, Vera, I'm so sorry. No wonder you are distraught."

A fresh sob broke free. Stephen moved his chair closer to mine and put his arm around me.

"What do the doctors say?"

"They say all we can do is wait."

"Do you want to leave and go back to the hospital now?"

"No lectures about falling in love with the help?" I asked, more bitterly than I intended.

"You insult me, Vera. That might be your mother's style, but you know I couldn't care less about his social standing. As long as he is a good man who treats you as well as you deserve."

A jeweler, I thought, but yes, a good man.

"What is it?"

"What do you mean?" I asked.

"Is there something you aren't telling me?"

There's so much I haven't told you, a guilty voice echoed inside my head. I hadn't shared my plan to entrap Oxley. Or my thoughts about what really happened the night of the robbery. But how could I? I didn't want him to become overprotective and lawyerlike and try to stop me for any one of a dozen reasons I knew would all be valid.

Stephen and I stayed at the club drinking champagne through the first act. He'd stepped

351

into my father's role, asking me more questions. I almost laughed when I realized he wanted to be sure Jacob wasn't taking advantage of me.

We joined the rest of the family at intermission. Letty and Jack had more questions about the robbery and the subsequent recovery of the stone. I told them we could talk about it at dinner and complimented my sister on her amethyst anniversary earrings. As we chatted on, I continued to take notice of who came and went, but at the same time, my mind kept returning to the man I'd taken as a lover, who was lying in a hospital bed only a few dozen blocks away, sleeping as deeply as one could and still be alive.

And what if he died? Died trying to protect me from a thief with a gun? Died before I ever felt his arms around me again? Before we ever spoke of what had occurred between us? Before—

Aunt Carrie approached and pulled me into a tight embrace.

"I told you that stone was bad luck," she whispered. "You tried it on, didn't you? Look what happened to you. And what happened to that jeweler? Evalyn said it's all so exciting she's even more determined to buy it. Even after she's read all the news. What am I going to do? You're not still thinking about buying it, are you? I want someone to so Evalyn can't. But I wouldn't want you to take a risk like that." She stepped back and began wringing her hands.

"I'm not sure what I'm going to do," I told her.

I had to keep the charade going that I was a potential buyer to get the information that still eluded me.

"I don't believe what happened was bad luck, Aunt Carrie. If it had been, I'd be dead, not standing here talking to you. It's a valuable stone, so of course, people are going to try to steal it—"

Her eyes filled with tears. "Exactly. And if Evalyn buys it, they will try to steal it from her. Vera, you have to help me. I wish I could persuade Mr. Cartier to make a paste copy of the stupid stone and give her that. You said you were going to talk to him. Did you? Tell him I'll double what he's asking."

Suddenly, I had an idea. I tucked it away in my mind as I finished chatting with Aunt Carrie. When the bell rang to signal the end of intermission, I kissed her good-bye and returned to our box.

At dinner, in the now-crowded club room, my mother asked me what kind of repair had brought me to Cartier's shop. I told her and showed her the pearls and the new clasp.

She admonished me for having treated her gift so carelessly, and I bit the inside of my cheek to keep from talking back to her. It was my sister's night, and I didn't want to ruin it by fighting with my mother.

I missed my father so much that evening. For so many reasons. If he were alive, I would have told him the truth about what I was planning. My confidant, who knew all my secrets, might have even helped me plot the perfect undoing of Mr. Oxley. My father had been so clever. I remembered several times when he exposed merchants who sold him inferior goods.

As one of the founding club members, his portrait hung in the dining room. It was one my mother liked but which he and I had thought made him look too stiff and senatorial. My father was full of life. He hated to sit still and was always jumping up to inspect something, a new bolt of fabric, a perfume, a piece of jewelry. I remembered him in Garland's, going from counter to counter every morning, greeting every single member of the staff by name, asking after sick mothers, pregnant wives, and children in school. He treated everyone who worked for him like family, and they, in turn, had so much respect for him.

My brother-in-law, now sitting in my father's place at the head of the table, saw me looking at the portrait. "I miss him, too," he said. "It's still so hard stepping into his shoes."

"Jack, he didn't want you to step into his shoes," I said. "I heard him tell you he wanted you to go down to the men's shoe department and pick out a pair of new shoes that fit you. He expected you to find your own style. And he knew that whatever it was, Garland's would accept it."

Jack gave me a grateful look. "Thank you for remembering that. I can always count on you," he said.

"Well, I can't," my mother said bitterly. "So I'm glad someone can."

"What else is wrong?" I asked her.

"I heard you turned down the opportunity to chair the ladies auxiliary luncheon when I specifically suggested to Marjorie Grant that you would be happy to do it."

"Which you did without asking me."

"Vera, you have nothing else to do, no reason not to accept."

"I do, in fact, have something else to do. I told you I've gone back to work."

"So you said. At the newspaper?"

"No, I'm working freelance. The article about the robbery was a one-off. I'm working on a longer piece for a magazine."

"And you're incognito again," Letty said. "I'm always wishing I might run into you and see you in action. But I never do. Can't we arrange a rendezvous?" Her eyes lit up. "Then I can tell all my friends I met—"

"Shh," I said, before she spoke my pseudonym out loud in public.

Our mother shot her an angry look. "Must you glorify what she does?"

"What she does is admirable, Mother."

"What she does debases this family."

"It's been a decade, and no one even knows Vee Swann is part of this family. Don't be ridiculous," I said, *sotto voce* but in an angry hiss.

"It is enough that your sister and brother-in-law and cousin know. That I know and your father knew."

I burst out laughing. "Father? Don't you dare suggest that he had any problem with what I did. He did nothing but encourage me, and you know it."

She sighed and turned to look for a waiter, raising her hand and signaling the maître d' that we were done with the main course and ready for dessert. Floating Island soon arrived, and we were quiet as it was served.

"Your situation is my fault," my mother said morosely.

"Not this again," Letty said, knowing, as I did, where this was going. She motioned to the wine carafe, and I nodded. She wanted me to prevent my mother from having any more wine. My mother must have had another glass of burgundy when no one noticed.

"No one failed me, Mother. I have the life I want," I said by rote. I had been telling her the same thing for the last eight years, ever since I ended my relationship with Max.

"You say that, but you don't know the life you are missing, and—"

"Mother, tonight is my anniversary, and Jack and I want to enjoy this supper. Not have you and Vera end up in another squabble," Letty cut in.

"With my example of how rewarding being a wife and mother is, it confounds me that you wouldn't want what I have," Mother said, ignoring Letty's request.

"If you had been a saint as a mother and a wife, it still would not have changed my mind. I'm missing some essential womanly characteristic. I don't have the constitution to run a household and have children and see to a man's needs. I thrive on being on my own and working and trying to effect some change. There's so much that is unfair—"

"Yes, I know," she said. "It's always been that. It's not fair that I can't wear pants, it's not fair that I can't play baseball, it's not fair that I have to have long hair, it's not fair that I can't go to school at Andover and study with Stephen. I heard it all."

Letty had had enough. "We've all heard it. We've all heard this argument. Do we have to hear it all over again?"

Jack agreed.

I got up. "I think I'll go."

My sister started to protest.

"No," I said. "It is late, and so far, we've

357

mostly had a lovely evening. I don't want to ruin any more of it with bickering. I'll see you later this week."

"Let me take you home," Stephen said.

"No, you stay. I made you miss the first act as it is."

I leaned down and kissed him on the cheek, and then my sister and then Jack, and finally bent to my mother, who sat stone-faced. She started to say something about my father and how he wouldn't have stood for me leaving, but I cut her off.

"Tell me what you want, but if you ever try to suggest that Father wouldn't approve of me again, I'll walk out and not come back. I mean it."

I saw her mouth fall open as I turned and left. It was one thing for her to express her constant disapproval. I'd learned not to care anymore. We were from different generations, and almost every friend I had who was a reporter had a similar problem with her parents about her life choice. But the one thing I wouldn't stand for was my mother suggesting how my father would feel.

I knew exactly how he would have felt. He was proud of me. But what I didn't know was how *I* felt about *his* choices. Hurt that he had to keep them secret. Distraught that he had died for them. Determined to defend them and avenge them and right the wrong that had been done to him and my uncle.

And so, still wearing my evening finery, I went to the hospital to spend another night by the bedside of the man who might be able to help me do exactly that.

CHAPTER 24

I was reading the newspaper the next morning in Jacob's room when I heard the question.

"Where am I?"

I rushed to his bed.

"Oh, Jacob, thank God."

"Where am I?"

"The hospital."

He looked at me. Closed his eyes. And then opened them again.

"Do you know who I am?" I asked.

"Of course. Why wouldn't I?"

"The doctors said you might have some memory loss." I stood up. "Don't move. Let me get them."

I started for the door, a sob escaping my mouth.

"Vera?"

I turned.

"Why are you crying?"

"It's been seven days."

"I've been here for *seven days?*"

"Yes, unconscious. We didn't know—" I broke off and went back to the bed, sat by his side, and took his hands. "I was so frightened," I whispered. "This was all because of me."

"What was?" he asked.

"Do you remember the break-in at the shop?"

He looked confused at first, but seconds later, I watched his eyes widen as he remembered.

"Yes, yes, the break-in. But that wasn't your fault. It shouldn't have happened at all. You weren't supposed to be there."

I lifted his hand and kissed the top of it. "If I wasn't there, you wouldn't have needed to protect me and wouldn't have been hurt . . ."

He paused, thought. Then: "My head aches."

"I would expect it does. Let me go get the doctor."

"Wait, please. Just a minute more. Have you been here the whole time? I was dreaming—or thought I was dreaming, now I'm not sure—but I kept hearing your voice, as if you were on the other side of a waterfall, and I kept trying to swim through it to find you."

I smiled. "Yes, I did a lot of talking to you. The nurse suggested it, on the off chance you could hear me. She said it would be helpful."

"It was. So you *have* been here the whole time?"

"Of course not. But I stopped in as often as I could."

"Why?"

It was a good question. A logical question. We'd spent only a little time together and had made no pledges to each other. I wondered why I'd been so drawn to his bedside and insistent on spending almost every waking minute here.

Would I have done the same if it had been Mr. Cartier who'd protected me from harm? Was I there because I had taken Jacob as my lover or because I considered him a key figure in taking down Mr. Oxley? I had been lonely, and Jacob had touched me in a way no one had in a long time. And I was an intrepid reporter following a lead. I felt instantly guilty, because there would be nothing wrong with any of those reasons coming into play if Jacob knew the whole truth. If he knew that I cared for him. And that I was a reporter. And that I needed his help and why.

But he didn't even know the half of it. I was hiding so very much from him.

I stood and went out into the hallway, found the nurse, and gave her the news. Then I went back inside his room, and while we waited for the doctor, I told him that the Hope had been stolen but recovered.

"Wait, are you saying the diamond was taken?" he asked.

"Yes."

The doctors had told me and Mr. Cartier that Jacob might be confused when he regained consciousness, so I didn't question his odd response. It didn't occur to me to wonder if he was lying.

"The thieves who took the stone sent Mr. Cartier a ransom note the following day. He paid it, and now the stone is back on Fifth

Avenue with Pinkerton men guarding it night and day."

Jacob looked as if he was still processing this information when the nurse arrived a few seconds later. She made quite a fuss about Jacob regaining consciousness and informed me that the doctors would be keeping the patient busy with tests for quite a while. "So now would be a good time for you to go home, Miss Garland," she told me.

"I think I will," I told her. "I could use a hot bath and a nap." I looked at Jacob. "I'll call Mr. Cartier and let him know you're all right. He's been worried sick about you, blaming himself as much as I have been blaming myself. We nearly argued over which of us was more to blame. He's been here whenever he could spare time from the shop."

"Will you—" Jacob started to say, and then broke off.

"Come back?" I asked.

"I don't want to impose."

I laughed. "You saved my life, Jacob. I'll be back later this afternoon."

"Vera," he said when I reached the door.

I turned.

"If I had to save someone's life, I'm very glad it was yours."

The next morning, Mr. Cartier and I were visiting when Dr. Lipskar was making his rounds. After a thorough examination, he gave Jacob the go-ahead to leave the hospital.

"Other than the scar on your forehead, there doesn't seem to be any damage," the doctor said.

"Despite being unconscious for so long?" Mr. Cartier asked.

"It's not usual. But Mr. Asher, you might very well suffer intermittent headaches. You should spend a couple of days resting up before you go back to work."

Mr. Cartier insisted that Jacob rest for the remainder of the week and not worry about the workshop.

And so, an hour later, ten days after Jacob had first been admitted, the three of us left the hospital together. Mr. Cartier's carriage was downstairs waiting, and we all got in. When the driver pulled up in front of Jacob's apartment, I offered to go upstairs with him to see what kind of foodstuffs he had and then go out and bring some things in.

Mr. Cartier said no, he would do that. I was, after all, a client. But I insisted.

"As a woman who keeps an apartment myself, I would bet I'm better equipped than you are in that capacity, Mr. Cartier. Don't you think?"

He laughed and said he did. "But I don't want you to be put out."

"For the man who saved my life?" I asked. *And who was my lover?* I thought.

Jacob's Greenwich Village building faced Washington Square Park. His second-floor, light-filled apartment consisted of a bedroom, a water closet, a kitchen, a parlor, and a dining room, which he'd converted into a workshop.

"Don't you work hard enough at Mr. Cartier's?" I asked as he gave me a tour.

"I do, but I have projects of my own as well."

"Can I see?"

"Maybe later."

"You're right. You need to get into bed, and I need to go get some groceries," I said.

"Are you always so efficient?"

"I am."

"Well, if I need to get into bed, I need company." The light I remembered but hadn't seen for days glinted in his eye.

"You need rest."

"Vera, come sit with me a minute." He sat down on the couch opposite the long work table.

I sat beside him. He took my hand and pulled me toward him. For a few moments, we just sat there together quietly, not speaking. I closed my eyes and felt relief flood through me. He really was all right. The worst of the ordeal was truly behind us.

With his fingers laced in mine, he said, "I am so sorry for what you've been through. And I can't thank you enough for your vigil at the hospital."

"You saved my life."

"You should never have been there."

He'd said that before. "I have questions about what happened," I said, finally willing to broach the subject.

"I would imagine."

"But I think I should go out and buy supplies first. We'll talk after."

He nodded.

"In the meantime, why don't you be a good patient and do as the doctor ordered? Rest."

I went into the kitchen and inspected the larder. It was so well stocked that for a moment, I just stared at it. There were rows of spices and staples, shelves of pots and pans. So different from any kitchen I'd ever kept. When I'd lived in Chelsea, I was never around at regular hours, because I spent so much time in the newsroom and uptown at my father's penthouse. Margery Tuttle brought in what she intended to cook and cleaned up afterward. Or I ordered up one meal at a time from the Birdcage. But I rarely went shopping for supplies. From what I could see, Jacob's kitchen had been stocked with fresh food, but the loaf of bread was rock hard. The lemons, oranges, and apples sitting in a bowl on the counter had shriveled. The jar of coffee beans beside the grinder would be fine, but the milk in the icebox had turned, and the water pan underneath it was full. Since Jacob had been in the hospital for more than a week, he'd obviously missed the ice delivery. I found moldy cheese and rancid butter.

"Where is the closest shop?"

I had walked from the kitchen back out into the parlor, but Jacob wasn't there. Hearing noises, I followed the sounds to the workshop. Jacob was leaning over a large box on his desk. As soon as I took a step into the room, he quickly closed it. I thought I heard the slight noise of turning a key in the lock.

What odd behavior, I thought.

"I'm sorry, what did you say?" Jacob asked as he stood up.

"Where is the closest shop?" I repeated the question.

"I really don't want you to go to any trouble," he said, turning around to face me. His hand was in his pocket now. "I can ask the superintendent's wife to run out."

Coming closer, I took in what he'd been fussing with—a medium-size box made of Moroccan leather with fine tooling on the top and sides, something old and precious.

"It's no trouble." I pointed to the box. "That's beautiful."

"It belonged to my father."

I remembered the story he'd told me about his father's death. "It must mean the world to you."

"It does."

There was an awkward silence while I waited for him to tell me more. But he didn't.

"The market?" I asked.

"Right, there's one just a block away on Bleecker . . ." He subtly moved me out of the room and toward the front hall. "And next door is a tea shop that sells sandwiches if you would rather not fuss with cooking."

"I think you deserve me fussing. You saved my life."

"You have to promise me one thing, or I won't let you back inside."

"What is that?"

"You're to stop mentioning that I saved your life. Anyone in that situation would have done what I did."

"I don't agree."

"Nonetheless. No more mentioning it."

"I'll think about it," I said, as I took my coat off the hook.

"No thinking about it. I won't let you back in unless you promise."

I moved in front of him, opened the front door, and stepped out.

"Vera?"

I turned.

"I *will* let you back in."

"I figured."

On the way to the store, I thought about how Jacob had so abruptly closed the lid on the box. He was obviously hiding something. His silent ways gave him a mysterious air that I wasn't sure I trusted. Yet I'd probably been drawn to him precisely for how enigmatic he was. I was always, much to my detriment, attracted to people who had secrets. Only those who lived boring lives were open books.

I found the grocer, baker, fish market, and butcher within two blocks, and I returned with two bags of food. I'd bought basics—eggs, bread, butter, milk, cream, potatoes, cheese, apples—and some surprises, including shrimp and oysters. Then I stopped in at the tea shop and picked up sandwiches and chocolate doughnuts.

Back in the apartment, Jacob took the packages from me, and we unpacked them in the kitchen. Since the ice wouldn't be delivered for another day, he said, we put the cold items on the window ledge—the November air would keep them fresh. The rest we put away in the cabinets.

Jacob took out plates for the sandwiches. I unwrapped them while he set the table in the corner with silverware, napkins, a pitcher of water, and two glasses.

"How long have you lived in this apartment?" I asked, once we were seated and had begun eating.

"Since arriving in America. Two years ago. I chose it for the neighborhood. I like that a lot of artists live here."

I'd been distracted by the box but remembered

then that there had been art supplies on the table in his workshop. "Do you paint?"

"Not really. I do sketches of my designs with pencils and gouache, but I don't consider that really painting."

"Do you have any of your designs here?"

"I do, and I'm going to guess your next question is to ask if you can see them. Am I right?" He laughed.

"I'm that predictable?"

"Well, your inquisitiveness knows no bounds. You ask so many questions it makes my head spin. It wasn't hard to guess what you were going to ask next. Are you always so curious?"

"When I was sixteen, my father had a brooch made for me, a question mark set with tiny diamonds."

Jacob laughed again. "Wear it the next time we meet. I'd love to see it."

"I will."

"Your father must have been a wonderful man."

I nodded, not trusting my voice to answer without cracking.

"What happens when you ask all those questions and get answers you don't like?"

"I try to keep an open mind. To focus rather on the discovery and where that will lead."

He cocked his head and stared at me for a moment. "You should be a reporter," he said. Then he reached for another sandwich.

Instead of responding, I took a bite of my own sandwich and chewed.

"Have you ever thought of working?" he asked.

No one had ever asked me that. The people I met as Vera Garland rarely considered that a woman might have a calling besides motherhood.

I didn't even consider telling him the truth, given how deep I was into the lie already. And I was good at lying. I'd been practicing for years. I'd lied my way through factories and tenements and abortion clinics, as well as other nefarious and hazardous places.

"I can't imagine working that hard or doing anything that dangerous," I said.

"No, I suppose that wouldn't be typical for one of your set."

I bristled and was suddenly sorry I'd answered the way I had. I sensed a bias that I hadn't guessed at before. But of course, he would have some resentment toward high society and the fashionable set. He had to deal with the likes of them all day long in the shop. And I was certain that he'd endured more than his share of rude treatment.

"Do you have a secret?" I asked him.

He cocked his head. "What an odd question to come out of the blue."

"Do you?"

"Yes," he said, without hesitation.

"Is it a big secret or a small one?"

He hesitated this time, then sighed, as if debating whether to tell me the truth. "I have one very large secret with many compartments."

"And have you ever told anyone?"

"No. In fact, I've never admitted to anyone but you that I even have a secret at all."

"Why did you tell me?"

"You asked."

"I doubt it is that simple," I said.

"No, Vera. It's not that simple. I don't think anything about you or me is simple, do you?"

"No, I don't suppose it is."

He took another bite of his sandwich and then a sip of water. "Your turn now. Do you have many secrets?" he asked.

I hesitated.

"Ah, so you don't like having the tables turned? You can ask all the questions you want but become shy as soon as I start asking them?"

I had a sudden memory and with it a realization. We were at the dinner table. My mother had asked my father something he hadn't wanted to answer. I could distinctly remember my mother saying almost the same thing to him that Jacob had said to me just now. That it was fine for him to ask questions but not her, and was that fair? My mother asking my father if it was fair. How had I forgotten that after all these years?

"Vera?"

"Yes, sorry. I just remembered something. My

father loved asking questions, too, but my mother complained that he didn't like to answer them. Odd that you would say the same thing about me."

"Not so odd. You probably take after him."

It struck me then to wonder if I had become a reporter to deflect the questions being asked of me.

"Well, I do take after him much more than I do my mother."

"So do you have any secrets? Answer me, or else you don't get a doughnut," he teased.

"Yes, then, I do. Quite a few."

"And have you ever shared them?"

"Yes, I have. My father knew all but one of them." I thought of my abortion. "But my mother and sister only know one."

"Cryptic . . . and interesting."

"My turn for another question. Have you told many lies?"

He paused, as if he were figuring out how to answer. "Yes, I suppose I have, but I hardly think that's very unusual. Don't you think in the course of a life one does? Many of them are kind. For instance, what am I supposed to say when a client asks, 'Do you think these earrings flatter me?' Or 'Do you think I'm too old for these pearls?' "

"Are there any pearls a woman is too old for?"

Jacob laughed. "I supposed that wasn't the best example."

373

"What are other types of acceptable lies?"

"Well, there are the lies you tell yourself when dealing with various situations. Telling yourself that someone isn't worth bothering with, even though you know in your heart they are, but maybe they've hurt you and you can't get past it. Convincing yourself that sometimes it's OK to do the wrong thing if it's for the right reason. Or the kind of lie that gets you through dark nights, telling yourself that there is nothing to fear when you know there is."

I was silent for a moment. I knew those kinds of lies. All too well.

"What other kinds of lies are there?" I finally asked.

"Vera, where is this all going?"

"I'm curious, that's all."

"I think it's more than that. I think you are struggling with your secret and want to tell me but aren't sure you can trust me."

I shook my head. "I think the question is more likely if you can trust me."

"That is a damnable habit, to keep turning my questions back at me."

"I'm just full of damnable habits, or so my mother always tells me."

I took another bite of my sandwich. Jacob finished his second.

"I'm going to make some coffee to go with those doughnuts," he said. "And don't try to stop me. I saw your kitchen. I know which of us will make the better brew."

A few minutes later, he brought in a tray with the plate of doughnuts, two mugs of hot black coffee, a little pitcher of milk, and a pot of sugar. I watched him make his coffee sweet and very light. I drank mine black. Too many newsrooms ran out of milk and sugar over long nights, and I'd gotten used to going without.

"Now," I said when we finished eating, "you need to take a nap. The doctor was quite clear about that. At least for the rest of the week, you need to do nothing but eat and sleep, read novels, and let your body get over the shock of the attack."

I shivered without realizing it.

"What about you? Are you over the shock of the attack?"

"I don't think so. I couldn't get past it while you were lying there in that hospital bed, worried if you were ever . . ." I couldn't finish the thought.

"Tell you what: I'll take a nap if you take one with me. The nurse told me how much time you spent at the hospital. More than you told me. Every night, Vera?"

He took my hand and ran his thumb across my knuckles, sending shivers up my arm.

What was I doing? Jacob might be the key to unlocking the story I was chasing. What would he say if he knew I was pretending to be interested in purchasing jewelry, all so I could gather information about Cartier? And I was on the verge of getting the sordid facts I needed. But at the same time, I was honestly and truly attracted to Jacob. Not just because of who he was but because of who I was with him, and I could imagine spending more time with him. Much more time, and it had been so long since I'd thought that about any man.

Was I taking advantage of my attraction to him and risking it all for a story? Except it wasn't just a story. This was about my father's life. My uncle's life. It was about right and wrong.

"Come on," Jacob cajoled, as he took my hand and led me toward the bedroom. And I, responding to his touch, shut down my thoughts and followed.

He sat down on the edge of the bed and, still holding my hand, pulled me with him. He took off his shoes and then leaned down and took off mine. He put his arm around my shoulders and drew me back onto the pillows with him.

We were both still fully dressed, lying on top of the bed. He rolled toward me, got up on one elbow, looked down at me, and then with his forefinger traced the lines of my face—eyebrows, nose, cheekbones, chin, and finally my mouth. Leaning down, he pressed his lips against mine, softly, then more firmly.

All the questions still swirling around in my

mind came to roost like birds settling on the grass. As we undressed each other I forgot about my confusion and guilt, my duplicity and guile. I just wanted to feel all the sensations Jacob roused. I just wanted to revel in his touch, in his presence, in his scent, in his attention.

One kiss led to more. I leaned so far into him that we were pressed together without any space between us. I wasn't playing at anything with him. I was as attracted to him as to any man I'd ever met. I wanted him, the flesh and blood of him. I wanted the man who was touching me, and now undressing me, and now caressing me. But when he raised himself up and looked down at me, with his secret smile on his lips, as he lowered his naked body onto mine and slipped inside me and I felt the first shudder, I knew that I also wanted what he might be able to give me: his help, his secrets, and Mr. Cartier's.

And wasn't that part of what made being with him so desirable? So decadent and dangerous? This was far more complicated than just passion. Someone like Vera Garland, a member of the 400, was not supposed to mix and mingle with a Russian Jewish jeweler. Someone like Vee Swann, a female journalist trying to make her way in a male-dominated profession, was not supposed to enter into a personal relationship with a source. This was far worse than befriending a seven-year-old schoolgirl. I was on new ground, and it kept shifting beneath me.

But as Jacob moved inside me, I lost focus on my duplicity and ethics. Our two rhythms synchronized into one. Our breaths coming at the same time. Our hearts hitting the same beats.

I felt both lost and found. He was letting me float in the great wide-open space of sensation and then pulling me back. I was tethered to him by the places where our flesh touched, where he moved, where his fingers explored, where his tongue teased, where his heat warmed me, and where I absorbed his fire.

I'd never experienced anything at this level of feeling before. Was it because I had so recently faced my mortality? Was it because staring down that gun barrel had made me understand that no single moment in life should ever be taken for granted? Was it because this man I was with, this man who my mother would remind me was nothing but a working man, and a foreigner at that, had stepped in front of that gun and taken a blow for me? Almost died for me. For *me*.

Every single tingle and flutter and wave and throb I was experiencing was a gift. But none so great that if not for him I might be able to receive any of them. The enormity of that suddenly overwhelmed me. As I angled my hips to take him further and deeper, so that he could reach my core, I kept thinking that this man had saved me and was saving me again and again and again, and it became a song in my head as the explosions came, followed all too soon by my tears.

CHAPTER 25

We both fell asleep and woke several hours later, hungry once more. First for each other. And then for food. I made us scrambled eggs with cheese and toasted slices of bread, and Jacob made coffee. While we ate, he asked me not to leave but to stay with him for the night. I said I would. After we finished our supper, Jacob went back to sleep, and I went into the parlor, looking over his bookshelf to find something to read and entertain myself with.

I helped myself to a book called *Mr. Justice Raffles* by E. W. Hornung. I'd read some of the author's short stories a few years before, when a fellow reporter at the *World* had reviewed them, and remembered finding them easygoing and clever. Perfect for that evening.

Raffles was a "gentleman thief," as he referred to himself. A rakish, charming, and cunning man who never seemed to get caught—or get caught for long. There was something Sherlock Holmesian about Raffles, which was no surprise, because Hornung was Arthur Conan Doyle's brother-in-law. When the first Raffles story had been published, there was a lot of talk in the newsroom about the family connection. There was also quite a bit of speculation that Raffles and his sidekick were patterned after Oscar Wilde and his lover Lord Alfred Douglas. At the time, that hadn't held much meaning for me, but now it did.

As I read Raffles's first escapade and recognized the homosexual theme between Raffles and his younger friend Bunny Manders, I couldn't help but think about my father and the letter I'd read from Uncle Percy. I so wished that my father had confided in me and wondered, not for the first time, how unhappy he had been and how difficult a time of it he'd had being married to my mother. He was such an accomplished, generous, and creative man, who always seemed to enjoy life—food, beautiful things, the store he'd created, reveling in his grandchildren and my writing. Yet there was an entire other side to him that I'd never seen. Worse, never sensed. How perceptive could I have been not to be aware of it? What kind of reporter did that make me?

And with that question, the old doubts came back. I'd broken the cardinal rule of getting involved with my story about Charlotte and trying to swoop in like Lady Bountiful and help her. No, more than help her—save her, change her circumstances. It wasn't up to me to change the world. But to report on it so that the proper authorities could change it. So that popular opinion would change it. Just thinking about Charlotte, my back twinged. My forever reminder of the little girl I'd loved and lost.

And yet here I was again, involved with Jacob while chasing a story. Except he wasn't the subject of the story, I thought. And then I almost laughed out loud at the pathetic way I was trying to justify my actions.

I returned to the book, read another chapter. How very charming this character Raffles was. My father had been charming. Charisma hides quite a bit of darkness in people. My mother, for instance, was beautiful, accomplished, determined, and smart. But she wasn't charming. Perhaps charm was really just another kind of lie. A way to put on a false front to hide the reality underneath. Jacob was charming, too. Did he use charm to hide his broken, tragic past? Or something else?

I put the book down. Thinking about Jacob's past made me think about his secrets and the fancy leather box that he'd closed and locked without explanation earlier that day.

I rose and wandered into his workshop. I stood on the threshold, where I told myself not to go. To resist the temptation of snooping. I turned, retreated to the bedroom. I would get back into bed and go to sleep beside Jacob. But that wasn't what I wanted to do.

Jacob's jacket was hanging on the silent butler where he'd left it. I quietly lifted it and walked out of the bedroom with it on my arm. I shut the door behind me and walked down the hall and into the kitchen, where I hung the jacket on the back of a chair at the table in the corner where we'd eaten.

Yes, it appeared natural there. As if he'd taken it off and slung it around the chair back. If he came out now and looked at it, he probably wouldn't even remember that he had worn it into the bedroom and taken it off there.

Even as I sat down in that chair, I was telling myself I couldn't do what I was contemplating. Everything about it was wrong. I would be betraying a man who had done nothing but help me. Who cared for me. Whose bed I had sat beside for days and nights.

I wasn't going to give in. I couldn't intrude on his life this way. And yet I wanted to know. I had to know. I could no longer trust that what I saw was all that was there, and without searching, I would never discover Jacob's secrets.

But that wasn't the way to get them. Or was it?

I took a breath and then reached into the jacket pocket and pulled out the key that I'd seen him hide when I'd walked into the room. Inspecting it, I thought it resembled the one I'd found in my father's pocket. The coincidence unnerved me.

Holding it tightly in my hand, so tightly that it cut into the fleshy part of my palm, I got up and left the kitchen.

For the second time in less than a half hour, I stood in the doorway to his workshop. And then I stepped over the threshold and walked toward the worktable. Everything was put away so neatly. The shelves behind the table were filled with tools of various sizes. While I had no idea what all of them were for, I recognized files and pliers and metal cutters. To the right of the table was a tall, narrow cabinet with double doors.

I tried them. They were unlocked.

Inside were four shelves on the right. The top was filled with a vast assortment of rough-hewn, nearly translucent rocks in various shades of blue, green, and red. Some were uncolored. Most were the size of my fist. Some were more polished than others. I picked one up, held it to the light, and wondered if it was in fact glass, not a rock at all. But I couldn't tell.

The next three shelves were full of beakers and Bunsen burners and other scientific equipment. I wondered why a jeweler would need items like that. The bottom shelf was stuffed with sketch pads. I sat on the floor and picked out one of them at random. Inside, I found drawings of faceted stones, all meticulously rendered in pencil and watercolors. I put it back and noticed an old journal. I pulled it out and opened it to find pages of notes and formulas written in an unrecognizable script. It took me a few seconds to realize it was Cyrillic. The pages were dog-eared and often stained. The leather cover was well worn, with a tiny tear in the bottom right.

I put the journal and sketch pads back. On the left side of the cabinet was only one shelf, and on it sat the leather box that Jacob had closed so suddenly when I'd walked in on him. I put the key in the lock, turned it, and heard the small but distinct click I'd heard before.

I lifted the lid.

Inside were three rows of five compartments each, all lined in midnight-blue velvet. I sucked in my breath. Five of the fifteen compartments were filled with glittering diamonds.

One by one, I took them out, examining each. It was like holding magic in my hands. They were droplets of frozen light. Even with my untrained eye, I knew the chest contained extremely valuable treasure.

All the stones were larger than average but none as big as the Hope. Three were pure white. One was an emerald cut, two others were round. A fourth was pink and pear-shaped. The last was square. I held it up to the lamp and sent rainbows dancing on the wall as I turned the stone this way and that.

I had done quite a bit of research so far for the Cartier story, and all the facts I had gathered about diamonds were top of mind. But they were all just scientific explanations of how the earth's pressure had formed the gems over millennia. One of the articles I'd read posed the question, if glass were more precious than diamonds, would we revere glass and eschew diamonds? A crystal chandelier cast the same rainbows on the wall, after all. Was our obsession with gems simply about supply and demand? Or was it something more elemental?

"Vera?"

I turned. Jacob stood by the door, looking at the cabinet with an expression that was half horror, half anger.

"What are you doing?" he asked in a tone I'd never heard from him.

"I . . . I was curious."

"And that's enough of a reason for you to take it upon yourself to break into my personal effects?"

"I'm sorry."

Jacob strode over to me, took the diamond I was holding out of my hands, and put it back in the box. He slammed the cover shut.

"What the hell are you doing? For real, Vera. No lies."

I couldn't tell him the truth. Not yet, not like that.

"I was curious."

"And so you went searching in my things?"

I shrugged. "I probably shouldn't have, but why are you reacting like this?" I asked, hoping I could shift the conversation.

"That is of no concern to you."

I spread my arms out. "Jacob, what's going on? You don't just have a studio here but a whole laboratory. And a box of what look like priceless diamonds."

His face was a mask. He looked like the jeweler I had first met in Cartier's shop. Removed and distant, simply doing a job politely and with reserve. "I am thankful to you for staying with me at the hospital and for bringing me home and bringing in food. But I'm fine now. I think you should go."

"Not until I understand."

"Actually no. Now. There's nothing I wish you to understand."

"Won't you explain?"

"No, I won't."

I knew he didn't owe me an explanation, but that didn't stop me from wanting one.

"Are these your diamonds?"

"Please leave."

"And this equipment and the formulas? What do you do with them?"

He laughed sardonically. "This isn't a court of law, Miss Garland."

"Miss Garland, is it now? My, how formally you address your lovers once they get near your secrets."

Jacob's face remained impassive. I knew I'd made a terrible mistake invading the privacy of this very private man, but I couldn't bear the idea of him keeping secrets from me.

"My father had had secrets . . . you need to understand . . ." I tried to explain.

"That's irrelevant."

He sat down on the couch, looking as if all the fight had gone out of him, and put his head in his hands. I walked over and sat down next to him, surprised he allowed it.

"Oh, God, Vera," he said. "I wish you hadn't looked. I wish you had just stayed in bed with me. But now that you have . . ."

"What's wrong? What did I see?"

"I've managed for a long time without having to explain myself to anyone. And that's how I prefer it," he said, not really giving me an answer.

"That can't work with us."

He shook his head. "There is no us."

"Because I saw all this, or because you never let anyone in?"

"Why would you think that?"

"Because I'm resourceful and smart, and I can see from your things and the way the apartment is that you don't have guests. And because you are thirty-three with no wife. And because Mr. Cartier didn't know a single person to ask the nurses to notify about the accident. And there were no notes on your doorstep asking if you were all right or why you'd missed this dinner or that play. And because of the haunted look in your eyes that I see when you think I'm not looking."

He was silent for a moment.

"There are reasons I can't be with anyone. Why I don't have a wife."

"An illness?" I asked, not imagining what it might be.

"Nothing like that."

"What, then?"

"Can't it just be that I enjoy my solitude? That I do not wish for responsibilities? Maybe I want to stay open to moving around. If I had a wife in London, I couldn't have come here."

"Actually, you could have. You could have just brought her."

"Yes, but that might have made her unhappy. People have roots and families and friends, and not everyone wants to just pick up and move."

He was talking about someone specific.

"Did you have a girlfriend who wouldn't leave London?"

He laughed cruelly. "No, but I saw my father try to get my mother to move. It would have saved all our lives, but she was determined to stay in the town where she had been born. Where her family lived."

"And so because your mother was stubborn, you have sworn off all relationships?"

"I like my life."

He sounded so definitive that I felt sad.

"So are you going to have to kill me to silence me so I don't tell anyone about your stash of stones?" I joked, trying to lighten the moment.

"I might," he said.

I knew he was joking as well, but his voice didn't have the rakish tone it usually did.

"I am sorry," I said.

He nodded. "I know. And—" He broke off.

"What is it?"

"It's the damnedest thing," he said. "I actually want to tell you. And I've never wanted to tell a soul before."

"You can trust me," I said. But could he? I thought. What if he told me something that would make a better story?

"If you want to hear my secret, you have to give up one of yours."

"A bargain?"

"A trade."

I hesitated. There was one I *should* share. He deserved to know who I really was. Except telling him would ruin any chance I had of accomplishing what I was so determined to do. And then I realized there was another secret that only one other person in this world knew about. Another lover, no less.

"All right," I said. I would tell him the secret of my heart.

"You go first," he said.

"Years ago, I thought I was in love. I got pregnant, and I had an abortion."

It had been eight years. That little baby would have already been in school. But there was no baby. There was no child of mine and Maximilian Ritter's. And that was all right. It was as it should be. There was, instead, a career. But it still pained me to say the words. I'd never uttered them out loud before.

"I'm sorry," Jacob said in a low, compassionate voice. "Was the scoundrel already married?"

"Not at all." That was someone else, I thought but didn't say. "He wanted to marry me."

"But?"

"He tricked me into getting pregnant so he could marry me and collect an inheritance. And that's not the worst part. He had help tricking me. From my own mother."

"What do you mean?"

I told him the story.

He took my hand. "You must hate her," he said.

"For a while, I did, violently. I couldn't look at her. Or speak to her. For months. My father didn't know about the abortion, but he knew something was terribly wrong. I admitted only that she had interfered in my relationship in an extremely intrusive way. Eventually, my father helped me realize that she still was my mother." I shrugged. "And that she was acting out of her own warped desire to do the right thing. We have a problem in our family—doing the wrong thing but thinking it is for the right reason."

"We? You do it, too?"

I nodded, about to say something else, but that would have been too telling.

"Now your turn," I said to him.

"The diamonds in the case were stolen." He said it the way he might have said the milk had gone bad or that he needed to buy new towels.

"You stole them?"

"Four of them. One I traded to get back."

"What do you mean, 'get back'?"

"I told you my father and his father before him and his father before him were jewelers. And diamond dealers. Our family legacy was the stones they kept for themselves. Only the best of the best passed down from one generation to the next. The first stone in the collection was purchased in the 1700s. By the time my father inherited it, the collection was incalculably rare and valuable. But we didn't treasure it simply for its monetary worth. The stones were our heritage. Woven into our family stories. There were legends about the tragedies and triumphs that befell our ancestors in their quest for acquisitions. Each diamond meant something to us. Every one was a symbol of our family's commitment to the generations to come. The diamonds were part of us. I can't explain it better than that. And when the thugs came and killed my father and stole the stones, it was as if they stole my whole family. As if every one of my ancestors died all over again."

Jacob fell silent. I sensed he was not finished but that he needed a moment before he moved on.

"Our family heritage was gone in a mad, wild minute. They murdered my father, and they stole our soul. Hundreds of years of hard work and honesty and fairness meant nothing."

"I don't know what to say. That's horrible. But . . ." I pointed to the diamonds. "How did you get these, and if they were yours, why did you say they were stolen?"

"When it first happened, I was too shocked and then too sad to do anything but mourn. But in time, I became angry. About a year later, I was working in London at Mappin and Webb. One day, a client came in with a ring she needed reset. The diamond was so much like one that had belonged to my father that I was startled. She asked me how long it would take to repair, but I hadn't heard her. She had to ask again and was angry at me for that. She shopped there often, so everyone endured her, but she was a difficult woman, married to a wealthy, miserable member of Parliament, a well-known anti-Semite, who stood for everything I hated.

"I took the ring into the workroom and sat there, taking it apart, seething. Of course, there was no way to know absolutely, but I was certain this was one of ours. I knew each facet and nuance and color and shape of every one of the fifty diamond treasures my family owned. I had no doubt. I hadn't thought about it before, but of course, whoever had taken them from my father would eventually sell them, and they'd start showing up on the market. I wanted that stone the way I never had wanted anything before."

"And so you just took it?"

"I couldn't just take it."

"What did you do?"

"First, I did some research into the history of the ring and found out when it had been made and where the diamond had been originally purchased. It all matched up to being part of my family's property."

"And then?"

"I got busy making a paste copy of the stone using my grandfather's formula. He'd taught me how. Not for nefarious reasons, but often we used it to create less expensive pieces. Or for clients who wanted copies of their own pieces to wear while they kept the real ones safe. And then there were the women my grandfather told me we always had to help, because they often had nowhere else to turn. Women who were so desperate they needed to sell their real jewels behind their husbands' backs in order to build a nest egg so they could run away."

There was a faraway look in his eye.

"What is it?"

"A story I'll tell you another time about my grandfather and one of those women." He resumed his explanation. "So I used the paste in our client's new setting, and I kept the diamond."

"You actually switched the stone?"

He nodded.

"No one knew?"

"No one knew."

"You got all of these that way?" I asked.

"All but one, which, as I said, I traded. When I left Russia as a boy, my father gave me a cache of diamonds to bring to England. In case I ever needed money, I could sell them. My father wasn't prescient, but he was wise. There had been problems for Jews in Russia before. He knew there would be again. The diamonds were my insurance. I never needed them, and their value increased over the years. I traded three of them for the pink diamond in the chest."

I sat there, stunned.

"So all five were from your family's collection?"

"As far as I can tell, yes. I've come across others that looked right at first, but when I researched them, their provenance didn't match up. I made up some rules along the way as well. I would only take a stone from someone who could afford to have it taken, and even if it was a stone that I thought belonged to us, I would never take one from a philanthropist who puts more good into the world than he takes out."

"How could you learn all that?"

"I read the papers, studied the society columns, read the scandal sheets."

I wondered if he read Silk, Satin and Scandals.

"I have other rules as well. No matter how certain I am that a stone belongs to us, I only allow myself one stone a year. I don't want to get discovered and lose my job."

"So other than the stone you traded for, you have been doing this for four years?"

"For twelve years. But I only found these five stones."

"So you are a . . ." It had never occurred to me, and I couldn't say the word.

He knew what I was going to say and said it for me. "A thief? Yes, I am."

"What if you get caught?"

"How?"

"One of the women could go to sell her stone, and another jeweler could tell her it was paste."

"Then she'd blame the jeweler she bought it from."

"Who would in turn blame you."

"Why me, specifically? How would the jeweler know when the switch had happened? How could the jeweler know the woman hadn't had it switched herself and was trying to pull a scam?" He shrugged. "I suppose, of course, it is possible, but remember, I always do my homework. None of our clients was in a financial situation where they would need to sell their jewels."

"That could always change."

"But in the future."

"So you take it upon yourself to be judge and jury and decide certain people deserve to have some of their riches taken from them."

"I suppose if you want to look at it that way, then yes, I do."

"Because what happened to you was unfair?"

"Not just to me. What happened to our *people* was unfair. The massacre was unfair. What happened to my grandfather, my father, and my mother was unfair. And not just unfair but criminal, tragic, horrific . . ."

I was sitting on a story that my fingers itched to write. An absolute scandal that had occurred in the most exclusive jewelry stores in the world, in Cartier's in New York and Mappin & Webb and Boodles in London. How many stores had he worked for in the last dozen years? Jacob Asher was a scoundrel. And if I wrote up his story, Oxley could blackmail Cartier with it—and Cartier would pay, wouldn't he? My mind was working too fast.

But I didn't want a story that Cartier would pay Oxley to keep quiet. That wouldn't accomplish my goal. Damn, this wasn't the story I needed. Cartier had to be willing to take the story public.

But there was another way to use this. I could get Jacob to create a paste copy of the Hope for my aunt Carrie and then somehow use that to get a story about the stone being fake, letting Mr. Cartier in on it.

There was only one problem. A problem I'd encountered before. Last time, it was a little girl I had fallen in love with. This time, it was a thief.

CHAPTER 26

After Jacob told me about his thievery, he forgave me for invading his privacy. With his rakish smile, he said it would be hypocritical to damn me for such a minor crime compared to his larceny. I think he was relieved to have finally unburdened himself. I stayed with him that night, and for the rest of the week, I spent most of my time at his apartment, helping him heal while he taught me to cook a few of his favorite dishes—chicken soup with matzo balls, carrots, and chunks of celery; an overcooked brisket that should have been tough considering how long it cooked but was instead so tender it didn't need a knife. There was a noodle casserole with eggs, raisins, and cheese that I told him I could eat for the rest of my life. I'd never enjoyed being in a kitchen before, but being in one with Jacob was different.

Everything with Jacob was different.

I was a wordsmith; he was a visual artist. Even the way he cut carrots and put them on a plate was beautiful. Every corner of every room was artfully designed, down to the way the crystal candle holders were arranged on the mantel.

Jacob reminded me of my father in that way. Like him, he was an aesthete who reveled in finding beauty in everything in his life. Jacob was also an expert in subjects I knew nothing about, which made our conversations fascinating. He had an encyclopedic knowledge of the history of the Jews, as well as an understanding of European politics that sometimes was hard for me to follow.

Often after supper, we would take glasses of brandy into the parlor, light the fire, and sit beside each other on the couch, and he would tell me a story about a missing tiara or a jewel theft or a gift that had ruined a marriage. He kept me enthralled recounting these tales about famous jewels and the men and women who owned them and wore them.

My interest didn't have anything to do with the article I was researching; rather, it was that Jacob was a natural storyteller who could spin a tale that combined both sweeping emotions and detailed descriptions.

After a little more than a week, on a Friday, I accompanied him for his follow-up visit with the doctor, who gave him the all clear to go back to work the following Monday. When we left the hospital, Jacob hailed a carriage and gave the driver an address different from his apartment.

"Where are we going?" I asked.

"You'll see," he said.

The carriage pulled up on Central Park West

in front of the Gothic castle, otherwise known as the Museum of Natural History.

"I haven't been here since I was a child. What are we doing?"

"You have so many questions about stones, and I don't have enough examples to really show you. So . . ." He opened his arms, indicating the building.

He took my hand, and we walked up the imposing stairs and into the great hall. Without having to ask for directions, he led me down one corridor, through several galleries of dioramas of preserved animals and birds in recreations of their natural habitats, until finally we reached our destination, the department of mineralogy.

"This gem collection here is a combination of donations from Tiffany and Company, Bement, and J. P. Morgan. I first saw some of these pieces in 1889 in the America section of the Paris Exhibition. It won two golden awards and was one of the highlights of the fair. There were important specimens of all kinds of stones, but especially noteworthy were the sapphires, topazes, beryls, tourmalines, and garnets. Everyone, from the public to important scholars and lapidaries, was amazed by the assemblage. Mr. Morgan paid one hundred thousand dollars for the entire collection and donated it to the museum. He also donated the Bement collection of gems, which he'd already owned. Altogether, the gifts consisted of more than two thousand gems, two thousand pearls, and twelve thousand mineral samples. Other donations and purchases have made this the largest collection of its size in any museum."

We were the only visitors at the exhibit, so we had the hall to ourselves. I watched Jacob's face as he described the properties of the different stones and explained how they were mined, as well as the methods used for cutting and polishing. We spent a long time in front of the diamond exhibit, which had examples of gems in various states, from rough to a fully faceted and polished gem.

"This is what they look like when they are found in the mine." He pointed to an unimpressive rough. "Michelangelo once said that when he looked at a piece of marble, he could see the figure deep inside and that his job was to take away the stone hiding it. A gem cutter feels the same way."

He pointed to each example in the case, explaining the processes involved at every step, finishing with what it took to create the final, polished gem.

We moved on to the next case. "These look like different kinds of stones, but they're all colored diamonds." One by one, he explained the rarity of each. "And then there are blue diamonds," he said, pointing. "These are excellent examples, but none, I think, has the magical lavender cast of the Hope."

"How difficult would it be to make a paste copy with that same hue?" I asked.

"Very difficult."

"But it could be done?"

He turned to me. "Why are you asking?"

"To find out if it would be possible for you to make a copy of the Hope Diamond."

"Why would I do that?"

"To help out a friend of mine."

"You're going to have to be more explicit than that."

I took a deep breath. "You know one of the people who wants to buy the stone is Evalyn Walsh McLean."

"I am not supposed to talk about our clients."

"OK, but I know she is interested. Our families are friends. Evalyn's mother is like an aunt to me. She's very worried about her daughter buying something with so much bad luck attached to it."

"That I can understand."

"So I had this crazy idea. You could make a copy and switch it with the real diamond, which Mrs. Walsh will take. Evalyn will get the paste copy. Without knowing it, of course. Everyone would have what they want. Mr. Cartier will have sold the stone at the price he asked. Evalyn will own what she believes is the Hope. Mrs. Walsh will be able to sleep at night."

And, I thought, I could write up a story about Evalyn Walsh McLean owning a fake Hope Diamond and use that to tempt Mr. Oxley into blackmailing Mr. Cartier. I would make it a condition of doing the favor for Aunt Carrie that she would agree to go public if, in fact, Mr. Cartier insisted on it. That way, Mr. Cartier could call Mr. Oxley's bluff without any fear of having his reputation besmirched.

"Isn't Mrs. Walsh worried about having the Hope in her possession and tempting the bad luck herself?" Jacob asked.

"She'll keep it in a vault and not ever touch it. Wearing it is the only way to invite the bad luck, correct?"

"So Mr. Cartier says."

"Will you do it?" I asked.

Jacob didn't answer.

We walked past a display case of emeralds.

"These are interesting gems," Jacob said as he stopped. "Unlike diamonds, every stone has some type of inclusion visible to the naked eye. Instead of using the word *flaw,* dealers and jewelers use the expression *jardin*, which, as you probably know, is French for *garden*. Ancient Egyptians believed they were symbols of eternal youth. And according to legend, it was believed that putting an emerald under the tongue would protect against evil spirits and give some the gift of clairvoyance."

It wasn't lost on me that Jacob had chosen not to give me an answer regarding the Hope. Somehow I had to convince him. While I hadn't worked out all the details, I knew the first step in my success was putting a fake Hope Diamond into play.

"Can you make paste emeralds?" I asked.

"Yes, but they are more difficult to create than diamonds. All the colored stones are. But Vera, please don't ask me questions like these in public."

"All right, I'm sorry."

We walked over to another case, and Jacob began lecturing on topaz.

"Actually," I interrupted, "I admire your pluck. You must have nerves of steel to do what you do."

"No, what I have is an amplified sense of injustice."

"I share that," I said.

"What do you do about it?" he asked in a tone that was almost judgmental.

"My family and I support several charities. I've told you about the ones my father founded," I snapped back defensively. It wasn't the answer I wanted to give him, but it was all I could say.

He didn't respond. Was he thinking that wasn't enough? I certainly wouldn't have been impressed by a wealthy socialite giving away money in between teas, galas, operas, and summers in Newport.

"I care very much about changing the world," I added.

"I suppose caring is the first step."

"Yes, it is."

"But you could get more involved," he suggested.

I wanted to tell him just how involved I was. But to do that, I would have to tell him that I had been lying to him all along. And that even when he had shared his secret with me, I still had held on tightly to the one I had that really mattered.

"This is one of my favorite places to come when I'm upset," Jacob said. "The rocks are ageless. Scientists can't even guess how old some of them are. Yet we mortals think we are all so important and powerful. We think we matter. Have you ever considered that we are not even grains of sand in the history of who has come before us and who will come after? Our time here is not even a fraction of a fraction of how long these rocks and crystals have existed on earth. I think I love gemstones most because of their timeless grandeur. They put my life in perspective. They make me realize how petty I am. How petty we all are . . ." He paused.

Jacob was staring into a star sapphire. As I examined its depths, I thought about what he'd said. To Jacob, gems weren't about money or fame or status. They were a connection to the earth. To history. He found peace studying and reflecting on these stones. They gave him a way to live through tragedy. A way I hadn't yet found and might never find.

"Your whole life has been about stones, hasn't it?" I asked.

He nodded. "I suppose it has."

"What will you do when you have filled all fifteen of those boxes?"

"I'll retire."

"From being a jeweler?"

"No, that's in my blood."

"From what, then?"

He winked.

"Ah. Turn to a life of virtue."

He laughed. "What is your whole life about?" he asked me.

"I don't know, exactly."

I did, of course. And this was the moment to tell him. And oh, how I wanted to. I yearned to tell him about Charlotte and the abortion clinic and the factories and the tenements and the articles that I and my sisters in arms had been writing since my hero Nellie Bly had herself interred in the mental institution to expose it. I desperately wanted to tell him about the risks I'd taken to help right injustices and watch his face as I listed the changes I'd helped bring about.

But I couldn't tell Jacob any of that now. It was too provocative for someone he thought didn't do much but who lived off her family fortune and dabbled in charitable work. I wanted to tell him what I did and who I was so he could be proud of me, and that realization surprised me. I cared what Jacob Asher thought of me. But it would have to wait until I accomplished what I had set out to do.

We were in front of a case filled with ruby crystals in various formations.

"I think you do know but don't want to tell me. Is that possible?"

"Why wouldn't I?"

"The thing about precious gems, Vera, is that they don't look precious or even special to the uninformed. Look at these." He took me by the arm and guided me over to another case, positioning me so that I was looking at a single, plain, gray, roundish rock.

"What do you see?" he asked.

"A rock."

"Pretty?"

"Not particularly."

"Valuable?"

"Well, it is here."

"All right, Miss Smarty Pants, suppose it was in the park."

"No, not valuable."

"Now look," he said, moving me a few inches to the right so I could see a similar gray stone, but this one was cracked open, revealing an interior of royal purple crystals.

"It's a treasure trove of amethyst," he said.

"Now look at this." He pointed to a dark gray rock that I would never notice if it were in the woods.

"What gems do you see in its surface?" he asked.

"I don't see any."

He pointed. "Look harder. Do you see those bluish bits there?"

"Yes?"

"Those will be priceless sapphires when they have been cut out and polished."

"So we're walking over millions of dollars of precious gems all the time? Not seeing any of them because we don't know how to look?"

"Exactly. But we can learn to see what others don't. Not just with rocks. But with people, too."

And the way he was looking at me made me shiver. I just couldn't tell if it was with fear, or longing, or a bit of both.

CHAPTER 27

Jacob and I had dinner together that night. Afterward, I told him I was going to attend to some family matters. But that wasn't true. I left him so I could go home, change into Vee's clothes, and then attend a meeting at the Woman's Press Club. Even though our previous march had resulted in a lot of coverage, Betty's editor hadn't dropped his suit. We were there to organize the next protest, to be held three days hence, on a Saturday. The hope was that if we kept up our marches and made more noise and reached more women each time, we could bring about change.

"We need to alert the rest of the press corps in advance for this one and get coverage before, during, and after the march," Martha insisted, "and not just from female journalists from our own ranks. As much as I hate to say it, we need the gravitas of newsmen writing about this."

Despite knowing that was true, it irked us, and we sat for the next half hour discussing the pros and cons of giving up some of our exclusives to get broader coverage.

In the end, we decided to alert our male counterparts. If we were heckled again, all the papers would be there with both a participating reporter and one watching from the sidelines. It ensured that our story would be told in full this time, with no one able to dismiss the articles as "sob sister" laments.

We also decided that this time, we'd march through a residential neighborhood instead of a business district. A vote was taken, and Greenwich Village won as the destination. We'd start at Grace Church on Broadway and work our way south and west, culminating with a rally in Washington Square Park. I was nervous at the idea of our march ending so near Jacob's apartment, but I had no good reason to talk the group out of it.

Besides, I reassured myself, I'd be in my Vee Swann disguise, and Jacob wouldn't even be home. He worked at Cartier's on Saturdays.

Fanny and Martha and I made plans to meet an hour before the one p.m. call time, have lunch in a tea shop near the church, then join our sisters with our placards and pamphlets.

That morning dawned chilly and gray, with clouds that threatened rain. By noon, the weather was no better. I dressed in Vee's modest clothes, donned my wig and glasses, and added a heavy coat, sturdy boots, and a warm scarf.

The march had been well publicized, which had its pluses but also created a problem we hadn't anticipated. We had even more hecklers marching alongside us.

By the time we reached the arch in Washington

Square Park, at least a hundred more women had joined us. Unfortunately, an equal number of men were marching against us. Their shouts drowned out ours, making it impossible for our message to be heard.

Inside the park, reporters were waiting for us. And so were more hecklers. As we reached the fountain, where we planned to stage the last part of the protest, the agitators started throwing pebbles and sticks at us, trying to get us to disperse.

As planned, we encircled the round fountain and linked arms, determined not to give in to the hecklers. But the men were just as determined, and a melee broke out when they physically approached us and pushed first one and then another and then another of us backward and toward the freezing-cold water in the fountain.

The police who'd been stationed in the park in advance of the rally ran forward, waving their billy clubs, breaking apart the skirmishes one by one. But there were more protesters and hecklers than police, and so the clashes continued. Some of the male reporters and gentlemen bystanders came to our rescue and tried to contain the troublemakers.

We all tried to fight back. Not everyone was strong enough. Fanny and Martha, working together, managed to punch one contentious bastard hard enough to send him sprawling.

I didn't fare as well. A man gave me a shove, and while I struggled to twist away from the water, I lost my balance and fell.

I was sitting on the ground, dazed, in terrible pain, aware that I was in danger of being trampled. I tried to stand, but my back wasn't cooperating. How was I going to get up? I tried to push forward onto my knees. But before I could make the effort, a woman near me fell right beside me, pushing me and upsetting my balance yet again.

And then two gloved hands reached down.

"Let me help you up," the man said as he grabbed my hands.

I didn't need to look. I recognized his voice instantly. But wasn't Jacob supposed to be at the store? Hadn't he told me that? Or had he? Perhaps I had just assumed that because the shop was open on Saturdays, he worked then.

I could tell that he didn't know who I was and kept my face angled down. Even though I didn't want to, I had no choice but to allow him to hoist me into a standing position.

"Are you hurt?" he asked.

I shook my head.

"Let's get you to a bench."

Just then, the wintry sun broke through the clouds and shone down on us. I put my hand up to my eyes to shield my vision, but the action strained my back, and it spasmed. I moaned in terrible pain and saw him start. Had he recognized my voice?

Before another moment passed, Fanny and Martha were there.

"We can take care of her, thank you very much!" Fanny shouted.

"I just wanted to help you with Miss—"

"Miss Vee Swann," Martha answered sharply before I could stop her. "But we don't actually need help from your kind."

"I wasn't one of the men who—"

But the two of them whisked me away, each with an arm around my waist, helping me walk with them toward the park exit.

"We'll get a carriage," Fanny said.

I turned back and searched the crowd looking for Jacob, but he had disappeared.

CHAPTER 28

The note came at five that afternoon, shortly after I arrived back home from the clinic where Fanny and Martha had taken me to make sure my back was all right. The doctor had assured me I hadn't done any serious damage but told me to rest and prescribed a hot bath with Epsom salts.

As soon as my friends had left, I discarded Vee's clothes, wig, and glasses, and I was in my robe, running the water, when the doorbell rang.

The store's concierge, Mr. Davis, was there with an envelope.

"He asked me to wait for a reply, Miss Garland."

I recognized the handwriting and opened the envelope with a trembling hand: *May I come up? We have things to discuss—Jacob.*

I told Mr. Davis to show the gentleman up and was waiting by the door when the elevator opened.

Jacob looked grim, and I knew instantly that he had, in fact, recognized me.

I let him in, and he followed me to the sitting room, where I poured us both whiskies without asking if he wanted one. I handed him the tumbler, and he drank half of it down in one gulp.

Then he rested the glass on the coffee table. The look on his face made me tie my dressing gown more tightly around my waist and raise my collar. One should always be dressed for one's trial.

"I told you my secret," he said in a monotone.

"Yes. But only because I stumbled on it."

"That's immaterial. I told you my secret. Why didn't you share yours with me?"

"I did share my secret. My most heartbreaking one."

"But you have two."

"You didn't ask me if I had two."

"Stop being so literal. You know exactly what I am asking you. Why did you share the one you did instead of the much more important one?"

"Important? That's your judgment. I shared the one that was the most private." It was a feeble excuse, and I knew it. So did he.

"How about we try for the real reason, Vera? Or should I call you Vee?"

I didn't respond.

"When you were snooping around in my apartment, were you doing it as Miss Vera Garland or the reporter Miss Vee Swann? Which one of you so willingly allowed me into your bed? And if it was Vee Swann, I have to ask what she wants with me."

I had done much more dangerous work as Vee Swann. This whole effort to write a story for Mr. Oxley with which to frame him had been so tame compared to previous assignments. And yet, other than the tenement story, none had ever become as complicated. I had thought I'd learned my lesson with Charlotte, but I hadn't at all.

"I invaded your privacy for a story, yes. But the truth is, I care about you. I even—"

"What story?" he interrupted, saving me, I thought later, from embarrassing myself.

"What story?" he repeated when I didn't answer. His face was pulled tight, and a vein throbbed in his forehead. I could feel his tension across the room. "A story about me?"

"Not about you, no."

"But you were in my apartment looking around."

"Yes, but . . ." I knew I had to tell him, and I also knew that it would probably be the end of everything. Of the story, of getting my revenge, of seeing him again. But be that as it may, I owed him an explanation, and so I explained.

Jacob sat listening, his hands clasped together, his eyes never leaving my face as I told him about my life—my two lives—and then about Charlotte and my father's illness and death and about finding the letter and learning about the blackmail and, finally, my plan.

When I finished, he stood up and went to the bar, took the decanter of whisky, and refilled his glass.

For a few moments, he just stood across the room, watching me, assessing me, relearning me.

"I feel as if I don't know you at all," he said.

"I can understand that."

He seemed to be weighing something in his mind.

"I am going to leave," he said.

I wanted to argue. To plead. Or cajole. But I did none of those things. "I understand that you are angry," I said. "Are you going to tell Mr. Cartier?"

"Is that all that matters to you? The story? Your plan?"

"No." I shook my head, fighting back tears. "But that doesn't mean that I am going to abandon—"

He interrupted. "Don't worry. Your secret is safe with me. I won't tell him who you are and what you are doing. Not because I am protecting you but because I am protecting myself. He would fire me in a minute if he knew that I had allowed myself to spend time with you. So go ahead and play whatever game you want—just don't ask me to play with you."

And with that, he turned his back to me, walked to the front door, opened it, and exited into the hall. Instead of waiting for the elevator, he took the stairs.

As I listened to his footsteps on the marble, something inside me panicked. I didn't want him to go.

I took off as fast as I could, running after him. Too distressed to be careful. I'd almost reached him at the bottom of the second flight when I slipped down four steps to the landing. Agonizing pains shot up my back. I tried to breathe through them as I waited for him to come back and save me for the second time that day. But I must not have made enough of a commotion when I fell, or he'd been farther down than I thought. Because I couldn't hear his footsteps anymore. I knew he was gone.

That was fine, I told myself. I didn't need his help. Not to get to my feet or to figure out what was going on at Cartier's. I would just sit there and wait until the spasms stopped. I knew I needed to be still and allow the muscles to relax. I remained there for the next half hour, hoping that Jacob had reached the street, or the next block, or had gotten three blocks away and changed his mind and would come back to find me and forgive me.

Finally, the pain receded. Carefully, tentatively, I pulled myself up by the banister, walked out to the landing, and rang the bell for the elevator to take me back to my tower.

CHAPTER 29

I spent the next day nursing my aches and pains. In an effort not to think about Jacob, I picked up *The Moonstone*, which I'd never finished reading. I read until late that night and went to sleep thinking there was something that had happened in the last few weeks that I'd missed.

I awoke the next morning with a start. I knew what it was. Maybe it didn't mean anything, but maybe it did. Either way, I wanted an answer.

On Monday afternoon, at closing time, I went to Cartier's. I waited in front of the building for twenty minutes before Jacob emerged just before six. He saw me but kept walking. I followed him for two blocks and onto a streetcar. I stood next to him. He wouldn't look at me, even though I kept my eyes locked on him. When he got off at Eighth Street and Fifth Avenue, I did, too. As he walked south on the avenue, I walked beside him. He sped up, I sped up. It started to rain. I ignored it. We reached his apartment building, and he ran ahead, reaching the front door with enough time to let himself in and then closed and locked it behind him.

I stood on the stoop, huddled under the narrow overhang, trying not to get wet. I was not going to leave.

After a half hour, he came downstairs and opened the door but stood blocking me from going inside.

"What do you want?"

"To apologize."

"You are something else, aren't you?"

"No. I want to apologize." I couldn't tell him another lie, even one of omission. "And ask you a question. Can I come up?"

"Why should I let you?"

"Because it is cold and wet out here. And because you and I are not that different. We only told each other some of our truths."

He opened the door wider. I walked in.

Without saying anything, he led the way up the stairs, and I followed. Inside his apartment, I sat on the couch in the living room, and he stood by the window.

"When does devotion turn into obsession, Jacob?"

He didn't respond.

"When does desire overtake reason? When does it become a compulsion? When do we lose our ability to see that we have become victims of our own passion for that object, that response, that solution, that end?"

He still didn't respond, but I could tell he was listening.

"You, me, Mr. Cartier, Evalyn Walsh McLean, we are all the same. All obsessed. You and I with revenge. Mr. Cartier with success. Evalyn with an object. How dare you suggest that what I did was different from what you do? Mr. Cartier treats you like a son, and you have a secret that is an abuse of his largesse. Yes, I started talking to you for my story. I even thought about charming you for my story. But something else happened between us. Something very real."

He was still quiet.

"There's more to what is going on with Mr. Cartier and that diamond, isn't there? There are other stories he hasn't told me or anyone else. You said something in the hospital when you came to that I didn't understand and have been mulling over ever since. You said, and this is exact, *You weren't supposed to be there.* All this time, I was thinking you meant it in the context of fate. But you don't believe in fate. You are a realist. You meant something quite different, didn't you?"

"What I said coming out of brain trauma doesn't let you off the hook for your duplicity."

I laughed, but it was an ugly laugh. One I'd learned listening to people lie and cheat to protect their greed or weaknesses over the years. I didn't want Jacob to be weak. I could accept his larceny, his mania for righting a personal wrong, but not weakness.

"You meant that I wasn't supposed to be at the store *that late*. That no one was supposed to be there to get in the way of yet another of Mr. Cartier's plans to imbue the diamond with more terrible luck. There was never supposed to be an actual robbery, was there? It was all staged. A robbery *attempt*. Just like in the book *The Moonstone*. He's using Wilkie Collins's plot to enliven the legends about the Hope. It's just more salesmanship. So what went wrong?"

Jacob didn't answer. He didn't have to. I'd figured it out. The novel had given me all the clues I'd needed.

"The men Mr. Cartier hired panicked and didn't know how to proceed when they saw me, right? The plan was for them to break in and threaten you, but you'd scare them off. Mr. Cartier would report the attempted robbery and the story about his brave jeweler who'd protected the Hope Diamond. More front-page headlines," I said sarcastically. "But something went wrong. Mr. Cartier never planned on his jeweler almost being killed in the process, and he didn't expect the stone to actually be stolen. Am I right?"

Jacob shrugged. "I suppose it doesn't matter anymore if you do know. Yes, you are right. The men Mr. Fontaine hired panicked when they saw you."

"But who took the stone? You didn't open the safe. You were with me the whole time in the showroom."

He didn't answer.

"Was someone else there?"

"Mr. Fontaine."

"He took the diamond?"

"Or thought he did," Jacob said with a sad smile.

"What are you talking about?"

"Who is asking me? Vee Swann?"

"I'm not trying to break another story. I'm trying to set up Mr. Oxley, remember?"

"Can I believe you?"

It was a fair question. Could he believe me? I'd lied to him so many times in so many ways. I didn't bother to answer.

"I guess it doesn't matter anymore. Mr. Fontaine is gone, and we'll never find him. It appears he was in the back, using the staged event as a distraction from a plan of his own. He stole what he thought was the Hope Diamond. But as it turns out, it was, in fact, a paste copy I'd made."

Jacob must have seen my eyes widen.

"Yes, there is already a paste version."

"So when I asked you at the museum . . ."

"I couldn't tell you. Mr. Cartier had me make it once he brought the stone here from Paris. The stone in the necklace he has let everyone try on is paste. He may exaggerate the bad-luck stories, but at the same time, he doesn't want to take any chances. Once a client expresses serious interest and makes a viable offer, Mr.

Cartier invites them to his home to show them the actual stone."

"Didn't Mr. Fontaine know that?" I asked.

"No. He never knew there was a copy. Only Mr. Cartier and I knew the real Hope was safe in Mr. Cartier's mansion."

"So Mr. Cartier paid a ransom for a fake stone?"

"Fake money for a fake stone."

"All to keep the story on the front pages?"

Jacob nodded.

"So now Mr. Cartier has the fake back?"

"Yes, and Mr. Fontaine—or whatever his real name is—is gone."

"Hadn't he worked in the jewelry business before? How was it possible he didn't know the stone in the vault wasn't real?"

"It's very difficult to tell one of my paste pieces with the naked eye. Especially for someone who isn't a trained gemologist. Mr. Fontaine was the manager, not a jeweler at all."

"How does a jeweler tell paste from the real thing?"

"A real diamond will drop to the bottom of a glass of water. Paste will float. And now you have your story," he said. "Oh, there's one more piece. The men who broke in? They were actors, not Hindus at all. Just three men wearing dark stage makeup and elaborate costumes."

"So the police have been looking for three men

who don't exist? The detective on the case had me go to the police station, Jacob. They had an Indian man they were questioning and wanted me to identify. What if I had? What if someone innocent is arrested?"

"But no one has been arrested. And if anyone is, I'll be the one who is asked to identify them, and I won't be able to."

I was having a hard time processing the enormity of the deception. "All this to get front-page stories."

"You can write your article about how everyone has been trying on a paste stone and that the robbery attempt was part of Mr. Cartier's outrageous theatrics used to build excitement around the Hope."

"Why have you told me all of this?"

"Because I want you to know you have everything there is to get out of me, so you don't come back trying to get more information. Because I don't want to be used any more than I already have been." He stood up, walked to the door, and opened it, inviting me to leave.

I rose. Gathered my purse and coat. Walking toward Jacob, I realized that I might be seeing him for the last time. Despite everything, I wanted to stop, reach out, take his hands, and beg him to forgive me. And have him ask the same of me in return. I wanted to smell his scent again and feel his arms embrace me. Instead, I walked past him and over the threshold and stepped out into the hallway. I reached the staircase and only then turned back.

"Good-bye." It took all of my will to keep my voice from cracking. *You can cry on the street,* I told myself. *You can weep in your pillows once all this is over.* "Thank you for giving me what I needed." I kept my voice even.

He sighed. "I hope you'll feel it was worth what it cost you when you realize that you can't save your uncle's life. And that you can't bring your father back."

CHAPTER 30

In the rarefied showrooms of Cartier's at 712 Fifth Avenue, the Hope Diamond sits in a safe behind one of the many paneled, silk-covered walls. The stone, according to Mr. Pierre Cartier, brings bad luck to anyone who owns it. But is that luck real or manufactured? Are the stories Mr. Cartier has been telling clients true? Or fabrications of his own making? And is the stone in the safe even real?

We took a certain novel written in 1868 by Wilkie Collins and examined it page by page against the stories circulating about the Hope Diamond and have found that there are several curious similarities. We've listed them below.

The question is, are the stories Mr. Cartier tells stolen from the book? Or are they real? And if they are real, then are there stories even worse that Mr. Cartier is not telling for fear he will not be able to sell the stone if the truth comes out?

Was the robbery at 712 Fifth Avenue legitimate? Was it staged? Was Jacob Asher, the jeweler attacked in that robbery, really injured, or was that staged as well?

And the greatest question of all: If the stone is the harbinger of terrible luck, why haven't any of the women who have tried it on come to any dire *fate? Or is the stone Mr. Cartier is showing to all of high society a paste copy?*

Mr. Asher, the head jeweler for the firm, is of Russian descent and is an expert in creating fabulous fakes in the form of paste. And we all know what paste is—most women have some of it in their jewel boxes. It's quite beautiful and reputable. It is, in fact, very valuable and has been since the 1700s. But it has been valued for what it is, not what it is not.

My article went on to outline what Mr. Cartier had done, including all the details of how the robbery was staged, how Mr. Cartier had been double-crossed by his store manager, and how in the end, Mr. Fontaine had been the one duped. But even with all the facts, I worried that the article wasn't strong enough.

I had been working on it nonstop for more than a week, and Mr. Oxley was pressuring me to turn it in.

Had I achieved my goal? Would Mr. Oxley decide it would be better used as blackmail rather than gossip for his magazine? Would Mr. Cartier call his bluff, knowing more press would only fuel the excitement about the stone? Only Mr. Cartier's refusing to pay the extortion fee would be the proof I required so I could write the real story I'd been going for all along—the one exposing Oxley's years of deception.

On the first Tuesday in December, I—or, rather, Vee Swann—personally delivered the article to Mr. Oxley. He thanked me and said he would read it and be in touch. Two days passed before I finally received a note from him, requesting a meeting.

I sat in the anteroom for twenty minutes after the appointed time before his secretary showed me into his office. Seeing me, Oxley fished around on his messy desk, finally finding my six-page manuscript under a pile of other papers. He patted it with his bearlike claw.

"Excellent work, Miss Swann. No less than what I expected, knowing your reputation," Mr. Oxley said. "This was worth waiting for."

"Thank you," I said, feeling a wave of relief.

"And this is all true?" he asked.

"All true."

"Does any other reporter have access to this information?"

"No," I said.

"No chance? It's absolutely a scoop?"

"Absolutely."

"How *did* you get this information?" he asked.

"I did what I told you I was going to do. I pretended to be a member of society interested in buying the stone. And in the process, I befriended Mr. Cartier's jeweler."

"Why would the jeweler confess all this to you?" Mr. Oxley asked with a lascivious smile.

I knew what he was thinking. The worst part

was that he wasn't all wrong. Except it hadn't been like that, I wanted to tell him. It hadn't all been for the story. There had been a true and honest connection between us. And I had destroyed it for what he was holding in his hands.

Of course, I didn't say any of that. "He didn't know who I was," was all I could manage.

"I'll be mailing you a check posthaste, Miss Swann."

"And when will you be running the story?"

Mr. Oxley looked down at the typed papers. I held my breath.

"Now, that I'm not certain of, but it's of no concern to you. Remember our contract. You can't shop this anywhere else, even if I choose not to run it."

"But if you're happy with it, why wouldn't you run it?" I was pushing my luck by asking, but wouldn't any reporter want to know?

"You leave that to me. And if you get any other story ideas, Miss Swann, my door is always open."

I was trembling as I stood up and was afraid that if he shook my hand, he'd notice. But he didn't offer a handshake. His secretary appeared to usher me out. I'd been dismissed.

I returned home via the tunnel. Upstairs, I changed out of my Vee Swann clothes and into my Vera Garland dress, shoes, and overcoat and took the elevator down to the street. Walking

431

from Fifty-seventh to Fifty-sixth Street, I hoped that Jacob would be at Mr. Cartier's and make an appearance while I was there. From Fifty-sixth to Fifty-fifth Street, I hoped he wouldn't. I changed my mind back and forth, working myself up into an agitated state by the time I arrived at 712 Fifth Avenue.

There were two Pinkerton guards standing sentry when the elevator opened onto the jeweler's floor. One asked me my name and went inside to get instructions while I waited in the hallway with the other guard.

Mr. Cartier himself came out to greet me.

"Mademoiselle Garland," he said, taking my hand and bowing over it. "Do come in."

I entered before him, and he shut the door behind us.

Mr. Fontaine was no longer there to take care of the amenities, but Mr. Cartier introduced me to the new manager, who took my coat.

"Can Mr. Marcus get you some coffee or tea? It's quite cold out today."

"No, I'm fine."

"How may I help you?" Mr. Cartier asked.

"First, I wanted you to know that I'm no longer interested in the Hope."

He nodded, not at all surprised.

"And I need to ask for your help."

In halting phrases, I explained to Mr. Cartier who I was, which shocked him. And what had happened and what I had done, which shocked him even more.

"I've brought you a copy of the article," I said. "I want you to know exactly what is in it so you have time to decide what you'll do when Mr. Oxley gives you his ultimatum. I'd like to ask you to allow me to be there when you meet with him—as Vee Swann, the reporter—so that I can write up what happens in order to expose Mr. Oxley for what he is."

I held out the article.

Mr. Cartier hesitated and then took the sheaf of papers from me. He stared down at the top sheet, reading the first few sentences. Then he looked up at me.

"I knew your father, Mademoiselle Garland. I was impressed with his business ethics. He would never have done anything like what you have done. Even for the right reason, some things are still wrong."

I nodded. "So you won't help me?"

"Do I have a choice?" he asked.

"You do. On your say-so, I'll go to Mr. Oxley and tell him that I had an attack of conscience and that the bulk of the story is false. I'll tell him I was so desperate to get back to my career that I let my imagination get the better of me to ensure he'd like the story."

"More lies," Mr. Cartier said.

I didn't know what to say.

"I'll let you know how I want to handle this by tomorrow," Mr. Cartier said. And then, still treating me deferentially like a client, he showed me out.

I walked home, saddened and depressed. I had thought I was trying to right a wrong. But to do it, I'd tricked people. I'd used the enemy's tactics to satisfy some longing for revenge that, as Jacob had said, would never be satisfied.

That evening, I was in the conservatory, pruning my father's orchids, which I had sorely neglected over these past weeks, despite my intention to take care of them. The doorbell rang, and when I answered it, the elevator operator handed me a note.

Mr. Cartier was downstairs, requesting an appointment.

When he came in, I took his hat and coat and brought him into the parlor. It had only been a week since Jacob had been here to bring our affair to an end. Mr. Cartier and I had a very different relationship, but I feared this visit would lead to yet another ending.

I offered him refreshments. He told me the last time he'd been here to see my father, he had offered him a fine Armagnac from France and asked if I had any of that.

I poured a snifter of the brandy for him and one for myself. The first sip would burn, I knew, but that seemed more than appropriate.

Mr. Cartier looked around the room before speaking. "As it turned out, that visit was a week before your father's death. He was still weak but told me he was certain he was going to get better. He was such an optimist, wasn't he?"

"Yes." I smiled, remembering how my father had tried to reassure me of the same thing in those last days.

"We talked about the retail business and shared ideas. Two merchants believing the future ahead of them was so very bright."

I nodded.

"Your father was my own father's client in our Paris shop, and also his good friend. And when I arrived here in New York, your father helped me immeasurably. Especially in the early days. I had a very influential client refuse to pay a very large bill, and quite honestly, I didn't know what to do. I was reluctant to go to the police, because I didn't want that kind of press so early upon opening my store. And I didn't know how far I could push the client without him spreading false rumors about us. I came to your father for advice, and he took care of everything. He'd had similar dealings with the same man over the years and knew exactly how to handle him. I can't imagine what it would have been like for our shop to be embroiled in scandal so soon after arriving in America."

Mr. Cartier stopped and took another sip of his

brandy. "We became good friends and had many conversations about commerce in America versus England and France. Lessons I never would have learned any other way. We talked strategy and marketing and customer relations. And we talked about theatrics."

"Yes?"

"We both did things differently, but in his own way, your father was a master at using theatrics, wasn't he?"

I thought about how my father set the scene in every nook and cranny of the store. How he used sales and specials to build excitement and anticipation. I nodded.

"I can't turn my back on you now that I know the story behind your father's last weeks and what this Mr. Oxley did to your uncle. I would rather you had handled this in quite a different way. But here we are . . . and when I needed your father, he was there for me. So I've decided that I will do what you've asked. I'm not sure your father would agree that you went about this the right way. But I am certain he would understand your motivation. As do I."

After all the weeks of effort to bring it about, I was surprised by how anticlimactic the moment was when I sat behind a screen in Mr. Cartier's office and listened to Mr. Oxley present the accusations I'd included in my article.

"It doesn't paint you in the best light, which is why I have an offer for you. A way for you to keep this piece from being printed and ruining your reputation."

Mr. Cartier held out his hand. "Can I at least read this damning piece before we discuss it any further?"

Mr. Oxley handed him the sheaf of papers. Even though I'd given it to Mr. Cartier three days before, he pretended to read it for the first time. He didn't rush but lingered, sometimes frowning, once smiling. Finally finished, he handed it back. "Not very flattering, is it?"

"Not at all," Mr. Oxley said. "In fact, it's quite unflattering. It shows how you manufactured an entire drama around the stone to get attention for it. How you lied. How you played on people's prejudice about men of a certain race. How you put people's lives in danger to perpetuate the farce. These are facts the public has every right to know."

"What I did is called merchandising," Mr. Cartier said.

"But our readers won't understand that. They will see you as a dishonest jeweler. Unless . . ." He paused and cleared his throat.

Mr. Cartier said, "Unless?"

"Well, there is another solution. If you were to consider advertising in the *Gotham Gazette*, say, to the tune of three thousand dollars a month for a year guaranteed, I would consider putting the story in my vault."

"You'd sell me the story in exchange for ads?"

"I wouldn't put it so crassly."

"How would you put it?"

"I would be extending a courtesy to one of our advertisers."

"Thirty-six thousand dollars is quite a lot of advertising."

"We have many other advertisers who pay that and more."

"What kinds of stories do you have on them?" Mr. Cartier asked.

"You insult me."

"Well, you have insulted me, Mr. Oxley. Your reporter, whoever she is, has no proof of any of this. For all she knows, the stone is truly a magnet for bad luck. That it is a dangerous, terrifying charm. After all, our jeweler did wind up in the hospital, unconscious for days. You call that good luck?"

"I believe my reporter and stand by her work," Mr. Oxley said, but didn't sound as sure as he had when he'd blustered in. Mr. Cartier's poise must have disarmed him.

"All right, then, Mr. Oxley. If you stand by her work and believe her story, then you'd have no problem touching the Hope yourself."

I held back a gasp of surprise. I'd had no idea Mr. Cartier was going to do any of this. I watched

438

through the crack in the panel of the coromandel screen as Mr. Cartier opened his desk drawer and withdrew a velvet tray with the kind of dramatic motion my father would have appreciated. He knew exactly where the light from the chandelier fell and positioned the Hope right beneath it. It was as if the stone had suddenly come alive, drinking up all the illumination in the room and leaving the two men in shadow.

"If you think I've invented all that bad luck and the legends about the stone are exaggerations and coincidences and scenes borrowed from a novel written more than forty years ago, then go ahead and touch it, Mr. Oxley."

"What I think is that you are lying to the public about the bad luck and everything else, and they have a right to know."

"Then touch the stone, Mr. Oxley."

With a grand gesture, Mr. Oxley reached out, plucked the Hope Diamond off the display, and held it in his hand.

"There. You see? Bad luck, phooey. Cartier, you've invented a whole lot of something based on nothing to drive up interest and the price for this rock, and you know it."

"You are more than entitled to believe what you will. Your article accuses me of lying. That is not the case, and I'm happy to refute that in the court of public opinion. Please, go ahead and print your story."

Mr. Oxley looked shocked. "What?"

Mr. Cartier pulled on a pair of white gloves. He rose and took the Hope from Mr. Oxley's hands.

"I won't pay your price. Print your story. If anything, it will just bring more attention to the stone. I will, of course, deny the article and stand by the legend. I'll be interviewed by other reporters, who will be all too happy to refute Mademoiselle—what was her name?" He thought for a moment. "Ah, yes, they will all be too happy to refute Mademoiselle Swann's suppositions. After all, no one can prove or disprove a theory like bad luck."

"What about the fact that you paid actors to dress as Indian robbers and staged the whole event?"

"There is no proof of any of that, so if you print that part of the story, I will sue you for slander. There are no witnesses, no suspects. There have been no charges and no trial. It's my word against Mademoiselle Swann's."

Mr. Oxley looked apoplectic. I guessed this didn't happen to him very often.

Standing, he grabbed the article and stormed out the door, slamming it behind him.

Mr. Cartier waited for a few moments, until we heard the outside door also slam, and then came around to where I was seated.

"Did you get your story?"

"Yes. I just hope you don't regret this when he publishes his."

"I don't think he will. But if he does, we have our story to follow on its heels. And ours is the one everyone will believe. Mr. Oxley has been terrorizing people for a long time, Mademoiselle Garland. Everyone will cheer when he's exposed."

"Why don't you think he'll publish?" I asked.

"Mr. Oxley is the type of man who doesn't mind threatening others but has a very thin skin when it comes to someone turning the tables on him. And we did that."

"I couldn't believe that you got him to touch the diamond . . . he looked terrified," I said. "I guess he does believe in bad luck, despite what he said."

"Ah, yes, about that. The last laugh is on him there as well," Mr. Cartier said. "That wasn't the Hope. That was Jacob Asher's paste replica."

CHAPTER 31

As I gathered up my things, I asked Mr. Cartier what he was planning to do with the paste version of the Hope.

"I'm going to give it to whoever buys the real one. I'm sure they'll appreciate having it for the same reason I had it made, as a decoy. So many of our clients request them. I'm going to have a hard time, though, finding someone new to produce them."

"Someone new?" I looked up from my satchel.

"Mr. Asher has left the shop and sworn off paste. It's a shame, too, because no one was as good as he was."

"What do you mean, he left the shop?"

"He's going back to Paris to work for a friend of mine, a Russian jeweler named Orlov. I didn't want him to go, but he said he was ready for a change. He's never really stayed in one place for long," Mr. Cartier said.

I walked home, feeling lost. Inside my apartment, the loss turned to anger that Jacob had left without telling me. And then the anger turned to loneliness. But I was used to that, wasn't I?

I considered this notion of fortune that I and so many others I knew had been fixated on for months. Was it good luck that Jacob had survived the robbery, or bad luck that he'd been hurt? Good luck that I had met him and had even those brief moments with him, or bad luck that I had failed so miserably?

I couldn't help but wonder if Mr. Oxley was thinking about luck that night, too. If he'd thought about it after leaving Mr. Cartier's office when his plan had backfired and mine had succeeded.

And I wondered about it again a week later.

I had gone to the *World* office to meet with Ronald Nevins and talk about going back to full-time reporting. I was ready to work for a real newspaper, not a rag like Oxley's. And as a return offering, I had the Oxley exposé in my bag. Mr. Cartier had given me carte blanche to publicly unmask the publisher's scheme using the jeweler's story as the main example.

As I walked through the *World*'s city room, I smelled the welcoming scent of fresh ink, stale cigarette smoke, and energy. I said hello to the reporters I passed, stopping to exchange a few words with those I knew best. I was thankful for their heartfelt welcomes. I hadn't realized until then how much I'd missed the camaraderie of being on staff during the long, sad months I'd been away.

I'd felt even more lost than usual for the last eight days since learning that Jacob had gone to Europe, but that morning, with each step

I took toward Mr. Nevins's office, the more it seemed I was on the right path and back where I belonged.

Mr. Nevins looked up when I knocked on the door, smiled, and waved me in. His desk was filled with papers, and he had a pencil in his hand.

"Have a seat, Miss Swann. Let me just finish proofing this story, and I'll be right with you."

As I sat down, I glanced at what he was working on. I could read the headline upside down.

Thelonious Oxley Dead at 72.

Chills went up and down my arms.

"Mr. Oxley is dead?" I blurted out. "But I have an article about him. I was bringing it to you. An exposé."

Mr. Nevins looked up. "He died of food poisoning last night. But that doesn't mean I don't want your story. I know it's wrong to speak ill of the dead, but he was a bastard." He held out his hand.

I opened my satchel, retrieved the piece I'd been working on, and handed it over to him.

"I think this will be a perfect follow-up to the story you're going to write covering his funeral," he said after skimming it. "Do you think you're up for that?" he asked with a discernible twinkle in his eye.

"Does that mean you're taking me back?"

"That was never in question, Miss Swann. So

tell me, do you have any ideas for what you'd like to tackle next?"

"More pieces on the garment industry's factory conditions for women workers. Too many establishments like the Triangle Shirtwaist Company are ignoring basic safety conditions and putting their employees at risk every day."

I managed to put Mr. Oxley's death out of my mind while Mr. Nevins and I worked out the details of my return to the newsroom. But after my meeting, as I walked back uptown, I couldn't help thinking about the magazine mogul. I kept picturing him the week before, grabbing the fake Hope Diamond with all that false bravado.

I wondered if he thought about that moment when he suddenly felt so ill he had to call for help. If he thought about it in the ambulance on the way to the hospital. How ironic that he'd died from food poisoning—the very cover-up for my own uncle's death. If I could have asked Thelonious Oxley anything while he lay dying, it would have been if he believed that touching the Hope Diamond had brought him the bad luck that had felled him. Or if it was something much more substantial than luck, if it was his own need for power, his own greed, and his own actions that had destroyed him.

CHAPTER 32

The morning of December 30, I woke up with dread. In a few hours, we would be interring my father in the mausoleum my mother had built. She'd requested that we all meet at her house for a light lunch at noon and then go to the cemetery together.

I took the train up from Manhattan and arrived on time. Letty and Jack and their children were already there, since they only lived next door. We sat at the dining-room table and feasted, as one always did at my mother's house. The meal began with salmon and mousseline sauce, followed by roast duck with new potatoes in their jackets. Rice custard with brandied raisins was served for dessert.

I didn't realize until I was halfway finished with the custard that everything she'd served had been one of my father's favorites dishes.

Over coffee, I noticed that my sister was wearing the amethyst earrings Jack had given her, the earrings I'd gone to look at with her in October the first time I met Jacob Asher.

Letty noticed me looking at them.

"Can you believe it? One of the stones came out last week, and I found the baby playing with it. He might have eaten it!"

We all responded with appropriate expressions of relief.

"I took it up to Mr. Cartier's, and that nice jeweler fixed it for me while I waited."

"Which nice jeweler?" Since Jacob was in Paris, I wondered who had replaced him. The way she'd said it suggested we knew him.

"Mr. Asher. He wasn't quite as charming, though."

"Charming? A jeweler? Doesn't he know his place?" our mother asked.

"Was he flirting with you?" Jack inquired right on my mother's heels.

Letty laughed at both of them. "He does," she told our mother. "And no," she said to Jack.

"Mr. Asher's there?" I asked.

Letty cocked her head. "Why wouldn't he be?"

I tried to control my voice, afraid it was shaking. "The last time I talked to Mr. Cartier, I thought he mentioned that Ja—Mr. Asher was going back to Europe. To Paris."

I couldn't think about this now. Not here. Not today. Not ever. That he hadn't left made it even more clear that there was nothing between us. He'd been here all this time and made no effort to contact me?

"Well, either way, he's back," Letty said, giving me a curious look.

"We should get ready to leave," my mother said, bringing an end to the conversation.

"Reverend Vestry is meeting us there at two."

My mother and I were going to ride to the cemetery in my father's automobile—a Johnson Empress Touring car. Since there wasn't room for all of us, my sister and Jack and their children would be driving in their own vehicle.

Just as we were leaving, Letty said the baby seemed feverish and that she wanted to drop him home with the nanny. She said she and Jack and the older boys would meet us there.

"Don't linger," Mother admonished her.

Snow began falling as we left the house, and I worried it would make the roads to Woodlawn treacherous, but we arrived without incident. Inside the elaborate gates, the chauffeur navigated through the heavily wooded cemetery, up and down various narrow roads until he eventually pulled to a stop.

As the driver stepped out of the car to open the door for my mother, I asked her if we shouldn't wait for the rest of the family.

"It's too cold to sit and wait in the car. Let's walk up and wait there. At least we can be inside."

My mother had not told me much about the mausoleum she was having built, nor had I asked her. I had assumed it would be an over-the-top extravaganza that she felt was befitting her stature. And when she'd informed all of us at dinner two weeks before that the construction

448

was complete and she'd arranged an interment service, I'd, of course, agreed to come, but with dread.

It had been bad enough burying my father the first time. But after the past year of shocks and tragedies, conflicts and loss, the last thing I wanted to do was visit my father's gravesite and feel all that grief anew.

The snow was still falling lightly as I got out of the car, but the sun had come out, and the whole world of Woodlawn appeared to be covered with diamond dust. Every tree and bush and tombstone and mausoleum glittered as if we were in a fairy tale instead of a place of death and mourning.

So it was with a lighter heart than I'd imagined that I walked with my mother up a pine-tree-lined path and came around a curve. I stopped. I couldn't understand what I was looking at. I recognized the building in front of me. I knew it intimately, but how could it be here? And then I realized what I was seeing.

The recently completed Garland mausoleum was a quarter-size replica of the store my uncle had designed and my father had turned into a fashion emporium like no other. Every single detail, from the bronze doors to the motif engraved on the granite, was identical to the Fifth Avenue building but miniaturized.

And there on the snow-covered path, I began to weep.

My mother, who rarely showed emotion, opened her purse and handed me her embroidered lace handkerchief and then took my arm and walked the rest of the pathway with me. When we reached the doors, she opened them, and we stepped inside together.

The interior of the sepulcher took my breath away. It was bathed in color—emerald, sapphire, ruby, and amethyst reflections streaming from the full-length stained-glass window on the east wall. I recognized the style from the windows in Garland's.

"Mr. Tiffany did this?" I asked.

"Yes. He's called it *The Voyage of Life*," my mother said.

The three-part window followed a river through a mountain to a valley and finally to a waterfall, where it pooled in a pond surrounded by my father's favorite flowers, irises and roses. The window was created in Tiffany's iconic favrile style, with layered pieces of colored glass—some opalescent, some iridescent—creating the depth and intensity he was known for. The watery reflections spilled across the floor, reaching our feet. I put out my hands and saw how the sunset hues in the windows turned them to gold.

"Father would have loved this," I said, as I took in the rest of the crypt.

There were four white marble benches, and where an altar might be was a sculpture of an angel, also in white marble, but, like my hands, she was bathed in the colors of the window, awash in the reflected blues of the river—the color metaphor for grief.

I took a step closer to her kneeling form. I knew her oversized wings were carved in stone, but they looked like gossamer feathers. I wanted to touch them, certain they would be feathery against my fingertips, but at the same time, I didn't want to destroy the illusion.

"Mr. Tiffany designed the whole crypt," my mother said. "And found the sculpture as well. There is room for thirty vaults, and here is where I'll be when my time comes. Right next to your father."

She had walked over to the south wall. I turned and looked where she was standing. Behind her was a shoulder-height marble scroll with two words and two dates engraved on its surface, along with roses and ivy relief work.

Granville Garland 1844–1909

Despite the fact that I had known of the plan to reinter my father here, it still gave me pause to realize that his mortal remains had been moved here in the last few days. I didn't believe in ghosts, but I wondered if his spirit knew. If he somehow sensed he was in this beautiful place now. My eye went to the space to the right of my father's vault. An identical scroll affixed to the wall was blank—awaiting my mother's fate.

451

Logically, my eye then traveled to the left of my father's vault, to another scroll.

This one was carved as well. I read the two words and two dates.

Percy Winthrop 1843–1909

I turned to my mother. "But Uncle Percy was entombed in your family crypt, where your parents and grandparents are," I said. "Why did you move him here? I don't understand."

"I moved my brother here to be beside your father. Where I know he would have wanted to be—" Her voice broke. For the first time in a very long time, maybe in forever, I saw my mother lose her composure.

I didn't say anything, but even though we had our differences, my mother knew her daughter and had read the astonished expression on my face.

"Yes, Vera, I knew. I always knew. I saw them together once, years and years ago, about two years after we were married, shortly after you were born. We were all at Newport. I'd gone to sleep and woke up around midnight. I didn't know why. The room was stuffy, and I went to the window to open it. They were swimming in the pool under an almost full moon. The water drops glistened on their skin. It was like a painting come to life. We were all so young then, and oh, they were both so beautiful. Like two Greek statues come to life. And then I saw Percy reach out and brush Granville's hair off his forehead. I could see how his fingertips lingered. And the way Granville leaned in to be closer to him. I'd never wondered before. Never guessed. But the way they were looking at each other, I suddenly understood so much. They didn't know that I was watching." Her voice was distant, as if she had actually returned to that time. Then, as if it was all too much to bear, she sat, suddenly, on one of the benches.

I hesitated and then sat beside her.

"Did Father know that you'd found out?"

"Not then. But I asked him after your sister was born . . ." She waved her hand as if she was dismissing the rest of that particular memory. "Your father loved you girls. He loved his family. He even loved me, in his fashion. And I made that enough."

Tears were rolling down her cheeks. I thought about reaching out to her, but that wasn't our way. I knew she would push me away. My mother never wanted comforting, she never offered it. She was like that stone angel, I thought. Alone in her grief. But I took the handkerchief she had given me and handed it to her.

"So I decided to have Percy taken out of the family crypt and put here next to your father. Percy on one side. Me on the other. How it was in life it will always be."

She rose, walked over to the wall, reached out,

and smoothed the marble slab with her brother's name engraved on it and then did the same thing to my father's. She turned back to me.

"That monster didn't win, you see? Even though he took time away from them, I've given it back. I've given them eternity. And I took it away from Oxley."

"Oxley?" I wasn't sure I was hearing her right. She nodded.

"You knew about the blackmail?"

"After your father's first heart attack, he told me about it and showed me Percy's letter. I was so overcome with rage. Your father swore he was going to get him back. We talked about it. Even plotted it together. Then Granville had his second attack.

"When you asked me about Percy that day at the Waldorf, I realized you knew. But it never occurred to me that you would really get involved, at least not against my wishes. And then I read that story in your gossip column about visiting Cartier and thinking about buying the Hope Diamond.

"Don't look at me like that. Of course, I knew you were writing that blasted column. But the idea of you buying something as extravagant as the Hope didn't make any sense. You're not indulgent like that. And when I asked you about it at dinner, you reacted strangely. I know you think you are so good at keeping secrets, Vera, but I can tell when you're hiding something. When you were there during that horrible robbery and wrote it up, I became convinced you were planning something. And I couldn't let you assume the responsibility . . . I couldn't, so . . ." She lifted her hands in a gesture of supplication.

"What did you do?" I asked, suddenly frightened of what she was going to say.

"I organized a lovely luncheon for a small group of twenty. As an appetizer, I served chilled oysters. On those wonderful Limoges oyster plates I bought in Paris. You know the ones? Each plate has six depressions. So everyone was served six. Oxley's first six were the same as everyone else's. Then I asked if anyone would like more. He was the only one who took another six. I'd known he would. We'd eaten with him before. He always took second helpings. No one else ever does. But he was such a pig. A greedy man in every way. He had a choice to take a second helping or not, you see. He could have been satisfied with one plate like everyone else. I left his fate up to him, and he made his choice . . . and so I myself got up and went into the kitchen and arranged his second plate of cold oysters. Mr. Oxley still had a choice. He didn't have to eat every single one. But he did. He sat at my table, and he slurped them down with his fat lips and fat fingers. I watched him pick up one after the other, barely taking a breath between them, except to wash one down with another gulp of your father's best Sancerre imported from France. He never sipped. That was too refined for him. I don't know which of those last six it was, but one had a perfect little pearl of cyanide tucked under its flesh. I'd arranged it all myself in the kitchen. And you know what, Vera? I slept so well that night, I didn't even dream."

I sat stunned. And then, as they always did, the questions started bubbling up. "But how did you know for sure he'd get that plate? What if someone else had asked for seconds?"

"But no one else ever does, dear."

"What if they had?"

"I would have said that on second thought, I'd realized my oysters tasted off and refused to serve any more, and then I would have come up with another plan. But as I expected, no one else did ask for seconds."

"Oh, my God . . . you—" I broke off, unable to truly process what she had told me.

She smiled at my shock. "Quite a story I've given you for the front page, isn't it? Society matron kills—"

"Stop!" I shouted at her. "Don't say it."

"Why?"

"If you don't say it, I won't hear it. I won't really know."

"And why can't you know? Because then you'd

have to write it up? Make an even bigger name for yourself?"

I shook my head. The thought of it was absurd. Insulting. And I didn't want to be mad at my mother, not now. I wanted to feel something for her other than anger and incredulity. Except I couldn't. "How could you be so calculating?"

My mother did the very last thing I imagined she would do. She reached out for me and pulled me to her and embraced me, holding me tightly, ferociously.

"I loved my brother," she said in a soft voice. "And I loved my husband. I did everything I could in my life to give them a safe place and make them both as happy as possible. I did that while they were alive, and I am doing it now, here." Her voice dropped to an even lower register. I heard her confession in a whisper soft and warm against my skin and in my ear. "Their revenge was mine to take, and its repercussions are mine to bear. I had to protect you from that . . . and I did."

CHAPTER 33

February 3, 1911

I have been back at work, investigating stories for the *New York World* under the name Vee Swann since early December. But I'd outed myself to my friends. I couldn't pretend with them anymore. There had been enough lies. I didn't want any more in my life. At first, Fanny and Martha were furious with me for the deception, and I thought I'd lose their friendship forever. But the more we talked it out, the more they came to understand why I'd felt I had to create an alternative persona, and they had forgiven me.

I've also retired Silk, Satin and Scandals. I will have to steer my sister and my mother to their charitable events without the column's push. After all that had happened, it seemed silly to continue with it.

I still think about Jacob. Often, if I am honest. But that story is better left alone. I now avoid walking past Mr. Cartier's shop during closing times. I certainly don't want to run into Jacob on the street and endure an impersonal greeting from him.

My mother and I have never spoken again of

her confession, but our relationship has changed because of it. Of course, I've kept what she did to myself. She's not a danger to society. She was a grief-ravaged wife and sister. She is a mother determined to safeguard her children. We've reached a truce. She trusts me, and in her trust I've found compassion for her. And yes, love. Tempered, but much more real because of its honesty. Without the pretense, she has become someone I can understand. A woman who once wanted desperately to be an artist but didn't know how to break out of society's pressures. Who fell passionately in love with a man who married her with the best of intentions but ultimately failed her in a profound way, through no fault of his own. A woman who, despite all that, scripted her own story and endured. She accepted who my father was yet never stopped loving him. She alone gave my father the safe place he needed so that he could navigate the treacherous but fulfilling path he chose. She provided him with the family he so badly wanted. Allowed him his passion, and in return, she survived her loneliness.

And I understand that. I, too, suffer from loneliness, as I have for so long except during those precious days when Jacob Asher's arms were wrapped around me and I thought I'd found a gem. A man I could accept for who he was despite his flaws and who I hoped could accept me despite mine. But I was wrong.

It's been two months since my mother's confession. Two months and three weeks since the confrontation with Oxley at Cartier's. Three months since I last spoke to Jacob. Five months since I found the letter from my uncle to my father.

Two weeks ago, Cartier announced the sale of the Hope Diamond to Evalyn Walsh McLean for $40,000 in cash, the return of an emerald and pearl pendant the McLeans had previously purchased from him, and $114,000 payable in three annual installments. It came to a total value of $180,000. Well below what he'd told me he expected to get for the stone.

Yesterday, Evalyn wore her brand-new diamond for the first time in public at a gala in Washington, D.C. I attended that party as a guest of Aunt Carrie and wrote about it for the *World*.

I left the capital this morning by train and returned home late this afternoon. I unpacked my gown and hung it up in the closet. Calling downstairs, I ordered some food. I poured myself a glass of wine, and while I waited for the meal to arrive, I reread the notes I'd taken before I left. I'm currently working on an exposé about a fake Rembrandt painting recently discovered at the Metropolitan Museum. While I have a lot of source material, I thought it would help for me to obtain some background on the painter's life.

That was when I remembered seeing a biography of the artist in my father's library.

Out of all the rooms in the apartment, the library is the one that most brings my father back to life, along with my grief. Usually, I simply go in and out, careful not to linger. But earlier tonight, I took the biography off the shelf and sat down in my father's big armchair to read.

From where the chair was positioned, I could see around the side of his desk and noticed a pile of books there. Getting up, I inspected them. They were the books that had led to my discovery of my father's other life, that had led to all of what had happened. I'd never replaced them on the shelf.

It was time.

My father had organized them chronologically, but I'd gotten them out of sequence. I decided to put them back the way he had wanted them, for no other reason but to honor his love of order. And that meant going through all the books, one at a time, to get their publication dates from the copyright pages.

I picked up the last book. The letter from my uncle had been in the second-to-last one. I didn't have that anymore. I'd done as Stephen had asked and given it to him for safekeeping in the law firm's vault. Now I was glad. As much as the letter might serve as proof of Oxley's crimes, it might also implicate my mother.

I shivered as I reached up to place the last book on the shelf with the others, but it slipped out of my hand and fell to the floor. As it did, an envelope fell out, fluttered down, and landed a few feet away from the ladder.

I descended and picked up the envelope.

It was addressed to me, with *Vera* written in my father's elegant script in the dark green ink he always used.

With a shaking hand, I took it to his desk. And using his jade letter opener, I slit the paper.

Dear Vera . . .

I put the paper down. The words swam before my eyes. I needed a moment and took a deep breath. Then I looked down again. All this time, it had been here and I'd never known.

Dear Vera,

If you have found this, then I am going to assume you found the other letter. I've tried in my way in my life to share who I am with you in all the ways that would matter. But I never told you, face-to-face, the truth of who I am, and that was a mistake. I should have told you so that I could talk to you about love. I have loved so many people in my life in so many ways. I don't want you to think that I didn't love your mother. In my fashion,

I did. She has been a fine and honorable wife to me. And a wonderful mother to both you girls. We all have shortcomings, darling Vera. We can only be who we are. That's the hardest lesson I've learned. I could only be who I was, but in doing so, I've caused much pain, and for that I have regrets. But I know I've also given pleasure and joy and to you and your sister, nothing but pure, deep, and abiding love.

I am not a philosopher. Not a brave man who challenged the system or tried to make a difference. But you are someone who can do that. I know how much pain you have suffered trying to make a difference. I know you focus too often on when you've failed instead of when you've succeeded. And you have succeeded so often. And I've been so proud of you—not for the success or the failure but for the effort. Don't stop trying, my dearest daughter. Keep fighting for everyone who can't bring their own story to the people, for everyone who doesn't have the words to move people and change the world the way you can.

But don't, in the process of saving the world, forget to save yourself. I have watched you, your whole adult life, treat yourself with less insight and thought than the people you write about. Please turn your keen eye on yourself. Don't shy away from love because you are looking for an ideal. There is no one capable of satisfying you if you look for perfection. We all have our faults. Even you. I'm smiling as I write this, thinking of you reading it and getting to this sentence and wanting to argue with me. You would tell me that I never disappointed you, that I lived up to the ideals you hold so dear. But that's not true. I lied, to myself and your mother. I thought I could have it all and not hurt anyone. But I hurt all of you with my selfishness. I tell you this now so that I can leave you with one lesson, if I may.

Living alone with your ideals is noble. But it is also lonely. I want you to open yourself up to the idea that you might find someone one day whose strengths outweigh their weaknesses. Whose love for you overwhelms your fears. Don't give up hope that there is happiness waiting for you. I am not going to give up my own hope that you will go forth and find that happiness and that when you do, you will embrace it for all its potential and possibility. Try, darling Vera. Just try, for me.

Your loving father

I held the letter in my hand and thought about everything that had happened since Charlotte Danzinger's death, my uncle's, my father's, and Mr. Oxley's. I thought about Mr. Cartier's exaggerations. About Jacob's larceny and my mother's crime.

There is fate, and there is choice. There is chance, and there is determination. We can't prove the absence of something. Does bad luck exist? Or good luck? Was dear Mrs. Walsh right to want to trick her own daughter to ensure she would never touch the actual Hope but would wear a glass reproduction of an object that had such a storied history behind it?

I will never know if luck is real or not, but I have learned that hope is. And that in order to have any kind of life worth living, hope is the thing that you must hold on to for dear life. Hope that you'll do the right thing and take care of the people you love well enough that they will know it and will love you back.

I had that for a minute with Jacob. I had felt that soaring hope that we might fulfill each other.

I didn't finish putting the books away. I didn't check in the mirror or fix my hair. I threw on my coat and, still clutching the letter, let myself out of the apartment. Snow had started to fall. I didn't know where to go or what to do. I just knew I had to get out of the apartment to think. I started to walk.

Now, standing here in the cold, staring at the fountain in front of the Plaza Hotel, I'm trying to pretend that I'm not really crying. That what appear to be tears are snowflakes melting on my cheeks.

I know what I want to do, but should I? Dare I?

I see a carriage pull up across the street in front of the Plaza and start for it, but a couple exiting the hotel reach it before I do, and they get in without so much as a glance my way.

Another carriage pulls up. I climb in and give the driver the address.

We drive down Fifth Avenue past Cartier's and continue on until we reach Greenwich Village and pull up on the west side of the park.

Upstairs, I ring the doorbell. For a moment, there is no noise inside. What if he isn't home? Will I find the courage to do this again? Ever? But after a moment, I hear footsteps, and then the door opens.

Jacob looks at me, at my disheveled outfit and my hatless head and my hands, the right one still clutching the letter, and he leads me inside.

"Are you all right?" he asks without any preamble at all. Without any surprise that I am here. Almost as if he has been waiting for me.

"You once told me how there is no such thing as a totally flawless gemstone," I say, not offering any explanation, just launching into what I want to tell him.

"That's true."

"And that even if it takes the highest magnifier to see it, there is always an occlusion or fissure or starburst or something inside that makes a stone slightly imperfect. But that doesn't mean it has no value."

"Yes." He nods, and I wonder if he understands what I'm not saying as much as what I am.

"I'm sorry that I didn't trust you enough to tell you who I was," I say, and take a step forward as he takes one, too. We don't quite meet in the middle.

"Considering everything, I understand," he says.

"Mr. Cartier told me you were going to Paris," I say.

"I made it all the way to the ship, but I turned around."

"Why?"

"It was too great a distance to put between us. And I was praying—" He breaks off.

"That we could find a way back to each other?" I ask.

"Yes. Do you think we can?" Jacob asks.

"I hope so . . ."

He reaches out to pull me the last few inches toward him, but as luck would have it, I have already stepped into the warm, welcoming circle of his arms. And there I stay.

HOPE DIAMOND WORN
AT McLEAN DINNER

Famous Gem Seen for the First time in Public Since It Changed Owners

---

A NOTABLE GATHERING

Guest Members of Diplomatic Corps Entertained by Metropolitan Singers.

Special to The New York Times

WASHINGTON, D.C., Feb. 2.—Mrs. Edward B. McLean wore the Hope diamond tonight. The occasion was the brilliant reception in the Walsh mansion on Massachusetts Avenue, given to her husband's uncle and aunt, Ambassador and Mme. Bakhmatlef.

It was the first time the famous gem was worn in the United States and the first time that its new possessor has worn it in public. Besides this world-famous jewel Mrs. McLean wore the famous Star of the East diamond, which weighs 98 carats, and which is regarded as one of the most valuable stones in the world.

The reception to the Russian Ambassador and his wife was held at the residence of the late Thomas F. Walsh in the ultra-fashionable residential section, where Mr. and Mrs. McLean, the hosts, make their home, Mrs. McLean being the only daughter of Mr. Walsh and the heir to the fortune left by her father.

AUTHOR'S NOTE

During the Gilded Age, New York was a city of skyscrapers, subways, streetlights, and Central Park. Where more than a million poor immigrants were crammed into tenements and half of the millionaires in the entire country lived in mansions on Fifth Avenue.

And so while *Cartier's Hope* is very much a work of fiction, its backdrop is real, as are many of the facts woven into the story.

The history of the Hope Diamond in my book, up to the attempted robbery, is not my invention. The legends recounted here come from what has been written over the last four centuries. Was the stone unlucky? Some believed so. Others didn't. Certainly, there are lists of terrible episodes, events, and ends that befell those who owned it, worked with it, and in some cases simply touched it.

Pierre Cartier was known to have exaggerated those legends in order to increase the price of the stone, convinced there would be people who would covet the Hope all the more to prove bad luck wasn't real or to stare it down.

According to books and articles I read about him, Cartier was a genius marketer who went on to trade a string of magnificent pearls for a choice piece of Fifth Avenue real estate and to become the first to dress stars in his jewels free of charge for the attention the House of Cartier would receive.

Except for the famous jeweler, Evalyn Walsh McLean, her mother Carrie Walsh, the writer O. Henry, and some of the female journalists quoted in the book, most of the other characters come from my imagination. Evalyn's mother, who did visit psychics, was afraid of her daughter purchasing the Hope. However, there is no evidence that she tried to trick Evalyn out of buying it.

The Garland family and its emporium didn't exist in reality, but I based them on the great department stores of the era—Saks Fifth Avenue, Lord & Taylor, and Henri Bendel.

Thelonious Oxley and his *Gotham Gazette* were inspired by *Town Topics* and its publisher, Colonel William d'Alton Mann, a Civil War veteran and businessman. The weekly not only reported on literature and sporting news and offered financial advice, but it also printed detailed and often salacious gossip about society's finest. For decades, Colonel Mann successfully blackmailed business leaders, politicians, and other members of the elite into buying advertising in his journal or risking exposure. Some of America's wealthiest men paid staggering amounts to squelch Mann's stories—as much as what today would be equivalent to a quarter of a million to half a million dollars.

The state of female journalists—and women in general—as described in the book is based on extensive research. Women didn't have the vote in 1910—and wouldn't for ten more years—and their fight for equality at work and at home was both real and urgent.

The early twentieth century was a study in contrasts between the haves and the have-nots. Between people of enormous wealth and families of ten living in two-room tenements. Between women who were forced to adhere to one set of rules and men who lived by another. Society was all too often cruel and unforgiving.

A last note. The Cartier family is royalty in the jewelry business, purveyors of some of the most magnificent stones and makers of some of the most beautiful pieces ever created. Pierre was a beloved figure in the industry as well as in New York society. He was a generous philanthropist, a highly respected businessman, and a gentleman in every sense of the word. Any suggestions otherwise are totally my invention in order to progress the story. I have nothing but admiration for him, his work ethic, his creativity, and his business acumen.

ACKNOWLEDGMENTS

First, to my fabulous editor, Rakesh Satyal, for great insight, brilliant edits, amazing support, and enthusiasm for which I am so grateful.

Thank you all for all you do—Carolyn Reidy, Libby McGuire, Lisa Keim, Lisa Sciambra, Suzanne Donahue, Loan Le, Milina Brown, Kristin Fassler, Wendy Sheanin, and everyone at Atria Books.

To Alan Dingman for truly beautiful covers that always surpass my expectations.

As always, to Dan Conaway, my amazing agent and knight in shining armor and to everyone at Writers House whose help is invaluable.

Thank you, thank you to the indefatigable Ann-Marie Nieves.

To all the amazing book influencers, shouters, reviewers, and readers, including Pamela Klinger Horn, Andrea Peskind Katz, Bobbi Dumas, Debbie Haupt, and Amy Bruno.

To all the jewelers and jewelry experts who have been so generous with their time and knowledge, including Stephanie Sporn, Inezita Gay-Eckel, Benjamin and Hilary Macklowe, Wendy Epstein, Warren Lagerloef, Daniel Morris at HD Gallery, and especially Marion Fasel.

And to my A+ think tank and dear friends: Liz

and Steve Berry, Doug Clegg, Alyson Richman, Randy Susan Meyers, Lauren Willig, Linda Francis Lee, and Lucinda Riley.

To Natalie White, who helps run AuthorBuzz. com so very, very well so that I have time to write.

To every single bookseller and librarian without whom the world would be a sadder place.

And I very much want to thank my readers who make all the work worthwhile. Please visit MJRose.com for a signed bookplate and sign up for my newsletter at MJEmail.me.

Lastly, and as always, I'm very grateful to my family and most of all, Doug.

ABOUT THE AUTHOR

New York Times bestselling author M. J. Rose grew up in New York City exploring the labyrinthine galleries of the Metropolitan Museum and the dark tunnels and lush gardens of Central Park. She is the author of more than a dozen novels, a founding board member of International Thriller Writers, co-founder of 1001DarkNights.com, and the founder of the first marketing company for authors, AuthorBuzz.com. She lives in Connecticut. Visit her online at MJRose.com.

Center Point Large Print
600 Brooks Road / PO Box 1
Thorndike, ME 04986-0001 USA

(207) 568-3717

US & Canada:
1 800 929-9108
www.centerpointlargeprint.com